DON'T SAY A WORD

A DS JACK TOWNSEND NOVEL

ROBERT ENRIGHT

In loving memory of Trevor John Lay.

CHAPTER ONE

This was the job.

That was what Detective Sergeant Jack Townsend reminded himself as he dropped his phone onto his desk and then rocked back in his chair. His hands clasped to the sides of his face, the palms gliding over the thick stubble as he drew them up over his eyes, and then ran his fingers through his dark hair. It was longer than he'd usually keep it, with his natural curls beginning to twist across his forehead, and along with the thickening stubble, a sign that he'd neglected his usual routine.

He'd neglected a lot recently, and the phone call he'd just received meant it was only going to continue.

The evening had just lurched past seven o'clock, and although he'd wanted nothing more than to march through the Thames Valley Police Station in High Wycombe, hop in his car, and head for home, he was needed elsewhere. It meant that his wife, Mandy, would be tasked with once again putting their precocious eight-year-old daughter, Eve, to bed. It was actually a job Townsend enjoyed. Her constant banter and backchat often causing him to break into a smile.

She was a good kid.

In the five months since they'd relocated from Liverpool to Buckinghamshire, she'd really blossomed, making friends quickly in her new school and letting down her guard more. For a few years, it had been tough, which Townsend knew was his own fault. He was the one who'd gone undercover for over three important years of her childhood, but the little-by-little restoration of their relationship had taken giant leaps over the past few months.

He'd help her with her homework.

Take her to gymnastics, which she was fast becoming obsessed with.

Whenever they went out as a family, it was his hand she would hold.

Mandy was a huge factor in it all. His wife was more than just his rock. She was his gravity, keeping him locked on what was important and constantly reminding him of her pride in what he did. She'd made it work all those years, helping patch up the cuts and bruises, as well as the broken heart that the years of distance had caused. Now, she was flourishing in her new job as a virtual assistant for the CEO of a tech start-up, which were still words that even he, as a detective, couldn't work out. But she was enjoying being back in the working world, and he often found her sitting on their corner sofa, laptop on the cushion across her thighs, tapping away in the evening.

He wished that was where he was right then.

Walking into his home in Flackwell Heath, a sleepy little village only a few miles from the station. Instead, as he threw his arms into his black parka coat, he knew he'd be heading in the opposite direction. The rest of the Specialist Crime's Unit were either off shift, or elsewhere, and he blew out his cheeks as he surveyed the quiet room. The new office wasn't exactly the Ritz, but it was bigger than the cramped room they'd occupied in the basement, although the promise of better coffee had been broken when the machine in the hallway offered the same brown sludge as the one underground. His desk was pressed against the wall nearest to the door and the minimal paperwork or stationery was a testament to his belief that his true job was out on the streets. Opposite his desk were both DS Nicola Hannon's and DS Michelle Swaby's desks, and on most days, he'd often find them mid-conversation as he entered the room. Hannon had grown in confidence over the past few months, as the young officer had been paralysed by fear after a brutal attack in her early years as a police officer. Townsend had helped her, bringing her along on a number of house calls and crime scenes, but her true talent was combing through archives and documents, and she'd shone in recent months. Swaby was only a few years older than Townsend, and her almost annoying commitment to being bubbly spat in the face of a hard-working detective with two kids approaching their teens. The duo was the hub of the office, and with Hannon off duty and Swaby on personal leave due to a family bereavement, the station was a quieter place without them. Detective Inspector Isabella King was elsewhere. Her diary blocked out for the evening. Undoubtedly sitting in a meeting and rolling her eyes at the dick-swinging as the other senior officers politicked for prominence. Ever since Townsend had saved her life by foiling Baycroft as he lunged to murder her, the two of them had formed a strong bond that had served the SCU well. King may have been as tough as stone, but she was smart enough to read a room, and her command over the unit had seen them become one of the Thames Valley Police Force's most important functions.

Much to the ire of DCI Marcus Lowe, her ex-husband, and head of CID, whose arrogance was only rivalled by his embarrassment after Townsend had taken him down a peg or two in the boxing ring.

Since then, Lowe had kept quiet, and Townsend had noticed the respectful nods from the younger officer.

As he thought about the final blow that sent Lowe sprawling to the canvas, Townsend smirked.

Good times.

As he marched through the corridors of the station, a few uniformed officers nodded to him, which he reciprocated, as his reputation among them had grown since the summer.

Ever since he'd caught Gordon Baycroft, the delusional old priest who'd embarked on a brutal murder spree through the town.

It had not only solidified the SCU as a respectable branch of the police force, but it had given him the belief that he himself could be a good detective.

That he was a good detective.

The desk sergeant threw an obvious comment about the weather as Townsend approached the door, and with a grimace, he hauled it open and stepped out into the bitter chill of the winter's eve. The wind lashed against him, and he hunched his shoulder and dipped his head as he rounded the station to the private car park behind. Thankfully, rush hour had already subsided, and the route he needed to take to the incident would be relatively clear. As he unlocked his car and pulled open the door, he took one final pause, looking back across the car park to the exit.

If he turned right out of the station, he could head for home. Back to the warmth of his house and the love of his family, lazing on the sofa in front of the television and some bright Christmas film that he wouldn't remember.

But he knew he couldn't.

This was the job.

Mandy would understand, and more than likely, demand he do what was needed.

Evie would understand. Some day.

A man had been found in a local estate with his throat cut.

With a grunt, Townsend dropped into the driver's seat, slammed the door shut, and then headed to the exit, turning left and out of the town centre towards the numerous residential areas that surrounded High Wycombe. The first weekend of December was upon them, and already, the majority of the houses were illuminated in a blaze of festive lights, some more tastefully than others.

It was just another reminder to Townsend that he'd made another promise to his daughter. Evie was champing at the bit to decorate the house, but as he gazed through the drizzle that spattered his windscreen, he knew that he'd have to put it on hold.

At least for now.

A few miles up from High Wycombe Station, Townsend turned down towards Totteridge, heading towards the housing estates that bled into Micklefield. They reminded him a little of home, the mean streets of Toxteth where he had been raised by his own police officer father. It was a long time ago, and the edges of those memories had begun to blur, but Townsend held them dear.

Just like the watch that clung to his wrist, that his own father had worn on the beat.

Injuries and then cruelly, cancer, had cut short his father's career and life, but Townsend always held on to the strong, powerful image of the man who served his community with dedication.

This was Townsend's community now, and as he slowed the car and turned into the estate car park, he could see the blue flashes of the police cars already on the scene. The officers had done a great job in cordoning off the area, and as Townsend strode through the downpour, he gave a respectful nod to PC Harris, who lifted the yellow police tape for him to pass.

'It's not pretty,' she said, shaking her head solemnly.

Townsend frowned as he surveyed the scene.

Across the car park, two officers were ushering back a gang of youths, all with their hoods up and all with their phones out, trying their best to turn a tragedy into clout. It sickened him that that was where their heads immediately went, but then he couldn't blame them for the world that he and other generations had cultivated.

Affirmation and acceptance was what they craved, no matter how low they stooped for it.

Beyond them, he could see the ambulance arriving, carefully steering its way through the car park and causing more of an argument amongst the rowdy group.

The far side of the car park was lined with rusty garage doors, all of them belonging to various residences in the tall tower blocks that loomed behind him. The dreary building was a spiralling grey column that was speckled with a few depressingly low-effort Christmas decorations from those who had bothered.

At the far end of the garage, Townsend could see the legs of the prone body, before the edge of the wall obscured the rest of the victim. Another uniformed officer was standing beside him, trying their best to preserve a crime scene that was swiftly being washed away.

With a grimace, Townsend turned back to Harris, who sniffed under her bowler hat.

'It never is,' he grumbled, and then with the same purposeful gait that his father had used for years, Townsend marched across the concrete of the dilapidated car park to find out who'd been brutally murdered this close to Christmas, and more importantly, why.

CHAPTER TWO

'Just stay safe, okay?'

Townsend felt the smile creep across his face as his wife spoke. He looked through the rain-soaked windshield of his car at the address he'd been given and sighed.

'You know me.' He chuckled.

'Exactly.' He could sense the smile on her face. 'You want to speak to your daughter?'

'Is she still up?'

'It's Friday,' Mandy responded. 'She's adamant she can stay up at the weekends.'

'Go on then,' Townsend said and then listened with a twinge of guilt as his wife called for their daughter. A few moments later, and after a brief rustling sound, the voice of innocence echoed through the phone.

'Hi, Daddy.'

'Hello, Pickle.' Townsend felt his heart thump. 'You all right?'

'Yeah. I had gymnastics.'

'Was it good?'

'Yeah.' Her enthusiasm was palpable. 'Can you come and watch me next week? We have a show—'

'I know, and I have it in my diary.'

'Can you come?' Little by little, she'd begun to grasp the severity of his job. 'Will work let you?'

'If I have to lock every bad guy up in the country.' He heard her giggle. 'You be good, okay? I'll be home soon.'

'Goodnight, Daddy.' She paused. 'I love you.'

'You too, Pickle.'

As he heard the sound of Eve passing the phone back to his wife, the front door of the house opened, and DS Rebecca Ramsey leant out and beckoned him. With a grimace, he threw open the car door, just as Mandy returned to the call.

'Sorry, love,' Townsend said through gritted teeth as he stepped out into the rain. 'I have to go.'

'Go get em, Jack.'

With his wife's endorsement ringing in his ear, Townsend marched through the downpour and headed towards the house. He pushed open the rusty gate that was hanging from its flimsy hinges, and then walked up the small concrete path that was lined with potted plants that had long been forgotten. The house was one of many that were crammed into a long strip of cheap, affordable housing projects that lined the outskirts of High Wycombe. While Flackwell Heath was hardly the beacon of affluence in the way places like Marlow was, his street seemed a world away from this one. Nearly every house was in disrepair, crying out for the love or attention that the property developers would never hear. The council-assigned residence was just as ambivalent, seeing it as a place to live as opposed to a home to make.

As he approached the door, DS Ramsey greeted him with a handshake and a smile.

'Jack.'

'How you doing?' Townsend said as he stepped in, sliding off his drenched jacket and folding it over his arm.

DS Ramsey was one of the most experienced Family Liaison Officers within the force, and she'd been a valuable asset in their pursuit of Gordon Baycroft back in the summer. Now, in the home of the murder victim from the car park, Ramsey had already established a connection with Jamal Beckford's grieving family.

'I'm fine.' She ran a hand through her short, cropped hair. 'Simone's in the front room. She's pretty cut up, as you can imagine, but she said she's ready to take any questions.'

'Do I need to ask her where she was this evening?' Townsend said with a sigh.

'No. She was here, and her son, Tyler, can corroborate her story. He was upstairs on his computer,' Ramsey said with a firm nod. Townsend smiled and then placed his jacket over the one that was already hanging from the bannister. He ran a hand through his wet hair and then pushed open the door to the modest living room. It was a little cramped, with two large sofas fighting for space against the walls, and a large TV loomed over the room from its bracket on the wall. On one of the sofas, Simone Beckford sat, her eyes red from tears, and she shook a little as she tried to compose herself. A cup of tea was on the coffee table in front of her.

It was stone cold.

Beside her, her son sat, his eyes locked on the ground before him, clearly lost in his own grief.

As he stepped in, both of them both turned their attention to him, and Townsend offered them a comforting smile. Simone took a deep breath while her son looked away.

'Mrs Beckford. I'm Detective Sergeant Jack Townsend. My colleague told me you were willing to answer some questions.'

'Yes,' Simone stated, clearly trying to encourage

herself. She seemed less on edge when Ramsey appeared in the doorway, gave them a nod, and then pulled the door closed. 'You're not local, are you?'

'It's hard to hide, huh?' Townsend said with a grin. His Scouse accent always drew attention. 'First off, let me say I am very sorry for what's happened to your husband. I can't imagine what you're going through.'

'Thank you.' Simone choked, another wave of tears brewing.

'I just need to ask a few questions to help with my investigation. How long have you been married to Jamal?'

As Simone took another breath, her son fidgeted in his seat.

'Two years. Well, coming up to it.'

'And what did Jamal do for a living?'

'He worked for Amazon. He was a delivery driver.' She sighed. 'He actually really loved his job.'

'He must have been busy,' Townsend said as he scribbled on his pad. 'My wife has a delivery every day. Did he mention anything that was bothering him? Any problems at work? Or with friends?'

'No. None.'

Again, Simone's answers seemed to agitate her son.

'Are you sure? Maybe something he mentioned in passing?'

'I'm sure of it. He told me everything. We had a good marriage.'

That comment drew a scoff from her son, and Townsend turned his focus to him. As he did, Simone pulled her cardigan tight to her body.

'Tyler, right?' Townsend said warmly. 'How you holding up?'

'I'm fine.' The boy shrugged dismissively.

Teenagers.

'How old are you, Tyler?'

'Fifteen.'

'I wasn't too much older than you when I lost my dad and…'

'He *wasn't* my dad.'

The venom in the young boy's voice took the whole room by surprise, and as Simone turned to comfort her son, her cardigan slipped slightly to reveal a dark bruising at the top of her arm. Against her brown skin, it was hard to notice, but Townsend did.

He made a note.

Simone swiftly pulled it up, confident she'd hidden it.

'I understand,' Townsend said, closing his notepad. 'DS Ramsey will be here for you. Whatever you need, you ask her.'

As Townsend stood, Tyler looked at his mum in confusion.

'Just tell him.' Tyler protested, but before Townsend could dig deeper, Simone burst out into tears once more, her grief strangling her down to the sofa. Clearly guilt-ridden for making his mother cry, Tyler wrapped his arms around her and squeezed.

Simone's face contorted slightly with pain.

Just enough for Townsend to notice.

'I'll be back soon, okay?' Townsend said, as he made his way to the door.

'Just find out who did this,' Simone yelled through her heartbreak.

'I'll do everything I can.'

Meaning every word, Townsend stepped back into the hallway and closed the door behind him, shutting off the grieving cries of Simone. Ramsey was leaning against the wall, arms folded.

'You've got a way with the ladies, huh?' she joked.

'Apparently so. Did she mention much to you about her marriage?'

Ramsey frowned, searched her archives, and then shook her head slowly.

'Just they were happy.'

'I don't think that's quite true. She's covering up some bruising on her arms. Tyler seems very apathetic to his stepdad's murder and was very clear about their relationship. Plus, when he hugged her just now, she felt it.'

'Leave it with me,' Ramsey said confidently.. 'I'll do my thing and let you know what I find out. Good work, Jack.'

'This is the job, right?'

The two shared a respectful nod, and then Townsend stepped past Ramsey towards the bannister as they disappeared back into the front room. Townsend lifted his sodden coat and tutted at himself for how drenched the jacket beneath it now was. But in the grand scheme of things, there were bigger problems facing the family than a wet coat.

As he zipped it up and lifted the hood, Townsend stepped out into the cold, winter downpour, once again with his phone attached to his face, cursing as DI King still wasn't answering his calls.

It was going to be a long night.

And he needed all the help he could get.

CHAPTER THREE

Throughout her entire career, Detective Inspector Isabella King had had to deal with obstacles.

Whether it was her race, something that, as a proud black woman, she wore with pride. Especially in the face of the systemic racism that still clung to the underbelly of society like a fungus. Or her gender, where despite her clear ability and professionalism, a number of self-aggrandising senior officers would almost use it as an excuse to bypass her for opportunities.

Or the fact that her prick of an ex-husband, Marcus Lowe, just happened to be the Detective Chief Inspector who headed up the main function of CID at Thames Valley Police. Their divorce had been messy, their union crumbling under the pressures of their work within the investigation team and his wandering eye, compounded by their inability to conceive, which he used as an excuse to play away.

But every single one of those problems she'd faced and conquered.

Now, she drew respectful nods from her colleagues as she strode into the room.

The loyalty of her team was unquestioned, and the opportunity to head the Specialist Crimes Unit had blossomed into one of the most sought-after positions in the entire police service.

Younger officers stood to attention when she addressed them.

Nobody second-guessed her opinion without merit.

Even DCI Lowe had taken a step back, begrudgingly acknowledging that her credentials were watertight.

But as she sat in her umpteenth Alcoholics Anonymous meeting, she looked down at the faded floorboards of the old town hall, and wondered if this was one obstacle too far.

For nearly a year, her drinking had been constant.

Never enough to impede her from her duty as a detective, but constantly gnawing away at her like an escalating toothache.

It started off, as most vices do, as a coping mechanism.

As DCI Lowe settled down into his new relationship, King found solace in a bottle of wine, the cork being ripped off before the front door to her home in Marlow had even shut behind her.

Glasses soon turned to bottles.

Good night sleep was soon replaced with passing out on the sofa, with yesterday's clothes clinging to her sweaty body.

At work, her focus began to dip, constantly being asked if she was still in the room.

Comments that she looked tired replaced a usual greeting.

All the red flags were waving wildly in front of her, but when she looked at the world through the haze of red wine, they just looked like flags.

That had all changed five months ago.

With the SCU floundering as nothing more than a

dumping ground from CID, King had been assigned a young DS whose confidence had been shaken to its very core, and a newly arrived detective who had a questionable background.

It was the makings of a disaster, but fate handed her a chance.

It offered her a rope to pull her out of the mud.

The opportunity to lead the investigation of the murder of young Lauren Grainger soon turned into a full-blown manhunt, as Gordon Baycroft, a sweet and unassuming vicar, went on a murderous spree in the name of a god that King had long since given up on.

The brutality of his murders still hung heavily in her mind, flashing across her vision in the dead of night. The image of the murderous Baycroft looming over her on the rain-soaked mud of the Wycombe Rye with a knife in his hand should have been what scarred her.

But it wasn't *what* he tried to do that had haunted her.

It was *why* he did it.

During the investigation, panic had spread through the town of High Wycombe, and the local media had done its usual job of stoking the flames of fear among the locals. King's name soon came into the firing line, and a picture of her buying two bottles of red wine soon surfaced online.

Her boss, Detective Superintendent Geoff Hall, pulled her out of the firing line of the press, but Baycroft made it clear that her lack of control was a disgrace to the bodies he'd left behind.

The women who'd been murdered deserved better.

Not just from the horrible hand they were dealt, but from her. When the town was looking to her to bring justice for the innocent women snatched from this world, all she could do was lose herself in the bottom of a bottle.

That night, after she'd sat across from Baycroft as he

spat his vile reasoning, she'd poured the remaining wine down the sink and promised herself she would be better.

Promised the five dead women that she would be better.

But five months in, as she listened to another story from someone looking for validation and pity, she wondered if she'd be able to keep it together.

'Thanks for sharing,' the leader of the group said to a young man, who nodded thankfully to the group who all clapped his bravery. King kept her eyes to the ground, knowing that Glen would be looking for another sharer. If he locked eyes on you, there was no backing out.

It didn't seem to matter tonight.

'Izzy.' His voice was warm and gentle, perfectly suiting his portly, mid-fifties body. 'You've been quiet for the past few weeks.'

There's a reason for that, she thought, but took a breath, and met his gaze with a force smile. 'Sorry. It's just been a little tough.'

The eyes of the room fell on her, and although everyone was there for the same reason, she couldn't help but feel judged. Glen nodded thoughtfully, before sweeping his hand as he motioned to the circle of attendees.

'That's fine. That's what we're here for.'

'I know.' King nodded, trying to politely cut the conversation short.

'Why don't you share what's been tough?' Glen suggested, and a few murmurs of encouragement floated around her.

There was no point in fighting it.

If she wanted to get better, she had to actively try.

'Do you think people can truly change?' she finally asked. The room all looked to each other and then to Glen, who tilted his head carefully.

'I think people have the capacity to change.'

'But there is a difference between capacity and ability,' King replied. 'I know that I drink. Well, I used to. A lot. But I know that the moment something upsets my day, or like every functioning forty-three-year-old woman, if one of the many moments of self-doubt creep into my mind, my entire body, from my mind to my toes, wants to reach for the bottle.'

'That's normal for a—'

'For an alcoholic?' King cut him off. 'Sorry, but that's the point I'm trying to make. You say we have the capacity to change, but I will *always* be an alcoholic. Whether that's in recovery, whether it's five months sober, or whether it's lying in a ditch with a bottle of red in my hand. I know we come here for help and support, and it has given me both, but it's just hard. Every day is hard. I told myself I would never let myself go back to who I was, and I have five really good reasons why.'

'Then remember them,' Glen said with a broken-hearted smile.

'Oh, I do. Every day,' King said, feeling her eyes watering slightly. Her jacket began to vibrate. 'But sometimes, I don't want to remember them. And the easiest way to forget them would be to go back to the very reason I let them down in the first place…' She took her phone from her pocket.

Eight missed calls.

All from DS Townsend.

'Erm, phones aren't allowed in…' Glen started as she stood up. King lifted her hand to dismiss him, as she turned and marched towards the door of the town hall, knowing her abruptness would be misconstrued as rudeness.

She'd make amends.

The group was a sucker for a plate of biscuits. In a way, they reminded her of DS Hannon.

With the guilt and the grief for the five women who had fallen at Baycroft's hand following her like a shadow, she pushed her way through the doors and out into the rain-soaked car park. Instantly, she fell back against the wall, taking a few deep breaths before she pulled her vape out and pushed a plume of fruity vapour into the rain.

Lauren Grainger. Natasha Stokes. Michaela Woods. Irena Roslova.

She'd demanded her team remember the names of the victims and what had happened to them.

With the yearning for a drink growing, she knew she'd do well to follow her own advice.

After a few more puffs, and with her clothes soaked through, King lifted her phone to return Townsend's call, and within minutes, she was racing to her car to get to work.

CHAPTER FOUR

'Fucking hell. Look who it is.'

Connor Davis sighed as the voice boomed behind him, and then he put on his best smile and turned to face the open arms of Jason Gallagher. It was an inevitability of attending a school reunion that you'd run into the faces from your past, but Jason's was one he wasn't looking forward to.

'Jason.' Connor extended his hand.

'Come on…' Jason grinned, as he wrapped his large arms around Connor and gave him a one-way hug. 'Fucking hell, it's been too long.'

Connor nodded politely, and then made his way into the main hall where the music was playing and a crowd of men and women in their early forties were awkwardly relaying their uneventful lives to each other. It was a bizarre concept to host a reunion, as the friends that people made through school would eventually whittle down to a select group of people that you'd genuinely want to spend time with.

Connor had his friends.

None of them were in the room.

Instead, he'd spend his Friday night with total strangers and make small talk. Still, he slapped his sticker onto his jumper, letting everyone know that the man with the slightly greying hair before them was once sitting in the same class as them a quarter of a century ago.

A few people nodded politely, as he did in return, before he made his way across to the table that was lined with room temperature bottles of beer. He picked one up, thanked the person overseeing them, and then turned.

Jason Gallagher was beside him.

'Let's get on it, shall we?' Jason smirked, picking up two bottles and glaring at the makeshift barman.

He hadn't changed.

Back in high school, Jason Gallagher was the alpha male of their year. Standing at six foot three and built like a rugby player, he had the pick of the girls and friendship circles. With such popularity at a young age, Jason's arrogance skyrocketed, and when Connor looked back with his world-weary gaze at how they'd behaved, he was almost ashamed of what they'd done..

Disruptive.

Destructive.

They even bullied some of the more reserved kids.

But they didn't care, and over the years, Connor had often wondered what had become of the other four members of their circle. Jason was always going to stay the same, and it didn't surprise Connor one bit to hear that he and Rachel were still together, although from the way Jason slurred his description of their marriage, it didn't seem happy.

'She didn't even want to come tonight.' Jason gestured with his hand. 'She's a selfish cow. Always has been.'

Connor nodded politely.

Jason had spoken about his struggles with employment, flipping from job to job and how he and Rachel were struggling to make ends meet. Connor felt almost embarrassed to speak about his own life, where he was happily married with two beautiful daughters, both of whom were in a prestigious high school which he could afford from the successful accountancy firm he ran with his wife just outside of Marlow.

'Do you hear much from the others?'

'Penny's here. Somewhere.' Jason waggled his eyebrows. 'Maybe she'll give you a blowie for old time's sake.'

As Jason laughed at his own inappropriate comment, Connor did scan the room to see if he could find his high school sweetheart. Penny Durant had been Rachel's best friend, and the four of them had been joined at the hip for most of high school, before Shelly had joined them in the last few years. She was a better influence on Penny, the two of them bonding over their love of ballet, and when the original four fell back into their brash behaviour, Shelly was often the one to walk away.

Connor envied her then and still envied her now.

'Is Shelly here?' Connor asked, trying to change the conversation.

'Nah, don't think so.' Jason turned to who he thought was a friend. 'Why? Don't tell me you were shagging her as well?'

'You really haven't changed, have you, Jason?' Connor said with a shake of his head. In response, Jason opened his arms out almost in celebration.

'Why would I want to do a fucking thing like that?' He then looked around suspiciously before dipping his hand into the inside pocket of his jacket. He pulled out a small bag of cocaine.

'Jesus fucking Christ, Jason,' Connor snapped.

'Oh, come on you little bitch,' he said as he tucked it around. 'Let's go have a bump and get this place started. Some of these girls turned out all right.'

'Yeah, and I'm sure they're all just dying for a go on Gallagher.'

'Some people just can't let go, mate.' Jason smirked, but then his eyes bulged. 'Now, who is that?'

Connor turned to follow his gaze, and even he was startled at the stunning woman who had marched confidently into the hall. Her brown hair flowed down to her shoulders, which were covered by a tight fighting leather jacket that she wore over a low-cut blouse. Her jeans were so tight, they looked painted on, showing off an incredible figure as she sauntered past both of them to retrieve a drink from the table. As Jason leered, along with a few others albeit, more subtlety, Connor tried his best to place her.

She looked familiar.

'What you reckon?' Jason leant in as he spoke. 'Some bird got the wrong address?'

'I think…I think that's Miller's kid,' Connor said over the loud music.

'What? Diddler?' Gallagher laughed. 'No fucking way. She was a right state. Not surprising really.'

'I'm pretty sure it is,' Connor said with a nod. As he looked beyond the stunning, mysterious woman, his eyes finally locked with Penny, who offered a sheepish wave. They'd stayed in touch through the usual routes of social media and had long since established that their flame had died out. Both were married, both had families, and lives that would never involve the other.

But seeing her for the first time in over two decades did make him shiver a little.

With excitement?

Or nerves?

'I'll be back in a bit,' Connor said to Jason, stepping away before he could respond.

'Yeah, whatever.' Jason shrugged, before looking around for the woman in the leather jacket. The thought of heading home early, back to another row with Rachel over the money they didn't have or the sex life they'd long since abandoned had little appeal, and despite the creeping gut and the loosening of his muscles over the years, Jason still fancied himself as a ladies man. He'd cheated on his wife enough times to confirm to himself that he 'still had it', and after a cheeky bump of cocaine, he'd be well up for a crack at one of the women who'd flashed a few glances his way. They had all settled down, but there would be one of them who would want to thrash out a fantasy from twenty years ago, and he was more than willing to oblige them.

He glanced over at Connor and Penny and felt a twinge of envy as the two well-rounded adults were a world apart from the gobby teenagers they had been.

What, effectively, he still was.

Everyone was talking. A few were even dancing in the middle of the hall to some cheesy 90s song.

But nobody had made the effort to speak with him. The idea of breaking down why that was, or why his own wife didn't want to be seen in public with him was a thread he didn't want to pull at, and with his arm shaking with anger, he necked the rest of his beer, and then downed the second bottle before marching out of the hall and down the corridor towards the toilets. As he swayed on his feet, he welcomed the buzz of inebriation, and he fell against the door and stumbled into the bathroom.

Some guy he didn't recognise looked at him with a sneer before exiting.

'Yeah, fuck you too, buddy,' he called out and then laughed, as he tipped the cocaine out onto the sink, with zero regard to where he actually was. He leant forward and inhaled it up his nose, snapping his head back and gasping as the sensation shot straight to his brain. 'Fuck me.'

He did another line before splashing some water on his face and staring at himself in the mirror. The reflection wasn't the truth in his mind.

The gut.

The bad teeth and skin.

The thinning hair.

In his mind, he was still the stud he was twenty-five years ago, and with the drugs coursing through his veins, he sauntered to the door with a confidence that he didn't deserve. As he stepped out into the corridor, he felt the chill of the outside world, and he glanced down the corridor where the fire exit door was being held open by the woman in the leather jacket. She had a cigarette hanging from her blood-red lips, and as she pulled a lighter from her bag, she turned and looked back at Jason, and made sure she locked eyes with him.

They lingered for a moment, and then she slightly arched one eyebrow suggestively before pulling the hood up on her jacket before stepping out into the rain to the pitch-black car park.

The message was clear as day, and as Jason marched towards the open door, he could already feel himself getting hard. Part of him wanted to message his wife and tell her that it was her fault he couldn't get it up with her, but his wife was the furthest thing from his mind.

Whoever this bombshell was, she was going to get every bit of him, and he couldn't wait to feel like a man again.

He stepped out into the darkness; the rain crashing over him, and he looked around for her.

For the tip of a cigarette.

But he couldn't smell the smoke, and there was nobody around.

Then, he felt a small prick in the back of his neck, and before he could say anything, he slumped against the van that was beside him and he didn't even remember hitting the ground.

CHAPTER FIVE

After stopping off for a coffee at a small café on what passed as the high street in Flackwell Heath, Townsend sped through the empty Saturday morning roads of High Wycombe, heading towards Downley. As he passed the now familiar streets, he thought back to when he'd abandoned his car in the middle of a traffic jam, sprinting on foot to save his boss's life five months before.

It had been a key moment in the trust that had been forged between himself and King, not only because he'd been able to crack who the murderer was.

But because he was there for her.

In a job such as theirs, knowing the person you were stepping into the unknown with had your back was worth its weight in gold, and although King had never been particularly cold to Townsend, in the months since, she'd let her guard down.

She did seem different, however.

Townsend was his own worst critic, but his perception told him that his boss was going through something. King was a closed book when it came to her personal life, which Townsend completely respected and understood. Her ex-husband hardly helped matters at work, although King's success in leading the SCU was certainly a smack in his face.

As was the tuning up Townsend had given him in the boxing ring, which had spread through the station like wildfire. Despite the constant stream of questions from eager young officers wanting him to confirm it, Townsend had never spoken one word on the matter.

Lowe had done his best to play it off as either a friendly scuffle or a lucky punch depending which day you caught him on, but the legacy of that moment had become permanent.

Lowe hadn't run his mouth to Townsend since that fateful summer morning, but there were clear signs he was trying to get his own back in his own petty ways.

Delayed reports coming back from the lab had become more frequent.

On a near weekly basis, Townsend's access needed to be reset.

He couldn't prove it was Lowe, but just like he had a feeling that something was up with King, he had a strong suspicion that Lowe was massaging his own ego by making Townsend's life harder.

As he guided his car down the hill from Downley towards Hughenden Manor, Townsend's thoughts quickly shot to the beautiful vista on the hills beyond, and he was once again reminded of the beautiful town where he now lived. He couldn't be further from the concrete labyrinth that he grew up in, and the rundown streets of the Toxteth estates that he had once known as his home.

'You're a long way from home.'

A regular response to his thick, Scouse accent, but Townsend agreed wholeheartedly with that statement up to a point.

His home was wherever Mandy and Eve were safe and

happy, and with every passing day, High Wycombe felt more and more like home.

A pretty decent place to lay down their roots.

The colossal structure of Hughenden Manor loomed large through the woodlands that surrounded it, with the fifteen-hundred-acre estate a vast sea of green. The house was one of the major attractions of the town and was under the care and counsel of the National Trust. Townsend hadn't been to the house itself, but he had taken Eve and Mandy to the public park on the outskirts of the land, where a paid membership wasn't needed. On one of the many occasions he'd been sitting on a park bench as his daughter threw herself wildly down the zipline, he'd googled the stately home with interest.

It had housed a prime minister in the late 1800s.

It was used as an underground base throughout the Second World War, where 'Operation Hillside' undertook the task of producing bombing maps that apparently helped end the war.

It was all so fascinating, and the idea of underground bunkers and code names made Townsend envious. His job was mainly paperwork and interviewing people who hated every fibre of his being. But it was important work, and the gravity of that wasn't lost on him as he rounded the corner and into the small, circular, gravel car park that surrounded the entrance to the public part of the grounds. There was already an eager crowd gathered around, being held back by a few officers who seemed annoyed to be this busy on a Saturday morning. The SOCO van was already parked near to the entrance, as the team pulled on their overalls, ready to get to work. He lowered his window and flashed his lanyard to the officer who guided him into the car park. As he pulled the car to a stop, he took a swig of his now cold coffee, grimaced, and stepped out of the car.

'Have this instead.'

DC Nic Hannon was already waiting for him, a coffee in hand, and the usual warm smile across her face. Townsend gratefully took it and closed the door behind him. The brisk morning was thankfully free from rain, but the bitter chill on the wind beckoned him forward like an ominous sign of things to come.

'How you doing, Nic?' Townsend asked as he gratefully sipped the warm drink and scanned the mayhem.

'Not bad.' She shrugged, as the strong wind blew her short, ginger hair askew. 'You know how it is…wake up, get told about a dead body. Classic Saturday.'

'Yeah, it's fucking ace, isn't it?' Townsend said dryly. 'I'm missing Eve's gymnastics for this.'

'Ah, that sucks.' Hannon smiled. 'Although, Shilpa was supposed to be taking me to Hot Bikram Yoga this morning, so I feel like I've had a right result.'

Townsend chuckled and then headed towards the crime scene, thankful for Hannon's company. As a detective, her career had been stalled by her own lack of confidence. After suffering a brutal attack while a police constable, Hannon had gone into her shell, and although she'd excelled when it came to the desk work, she was seen as damaged goods in the eyes of CID. King had done wonders for the young woman, taking her under her wing, but it was Townsend who'd taken her by the hand and dragged her back out into the streets.

She'd never say it, but she was always thankful when she had Townsend alongside her. They'd worked closely on the Baycroft case and had fallen into an older brother/younger sister type relationship. So improved was her confidence, Hannon had come out as homosexual to the team, who simply shrugged, and carried on.

Townsend knew that was what she wanted, for them to think nothing of it, but he was proud of her for how far she'd come in the months that he'd known her.

As they crunched across the dying embers of the last leaves on the muddy path, he looked up through the corridor of trees to the group of his peers who were clearly working the crime scene. There was police tape being rolled around tree trunks, officers in white overalls scanning through the surrounding shrubbery, and what looked like a man's body slumped against the tree.

'What's the deal?' Townsend asked Hannon as they approached.

'Male. Early to mid-forties. Syringe marks in his arms. Paraphernalia nearby.'

'Overdose?' Townsend arched his eyebrow at Hannon.

'Looks like it.'

'We'll see,' Townsend said sceptically, and then quickened the pace towards the crime scene. As he strode up the muddy path, he frowned towards the cars that were slowing on the adjacent road. Human nature's voyeuristic need to see something out of the ordinary. Changing the subject, he looked at Hannon and smiled. 'How's Swaby?'

'I think she's okay. The funeral was yesterday—'

'Her father-in-law, right?'

'Yeah. Apparently, it's hit Rich pretty hard. And the boys.'

DS Michelle Swaby was the life and soul of every room she walked into. A beacon of positivity in a job that ground people down and spat them out. She was adored by both the SCU and CID where she'd worked previously. Alongside a well-respected career, she had a wonderful sounding home life, with her high-flying banker husband and their two teenage sons. If anyone was able to handle the death of a loved one, and rally around those who needed her most, it was Swaby.

'Well, until she's back, send her my best.'

Hannon nodded, and the two of them covered the final hundred yards or so in a contented silence. As they finally reached the caution tape, Townsend greeted PC Boyd who was acting like a makeshift bouncer.

'DS Townsend.' He nodded. 'Not sure you guys are needed for this?'

Boyd was a few years older than Townsend but had never had any inclination to climb the ranks of the service. Throwing on his vest and firing up the sirens was what he lived for, and despite his first interaction with Townsend being a little icy at the scene of Lauren Grainger's death, he'd turned out to be a pretty standup guy.

'Every death is serious, Simon,' Townsend responded.

'But not a crime,' Boyd offered. 'Looks like our matey over here got a little too greedy last night.'

'So it is an overdose?' Hannon asked with intrigue.

'Cut and dried.' Boyd turned to guide them towards the body. 'You're welcome to have a look yourself.'

'Thanks,' Townsend said dryly. 'This is my crime scene, but thanks.'

Boyd rolled his eyes and lifted the tape for them, and Townsend stepped under. As he approached the dead body, he made a point of stuffing his hands in his pockets and paid keen attention to the plastic, numbered markers that littered the ground. One was placed next to a needle.

Another next to an almost empty bag of an unknown drug.

The man was soaked through, slumped against the dead tree with his head hanging low. His bulky frame was wrapped in a tight fitted shirt that was stretched against his slightly bulging gut.

'Smartly dressed for a drug addict,' Townsend muttered to Hannon, who was making notes in her notepad.

'Charity shop?' Hannon offered. Townsend shook his head.

'Something doesn't feel right.' Townsend mused, as he

carefully approached the body and then squatted down for a closer look. 'Why would you do it out here?'

'People have been getting smashed or high in the park for a long time,' Hannon said.

'But it was pissing it down last night. I know, I was out in it. Most people, when they jack up, they want somewhere to lie back and pass out. At least somewhere sheltered.'

'Desperation?'

Townsend gazed a careful eye over the body once more.

'Maybe. But this isn't exactly drug central out here, is it? More likely to do it in the Rye, right?' Townsend then turned to one of the SOCOs working nearby. 'Do we have an ID on the body?'

The officer helpfully turned to the bagged evidence they'd begun to collect and handed Townsend the one with the wallet. Carefully, Townsend opened the wallet through the plastic to the driving license.

'Jason Gallagher,' he said coldly. 'Let's get him checked out straight away. We need to know who he is, who his next of kin is, and we need to let them know what's happened.'

'Yes, guv,' Hannon said, almost instinctively. She looked up tentatively.

'Jack will do.' He smiled back at her before turning back to the SOCO team. 'You guys finish up here. Get that body to Mitchell as soon as you can and then let me know the state of play.'

'Will do.' Came a voice from behind a mask. Townsend gave them the thumbs up. He strode towards Hannon and beckoned her to follow.

'We've got some bad news to break.'

As she fell in step behind him, a little cry of panic echoed behind them, and both Townsend and Hannon turned in time to see the limp body of Gallagher rock to the side and then collapse onto the sodden mud beside him. Gravity had done its job, and as the panic settled down, a few gasps of horror echoed around the crime scene.

Hannon looked on with wide eyes, and Townsend took a bold step forward, standing beside PC Boyd who looked horrified.

'I think we're in the right place,' Townsend finally said to him.

With his cheek pressed against the mud, Gallagher's slack jaw had fallen open to reveal that someone had cut out his tongue.

CHAPTER SIX

King was already waiting for them when they stepped through the door to the SCU, her arms folded as she propped herself on the edge of one of the desks.

'What have we got?' she asked, looking beyond Hannon to Townsend, who was already sliding off his coat.

'Two detectives who are just thrilled to be working this Saturday morning,' Townsend said dryly. Hannon chuckled as she lowered herself into her chair, adjusting the mandated back support she needed for her injuries.

'Ha ha,' King retorted. 'You think it's a murder?'

Townsend dropped into his own chair and swivelled round to face his boss.

'I think we have a guy, with no previous records for drug addiction, found with his tongue missing and bulging at the seams with heroin.' Townsend shrugged. 'I think he was murdered.'

'I ran the name. Jason Gallagher.' King pushed herself off the desk and strode to the glass screen that had been provided to them. She'd already printed off Gallagher's picture and stuck it to the top, as well as a map of Hughenden Manor's grounds. 'A few run-ins with our boys over the years. A DV accusation. A few slaps on the wrist for behaviour. Nothing we could ever really make stick. But we need to know what he was doing last night. Where he was and how the hell he ended up dead in the woods.'

'We need to go and speak to his wife.'

'Rachel. High school sweetheart. No kids.' King nodded. 'A FLO is already there, and I said we'd be along shortly to talk with her.'

Townsend nodded, and then frowned.

'What I don't get is why the theatrics?'

'What do you mean?' King asked. As always, she was coaching him, trying to guide his thought process out into the open. Townsend hadn't noticed it during the first few weeks of working together, but over time, he appreciated her constantly trying to develop him.

'If we're running on the basis that Jason Gallagher was murdered…why try to stage it like a suicide? Also, why pose the body in a way that hid the fact that they'd removed the tongue?'

'You think there's a meaning behind it?'

'I think it's worth looking in to.'

'Serial killers sometimes keep trophies?' Hannon said without looking up from her computer. 'Maybe our killer has a delightful tongue collection that they're just dying to share with us.'

'Charming.' King shook her head. 'But it's a decent theory.'

'Could be symbolic?' Townsend ventured. 'But if you have someone at your mercy to cut out their tongue, why then go through the rigmarole of the overdose?'

'Any chance it was removed after Gallagher was killed?'

'I don't think so. There was no blood on him. Nobody knew it was missing until he hit the mud.'

'Well, right now, we need to start looking at the facts we have and build out from there. We need to know where he was last night, where he went, who he was with. Everything. Hopefully, Rachel Gallagher can shed some light on him, but looking at some of the complaints she's made over the years, I don't think we'll be hearing about what a lovely husband he was.'

Behind King, Hannon was already clicking away on her keyboard.

'According to his social media, his last activity was to accept an invitation to the Cressex Community School reunion, which was…' Hannon raised her eyebrows.

'Last night,' King and Townsend said at the same time.

'Bingo.' Hannon sat back in her chair. 'God, I'm good.'

'Annoyingly, yes you are,' King said with a smile. 'I need a list of every single person who was at that reunion last night. Run the names, see what comes up, and pull out any people of interest.'

'On it, Guv,' Hannon said, as she reached for a custard cream biscuit from the personalised biscuit jar the team had brought her for her twenty-sixth birthday a few weeks before. King looked to Townsend and then beckoned him to her private office at the back of the SCU. Townsend looked to Hannon, who was already lost in her work, and then pushed himself up and obliged.

'Guv?' he asked as he stepped through the door. King had her arms folded.

'So before you two arrived back, I had a chat with Detective Superintendent Hall. He said he wants the SCU's *full* attention on this.'

'Understood.'

'*Full* attention, Jack,' King said with a sigh, and the penny began to drop.

'I promised Simone Miller I'd do everything I could and—'

'And you know you shouldn't make promises, Jack. Not in this job.'

'I gave her my word.'

'And I'm giving you an order,' King said firmly. 'This whole team, Jack. It has been built off what we did last summer in catching Baycroft. For us to continue to operate, we need to follow Hall's instructions and if he wants us on Gallagher's murder, then that's what we do.'

'So what…we're just going to give up finding out who killed Jamal Beckford?'

'Not exactly.'

Townsend's eyes closed in frustration, and without looking, he could already see the smarmy smirk plastered across DCI Marcus Lowe's face. With a gentle shake of the head, he turned to face the head of CID as he stepped into the office.

'Sir,' Townsend said, without hiding his disdain.

'DS Townsend. Izzy.' He smiled at his ex-wife, knowing it would make her skin crawl. 'I hear you've got a junkie's overdose to deal with.'

'It's a murder case…' Townsend snapped.

'Easy, Sherlock. I'm just pulling your plums.' Lowe smirked. 'But if you could pull together a lovely little report of all the work you did into the early hours of the morning, I'd really appreciate that.'

'Can we not do this?' King cut in. 'We'll send you over everything on the Beckford murder.'

'With respect, I'd like to be kept up to date with it,' Townsend said. Lowe raised his eyebrows.

'Would you now? Well, with no respect…I'll decide what you get up to date with.' He shot a frustrated glance at King and then smirked at Townsend. 'Now, if you could get that over to my team sharpish, that would be great.'

With an arrogant wobble of his head, Lowe turned and marched out of the office, through the rest of the SCU and out into the hall. Townsend clenched his fist, wondering if his wife would permit him one more round in the ring with him.

'Don't let him get to you, Jack,' King advised.

'I know. But he is a bellend.'

'On that, I will not argue with you.' King lifted her coat and began to slide her arms into it. 'I'll keep you in the loop as much as I can.'

'Cheers, Guv.'

'Now, get your coat on. We have to go and tell a wife that her abusive husband is dead.'

'This Saturday morning just keeps getting better and better, doesn't it?'

King chuckled, and Townsend whipped his coat from his seat and followed her out of the office. As they headed to the car park behind the High Wycombe Police Station, neither of them said a word, as a sense of dread began to loom over them.

There was something off about the whole thing.

The fake overdose.

The missing tongue.

As they got into Townsend's car and he started up the engine, he lowered King's window an inch as an invitation to allow her to vape. She smiled her thanks, but the smile soon faded as they made their way to Jason Gallagher's home address.

Both of them could feel it in their bones.

Something bad was coming.

They just didn't know what.

CHAPTER SEVEN

The drive out to Gallagher's home was riddled with the usual Saturday mid-morning traffic that ground the town of High Wycombe to a halt, as families dashed to the endless stream of activities, while busy shoppers descended upon the town centre. As they sat in the traffic, Townsend and King discussed Gallagher and what they knew about him.

The man's criminal record suggested he wasn't exactly an upstanding citizen, something that Townsend made the point of stating that it didn't mean he deserved to be murdered. King could appreciate that, and over the five months of working with the man, she admired his one true line of thinking as a detective.

Every victim deserves justice.

To Townsend, it didn't matter if the victim was rich or poor, Black or white, a boy scout, or a common criminal.

If someone had experienced a miscarriage of justice, or in the line of work that the SCU specialised in, had been stricken from the world by the hand of another human, that person deserved the truth to be found and the law to be applied.

In his eyes, there was no grey area when it came to the law.

As they sat at yet another temporary traffic light, with the construction crew nowhere in sight, King looked out over the rain-soaked Wycombe Rye, her eyes falling upon the very spot where Baycroft had come so close to killing her.

'You okay, guv?'

Townsend had sensed the tension in the car.

'Yeah, I'm fine,' she replied unconvincingly.

'You sure?' Townsend offered her a smile. 'It's been years since that bastard beat me to near death and not a day goes by that I don't get a flash of fear from it.'

King turned and looked at Townsend. The man was as tough as any detective or officer she'd met in her career, but his openness was refreshing. She knew fragments of his life before he moved to High Wycombe, the undercover work, the tentative link to the vigilante Sam Pope. The very near-death experience he had been through.

'It's just…' she began, but tapered off.

'It's hard to get past. I get it.' Townsend shrugged as the lights turned green and they crawled forward. 'But there are always ways to deal with it, you know? Some better than others.'

If it was meant to be a subtle reference, it hit like a sledgehammer and King squirmed a little in her seat. Her private life was always strictly that, and although she knew there were whispers of her drinking after the social media slurs against her, it had never been broached by a member of her team.

DSI Hall checked in with her regularly to ensure she was on the right path, and her dick of an ex-husband would often ask if she fancied going for a drink.

But never had her team made a reference to it.

It had caught her cold, and she felt her muscles tighten and an unwelcome annoyance flood through her.

'I'm fine,' she said curtly. 'I know how to look after myself.'

Townsend took the hint and nodded.

'I'm just saying, if you ever need to talk…'

'Let's just get to Rachel Gallagher and then we can talk.'

They drove in silence for the rest of the slow, twenty-minute journey to Totteridge, which was just outside of the town centre. It was a stone's throw away from the rather affluent Hazelmere, but it felt a century away in terms of its appeal. The small, winding roads were set on numerous hills, and the houses had been built decades ago and left to wither as the years went by. Numerous council estates had popped up over the years, and while other parts of High Wycombe had prospered, it felt like Totteridge had been left behind.

They turned on to Gallagher's street, and as they approached her house, Townsend pulled over and parked the car.

'This is it,' he said, looking up at the grotty looking house through the downpour. King offered him a nod, a half-hearted apology that she knew he'd accept, and then the two of them briskly made their way to the front door. DS Chopra, who worked closely with Ramsey, was the designated Family Liaison Officer, and she ushered them in from the rain. There wasn't much to update her on and she made the introduction between the two detectives and the widowed Rachel, who was sitting on a leather sofa in a cramped, tidy front room. Townsend was expecting to find a broken woman, yet she seemed relatively fresh faced, with her brown hair pulled into a ponytail and she looked at them with a bored expression.

'Rachel, can I just say how sorry we are for your loss,'

King started, taking a seat beside her on the sofa, as Townsend sat on the one opposite. Chopra entered with cups of tea and then made her exit as Townsend mouthed 'thank you'.

King continued. 'We understand this is a difficult time for you and…'

'Trust me, it's been a difficult time for a long time,' Rachel said coldly, sipping her tea.

'Oh?' Townsend leant forward. 'What do you mean?'

'Come on. You guys have probably spent more quality time with Jason than I have over the past few years. We weren't exactly happily married.'

Townsend looked to King, who, as ever, was the picture of calm.

'Are you referring to the domestic violence claim you mad—'

'Claim? That bastard knocked the shit out of me regularly and the one time I finally did call on you guys, nothing came of it. So I think it's a bit rich that you'd spend any time looking into who killed him.'

'I can only apologise for before,' King said, her fist clenching at the police's inability to keep a vulnerable woman safe. 'But we need to know as much as we can so we can ensure whoever did this is brought in.'

'Have you been down to Paradise?' Rachel shrugged. 'Whenever he'd have a drink, which was most nights, he'd end up in there.'

Townsend noted it down in his notepad and wondered if the owner would appreciate another visit from him or King so soon after the summer.

'Was there anything bothering Jason over the past few weeks?' Townsend asked. 'Anything that he was worried about?'

Rachel caught them both by surprise with a nasal laugh.

'Everything bothered him. Not earning enough money. Immigrants. How woke the world was. You name it, and he had a problem with it.'

'So he was easily antagonised?' Townsend offered.

'You could say that again. Once, he punched me in the face because I hadn't ironed a shirt he wanted to wear to a friend's wedding. He ended up going on his own because he didn't want them to see the black eye he gave me.'

Townsend drew his jaw tight and looked to King, and she could see he was struggling with his usual line of thinking.

Jason Gallagher deserved justice.

Even if he was a cowardly wife beater.

'Was there anyone who maybe wanted to hurt Jason? Did he mention having a falling out with someone?' King probed.

'Again, how long have you got?' Rachel shook her head. 'You don't have the manpower to go through the list of people who thought my husband was the shit on the bottom of their shoe. He drank. He gambled. He fucked around with other people's women.'

'It sounds like things have been difficult for you.' King tried to sound comforting, but Rachel waved them off.

'Trust me, I can deal with it.' Then she sighed. 'Well, I don't have to anymore.'

King looked to Townsend, who seemed deep in thought. After a few considered moments, he spoke.

'Jason was at a school reunion last night—'

'So he said.' Any effort she'd made to hide her irritation was slipping.

'Any reason why you didn't go, too? That's where you two met isn't it?'

'You think I want people to see that in the last twenty-five years I was still with him?' Rachel shook her head. 'I'd rather just stay here and let the world have him.'

'So you were here last night?'

'Yes. Thanks for enquiring if I had anything to do with it,' Rachel said with a mocking tone. 'Now, if that's everything you need to ask, I do have to call Jason's mum to tell her that her son is dead.'

King smiled warmly at Rachel and shut her notepad and then stood.

'We'll be in touch, Rachel,' she said softly. 'In the meantime, whatever you need, DS Chopra is on hand to help.'

'Does she need to be here?' Rachel said with a frown, not bothering to stand. 'I'm fine.'

'Like I said…we'll be in touch.' King turned to Townsend and nodded to the door. And he obligingly pulled it open and let her through before following. They said their goodbyes to Chopra before heading out into the freezing winter downpour.

'Well, that was awkward,' Townsend said gruffly, as they headed to his car.

'Yup.' King agreed, puffing on her vape. 'It seems like Mr Gallagher had a long list of people who hated his guts.'

As they both reached for their car doors, Townsend looked across the vehicle and into the eyes of his boss.

'Including his wife,' Townsend said coldly, before the two of them dropped into the car to head back to the station, knowing he was simply stating what they both were thinking.

Rachel Gallagher didn't seem at all shocked or upset that her husband was dead.

She seemed relieved.

CHAPTER EIGHT

'How was it?' Hannon asked, crunching on a custard cream biscuit as King and Townsend walked back into the office. She held the packet out invitingly, but both politely declined.

'Interesting,' Townsend said with a frown.

'It would appear that Rachel and Jason Gallagher weren't exactly happily married,' King said as she marched across to the glass board and looked up at the photo of the deceased. She reached for one of the dry-wipe marker pens and scribbled the name *Rachel Gallagher* on the board and drew a circle around it. 'In fact, I want us to do a little more digging.'

'You think she did it?' Hannon said with raised eyebrows. 'Classic.'

'I'm not ruling anything out. But she didn't exactly seem upset or surprised that he'd been killed.'

'Do we know where she was last night?' Hannon asked.

'She didn't go to the reunion. But we don't have anyone who can confirm she was at home.'

'If she was at home,' Townsend interjected. 'Gallagher wasn't killed at the reunion. As far as we know.'

'Good point.' King nodded and then turned to Hannon. 'Where are we on the guest list?'

'Oh, we're golden.' Hannon smiled. 'I've just sent a list of sixty-three names to our friends in uniform to go and knock on some doors. Suffice to say, I've ruined a number of Saturday afternoons.'

'Christ, is that the time?' King said, looking at her watch. Almost instantly, her stomach grumbled. 'Right, I need to grab some food and then I'm going to check in with Mitchell down at the morgue. I want to know the proper cause of death and try to figure out why the hell someone took Gallagher's tongue.'

'Need me to come with?' Townsend asked, his own stomach grumbling.

'No, I need you to go to the school. Get the CCTV. Ask some questions. I want to know who he was talking to, when, and where, he left the building and with who.' King shrugged. 'Chances are he tried his luck if his wife was telling us the truth about him.'

'I'll pop in and see our old buddy Sykes, too.' Townsend nodded. 'See if he can give us some dirt on him.'

'Sykes?' Hannon tried to place the name and then clearly found it. 'From Paradise?'

'Yep. Apparently, our man was a regular in there,' King answered and then turned to Townsend. 'Be nice.'

'I'm always nice, just in a slightly more challenging way than most.' Townsend grinned.

'Yeah. That'll be the Scouse.' Hannon joked, and Townsend shrugged his agreement.

'Right…let's crack on.' King clasped her hands together and marched out of the office. Once she was sufficiently out of earshot, Townsend turned back to Hannon, who was already digging up everything she could on Rachel Gallagher.

47

'Hey, Nic. Does the boss seem okay to you?'

'Who, King?' Hannon looked consumed. 'Same as ever. Why?'

'I don't know. I get this feeling she's struggling with something, but you know her…'

'Closed book.' Hannon agreed. 'My advice, Jack. Leave her to it. Or get Swaby to wrangle it out of her when she's back.'

The thought of it caused Townsend to chuckle. The irrepressibly joyous DS Swaby was always one for a good natter, and if anyone could get King's guard down, it would be her.

'Well, maybe I'll ask her when she gets back,' Townsend said and then headed towards the door, his stomach leading the way as he thought about the sandwich bar just up the road. As he ventured down the corridor, an unwelcome voice boomed behind him.

'Townsend.' With a sigh, DS Townsend turned to the approaching DCI Lowe, who walked purposefully towards him. He could tell his presence angered Townsend, and it clearly amused him. 'I'm not holding you up, am I?'

'No, sir.' Townsend refused to bite. 'I just have a murder investigation to get to.'

'Right. Of course. The junkie,' Lowe said in a belittling tone. 'Well, we've made some progress on the Beckford murder. Don't look so surprised. It's called good detective work.'

Again, Townsend refused to take the bait. Lowe continued.

'I would appear that our friend Jamal Beckford was part of the NX Crew, one of the most dangerous gangs in Wembley. Do you know Wembley, Jack?'

'Yes. Unsurprisingly, sir, I know where Wembley is.'

'Okay, calm down. No need to get shirty.' Lowe was clearly getting frustrated at the lack of Townsend's own.

'Well, I've got a mate who works that borough. We go way back from my days in the Met. I've reached out to him, but I should have something by close of play. I'll keep you posted.'

Townsend narrowed his eyes as he stared at Lowe, who held his strong, bearded jaw high. It wasn't the man's usual tactic to be cooperative, and Townsend trusted his gut more than anything in life.

'Thank you, sir.'

'As you were.' Lowe nodded before he swiftly turned on his heel and marched back through the station. Townsend watched him for a few moments before shaking his head and refocusing his mind on his own case.

King needed his full attention.

The death of Jason Gallagher demanded it.

The entire drive over to the imaginatively named High Wycombe High School had been entirely hijacked by Lowe, as Townsend spent the seventeen-minute drive pondering what exactly the man was up to. Despite being a celebrated detective by his seemingly endless number of supporters within the Thames Valley Police Service, Lowe was a petty and vindictive narcissist who seemed determined to undermine his ex-wife and the SCU at all times.

Townsend hadn't helped things in the long run by knocking him silly in a boxing ring, and as satisfying as it had been, he did worry about the consequences. But Lowe had been sincere when he spoke of his anger at seeing another young black man killed in a knife attack, and if Townsend needed to try his hardest to take Lowe sincerely, then he would at least try.

When he arrived at the high school, he let out an audible whistle at the facilities, with the plush, glass-panelled high school sitting between a pristine set of tennis courts, along with a number of artificial football pitches. It was a long way away from the concrete slab of his own high school in the worst part of Merseyside, but Townsend wouldn't begrudge the latest generation a better education than he had had. Mandy was already waxing lyrical about the tremendous schools within the county, and Townsend felt envious that she'd enjoyed school a lot more than he did.

Two vans from the same cleaning company were parked out front, no doubt there to clear away the mess from the party the night before, and Townsend knew that any hope of preserving what could be a crime scene would have long since been damaged. As he stepped into the reception area, one of the admin team, who seemed thoroughly unimpressed to be working on a Saturday changed her tune the second he flashed his ID. Clearly nursing a hangover from the night before, Carly Roberts, had attended last night and was now working in the school office during school hours while her own children attended the school. She didn't have much to offer on Jason Gallagher himself, remembering him as the "cool kid" all those years ago, but in hindsight, was a bit of a jerk. She had seen him that night, drunk as anything, and clearly on the gear, which didn't completely surprise Townsend given what Gallagher's own wife had said.

Beyond that, she didn't know much although she did mention the name Connor Davis which he noted down in his pad.

After having a look at the now nearly cleared main hall where the party had been held, he requested a look at the CCTV of the night before. When she booted up the system for him, he was blown away by the amount of surveillance within the school, comparing it to the odd teacher from his own who didn't give a damn about a fight breaking out as long as a weapon wasn't involved.

Times had certainly changed.

Carly helpfully pointed out Gallagher on the camera

overlooking the hall, and Townsend watched as the brutish man seemed to be pestering another, who he assumed, and Carly confirmed, was Connor Davis.

It wasn't until Gallagher left the party that they changed to a different camera, which overlooked the corridor where they watched him stumble into the bathroom. For obvious reasons, there was no CCTV within the school toilets, but Townsend made it clear no one was to enter or clean the bathroom before he had a SOCO team enter.

It was a formality, but he wanted them to check for traces of cocaine, which he was certain Emma Mitchell would confirm in her toxicology reports.

As he watched, a woman marched down the hallway, her brown hair cascading down into the hood of her leather jacket, and her jeans so tight they looked like they were painted on. She never turned to allow the camera to see her face, but Townsend watched with intrigue as she pushed open the door at the far end of the corridor and looked to fish out a cigarette.

She stood for a full two minutes, seemingly waiting, and it was only when a refreshed looking Gallagher emerged from the bathroom did she fish about for her lighter.

Gallagher watched her.

She lit the cigarette, and then disappeared out of the door, leaving it open for him to follow.

'Shit,' Townsend said under his breath.

'What?'

'Who is that woman?' He pointed to the screen where she'd stood and where Gallagher was now walking. 'Did you see her last night?'

Carly blew out her cheeks.

'To be honest, mate. It's all a little fuzzy.'

'I need copies of all this,' he demanded. 'Every camera. Can you download them for me?'

Her face dropped as if he'd just asked her to run a marathon.

'That'll take a while.' She tried to argue.

'Well, let's get started.' He flicked to the camera overlooking the car park, where the view of the door was obscured by a parked van. It didn't show much, except a sudden flash of pale skin dropping next to the tyre on the side, hidden by view.

A hand.

Gallagher's hand, which was swiftly dragged from view.

As Carly made an event of downloading the footage for him, Townsend pulled out his phone to call King to tell her that Gallagher wasn't killed randomly last night.

He was lured to his death.

CHAPTER NINE

As she walked through the Sexual Health Clinic of High Wycombe hospital, DI King tried to recount how many times she'd made this journey. When she'd moved from London to the cosy world of the Chilterns, she'd assumed that her life and career would calm down. Foolishly, she'd predicted that her cases would involve quaint mysteries, yet as she once again walked to the stairwell that led down to the morgue, she felt a shudder of horror at how many dead bodies she'd seen in her time at High Wycombe Police Station.

Evil wasn't just confined to the urban jungle that was London.

It bled through the country.

As she ascended the two staircases, she wondered how she'd get out of Dr Emma Mitchell's inevitable invitation for a drink after work. In the past, the two of them had shared many a bottle of wine in one of the local, police friendly pubs in the town. But with five months since both contact with Mitchell and an alcoholic beverage, King knew the offer was coming, and she'd had to make her excuses.

Perhaps Mitchell would be understanding to the fact that she was a recovering alcoholic?

Maybe talking to the people closest to her wasn't such a bad idea?

Before she could pull at that thread any further, King approached the thick, metal door to the morgue and pressed the buzzer. Moments later, it crackled to life.

'Hello?'

'It's me,' King said. No introduction necessary.

'Izzy! Give me a sec…'

As always, there was a bounce in Mitchell's voice, and despite spending her days slicing open dead bodies, the woman was a beacon of positivity, much in the same way that DS Swaby was back in the SCU. The thought of the two of them in the same room made King's head spin. With a buzz that echoed down the corridor, the door flew open, and Mitchell stepped out, decked in a white lab coat and with the usual smile plastered across her face.

'Well, well, well…we meet again,' she said with a grin.

'You knew I was coming, right?' King said with a raised eyebrow.

'Of course.' Mitchell pushed her glasses up her nose. 'I just like to spice the day up with a little improv. It's pretty dead in there.'

The joke pulled an unintentional smirk from King, and Mitchell turned and disappeared back through the door. King followed, taking a deep breath before she walked headfirst into the overpowering stench of sterilisation that always threatened to choke her. Mitchell didn't seem to notice it at all, which, through her twenty years as a forensic pathologist, was probably just a normal part of the day.

Like opening up a body and sifting through the pieces for clues.

As macabre as her world was, Mitchell embraced it

with an infectious enthusiasm and as she pulled on her gloves, she let them snap dramatically before she offered some to King.

'Shall we?' Mitchell said with an arched eyebrow, before she pushed open the final door that led to the morgue itself. King knew it well, but the sight of a body on one of the three metal slabs that were placed perfectly in the room always caught her a little off guard. She hadn't been present at the crime scene, and her only sight of Jason Gallagher to this point had been the photograph she'd pinned to the top of the investigation board.

But now here he was, a large lump under a white sheet which was illuminated by the fierce bulb above it. Without warning, Mitchell whipped the cloth from the body, exposing the man's naked corpse. Already, the body seemed paler than most, and despite being built like a rugby player, albeit one who had gone a little saggy around the seams, he didn't look as big as King had imagined.

Death had a funny way of reducing people in the eyes of the living.

'Do I need to introduce you?' Mitchell said with a shrug, trying to lighten the mood. It was an effective tactic and one that showed King Mitchell knew that those who visited her weren't as numb to the sight of death as she was.

For King, it was just part of the job.

'Jason Gallagher. Forty-one years old. Married. No kids. Lives in Totteridge,' King said as she slowly walked around the corpse. 'Heavy drinker. Drug taker.'

'Sounds like a catch,' Mitchell said sarcastically.

'Well, his wife didn't seem to care all that much that he'd been killed.' King stopped and looked at the rough needle marks on the inside of Gallagher's left arm, and the bruising that was building around it. 'Almost like she'd expected it.'

'Well, we can safely say that he was killed,' Mitchell said confidently. King's head snapped up.

'Can we?' King walked around to her expert friend. 'Because there are still some who want this swept away as a suicide.'

'Let me guess. Marcus.' Mitchell sighed. 'Twat. Anyway, like I said, it would appear Gallagher here was drugged, butchered, and then murdered. In that order.'

'Show me.'

'Well, you already looked at the arm just then. That was where the killer rammed a needle into him and over two hundred milligrams of heroin.'

'Jesus,' King uttered.

'It would have been pretty peaceful if that's any comfort to you.' Mitchell marched up to the top of the top of the body. 'This, however, would have hurt like hell.'

Expertly, she placed her fingers across either side of Gallagher's face and tipped his head back, opening his mouth to reveal the gaping wound where the man's tongue would have been. The jagged flesh that remained showed that it was hardly done by an expert hand, and King felt the lunch she'd quickly scoffed on the walk over, flipping in her stomach.

'Was he alive when this happened?' King asked, looking up at Mitchell.

'I believe so. Serrated blade judging from the cut itself, and as you can see, it's hardly the cleanest.'

'Any signs of a struggle?'

'Nope.' Mitchell gestured for King to grab a leg. After a nod, the two of them heaved the body up and onto its side. Gallagher's back was covered in a thin layer of fluffy brown hair, and also bore a couple of cheap, faded tattoos. It also had a significant bruise and scratch marks at the base of his spine that spread to the top of his buttocks. 'He clearly took a drop, as you can see by the state of his arse.'

'Emma,' King said with an audible tut. Mitchell shrugged. She steadied the body on its side and then beckoned King closer. 'There's also a fresh wound on the back of his skull here, and also grazing on his elbows. So he must have been unconscious when he hit the ground as he didn't try to stop himself.'

'Was he hit over the head?'

'Doubtful. The wound is in line with a fall, but this is where I can prove he was targeted. You know, beyond the tongue removal thing.' She pointed to a tiny mark on the back of his neck. 'A syringe mark.'

'You think he was drugged?' King said, stepping back from the corpse.

'I've got the toxicology reports to come back, but my guess would be that he was drugged, butchered, and then murdered. As I said.'

'Would take a pretty big hit to floor a guy this size.' King speculated. 'Any thoughts?'

'I'll put a rush on the report, as until we know for sure what's in his blood we're just guessing.'

'Good point.'

'Plus, whoever did this thought it through. Because the overriding substance will be heroin.'

'You think they were trying to cover their tracks?' King asked, truly valuing the expert opinion. For the first time since King had arrived, Mitchell paused for thought, and the usually chipper smile was replaced by a measured look of calm.

'I think whoever did this planned it out,' she said with a shrug. 'And I think they knew exactly when and where to find him, and how to do this to him.'

'So, in other words, a real dangerous bastard.'

'Bingo,' Mitchell said, shooting her finger at King before suddenly remembering something. 'Hey, you fancy a drink? Your treat for sending me a dead body to look at.'

King smiled politely as she wrestled with her inner demons.

'Not tonight, I'm afraid,' she said with a sigh. 'I've clearly got some work to do.'

'Ah yes. A killer to catch.' Mitchell led her towards the door. 'I'll get those toxicology reports to you pronto.'

'Thank you, Emma. I really appreciate it.'

'And tell Jack, that next time…I expect to see him here. I know he misses me.'

The two friends shared a laugh, but as King marched back towards the light and life of the outside world, she felt a shiver run down her spine, as if an ice cube had dropped down her collar from the heavens above.

There would be a next time.

Something, somewhere deep inside her, told her that this was only the beginning.

CHAPTER TEN

When DI King burst through the door of the SCU that Saturday afternoon, Townsend was already standing over Hannon's desk, his powerful arms folded across his broad chest and his eyes focused squarely on the two monitors before her. Hannon was glued to the screen too, scanning over a series of different windows, all containing CCTV footage.

'Is that from last night?' King asked as she slid out from her sodden jacket.

'Yup,' Townsend said without turning. 'You need to see this.'

King stepped forward, retying her black hair into a ponytail as she approached. Hannon enlarged one of the windows to show the corridor, where a woman who was too far out of focus stood in a doorway, patiently waiting.

'What is this?'

'This is Gallagher being lured outside,' Townsend said firmly. 'Watch.'

Sure enough, the footage played out, and as Gallagher emerged, the woman sparked to life, lighting her cigarette, and then, as the two looked at each other, she stepped outside, and he swiftly followed.

'Do we have any footage of her face?' King asked excitedly.

'Unfortunately, not,' Hannon said with a sigh. 'We just know that she's petite with dark hair.'

'Like Rachel,' Townsend suggested.

'It's a stretch.'

'You're the one who says we have to look at every possibility until they run out.' Townsend shrugged. 'Plus, it didn't come as much of a surprise that he was dead.'

'What happens next?' King said, pointing to the screen. Hannon swiftly moved from window to window.

'Not much. The camera in the car park is too far away to pick up any real details. Plus, she has her hood up. But if you look here, she disappears behind this van…Gallagher steps out and then…it looks like he hits the deck.'

'Lying in wait,' Townsend said grimly.

'Well, that is consistent with what Mitchell said,' King said as he stepped away and towards the board. 'Gallagher had bruising and markings that indicated a fall. He also had a gash on the back of his head.'

'You think she bashed him over the head?' Hannon asked, looking up from the screen. 'Would have needed a running jump based on the size of him—'

'That would have sent him forward.' Townsend interrupted. 'It looks like he falls backwards…'

'He was drugged,' King said. 'We don't know with what yet, but there's a clear syringe mark in the back of his neck that would indicate he was drugged and then took a drop. So whoever did do this, they'd planned it out. Which meant they knew where he was going to be and…'

'And where the cameras would be,' Hannon said.

'I take it when we roll that footage on and that van

does move, we won't see Gallagher's body?' King said sternly. 'Any luck with running down those names?'

'Uniform has come back to me on about a third of them so far,' Hannon said, shuffling through her notes. 'It's kind of hard to track down parents on a Saturday, but they're working through it. But so far, no dice.'

'What about Connor Davis?' Townsend asked, drawing King's attention.

'Who's that?'

'The admin lady at the school. She was there last night. She said Gallagher was talking to someone called Connor, and it tracks out through the footage.'

'Have we been able to track him down?'

'Not yet,' Hannon said. 'But he runs a well-respected accountancy firm not far from where you live, Guv.'

'Gallagher had debts?' King said with a shrug. 'But I think we need to speak to this Mr Davis as a priority.'

'We heading out?' Townsend asked. Before King could answer, Hannon lifted her hand.

'Before you go traumatising a nice family man, I did find something.'

King and Townsend turned to Hannon, both of them smirking with pride at how the young officer's confidence had blossomed over the past few months.

'Go on.'

'Well, like you just said, Gallagher had debts, right?' Hannon clicked her mouse to open a few documents on her screen. 'And his wife said he gambled and we're pretty sure he was a consistent drug user. Anyway, I managed to get access to his bank accounts…'

'And?' Townsend stepped forward to take a look.

'It's pretty bleak. Lots of cash withdrawals and a number of transactions at Paradise. I assume most drug dealers or working girls prefer cash in hand.' Hannon then pulled up another document. 'But you said his wife seemed pretty unmoved by his death, so I had a look through their joint account…'

'Same thing?' King asked.

'No.' Hannon shook her head. 'Probably because he doesn't have access to it, but I did find something interesting. She said she was at home last night, right? Well, a transaction was made through the account at a petrol station at around ten thirty less than a mile away from the school.'

King stepped forward, her brow furrowed.

'What time was Gallagher taken?'

Hannon swiftly returned to the CCTV footage.

'Ten fifty-five.'

Townsend and King both snapped their attention to each other, a spark of excitement at a possible breakthrough.

'We need to bring her in. Now,' King said with urgency. 'Jack, take uniform with you, and get her back here as soon as you can. I need to go and fill Hall in on our progress. Fantastic work, Nic. You're a diamond.'

'You could say I'm the jewel in the SCU crown,' Nic said with a wink.

'I could. But I won't,' King said with a smile, before bouncing out of the office as Townsend lifted his coat from his chair.

'Besides…' he said as he slid his arms in. 'I'm the jewel in this crown.'

'Yeah, yeah. You're an errand boy.'

Both of them laughed before Townsend turned and headed back to his car, knowing that every second counted. The first forty-eight hours in every murder case were crucial, and even if Hannon's discovery didn't mean Rachel was the killer, it did prove one thing.

Rachel Gallagher had lied about her whereabouts the night her husband was killed.

Thirty minutes later, and after a rather unpleasant exchange with Rachel and her mother, who had joined her during such a trying time, Townsend was following the patrol car that was taking her back to the station, leaving her aggressive mother in the more than capable hands of DS Chopra. As they pulled up in the station car park, Townsend ordered the officers to take her through to the interview room before he sent an apologetic text to his wife for another long day on the job.

She'd understand.

She always did.

But as he stood in the downpour, the yearning to get back into his car and treat his girls to a takeaway and a movie was pulling at him like a magnet.

But he slipped his phone and his keys back into his pocket and shook the thought from his head. Then he turned with purpose and marched back towards the station, ready to find out two things.

Where was Rachel Gallagher last night?

And did she kill her husband?

CHAPTER ELEVEN

Interrogation is an art form.

It was something Townsend was beginning to under-stand, and he often found himself marvelling at just how good DI King was at it. Although she wasn't physically the biggest woman in the world, the way she controlled the conversation and often drew what was needed from the unfortunate person on the other side of the table, made her seem ten feet tall. When he was made a detective in the Merseyside Police Service, it had always felt as nothing more than a make-good for the appalling betrayal that drew an end to his undercover work and almost cost him and his wife their lives. Inspector Reece Sanders had been in collusion with the very gang he'd been sent to infiltrate and had it not been for the intervention of the rogue vigi-lante, Sam Pope, there was a very good chance Eve would have been orphaned.

But once he'd recovered, and they gave him his shiny new position, they drowned him in busy work, under the false pretence that due to his undercover work, it was too dangerous for him to get involved in "real" police matters.

Truthfully, they didn't see him as a detective and neither did the Thames Valley Police when he was relocated down south. But King and Hannon had made him feel welcome and had drawn the detective out of him.

And by watching King in action, that development would only continue.

Once they'd entered the room, Rachel Gallagher had begun to aggressively remonstrate about the intrusion to her grief, but Rupa Patel had stopped her swiftly. Patel was a familiar face in the station as one of the duty solicitors often assigned to someone upon request. Rachel clearly had no intention of cooperating and had demanded representation even though she wasn't under arrest.

King had arranged it for her, and an hour after Townsend had brought her in, he and King sat opposite the woman who glared at them with hatred.

'Are we going to start or what?' Rachel snapped, as King sat quietly, shifting through a folder of notes. They weren't of any real use, but they did give the impression of importance. Slowly, she closed the file and fixed Rachel with a cold stare.

'Why did you lie to me, Rachel?'

'Excuse me?' Rachel looked at Patel, who stayed calm.

'Earlier this morning. You told my colleague and me that you were at home all last night.'

'Yes.' Rachel nodded, but she slightly shifted in her seat.

'That's not entirely true, is it?'

King sat patiently, looking at the woman who ran her tongue anxiously against her inner lip. To break the tension, Townsend leant forward, his hands clasped on the table.

'Rachel. There's a reason we didn't bring you here in cuffs, okay? I know today has been life shattering, and I know you must have a million things going through your head right now. But our job is to catch whoever killed your husband. He didn't overdose...he *was* murdered. And we need to work fast to find whoever did this.'

'So why aren't you out there doing that?' Rachel spat, and Patel reached out and placed a hand on her forearm to signal for her to calm down.

'Because you lied to us,' King repeated, her gaze locked on the agitated widow. 'So...where were you last night?'

Visibly distressed, Rachel looked to Patel for guidance. Townsend leant forward again, slipping easily into the role of good cop.

'Look, Rachel. We know you made a payment of thirty-three pounds and eighty-three pence at the petrol station just up from Handy Cross roundabout, last night at around ten thirty.' She squirmed again. 'It came from your joint account, which we checked with the bank, only has one card assigned to it and which we didn't find among your husband's belongings.'

'And the banking app's only been activated on one phone,' King said coldly. 'Yours.'

'And as it hasn't been reported stolen...' Townsend lifted his hand as he tailed off, his assumption clear.

'I...errr...' Rachel looked at Patel once again, who motioned for her to speak.

'It wasn't reported lost, either,' King said and sat forward. 'And if I was to search you right now, would I find—'

'Okay, fine,' Rachel interrupted. 'I went out last night. Is that a crime?'

'It depends,' King said, sitting back casually in her chair and in complete control of the interview. 'Because less than half an hour after you were at that petrol station, your husband was drugged and taken from somewhere a mile up the road.'

'Jesus fucking Christ, are you accusing *me* of doing this?' Rachel said, her eyes wide with fury. Her reaction was so genuine, Townsend almost felt bad for her.

But his personal feelings had no bearing on the facts. They needed to eliminate every possibility they could with complete certainty.

'You did confess earlier today that he hit you,' King stated, and Patel cut in.

'DI King, I appreciate you have a job to do, but please bear in mind that Mrs Gallagher has lost her husband today.'

'Yeah, the fucker hit me.' Rachel's words were laced with venom. 'But I didn't kill him.'

'Then fill in the blanks for me, Rachel,' King said, switching from cold to authoritative. 'Because trust me, nothing would make me happier than ticking your name off my list and letting you go home.'

All eyes fell on Rachel Gallagher, who dropped her head in shame. At once, the three other people in the room realised what the answer was going to be, and Rupa Patel leant towards the vulnerable woman and spoke softly.

'It's okay, Rachel,' she said tenderly. 'Just tell the truth.'

After a few moments, Rachel lifted her head, her eyes watering.

'Do you know what it's like to feel stuck? For the last twenty years of my life, I've had to watch friends, and people I used to love and care about, move on with their lives. You know, grow as people…into proper adults. They had families, got promoted, went on holidays.' She wiped a falling tear with the back of her sleeve. 'But Jason, he just never did. He looked in the mirror and he saw the same teenage kid who ruled high school and as time went on and I wanted more, he would just pick at me. Nasty comments which turned into degrading sex which eventually turned into balled fists. The idea of moving on from *who* he was to accepting *where* he was just sent him into a spiral. And he blamed me. When I said he was a piece of shit, I meant it.'

'I believe you,' King said, offering her a warm smile for the first time. Rachel nodded.

'I know you do. And I know you're both just doing your job. And these tears, these aren't of sadness. That might sound cruel, but they are of relief.' Rachel took a breath. 'But I didn't kill my husband. And if you need proof of that, you need to speak to Jamie Langley.'

'And who's Jamie?' Townsend asked.

'Jamie is the man I've been having an affair with for the past three years,' Rachel said bluntly. 'I'm not proud of myself but…'

She trailed off and King leant forward in her chair, her disposition changing from cold to caring in a heartbeat.

Townsend was almost in awe.

'Rachel,' she said with a warm nod. 'An affair isn't usually the cause of a marriage ending. It's usually a symptom of what's happened before. Trust me, as someone who's been through an unhappy marriage, it usually takes something big for it to eventually break.'

King's words drew more tears from Rachel, who tried to smile and nod but couldn't keep them in. Patel handed her a tissue before offering King a small, thankful nod.

'We'll speak to Jamie,' Townsend said. 'We'll need his number and address and once we can confirm everything, we'll be in touch. Thank you for your cooperation.'

The entire process seemed to have a cathartic effect on Rachel, who, after a few deep breaths, sat up straight as if a weight had been lifted from her shoulders.

'Does that mean I can go now?' she asked, looking at everyone in the room.

'Just one last thing…' Townsend lifted a finger. 'Does the name Connor Davis mean anything to you?'

The name caught Rachel by surprise, and her finely shaped eyebrows rose.

'Wow, now that's a blast from the past.' She racked her brain. 'Connor was Jason's best friend in high school. The two of them were inseparable. I was pretty good friends with his girlfriend, too. Penny. Penny Durant.'

'You said *was* his best friend?'

'Yeah. Like I said, Jason didn't want to move on from high school, but Connor…he was a smart guy. I think he got some degree in finance or something. Last I heard, he runs an accountancy firm, but we haven't heard from him in years.' Her eyes widened. 'Wait, do you think he had something to do with this?'

'It's just a name that came up,' Townsend said with a smile. 'Let's get you home, shall we?'

Rachel smiled, and she stood along with Patel, who ushered her towards the door. As they closed it behind them, Townsend blew out his cheeks, rubbed his eyes with the balls of his wrists, and then stood.

'Great work, Jack,' King said with a reassuring nod as she stood.

'What now?' he asked, pulling on his sodden coat to brave the elements once more.

'I'll follow up with Langley. Arrange for him to come in tomorrow…' She looked at her watch and frowned. 'Drop her off and then get yourself home. You've had a long few days.'

Townsend chuckled.

'The thing is, Guv.' He headed to the door, and as he pulled it open, he looked back at her with his cheeky grin. 'They're all long days.'

Townsend stepped out, briefly spoke to Patel and Rachel before leading them both down the corridor. King watched, impressed by the disarming charm of the man and his intrinsic good nature that drew people towards him.

Then, with a sigh, she uttered to herself.

'Right you are, Jack.'

Then she headed out of the interview room with a phone call to make and another avalanche of emails to sift through.

CHAPTER TWELVE

As she saw the lights of DS Townsend's car burst into life, Rachel Gallagher stood and watched as the rain lashed down on his car. It was only when she saw his tail lights disappear around the corner that the weight of the past twenty-four hours really hit her.

As she turned and headed towards the door, she felt her knees buckle and she dropped down onto the concrete, her hands slapping against the wet concrete to catch her from colliding. The door to her house flew open and her mother raced out, doing all the things a mother would do, fussing as she helped Rachel to her feet.

Rachel welcomed the comfort, and as her mum ushered her in from the rain, Rachel could feel her body shaking.

Jason was dead.

As tough as she'd tried to be throughout the day, she was suddenly presented with an enormous vacuum in her life. The love between them had long since turned to a disdain, but the idea that she'd never see the man or again, or hear his gravelly voice wasn't something she'd quite processed.

No longer would she need to prepare herself for a drunken argument with a man who loathed himself almost as much as he loathed her.

Never again would she feel her skin crawl as he slid a hand over her thigh in bed, trying to initiate a passion that had burnt out years ago.

As her mother boiled the kettle and made herself busy with the mugs in their sliver of a kitchen, Rachel sat at the small kitchen table and just stared into space.

She should have hated herself for it, but a smile crept across her face.

She wasn't happy that Jason had been murdered.

She was simply relieved.

In their teenage years, Jason seemed like a superstar, with his good looks and his athletic ability, but all that had faded swiftly and had been followed by decades of unemployment, drinking and bad decisions. The world was against him, he'd often said, and for a long time, Rachel had fallen under his spell and believed it. But then she'd seen others build lives for themselves, and the more she looked at her husband, the more she'd realised he'd dragged her down with him.

She'd never had the career she'd wanted.

Never had the children she thought they would.

The only fragments of happiness she'd experienced in the past decade were in the last three years since she'd met Jamie.

Back then, she'd been working as an office manager in a logistics company, and he'd been called in to do some plumbing work in the building. They'd instantly hit it off, and when he'd asked for her number, her desperation to feel good about herself once again had caused her to write it down.

Her longing for something even resembling true

passion was why she'd answered the call, and the first time they'd had sex had been transformative.

It wasn't because it was new or with someone else.

It was because she'd wanted to.

Lost in her thoughts, Rachel didn't realise her mother had placed a mug of tea in front of her and taken the seat opposite.

'What a mess,' her mother uttered.

'You can go home, Mum,' Rachel said with a smile. 'I'll be fine.'

'Nonsense,' her mother said, sipping her scalding tea. 'Poor Jason.'

'The police are doing all they can,' Rachel said calmly, her eyes darting to her phone.

'Pah. Sure they are. Dragging you in like a suspect.' Her mother shook her head. 'Mind you, that detective was a bit dishy, wasn't he?'

Rachel felt her lips lift into a smile. DS Townsend was easy on the eye, but it was actually his nature that had struck a chord with her.

He actually seemed to care. To want to know what had happened to her husband. Although a bit of her hated herself for not mourning the death of her husband, she was at least glad that his murder was being investigated by someone like him. Without saying a word, Rachel opened her phone, tapped out a message, and then set it down.

'Seriously, Mum. It's been a long day. I think I just need to get some rest.'

'Are you sure?' Her mum raised her tinted eyebrows. 'I'm happy to stay and—'

'I'm sure,' Rachel replied. 'I think I just need to be alone and get a good night's sleep.'

Clearly offended, her mother gave her a reassuring smile and a few minutes later, she was putting on her coat and promising Rachel she'd be back again in the morning.

Rachel thanked her, saw her to the door, and as soon as she'd closed it, she opened her phone once more and sent Jamie another message.

I need you.

It felt silly hiding Jamie from her mother, especially now there was no sense of betrayal.

She was finally free.

Free to be happy with the man she truly loved, and after a quick shower, she put on her nicest underwear and a baggy T-shirt and felt her heart skip when the doorbell went. Jamie was soaked through, but the two of them embraced in the hallway. Their lips locked harder and harder, and she felt her hands already pulling at the belt of his jeans as his own slid up her T-shirt. They made their way to what had been her and Jason's marital bed for over twenty years, and she pushed him down on it, removing the rest of her clothes as he slid off his trousers and underwear and beckoned her on.

She lowered herself on top of him, and for the next five minutes, she allowed all the pain and anger of the past twenty years to flow through her as she rocked back and forth wildly. They both groaned with pleasure, and every time his hands grasped her hips or her breasts, she felt a surge of happiness through her body.

It came to a loud and explosive end, and she collapsed on top of him, his hands clasping her sweaty back as their bodies pressed against one another.

'I love you,' she said through quick breaths.

'I love you too,' Jamie replied, also panting.

They laid in silence for the next few moments, their naked bodies linked until Rachel finally rolled to the side and rested her head on Jamie's muscular chest.

His heart was beating at a rate of knots.

It was likely due to the intense sex they'd just had, but a

bit of her knew it was due to the same thing that was causing hers to beat faster.

They could finally be together.

This could be their life from now on.

After a few more moments, Jamie leant upwards and turned to her, his face strewn with concern.

'The police called me this evening,' he said, with a small undercurrent of accusation. 'They said I need to go in tomorrow morning for a chat.'

'I told them about us,' Rachel said with a smile. 'They needed to know where I was last night and…'

'They don't think I did it do they?'

'No. Oh gosh, no.' Rachel sat up and gently cupped his strong jaw in her hand. 'I told them we were together and they just need to confirm it all. I guess we no longer need to keep this a secret, huh?'

Jamie smiled and placed his hand over hers. She looked beautiful in the golden light that cut through the curtains.

'I guess not.' He chuckled. 'Although, maybe let's wait a little while. I hardly think putting it up on Facebook the day your husband died is a good idea.'

Rachel laughed.

It had been the first time she'd laughed all day, and it felt amazing, and she then leant forward and planted a gentle kiss on Jamie's lips.

'Fancy a drink?' She raised an eyebrow.

'You read my mind.'

They kissed once more and then threw on their underwear before heading down to the kitchen to raid the cupboard. There wasn't much, but Rachel found a bottle of vodka in the back of one unit while Jamie found a few cans of cola in the fridge.

'Vodka and Coke it is,' Rachel said with a giggle, and without a care in the world, she sat with her true love at the small kitchen table in just their underwear, and she enjoyed a cigarette and a drink as he spoke to her about their future.

A holiday to Greece.

Trips into London to see shows.

Even the little idea about taking her out to a nice country pub for a Sunday roast made her heart flutter.

This was what it was like to be happy.

They poured themselves one more drink before they headed upstairs once again, this time for a longer, more adventurous sexual escapade, and by the time they'd finished, they were ready to sleep for a week.

As they collapsed onto the mattress, their naked bodies shuddering under a thin layer of sweat, he made a promise of a coffee and a croissant on his trip back from the police station.

As her eyes fell shut, it sounded like heaven.

Little did she know, she'd never open them again.

CHAPTER THIRTEEN

This was the job.

That was what Mandy told herself, as she woke up that Sunday morning and reached out to find her husband no longer lying next to her. A small twinge of sadness crept through her body, as the events of the previous evening had been so wonderful. Townsend had returned home, soaked through, but with a takeaway pizza and a smile on his face. As always, Mandy had chosen not to ask about his day, as he'd been called away early and had missed Eve's ballet session along with their afternoon playdate with one of her school friends. No doubt, he'd been once again dealing with a morbid situation, and her social media time-line had been filling up with news of the body found in Hughenden Park.

But he'd arrived home, spring in his step, and the three of them sat down in front of the TV, pizza on their laps, and watched the animated movie Eve had insisted on watching for the hundredth time.

But Mandy didn't watch it.

She watched Jack, who hadn't seen it, and consumed it with the same enjoyment and vigour as their daughter.

He was there for bath time, too, drawing countless giggles from Eve as he covered his face with bubbles, before she found him dozing next to her, the copy of *Matilda* open on his lap as he'd read her to sleep. That was when she'd taken his hand, led him to their bedroom and they'd made love and fallen asleep in each other's arms.

And now he was gone.

Taken once again by the severe responsibility that his position as a detective sergeant in the Thames Valley Police demanded from him.

As she sighed and went to push herself off the mattress, her heart skipped a beat at the sound of an egg sizzling on a frying pan, accompanied by the out-of-tune singing of her husband that echoed up the stairwell.

Eve was giggling once again, as her dad treated her to a rendition of his 'omelette song'. She quickly dressed and scurried down the stairs, just in time for him to hit a terrible high note that caused their daughter to jovially throw her hands over her ears. Mandy reciprocated before planting a kiss on Eve's forehead. She then wrapped her arms around Townsend's waist, catching him by surprise.

'Oh, you're up,' he exclaimed, tossing the perfect-looking omelette over to cook it through.

'Well, I could hardly sleep with all this noise, could I?' She nuzzled into his neck.

'Well, sit down. Breakfast is nearly ready,' he said with a grin, and she took the seat next to Eve, who was already crunching down on some toast. 'One picture-perfect omelette coming right up.'

Moments later, he placed her breakfast in front of her, and then went about fetching her a cup of tea. The trio sat around their kitchen table, and Eve recounted to Townsend the previous day, and how she couldn't wait for her ballet recital next Friday.

'You're still coming, aren't you, Daddy?' Eve asked, looking at Townsend with hope.

'I wouldn't miss it for the world, Pickle,' he said with a smile, before he locked eyes with Mandy who gave him a silent warning.

Don't make promises you can't keep.

Once they'd finished breakfast, they all got ready and Townsend booked them in for an hour-long session at the enormous trampoline park, hidden away in one of the industrial estates just outside of the town centre. Once they arrived and went through the needlessly over-the-top safety procedures, Eve burst onto the vast array of trampolines and began to show off for her parents, nailing some exceptional cartwheels and even a front flip. Townsend couldn't believe her skills but was completely taken aback by Mandy's prowess on the springs, and soon revealed she'd been a keen trampolinist throughout high school.

'What kind of high school did trampolining for an activity?' Townsend asked with an eyebrow raised.

'One that didn't encourage kids to box each other.' She shot back, and Townsend conceded that his own experiences of high school were very different to hers. Coming from a rougher part of Merseyside than she did, Townsend had found his calling in the boxing ring, a passion he'd abandoned at Mandy's request when they became expectant parents. As he watched his girls bounce wildly across the trampoline park, Townsend felt his heart bursting with pride and he wished that his own father could have spent some time with them both.

Malcolm Townsend had been a proud member of the Merseyside Police Service, but the stress fracture to his spine that he sustained during the Toxteth Riots in the early 80s soon caught up with him and his life spiralled after that. Townsend watched his father fall into a depression that would eventually lead to the breakdown of his marriage to Townsend's mother. When Malcolm Townsend was eventually diagnosed with bowel cancer, he put up little fight, and when he finally passed just after Townsend's seventeenth birthday, his son saw it as a mercy.

Thinking of his father drew a smile across Townsend's face, and he looked at the watch, strapped to his wrist, that had once belonged to his father, and figured he'd make the most of the last few minutes they had in the park. He raced Eve to the diving board, hurling himself off and crashing onto the air-filled mattress below.

His daughter, however, was a little more graceful, executing a perfect front flip that drew the ire of the staff, and Townsend half-heartedly apologised before he led his girls upstairs to the café. Eve raced to the glass counter, selecting the enormous chocolate chip cookie, before she rushed off to find them a table overlooking the neon-drenched trampoline park below. As Townsend waited in the queue to order, Mandy pushed up on her tiptoes and kissed his stubbly jaw.

'Love you, mister,' she said with a warm smile.

'You, too,' Townsend replied. 'What a lovely morning, eh?'

'Well, when they let us have you for a little while, it turns out we have quite a nice time,' Mandy joked. 'It's almost like we're a happy family.'

'Imagine that.' Townsend chuckled, and just as he took his place at the counter to order, his phone vibrated in his pocket. 'One sec…babe, can you order?'

Mandy stepped forward, but then watched with a sense of resignation as Townsend's face went from joyful to stern in a matter of milliseconds. She knew what was coming, and as much as she craved a full day of the three of them just enjoying each other's company, she knew that her husband was needed elsewhere.

The man was a hero, even if he hated the word.

Mandy ordered the two coffees, and the cookie, and as she tapped her phone to pay for them, a rueful Townsend marched back over, already holding up his hands in apology.

'Don't say sorry, babe,' Mandy said with a smile. She leant forward and kissed him on the lips. 'We understand.'

'I have to go,' he said with a sigh. 'Best cancel my coffee.'

Townsend rushed across the café area to Eve, and Mandy's heart cracked slightly at the immediate sadness that fell across their daughter's face as he gave her the news. It had been a long road for the both of them, Eve and Jack, but they were now as thick as thieves and the disappointment that was clearly emanating from both of them was a testament to the bond they'd forged. As he marched back towards her, Townsend blew out his cheeks as he battled his own anguish.

'She'll be fine,' Mandy said calmly to ease his worry and then handed him a takeaway cup. 'I got yours to go.'

'You're the best,' Townsend said smiling, then kissed his wife passionately and then darted towards the stairs. Mandy joined Eve at their table and watched with a mixture of sadness and pride as her husband pushed open the doors to the outside world and disappeared into the rain.

This was the job, she told herself.

This was the job.

CHAPTER FOURTEEN

By the time Townsend had arrived at Rachel Gallagher's address, the SOCO team were already buzzing around the property, getting ready to analyse the house with a fine-tooth comb. Uniformed officers were braving the elements, standing on the cordons that had been marked out with white and blue police tape, and ushering the nosy neighbours back from the crime scene. Word had already spread of Jason Gallagher's murder, with the curtain twitchers on the road spreading their uninformed rumours like another infectious disease. Townsend pulled his car over onto the curb before he marched through the rain, flashing his lanyard to one of the officers before ducking under the police tape. Usually, he wore a shirt, tie, and trousers in an attempt to look semi-professional, but the events of the morning had ripped him straight out of his normal life.

Hannon was the first to make a remark.

'Well, don't you look casual,' she said with a smirk. Townsend looked down at his black T-shirt, jeans, and trainers, and then gestured for them to move into the house out of the freezing rain. 'Do you not wear coats on the weekend?'

'It's in the car,' Townsend said as they stepped into the hallway of the home where he'd met with DS Chopra just the day before. He looked around the house and blew out his cheeks. 'Fucking hell.'

'You can say that again.' DS Chopra's voice cut through the hallway as she emerged from the kitchen. She jolted her thumb back over her shoulder. 'Rachel's mother is in there if you want to have a word. Poor woman, found them both this morning.'

'Are they still upstairs?' Hannon asked a little anxiously.

'Rachel is,' Chopra said sadly. 'Langley's already been arrested and taken to hospital.'

'Arrested?' Townsend snapped his head towards her.

'Yup. They found him next to her, unconscious with an empty bottle of pills in one hand and a straight razor in the other.' Chopra shook her head. 'I'm warning you both. It's not pretty up there.'

'Thank you,' Townsend said with a firm nod. 'Tell Rachel's mother we'll be down in a few moments. I want to see the crime scene before SOCO swarm all over it.'

'How bad is it?' Hannon asked, her voice cracking slightly with nerves.

'You'll be fine,' Townsend assured her. 'Just stay with me and if you feel yourself going, don't do it in the room.'

Townsend climbs the stairs with purpose, shoving his hands into his pockets as he did so as not to touch anything on the way, and Hannon followed behind. A few SOCOs were already on the landing, preparing their investigation, and one of them nodded for Townsend to go through.

'It's not a pretty sight.' The faceless voice warned them.

They weren't lying.

As Townsend pushed the door open with his broad shoulder, he felt his entire body stiffen at the sight that welcomed him. Behind, he heard Hannon gasp in shock and then the two of them made careful steps as they entered the bedroom. A blood-soaked duvet was hanging over the end of the bed, the drenching of the sheets now seeping into the worn white carpet. To the left of the bed was a dressing table, with a number of high-end moisturisers presented neatly in a row. The curtain was half open, allowing a little of the gloomy outside world to filter in and offer a further layer of dullness to the bleak scene.

On the ground beside the bed was an empty bottle of vodka.

On either of the bedside tables were empty glasses.

But on the bed itself lay Rachel, her naked body slathered in her own blood, which had also covered almost the entire sheet beneath her. Lying on her back with her arms by her side, the skin of each forearm had been sliced vertically, the deep slashing severing every major vein in her wrists in what was regarded as one of the most effective means of suicide. The damage done by a vertical cut was nearly irreparable, causing the victim to bleed out through uncontrollable blood loss, which was certainly the cause of death.

But it wasn't a suicide.

Rachel Gallagher had clearly been murdered, and although Townsend would pick up the finer details once he'd paid his silent respect to the deceased, he'd already been informed that her lover, Jamie Langley had been found beside her with the murder weapon in hand and most likely a stomach full of paracetamol.

But despite all the blood and the deep, horrific wounds up Rachel's arms, the one thing that really sent a shiver down Townsend's spine was the blood that had stained the woman's face.

Her eyes were shut, but her mouth was open.

And her tongue was missing.

'Poor woman.' Hannon eventually broke the silence,

and Townsend nodded in agreement. 'What you thinking, Jack?'

'I think someone's sending a message.'

'Like what?'

Townsend shook his head in defeat and sighed.

'I don't know. Not yet.' He nodded to the doorway. 'But we need to let these guys crack on.'

Townsend and Hannon stepped back out onto the landing, allowing the two SOCOs to enter the bedroom and get to their meticulous work. Slowly, the duo descended the staircase, their footsteps echoing through the morbid household, and Townsend gently knocked on the kitchen door. Chopra opened it and then beckoned them in. Sitting at the kitchen table, staring vacantly into a stone-cold cup of tea, was Rachel's mother, who Townsend had met the day before.

'Janet.' Chopra tried to speak through the woman's grief-stricken haze. 'Janet…you remember DS Townsend?'

Janet slowly lifted her head to Townsend, who offered her a sympathetic smile as he took the seat across the small table.

'Janet, I am so sorry for your loss.'

'Do you have kids, detective?' Janet spoke softly, looking down at her mug on the table.

'Yes, I do. A little girl.' Townsend tried to stymie the pride in his voice.

'Trust me. Even when you get to my age, you never stop being a parent to them. Never stop worrying about them.' The woman broke down in tears. 'Never stop loving them.'

As DS Chopra comforted the broken woman, Townsend looked to Hannon and nodded for her to wait outside. As Hannon stepped out into the hallway, Townsend waited patiently for Janet to compose herself and then he'd her walk through what happened. She'd left her daughter last night to get some rest and had then woken up early to pick up some shopping to come and fill Rachel's fridge and then treat her daughter to some breakfast. It was only after she'd called up a few times to no response did she notice the pair of men's shoes by the front door, and when she described opening the bedroom door, she broke down again, this time uncontrollably.

Townsend thanked her for her time, offered his condolences, and then promised DS Chopra they'd be in touch. As he stepped out into the hallway, Hannon winced at the mournful cries of Rachel's mother from beyond the door, and Townsend looked visibly shaken.

'You okay, Jack?' Hannon asked.

'I just…' Townsend shook his head. 'I can't imagine the pain, you know?'

Before Hannon could respond, Townsend's phone buzzed, and he held it up to show Hannon that King was calling. He answered, nodded a few times, and then hung up.

'I take it that wasn't a coffee order?' Hannon asked, trying to cut the tension.

'Guv wants us back for a debrief.' He pocketed his phone. 'Hope you didn't have plans today.'

'Come on now, Jack. You know we aren't allowed to make plans.'

Townsend smirked, once again grateful for Hannon's companionship, and the duo headed back out into the pouring rain. They felt all the eyes of the watching crowd on them as they made their way to their respective cars. As soon as Townsend dropped into the seat and slammed the door, he sent a quick message to Mandy to let her know he was gone for the day and then slammed his phone down on the passenger seat. He took a few deep breaths as he clenched the steering wheel and watched as his knuckles turned white with frustration.

Rachel Gallagher, once they'd broken through her hard outer shell, was just an unhappy woman who'd been beaten down by the life her husband had forced her into.

No happiness.

No family.

No way out.

She'd found comfort in the arms of another man, who was now their chief suspect behind her, and her husband's, murders.

But something didn't feel right to him, and Townsend started the car hating the fact that process dictated they follow the evidence. That Langley had the murder weapon in his hand and had seemingly tried to commit suicide to leave the earth with Rachel.

But in his gut, Townsend didn't think that Jamie Langley was the killer.

Which meant whoever had killed the Gallaghers was still out there.

CHAPTER FIFTEEN

As Townsend and Hannon pushed open the door to the SCU, King was already waiting, arms folded as she rested against the edge of Townsend's desk. Knowing full well that Hannon would have stopped at the coffee shop on the way in, King extended her hand to gratefully receive it.

'So…' King began, sipping her coffee and nodding her thanks to Hannon. 'Fill me in.'

'Rachel's wrists were sliced open,' Townsend said with a sigh. 'But I don't think it was a suicide.'

'No, I hear that her lover, Jamie Langley, was caught with the murder weapon and a stomach full of pills.' King stated, clearly already up to date on proceedings. She was just coaching the team, which Townsend realised was one of her natural gifts. 'He's up the road having his stomach pumped right now.'

'Good. Then he can rot in prison for what he did to that poor woman,' Hannon said through gritted teeth as she lowered herself into her chair, her longstanding back issues clearly giving her some discomfort.

'You think he did it?' Townsend asked with a raised eyebrow. King jumped in before Hannon.

'You don't?'

'It just doesn't feel right,' Townsend responded and then lifted his hand before King could respond. 'I know, I know. We need to go by the evidence, not by feeling, but it just doesn't add up. Why cut out her tongue?'

'Maybe she said something to him he didn't like?' Hannon suggested. 'We already know they'd been having an affair for the past few years—'

'Yeah, and now with Jason Gallagher dead, they'd be home free to actually be together,' Townsend said.

'So you think he killed Jason Gallagher?' King said with a frown.

'No. I don't think he's our guy, but I appreciate he was lying next to a dead woman with a straight razor in his hand and a clear attempt at taking his own life. I just…'

Townsend trailed off and dropped into his seat and rubbed his eyes with the balls of his wrists. King looked to Hannon and then pushed herself from his desk and approached the murder board.

'I get it, Jack. I'll be honest, I don't know what the hell is going on. But let's just look at the facts right now.' King unpinned Rachel's photo from its position on the board and then tacked it with authority next to her also deceased husband. 'Jason Gallagher was lured out of the school reunion by a mysterious woman and ten hours later, is found dead in Hughenden Park. We can rule out the suicide, as his tongue had been removed. So why was he killed?'

'Langley wanted Rachel for himself?' Hannon offered from over her computer screen.

'Maybe,' King said, arms folded and her eyes locked on the board. 'But she gave a pretty clear alibi that she was with him last night, so unless she's lying…'

'Maybe that's why he killed her?' Hannon said. 'Maybe

her conscience got the better of her and she threatened to go to the police?'

King nodded with encouragement.

'It's a good theory. The best one we have so far.'

'It would explain cutting out her tongue, I guess,' Townsend chipped in. 'Send her a message not to say anything.'

'I'm waiting for word from the uniforms at the hospital. As soon as Langley's well enough to talk, I want you to get it out of him.'

'Me?' Townsend pointed at himself. 'Sure. You not coming?'

'I've got Connor Davis coming in this morning. You know the friend from the reunion. I spoke with him last night and he offered to come in for a chat.'

'Isn't it nice when the public aren't dick-heads to us?' Hannon piped in, drawing a smile from the rest of her team. 'Want me to do some digging on him?'

'It couldn't hurt.' King shrugged. 'From what Rachel said, they've been estranged for a long time, but if there is a more recent link between the two of them and he doesn't offer that up freely…'

'Then it's another avenue of investigation,' Townsend said, and King clicked her fingers and pointed to him.

'Exactly. Follow the facts. It's all we can do.'

'I hope you're planning on doing more than just that.'

The booming, respect-commanding voice of Detective Superintendent Geoff Hall snapped all their attentions to the doorway, and the immaculately presented man stepped into the SCU office. Oozing authority, he nodded to the team who stood to attention, motioning for them to take their seats.

'Of course, sir,' King said with a smile. 'But we can't go shaking the wrong cages just yet.'

'Oh, I'm not doubting this team's ability to get this

done. Far from it.' He then shot a glance at Townsend with a wry smile. 'Even if you do have a certain knack for pissing people off.'

'Thank you, sir,' Townsend said with a grin. Hall straightened up, and took a few steps towards the board, gazing his expert eye over it. Although the man wielded immense power within the Thames Valley Police Service, he was as respected as he was feared, and over the past few months, Townsend had enjoyed witnessing the clear mutual respect that he shared with DI King. 'So... murdered couple?'

'Yes, sir.'

'I hear that the wife had a lover, who is now in our custody.'

'It's a little complicated...' Townsend began, but King held up her hand to stop him.

'That's correct, sir. He's currently getting medical treatment and then we'll be questioning him.'

Hall tutted as he shook his head.

'You know, Jill and I have been married nearly thirty years. The thought of playing away has never crossed my mind. Nasty business.'

'Tell that to my ex,' King joked, but it drew a scowl from Hall, who had made it clear to both her and DCI Lowe that the fallout of their messy divorce wasn't welcome within the police station. 'Sorry, sir.'

'No worries.' He grinned. 'But let's not let this get out of hand, shall we? Two murders within twenty-four hours...as soon as the media gets onto this, it will spread like wildfire. And we know how damaging that can be...to all of us.'

Hall's emphasis on the final point was for King's benefit, as he'd worked tirelessly to steer the media away from her during the Baycroft murders over the summer. Her drinking problem had been exposed, even if just for a moment, and Hall had pulled her out of the firing line to protect her.

She would be forever grateful, and although her team had no idea as to her struggles for sobriety, Hall had been a friendly shoulder and an encouraging voice in her battle.

'We're on it, sir,' King assured him.

'Fantastic.' He gave them all a respectful nod. 'This is the Specialist Crime Unit. Keep earning that name.'

With that, Hall took his leave, and although Townsend once again stood out of respect, Hall motioned to Hannon not to stand, which she smiled her appreciation for. Once Hall was gone, Townsend stayed standing, his hands on his hips and his eyes locked on the board. King's phone buzzed just as the office phone began to ring. King lifted her phone to her ear, while Hannon answered the one on her desk.

Both of them seemed to be agreeing to something or other, but Townsend wasn't listening.

The wheels in his head were turning.

His scepticism growing.

Almost in synchroneity, Hannon hung up the call as King lowered her phone. Hannon spoke first.

'Guv, Connor Davis is in reception.'

'Brilliant,' King said as she pocketed her phone. 'Can you take him into one of the interview rooms, please? I just need a quick five.'

'You got it, guv,' Hannon said as she eased out of her chair and disappeared into the hallway.

'Langley has had his stomach pumped and is now awake. I need you to get down to the hospital and find out what the hell happened last night.' King looked up at Townsend, who had lost himself in the board before him. 'Jack?'

He snapped out of it and turned to her.

'Yes, guv?'

'Did you hear me? Langley's awake. Off you go.'

'Yeah, sorry.' Townsend lifted his soaked jacket and then turned back to King. 'I have a question.'

'Yeah?'

'Why try to stage the deaths to look like suicides?'

'I don't know. For show?'

'But whoever did this would surely know we'd see the missing tongue. So we'd obviously be looking for a killer,' Townsend said. 'So why do it?'

'Why don't you ask Langley?' King said as she ushered him to the door. 'And remember, Jack. Play nice.'

Townsend chuckled as he marched out of the office, knowing full well what King was telling him to do.

Find the truth.

Try to do it as compliantly as possible.

But find the truth at all costs.

CHAPTER SIXTEEN

As he sat patiently in the interview room, Connor Davis blew out his cheeks and looked towards the mirror that ran along the far wall. He'd seen enough TV shows to know that it was two-way glass, but he doubted there was anyone behind it. He'd volunteered to come in to speak to the polite detective who'd called him and he understood, as one of the last people seen with Jason Gallagher before he died, he might have something to offer.

But why did he feel anxious?

He ran a hand through his neat, grey hair and then checked his reflection once more. He looked fine, if a little sleep deprived.

His wife, Abby, had been shocked to hear of Jason's death and agreed that speaking to the police was the right thing. Abby had only ever met Jason once, in the final throes of a dead friendship, and hadn't been particularly fond of the man. But by association, Connor knew someone who'd been killed and, as they were seen as upstanding members of their community, having a police car show up outside their house wasn't something she wanted the neighbours to be gossiping about.

She also didn't want their two daughters to witness their father being put in the back of a police car, regardless of the reason.

The door opened, and DC Hannon re-entered. The warm cup of tea she'd promised gripped in her hand, and her welcoming smile still plastered across her face.

'Thank you,' Connor said as he took the mug and then sipped it quietly as Hannon tapped away on the laptop that sat on the table between them. A few moments passed, and the door opened once more and in marched DI King.

'Sorry to keep you waiting, Mr Davis,' she said, offering a handshake across the table. Connor stood and took it.

'It's quite all right.'

'Thank you for coming in.' King gestured for him to take a seat. 'I understand it can be quite intimidating.'

'Look, anything to help. I mean…Jesus. Jason's dead.'

'I'm afraid so,' King replied, casually rested her hands on the table. 'You were friends with Jason?'

'Oh, that's err…that's a stretch,' Connor said with a sigh. 'We were. Way back when, you know. But over time, that just sort of fizzled out.'

'Any particular reason?'

'If I'm honest. I look back on the way we behaved at school and I'm pretty mortified. I guess, as I grew up and realised that I also realised that Jason was trapped in what he used to be.'

'And what was that exactly?' King asked, noticing Connor shift uncomfortably. 'I'm just trying to build a picture of the man. His wife, Rachel, she didn't have many good things to say about him…'

'I should think not,' Connor said glumly. 'I think she was just as trapped as I was. Look, back when we were kids, Jason was the alpha of the school. He was tall, he was strong, he was mouthy.'

'The whole 'guys want to be him and girls want to be with him' kind of thing?' Hannon interjected.

'Precisely. We both played on the school rugby team and yeah, we were close. But over time, you grow out of it all.'

'All of what?'

'Usual stuff. We picked on the weaker kids. Bullied the shy kids. Made life a living hell for some of the teachers.' Connor noticed their disapproving looks. 'It's not a crime to be a pain in the arse as a teenager.'

'True.' King agreed and adjusted herself, leaning forward to slightly unnerve him. 'So what happened on Friday night?'

'I don't know.'

'You saw Jason, didn't you?' King asked with a hint of accusation.

'Yes, at the reunion. I think he was waiting for me because he jumped on me as soon as I got there.'

'And how did he seem?'

'Seem?'

'Yeah. I mean, he turned up dead twelve hours later with a needle in his arm.'

'An overdose? Christ.' Connor looked genuinely perturbed. Hannon flashed a glance at King and understood straight away they weren't divulging more information. King nodded at her to follow on.

'Did Jason seem okay to you?' Hannon asked.

'I mean, he was wasted when I got there.' Connor looked around, trying to remember. 'He was pretty eager to 'get on it'.'

'You weren't so keen?' Hannon asked with a shrug.

'Those days are behind me,' Connor said with a shake of the head. 'I run my own business. I have a family. It would be pretty irresponsible for someone of my age and with my responsibility to drink that recklessly.'

King shuffled uncomfortably in her chair, as if those words had been meant for her.

'So he was drunk?' King continued. 'Did he mention anything that was bothering him or—'

'His wife. Rachel.' Connor sighed again. 'Took him two minutes to drag her name through the mud and then start making wild claims that he was going to crack on to some of the other women from school.'

'Anyone in particular?'

Connor blew out his cheeks.

'I mean, I don't really remember who was there. I didn't stay too long. I met an old friend, Penny Durant, who we used to hang around with and we caught up for a while. But I was home before midnight.'

King made a few notes in her book, underlining the name Penny Durant before smiling at Connor.

'Did Penny know Jason?' Hannon asked, and King smiled, knowing they were going down the same school of thought.

'Yeah, me and her dated back in secondary school. She was part of the group. Although she was pretty clear that she didn't want to speak to him again.'

'Any particular reason?'

'Take a guess.' Connor snapped.

From what they already knew of Jason Gallagher's behaviour, they could connect the dots themselves. The anger in Connor's voice however, registered with them both as well.

'Did Jason mention anyone who might have wanted to hurt him?'

'Hurt him?' Connor frowned in confusion. 'I thought you said he overdosed?'

'I did,' King confirmed. 'But we do know that Jason had some serious money problems. Did he mention anything about that?'

Connor shook his head.

But the spark of fear in his eye was enough for King to know there was more to it.

Not enough to ask right now. But enough to set Hannon on it like a rabid dog. Instead, King relaxed back in her chair and held up a hand in apology.

'We're just making sure we cover all angles,' King said. 'So, you run an accountancy firm in Marlow?'

'Yes. Started it up nearly fifteen years ago,' Connor said proudly. 'I run it with my wife, Abby.'

'I live in Marlow.' King smiled. 'It's a pretty good place to be an accountant.'

'I can't complain,' Connor said reservedly. He was smart enough to know when someone was fishing for information. 'Look, I'm sorry I can't be of more help. The only other thing I know is that the last time I saw Jason, he was heading to the bathroom to do some cocaine.'

'And before then?' Hannon asked, a little too curtly that it caught King's attention. 'When was the last time you saw Jason Gallagher before the reunion?'

Connor looked a little sideswiped by the question, and as he pretended to rack his brain, King instantly saw the performance of a man cooking up a lie.

'Umm…probably around when I started up my business. Fifteen years or so. Like I said…our friendship sort of died when I decided to grow up.'

'Thank you, Mr Davis.' King stood, extending her hand. Connor rose and took it. 'We really appreciate it.'

'No worries. If I can help in any other way, just let me know.' He offered King a smile. 'And if you need an accountant…'

King smiled warmly and showed him to the door, where a uniformed officer escorted him down the corridor and back to the rest of his Sunday. King closed the door and turned to Hannon, who had already spun in her seat.

'He's lying,' Hannon said curtly, and although King was inclined to believe her, she folded her arms across her chest and regarded her colleague with intrigue.

'What makes you say that?' King asked with encouragement, but Hannon had already opened the tab on her laptop, and she highlighted one line of data. It wasn't incriminating, but it did prove her right. King felt a pulse of pride echo through her body.

'What do you want to do?' Hannon asked with excitement.

King took a beat, knowing that walking towards the right decision was better than running towards the wrong one.

She took a puff on her vape, ignoring the myriad of 'No Smoking' signs throughout the station and then she nodded to Hannon.

'Keep digging.'

CHAPTER SEVENTEEN

The layout of High Wycombe Hospital was becoming slightly more familiar to Townsend, and his second visit in two days took him to the Urgent Treatment Centre, located in the main building that loomed large over an expensive car park. The hospital itself didn't have a walk-in A&E department, something that concerned Mandy when they'd first moved, but knowing that the hospital did offer an emergency service had soon put her mind at ease.

As Townsend made his way through the repetitive, faded white halls of the hospital, he emerged into the reception area of the UTC, clocking the dozen or so people who were there seeking treatment for their minor injuries. He followed their intrigued gaze towards the uniformed officers who were standing guard down the corridor, and Townsend made a beeline towards them, and as he approached, he realised that PC Boyd had been assigned to the security detail.

'Fuckin' hell, do they not give you a day off?' Boyd quipped as Townsend approached, and he gestured to the other officer that it was fine.

'I know. We keep meeting like this, and the missus will start asking questions.'

'Ha ha. You're a little out of my league, son,' Boyd said with a wry hint of self-deprecation. 'He's awake.'

'Has he said anything?' Townsend asked, peering through the sliver of glass at the man who was lying helplessly on the hospital bed.

'Just that he didn't do it.' Boyd shrugged. 'He's scared shitless mind, so be nice.'

'Why does everyone keep telling me that?' Townsend said with a shake of the head, before pushing open the door, startling Jamie who shot up on the bed, before the handcuff that bound him to the railing snapped him back. A nurse frowned at Townsend, who held up an apologetic hand before she quickly shuffled out of the room.

'I didn't do it,' Jamie barked, his voice stricken with panic.

'Jamie. I'm DS Jack Townsend.' Townsend gestured to the seat beside the bed. 'May I sit?'

'Whatever.' Jamie was a mixture of fear and anger. 'I haven't done anything.'

'Look, I'm just here based on the facts. I'm sorry to tell you that Rachel Gallagher was killed in the night. And I'm here to find out what happened.'

Townsend paused as he sat, allowing the gravity of the situation to engulf the suspect. The colour drained from Jamie's face as he stumbled for his words.

'I-I went round to Rachel's last night to…' He trailed off with embarrassment.

'Jamie, you need to tell me everything. Okay? Because right now, you are the person we found next to her with the murder weapon. So I need you to be *specific*.'

'Rachel had been unhappy with Jason for so long that when we met and the spark was there, we started seeing each other.'

'How long have you and Rachel been together?'

'About three years.'

'Specific, Jamie.'

'Three years and two months.' Jamie confirmed. 'Look, I didn't know Jason Gallagher, but from what she told me, he was a right prick. He drank. Did drugs. Even knocked her about and forced her to do things she didn't want to do.'

'So you had a problem with Jason Gallagher?' Townsend knew it was antagonistic, but his own belief that Langley didn't do it needed to be confirmed. By the wide-eyed fury that he was met with, he knew in his gut he was right.

'What?!' Jamie snapped. 'I didn't even know the fucker. But his wife hated his guts, and you know what…you want the truth. I went round there last night to celebrate with her.'

'Celebrate his death?'

'No. Celebrate her freedom.' Jamie's eyes began to water. 'We'd spoken so many times about running away and making a life together, but deep down, she was so scared of that man. Of the lengths he'd go to find her and what he'd do to both of us when he did. So, when she told me he'd been found dead, we both felt this weight lift.'

'Did you know that Jason Gallagher had been murdered?' Townsend asked, his eyes scanning the man's face for any hint of dishonesty.

'Rachel said you thought he'd been killed.' He wiped away a tear with a free hand. 'I guess I'm being pegged for that too, huh?'

'Tell me what happened, Jamie. How did you go from celebrating your relationship to holding the razor blade that killed Rachel and a stomach full of pills?'

Jamie broke.

Tears flooded down his stubbled cheeks and Townsend

sat patiently as he allowed the man to grieve. Even if he was a suspect, the man had lost the woman he clearly loved. After a few moments, Jamie shook himself straight and turned to Townsend.

'I went round there. We had a few drinks, had sex and then went to bed.'

'And then?'

'And then I don't know. I woke up in an ambulance with a tube down my fucking throat as an officer informed me I was under arrest. You ever had your stomach pumped before?' Jamie shook his head. 'It's not pleasant.'

'So you have no recollection of it?' Townsend leant forward.

'No. Look, I enjoy the occasional drink, but I don't go overboard. I don't do drugs and I'm pretty strict on living clean. The police said I murdered Rachel and tried to commit suicide, but I didn't.' Jamie's lip quivered again. 'We made love, fell asleep, and then…this.'

He lifted his arm, drawing the handcuff tight until it clanged against the metal railing.

'Can you think of any other way this could have happened? Did Rachel ever mention having suicidal thoughts?'

'No.' Jamie frowned. 'God, no. I mean, she was unhappy, but she didn't want out. She just wanted Jason gone. And she got it…for a day.'

'Jamie, I need you to understand that things don't look great right now. But I'll do *everything* in my power to find out the truth. Whether or not it's what you've told me today, I will go to the ends of the earth to find out. Do you have a lawyer?'

'No.'

'I suggest you get one.' Townsend suggested as he stood, offering Jamie a reassuring nod. 'Just hang in there.'

'What's going to happen to me, detective?'

Townsend sighed and looked around the hospital room. The usual selection of gadgets and apparatus lined the walls, along with a few ironic posters about hope.

'I don't know. Not yet.'

With that, Townsend headed back to the door, and as he pulled it open, he was met with the unmistakable chuckle of Dr Emma Mitchell, who was snorting through her nose at something PC Boyd had just said. She saw Townsend and jabbed a thumb in Boyd's direction.

'He's a cheeky bugger, ain't he?'

'That's one word for it,' Townsend said, frowning at their jovial encounter at such a time. He started off down the corridor, beckoning Mitchell to follow. 'You keeping tabs on me?'

'No. But I told Boyd to message me when you arrived.'

'Why?' Townsend stopped and turned to her.

'I'm in the process of writing up the report, but I've done the blood work on Jason Gallagher, and there were some pretty serious drugs pumping through his final minutes.'

'Yeah. We know. Cocaine. The heroin he was tanked up with…'

'No. Beyond that. You remember that syringe mark on the back of his neck I told Izzy about?' She looked to Townsend who nodded. 'Well, I believe the theory of him being drugged works out, because he had a number of intravenous drugs in his body. We're talking etomidate, propofol, ke…'

'I don't need the list. But he was drugged.'

'Yup…and the worst part is, the combination of those agents meant that although his body was paralysed, he was never under anaesthetic.'

'You mean…' Townsend shuddered slightly.

'Yup. He was conscious for it all. The tongue. The overdose. He felt everything but could do nothing about it.'

'That's why there were no signs of a struggle.' Townsend added, feeling a surge of adrenaline pump through his body. Mitchell could sense it, and she arched her neck back towards the hospital room where Jamie Langley was chained helplessly.

'So unless your buddy in there has a background in chemistry…I think you might have the wrong guy.'

CHAPTER EIGHTEEN

'You sure you don't want a proper drink?'

Townsend asked with a raised eyebrow as he lowered the Diet Coke in front of King, who waved him off in response. He slid the gin and tonic across to Hannon and then took his seat at the small wooden table and took a swig of his pint followed by a satisfying sigh.

'I'm on antibiotics,' King lied, cursing herself silently for being unable to open up to her team.

'That sucks,' Hannon said as she sipped her gin. 'After weekends like this one, I for one am grateful for the sweet elixir of life.'

The trio chuckled, and Townsend looked around the small pub. A few regulars were posted by the bar, engaging in conversation with the friendly landlord who'd served him. On the far wall, a TV was showing a football match from another country, with one person keeping an eye on the score as they thumbed through their phone. It was one of the few pubs that was crammed onto the busy high street a stone's throw from the station, but as he took another sip of his beer, Townsend couldn't help but feel like they were a world away from the chaos of the job.

'I'll drink to that,' he said with a smile.

'So…Langley…' King began.

'He didn't do it,' Townsend said with conviction.

'*He says* he didn't do it.' King corrected him. 'Until we can prove otherwise, we have to treat him as our main suspect.'

'I know, I know,' Townsend huffed. 'But it just doesn't make sense to me. Why stage it to look like a suicide? If he did do it, why did he make it look like both Jason and Rachel committed suicide if he was just going to kill himself next to them?'

'People do crazy things,' Hannon offered.

'But this doesn't feel crazy.' Townsend took another sip of his drink. 'I saw Mitchell at the hospital, and she said that Jason was drugged with a mixture of different shit that basically paralysed him but kept him conscious.'

'Meaning…' Hannon asked.

'Meaning he felt every goddamn thing that happened to him.' Townsend paused to let that sink in. 'So whoever did this to them both, they wanted them to feel what was happening but to be able to do absolutely nothing about it.'

'That's basically torture,' King said with a worried scowl.

'Yeah. And I know there's a lot of evidence pointing towards him, but Langley doesn't strike me as the type. He says the last thing he remembers was falling asleep next to Rachel and then boom…he's in the back of an ambulance, hands cuffed, and having his stomach pumped.'

'And you believe him?'

'I think that once Mitchell gets a look at what was in both Rachel's and Langley's system, we'll be able to prove that he didn't do it.'

A silence fell between the team, and as Townsend took

another long gulp of his beer, King shifted the ice in her glass with the straw.

'So what do we do then?' Hannon asked, looking to the two of them for guidance.

'If that's the case, then we need to start working out why the Gallaghers were targeted and by who.' King shook her head in frustration. 'Means, motive, and opportunity.'

'Langley had the opportunity…' Hannon shrugged.

'And the motive, if your theory of him offing Jason but Rachel having doubts is true.' King nodded.

'But not the means. I mean, the guy's a plumber…not a pharmacist,' Townsend said. 'The list Mitchell ran off didn't seem like the sort of stuff you could pick up at Asda.'

'True.' King frowned, deep in thought. 'Once she sends that across to me, I'll need you to go through every item and see how readily available it is.'

'On it,' Hannon said with a hint of excitement. The promise of desk work had a strange allure to her.

'And if the same stuff was used on both Rachel and Langley, then we'll have to move him from suspect to a victim who survived a murder attempt while his partner was killed next to him.'

'If so, why didn't they just kill him?' Hannon pondered out loud.

'Maybe he wasn't the target?' Townsend offered. The three of them shared another moment of silence, as the realisation of the ripple effects of the case were made clear. As the quiet began to verge on awkward, Townsend changed the subject.

'Any luck with Davis?'

'Oh yeah,' Hannon said with a grin. 'Turns out he's a lying little rat.'

'Oh, really?' Townsend looked to King who rolled her eyes.

'I wouldn't go that far. But yes, he's certainly on our list of people of interest.'

'Interest?' Hannon looked gobsmacked. 'The man sat in front of us as said he hadn't seen or dealt with Jason Gallagher in fifteen years, but it turns out, he and Gallagher had a financial interaction four years ago.'

'What was it?'

'I don't know just yet,' Hannon said, as if she was being challenged. 'But we do know that Davis transferred a substantial amount of money into a business that he had as a client on his books for a year or so. Guess who owned the business?'

'Gallagher.'

'Bingo.'

'So what…he owed him money?'

King took a discreet pull on her vape stick and blew the residual vapour into her lap before she looked up.

'It means he lied, which is what we need to focus on. Why? If he was so adamant that he didn't want anything to do with Jason Gallagher, why after all those years did he seemingly go into business with him? And why did he lie about it?'

'I don't know. But I really want to find out,' Townsend said with a smirk. 'Want me to go and kick his door down?'

The three of them laughed, and King shook her head playfully.

'That won't be necessary. Not yet, anyway.' She nodded to Hannon. 'Once you have everything we need, we'll call him back in again and grill him. But until then…it's just a thread for us to pull on.'

'And believe me, I'm going to pull the hell out of it,' Hannon said with gusto, drawing another chuckle from her team. As she laughed, she looked down at her phone and her eyes lit up. 'Hot off the press…it looks like Rachel's mum is throwing a remembrance service for her daughter tomorrow.'

'Really?' King leant forward and looked at the phone. She began to read aloud for the rest of the team. '*As you may have heard, my beautiful daughter, Rachel, was killed this past weekend. I cannot describe the pain I'm feeling right now, but I know she'd touched so many of you all. Tomorrow lunchtime from twelve, I'll be holding a small remembrance service for her at the Preistmead Church, with a small reception at the adjoining social club. Please feel free to come and pay your respects and be with each other during this awful time.*'

'It's really sad,' Hannon said with a sigh.

'It is.' Townsend agreed. 'I spoke to her, and she almost blamed herself.'

'I see there's no mention of her son-in-law,' King said accusingly.

'I don't think she was his biggest fan,' Townsend offered, and then quickly latched on to King's train of thought. 'But not enough to do something drastic if that's what you're thinking.'

'I wasn't, but we can't rule it out just yet.' King smiled. 'However, once her alibis are cleared, then, of course we will just let this woman grieve for her daughter. I also think we should go.'

'Agreed,' Townsend nodded as he spoke.

'To the service?' Hannon looked to them both. 'Will that not be a little…I don't know, intrusive?'

'We're investigating the murder of her daughter. I'm sure she won't mind us coming along to pay some respects and ask some questions.'

'Is Swaby back tomorrow?' Townsend asked.

'Probably not,' King said glumly. 'I think her husband is really struggling right now, so I've told her to play it by ear.'

'Fair enough.' Townsend sipped his beer. 'I remember when I lost my dad. It's a shitter.'

King nodded her agreement and then glanced at her watch and her face was suddenly awash with panic.

'Oh crap. Is that the time?' She quickly down the last of her Diet Coke and stood. 'I need to go.'

'Hot date?' Townsend asked. He turned and shrugged to Hannon.

'I don't like the idea of you dating,' Hannon said with a comical sneer on her face. 'It's too weird.'

'I know, right? Like your mother going on a date…'

King playfully clipped Townsend around the back of his head.

'Will you two shut up? No, I do not have a date. But I do have somewhere I need to be,' King said it with a smile, but there was a clear undercurrent of finality to her voice. 'Get some sleep. Both of you. Something tells me it's going to be a long week.'

With that, she pulled her jacket tight and marched towards the door, as Townsend turned and watched her leave. When he turned back to Hannon, she was thumbing through her phone.

'Does the guv seem off to you?' he asked.

'No more than usual.' Hannon looked up at him. 'Why?'

'I don't know. She just seems like she's struggling. Not with the case, but just…'

'She was nearly murdered a few months ago. Remember?' Hannon shrugged. 'You of all people must know that that has lasting effects.'

She was right.

Townsend had told Hannon what had happened to him when he was undercover, when he was beaten to within an inch of his life after his cover had been blown. Although it had been years since that moment, and he and

111

Mandy had moved away and begun a new, safer life for them and Eve, there were still echoes of that moment that appeared when he least expected it.

A bad dream.

The wrong word being used.

Trauma could be brought back to the forefront of the mind by the most minute act or word, and it always caught him by surprise.

But DI King was struggling with something.

And all Townsend wanted was for her to know that they were there if she needed them.

With a sigh, he turned back to Hannon, contemplating another drink and a taxi home when she began to pull on her coat.

'Are we done?'

'Yeah. Shilpa's got the arse with me…'

'Is it because you missed Hot Bikram Yoga?'

Hannon scoffed and shook her head.

'Jack…can I ask you a personal question?'

Townsend finished his beer and smiled.

'Is it about my feelings?'

'Er…no.'

'Then go ahead.'

'When did you and Mandy know you wanted a family?'

The age gap between the two of them never really showed, and Townsend and Hannon and managed to fall into a big brother/little sister relationship pretty easily. But now, just a few weeks shy of his thirty-ninth birthday, the near thirteen-year age gap between the two of them felt almost parental.

'We didn't,' he said with a smile. 'It just happened for us. Why?'

'No reason,' Hannon said with a sigh. She stepped past the table and Townsend looked up at her.

'Nic…remember. Never do anything you don't want to do. Okay?' He offered her a warm smile. 'You'll only live to regret it.'

She squeezed his shoulder and then took her leave, and Townsend had one last look around the pub, thought about another quiet beer, but quickly decided an evening with his girls was more appealing.

With a violent killer on the loose, the chances were, it might be awhile before he could have one again.

CHAPTER NINETEEN

It had been a hell of a weekend.

Connor Davis had taken a long drive after he'd left the police station that morning, hoping that the aimless venture would help him to clear his head. After so many years free from Jason Gallagher, the last few days had once again drawn him back into the man's orbit.

Four years.

Forty-eight months without having to deal with that lying, treacherous scumbag, but in just one evening, Jason Gallagher had become the centre of attention once again. What made Connor feel even worse was as he drove, couldn't even muster up one iota of sympathy for the man. After driving for an hour, Connor pulled the car into the car park of a country pub on the outskirts of Thame and went inside. After ordering a pint of his favourite lager, he found a quiet corner and took a seat, trying his best to collect his thoughts.

Abby had sent a few messages, each one more fraught than the one before.

He tapped out a message to put her mind to rest.

Everything is fine. Home this afternoon X

It didn't explain much, but what was there to explain?

Connor had answered all the questions they'd asked, and from what he could tell, he wasn't in any trouble. Jason had let his demons get the better of him and whatever sad state his life was in, he'd gone too far in pursuit of the dragon.

Despite his anger towards his dead friend, Connor lifted his pint up to the rainy window.

'Rest in peace, mate.'

Connor took a sip and put the pint down on the table before him. He'd hoped the drive out to the countryside would have cleared his head, but he shifted uncomfortably in his seat.

He knew he'd lied to the police, but even on reflection, it wouldn't have done them or him any good for him to have told the truth.

It wouldn't have helped with the investigation into Jason's death, and all it would do for him was bring his company into disrepute and put a strain on a marriage that wasn't as perfect as he often made out. As he sat quietly and tried to block out the situation, he found himself thumbing through Penny Durant's Instagram account. She was a frequent user of the app, proudly displaying pictures of the numerous charity runs she'd done, and the seemingly idyllic time she spent with her kids.

She was still so beautiful.

A small green dot had appeared next to her profile picture, indicating she was on the app at that very moment, and Connor tapped the *message* button and tapped out a message.

Lovely to see you on Friday. Like old times X

He hit sent, and instantly wrestled with the dollop of guilt that landed in his gut.

What did he hope to achieve?

His phone buzzed.

Penny.

You too. Loving the grey ;) xx

She was flirting. Connor felt a spasm of excitement shudder through his body, and for the next twenty minutes, the two of them traded compliments, skirting around the idea that they clearly were both thinking.

They didn't mention Jason.

As Connor finished his beer and promised to message her later, he headed to his car with a spring in his step, and the events of the morning firmly out of his mind. They didn't return until he walked through the door, where Abby instantly threw her arms around him and asked him what happened. He recounted to the best of his memory, purposefully omitting the question around the last time he'd seen Jason.

Abby didn't know they'd been in contact.

If she knew about the money, then she'd take his business and his children away from him.

'Well, you did the right thing, Connor. I'm proud of you,' Abby said with a smile, pouring gasoline onto the guilty fire that was roaring inside him.

The strain of running their own business and raising their girls had taken a toll on their marriage over the years, and although neither one of them would say it, it had felt like they'd been going through the motions for a while.

Same evening routines.

Same weekly sex on a Saturday if they could be bothered.

Same restaurants.

Same. Same. Same.

It was neither of their faults; it was just the easiest way through the life they'd built, and Connor had often wondered what the future would hold when the girls had flown the nest.

Would their passion rekindle? Or would they admit what they never would while the girls still needed them?

The rest of the afternoon was spent in the kitchen with his daughters, who had challenged him to a game of Monopoly, which stretched through a couple of hours. Abby flittered about behind them, expertly preparing the roast dinner that they would eat together before heading into the front room to watch the results of the latest dance show the girls were obsessed with.

As the day fell into the evening, Connor was helping their eldest with her homework when Abby let out a gasp from the kitchen. Connor quickly rushed in.

'What's wrong?'

'Rachel Gallagher is dead?!' she said, her eyes wide in shock. The announcement shook Connor, who tried his hardest to remember his old friend's face. She'd never been involved with the dealings he'd had with Jason over the years, and she hadn't been at the reunion. Back in the day, she'd been just as arrogant and brash as Jason, but in their quieter moments, he'd often found her to be the total opposite.

She was just lowering herself to Jason's level.

He felt a twinge of sadness in his chest for her, as the way Jason had spoken of her led him to believe the past few years hadn't been happy for her. Eventually, after registering the shock, he spoke.

'What happened?'

'I don't know,' Abby said as she scrolled her phone. 'But a friend of yours just posted his condolences on a memorial page set up by her mother.'

'Let me see…' Connor said as he reached for the phone. As he read through the message from Rachel's mother, and the plethora of heartbroken messages, Connor shuffled uncomfortably.

As you may have heard, my beautiful daughter, Rachel, was killed this past weekend. I cannot describe the pain I am feeling right now…

Rachel had been killed.

Not a suspected suicide like Jason.

Killed.

Which meant there would be an investigation, which meant every dark corner of her, and Jason's, life would be pulled apart and that included their finances.

They'd find out about what happened, and most likely, the threatening messages that Connor and Jason had exchanged.

Despite knowing that two people he'd spent his teenage years with were now dead, the only thing Connor could think about was the potential impact on his own life.

His marriage.

His kids.

His business.

Yet all he wanted to do, was to message Penny.

The evening went by as a blur, as one by one his kids took themselves off to bed, and then he feigned interest in the latest episode of whatever series he and his wife were watching. Clearly seeing him lost in his thoughts, Abby offered to open the office in the morning and make excuses for him until after lunchtime.

'You should go,' she said with a caring shrug. 'Pay your respects.'

'Thanks,' he replied. 'It's just a shock, is all.'

She squeezed his shoulder and headed upstairs to begin her multiple step skincare regime, and Connor went to his downstairs office and, as quietly as possible, locked the door.

He booted up his laptop, and then pulled up Instagram, and sure enough, Penny was online.

Are you going tomorrow? He typed out.

Three dots…

Yes. Of course. I can't believe it.

I know, he replied. *Raincheck on tonight?*

He sighed with disappointment as the thrill of a naughty conversation with his old flame had gotten him through the day. So when she replied with *Give me five minutes…* he felt a sudden surge of arousal.

He knew it was wrong.

With everything that had happened the past few days, and the avalanche of shit heading his way, the smartest thing to do was to close the laptop, head upstairs, and go to sleep.

Instead, he unzipped his trousers, had a swig of the cold bottle of beer sat beside him, and then the video call from Penny burst onto the screen.

With his heart beating faster than it had in years, he took a few moments to compose himself, and then clicked accept, not just for the call, but for the start of their affair.

CHAPTER TWENTY

It was always important to start a Monday off on the right foot.

That was what Townsend's father had told him from a young age, arguing that beginning the week in a negative way would only worsen as the week progressed. Most people worked long, arduous hours in jobs they didn't like, to sustain a life they were never fully happy with, and if each week began with a whimper, then things would never improve. It was a lesson Townsend had taken in his stride, and although he certainly loved his job and the life he was building with his family, it was all too easy to allow the physical and mental drain of life to pull you down with it.

Townsend had woken ten minutes before his five thirty alarm that morning and had carefully rolled out of bed to allow his wife the luxury of a lie in. After quickly washing and throwing on his gym clothes, he made a quick pit stop to check on his daughter, feeling his heart swell with pride as she lay in a peaceful sleep.

A quick coffee, and then Townsend entered the freezing cold garage that he called his gym, and after thirty minutes of intense weights, he strapped up his hands, slid them into his boxing gloves, and unloaded on the heavy, leather bag that swung from its hook. As his favourite workout playlist pumped from his ear buds, Townsend expertly exploded into a number of different combos, his muscle memory leading the way as he hammered the leather with ruthless proficiency. Although Mandy didn't want him fighting in the ring anymore, she knew how much boxing had given him, not only in his discipline and his control but also as an outlet for the rough upbringing he'd lived through, and the toll of a demanding job that he'd never walk away from.

His daily fitness routine and sparring session was why, on the rare occasion Mandy had permitted him, when he stepped in the ring with DCI Lowe that past summer, he was able to humble the man with minimal fuss.

But now, with each glove that collided with the bag, Townsend was working out the frustration of the escalating situation he and the SCU were faced with.

Two dead.

Murdered.

Their tongues removed and their deaths arranged to mimic a suicide.

A man was arrested but adamant he didn't do it.

Pieces of a puzzle that they had no point of reference for, and the majority of the others missing.

Townsend's pace quickened, his punches becoming more and more erratic as the name Jamal Beckford slid into the forefront of his mind.

The vision of the man, lying motionless in the rain, his throat slit, and his life long-gone.

The broken wife who sobbed as her heart broke.

A teenage boy, stricken with grief to the point of anger.

So many people relying on him.

Looking to him for the answer.

For the truth.

As he threw his final punch that sent the bag swinging to the point of toppling, Townsend gave a huge groan and hunched forward, resting his gloves on his thighs as he caught his breath. The smell of coffee caused him to turn, and he was greeted by his wife's beautiful smile.

'Here you go, Rocky.' She joked, as she placed the coffee down on the messy workbench that ran across the wall nearest to the door. 'You okay?'

Townsend ripped the Velcro off the glove with his teeth, slid his hand out, and then removed his ear buds.

'Never better.' He smiled, and he stepped forward and gave her a kiss before lifting his mug. 'Thanks.'

'No worries. Working out some stress?'

'In a way.' He shrugged. 'Just need to clear my head.'

'Well, if you want a real fight, missy is refusing to get out of bed. Any chance you can give her a kick on your way upstairs?'

Townsend laughed, downed his coffee, and then headed upstairs. Lacking the delicate touch of his wife, he pulled open the curtains in Eve's room and clapped loudly above her head to wake her, drawing an angry groan and a wild claim of hatred. Quickly, Townsend showered, and by the time he'd finished buttoning up his crisp, white shirt and headed downstairs, Eve was sitting at the table, shovelling cereal into her mouth. She fixed her father with a frown as he approached her.

'Morning, lazy,' he said with a grin as he leant down and kissed her on the top of the head. Eve didn't respond.

'She's mad at you.' Mandy smirked. 'I said maybe you'd make it up to her with a McDonald's on Friday…'

'I mean, yeah, but I don't think I've done anything wrong.'

Townsend turned back to Eve, who stuck her tongue out at him. He replied in kind, kissed his wife, and then headed out to the car. The journey through to the station was easy enough, as the school rush had yet to kick in, and Townsend found himself alone in the SCU office when he arrived. He made a cup of tea and then sat at his desk, using the hour before his workday began to look through the notes of the Beckford murder that had been uploaded to the Police National Computer. Despite their personal differences, Townsend did respect DCI Lowe as a detective, and his team were clearly working hard to find out who'd murdered Jamal Beckford, as there were countless reports and statements that they'd gathered over the weekend. While his and the rest of the SCU's world had revolved around the brutal murder of the Gallaghers, the world hadn't stood still, and Lowe was clearly pushing his department to find out what the hell had happened to see that man die a slow, painful death, alone in a wet and windy car park.

They were looking into the man's movements over the past few weeks, along with an in-depth look into his working life.

Building a picture.

Trying to connect the dots.

As Townsend opened up a report on Beckford's previous links to a North London gang, the sound of a bag dropping onto a desk broke his concentration and he spun in his seat.

'I did say hello,' Hannon said with a smirk, and then fished out a fresh packet of biscuits from her rucksack.

'Sorry.' Townsend shook his head clear. 'I was lost in this…'

'What you reading?' she asked with interest.

'It's the Beckford case. It looks like Lowe and his team are doing a good job so far.'

'Yeah, it's annoying, isn't it?' Hannon joked. 'I mean, the man is a grade-A twat, but he's a damn good detective. I know Lowe has granted you access to those files, but you do know that the guv will drag you over the coals if she knows you're still looking into this.'

'Looking into what?'

King's voice was swiftly followed by her appearance in the room, and she looked back and forth between her team expectantly. Hannon looked like a kid caught passing notes, and she mouthed 'sorry' to Townsend who sighed and turned on his chair.

'I was just going over the Beckford case and—'

'And I told you that I need you fully focused on the Gallaghers.'

'I know, Guv. It's just, I promised Simone Beckford and Tyler that I'd do everything I could—'

King held up her hand to cut him off and stomped through the office towards the murder board, which was beginning to fill up with photos, sheets of paper, and numerous drawn arrows. She slammed her hand beside the pictures of the deceased couple.

'Jason and Rachel Gallagher. Both murdered.' She turned and locked her eyes on Townsend. 'These two are the priority. I hate to say it, but DCI Lowe and his team are more than capable of handling that case and no matter what you promised, Jack...I need your full focus on this. Is that clear?'

Townsend shot a glance to Hannon, who already had her head down in her work. Begrudgingly, he nodded.

'Yes, guv.'

'I appreciate you made promises, Jack. But that's no longer your case. And take it from me, in this job, don't make promises you can't keep,' King said with authority. 'You're no good to me or to the Gallaghers if your focus is elsewhere.'

'Understood.'

The tension was palpable, and Townsend grunted as he turned back to his computer and shut down the reports that were displayed on his screen. King watched for a few moments, clearly thinking of a way to lighten the mood, before giving up and heading to her own office at the back of the room. As she passed the murder board, she shot another glance up and called back to Hannon.

'Let me know what time we need to go to the memorial service,' King said as she slid off her sodden jacket. 'I've got a department meeting with Hall in ten.'

'Will do, guv.'

As King disappeared into her office, Townsend felt a bitter sense of failure in his gut. Not just to the Beckfords, but to King. The week was just minutes old and already she'd questioned his judgment.

So much for starting the week on the right foot.

Behind him, he heard the squeaking of chair wheels and the rustle of a packet, and when he turned, Hannon was there with an open packet of custard creams.

'Biscuit?' She waggled her eyebrows comically.

Townsend couldn't help but chuckle.

CHAPTER TWENTY-ONE

Penny Durant took a deep breath as she stood outside the social club, wondering if giving up smoking over a decade ago had been a good idea after all. The cravings often returned when her anxiety kicked in, but she'd decided to kick the habit when she and Stephen had decided to start a family and the idea of purposefully risking her health while her kids were so young was enough to keep them at bay.

But this was different.

Sure, the anxiety was bubbling due to having not seen Janet in over a decade, a woman who had been like a second mother to her when she was growing up. But that relationship, much like her one with Rachel, had withered over the years, and she was certain that the bubbly woman she had once known would now be just another old lady, only one stricken with a grief that Penny could only imagine. As a mother of a daughter herself, the idea of laying her child to rest, whatever the age, was the one thing in life she never wanted to experience.

There would also be the questions about why she and Rachel lost contact over the years, and although Penny was never particularly fond of Jason, didn't want to speak ill of the dead. Despite the man's disgusting behaviour, and the multiple times he'd tried to force himself upon her during their brief friendship back in school, he still had people who would be mortified by his passing. But he had always been the reason that her friendship with Rachel deteriorated and even if she'd wanted to, she'd never shed a tear for his passing.

Then there was Connor.

Seeing him at the reunion had been like touching an exposed wire, and the sudden shock of excitement had startled her from her comfortable life. Daniel was a senior leader in a major marketing company, with a healthy salary and an attractive work ethic. Their home was spacious, shaped to her every design, and their beautiful children were excelling at school. Penny had also forged a lucrative business as a life coach, which she found ironic considering the crippling anxiety she suffered, but all in all, her life had been comfortably content.

Connor was still just as handsome as he had been in high school, and his trim physique and greying hair gave off the air of a man who looked after himself and was built for success. She knew it was wrong, and that he had a family, but it had become clear that, like her, he'd begun to tire of the everyday routines it demanded.

This was a chance for a little excitement.

Something new. But still familiar.

Less than sixteen hours had passed since they'd exposed themselves on camera to one another, stealing half an hour to reconnect sexually for the first time since their late teens, but seeing him so soon after caused her stomach to flip and her mind to tell her to head home.

But she needed to walk in.

Needed to pay her respects.

And as the anxiety loomed like the adjoining Priestmead Church that cut through the cloudy sky above,

Penny pulled her coat tight against the cold and stepped in. The morbid atmosphere welcomed her, and those who had been in attendance for the service turned and greeted her with disinterest. Family members and the few friends that Rachel still had were already congregated in their familiar circles, and Penny awkwardly shuffled towards the large picture of Rachel that was standing on a wooden easel. Just as Penny remembered her, Rachel's beautiful face was filled with life and happiness, a snapshot of a time before the crippling abuse of her husband had beaten her down.

Penny felt her eyes water as she looked at her lost friend, before a comforting hand rested on her shoulder.

'She always spoke of you.' Janet's voice was warm. 'Always telling me how well you were doing.'

Penny turned to the grieving mother and wrapped her arms around her, holding her tightly.

'I'm so sorry, Janet.' The two embraced for what felt like minutes, and Janet eventually rubbed Penny's back and broke away, dabbing away a tear.

'It's lovely to see you, dear.' She smiled through the pain. 'How are you?'

'Oh, you know. Life.' Penny forced a smiled. 'I just feel guilty that I wasn't around for her and…'

Janet waved her hand, dismissing Penny's guilt.

'Don't be. That bastard pushed everyone away. He even tried to cut me out. Good luck with that, I told him.'

Penny smiled again, instantly remembering how much she loved this woman and just as she was making a mental note to arrange a proper catch up, both of their attentions were drawn to the door of the community hall as three people strode in. Their demeanour screamed authority, and all eyes fell on them as they sheepishly held up hands and nodded uncomfortably. The man, tall, handsome and with a stubbled jaw, waved to Janet, who nodded politely.

'That's the detective.' Janet leant in to Penny, lowering her voice. 'He's a bit young for me, but you never know.'

The joke was appreciated, and as Janet broke away from Penny and headed across the room to speak to the people who were responsible for finding her a modicum of justice, Penny sighed, her chest heavy from the guilt that was breaking her heart.

'Those were the two women I spoke to you about yesterday.'

Penny spun and came face to face with Connor, who offered her a loving smile. Instantly, all the panic and anxiety ebbed away, and she realised that by his side, she felt comfortable.

That even two decades apart didn't detract from the connection they had.

'The detectives?' Penny said, looking back at them. 'That one's a bit young, isn't she?'

She was looking towards DS Hannon, who locked eyes with her and didn't budge until Penny broke the stare. She cursed herself slightly, knowing it was a power game, and she'd been easily beaten. Connor stood beside her, and rather sneakily, slid his hand across the bottom of her spine.

She felt a twinge of excitement.

'They're harmless enough,' Connor said, as he gave her a knowing glance. 'Although they'll want to talk to you.'

'Why?'

'Just because you were at the party. I said we spent the evening talking and…'

'But Rachel wasn't at the party.'

'I know. They're investigating both deaths,' Connor said, nodding cheerily to DI King, who didn't look as cheerful. 'But it's fine. We have nothing to hide.'

'Don't we?'

The words lingered between them, crackling with

forbidden passion. They'd taken a step beyond the line and knew they weren't stepping back from it.

'We're taking the kids to the Marlow lights tomorrow,' Connor said calmly. 'I've told Abby I'm meeting the guys for a few drinks afterwards…'

The invitation was clear, and Penny felt her body tremble.

Was it excitement?

Or guilt?

As she tossed the idea of a sordid meeting with the man who was gently rubbing the base of her spine, she looked up to the detectives, who were all standing, listening intently to Janet who was chewing their ear off. The woman was grieving, wanting to know what had happened to her beautiful daughter, and Penny knew that if she was in the same situation, she'd be giving them both barrels, too. The male detective suddenly reached for the inside of his jacket and pulled out his phone, made his apologies, and stepped out of the room, which had surprisingly begun to fill up. As the detective headed for the door, he held the door open for a woman who quickly scurried through and out into the rain.

Penny turned and looked back at Connor, and their eyes locked, making a silent agreement to take this affair to the next level the following evening.

'I'll figure something out,' she said, and as they both resisted the urge to kiss each other, their focus, and the focus of everyone in the room turned to the ear-piercing scream that exploded behind them.

Everyone turned, as Janet, who was now standing by the table that was covered in clingfilm wrapped trays of sandwiches, at the far end of the room, screamed in horror and dropped to her knees.

On the table before her was an open shoe box.

And inside it were two severed tongues.
One of them belonging to her murdered daughter.

CHAPTER TWENTY-TWO

The drive out to Priestmead Church had been a little tense, as Townsend kept his eyes on the road as he navigated through High Wycombe to where Rachel's mother had arranged her service. Although King felt a little bad about digging him out over his focus, she wouldn't apologise for it.

She didn't need to.

Despite his good intentions, she needed Townsend's full attention on the Gallaghers, and she'd seen too many detectives and police officers stretch themselves too thin.

That's how mistakes get made.

That's how they get it wrong.

Hannon did her best from the backseat to lighten the mood, but eventually, she gave up and the three of them sat with their own respective thoughts as they approached the venue. As Townsend pulled into the small courtyard just outside the social club, King threw open the door and stepped out into the rain.

'Remember, everyone here is mourning,' she said over the roof of the car as the others emerged. 'We're here to work, but let's be respectful.'

'Absolutely.' Townsend agreed.

'She liked you.' Hannon smiled at him. 'Janet.'

'I guess.'

'Well, let's be quiet, let's keep our ears open, and let's keep doing our jobs,' King said with a firm nod. Pep talk over, the three of them headed into the social club, and Townsend yanked open the door and ushered his colleagues through. As they stepped in, they felt all eyes fall on them, a mixture of hope and resentment flooding towards them like a tidal wave. Hannon tried to disarm them all with a charming smile, but Townsend and King just carefully scanned the room, which had splintered off into a number of different social groups. Family members sticking close together, while those on the fringes of Rachel's life had managed to make contact with others in the same boat.

The volume was low.

The mood was cold.

Adorning a plaque at the far end of the room was a large photo of the deceased woman, her bright smile and wide eyes a world away from the last time Townsend had seen her.

Naked.

Covered in blood.

He clocked Janet at the exact same moment she did him, and the old lady leant in to the woman she was talking to and then shuffled through the crowd of people toward them. As she did, King and Hannon both shared a look as they watched Connor Davis saddle up next to the woman Janet had just abandoned.

'Detective Townsend,' she said with a warm smile. 'Thank you for coming.'

Without warning, she threw her arms around his broad frame, and as he peeled back, Hannon raised an eyebrow just to add to his discomfort.

'Of course. This is DS Hannon and this…'

'Detective Inspector King.' She cut in, extending her hand that Janet felt obliged to take. 'First off, please accept my deepest condolences for your loss.'

'I didn't lose her, dear.' Janet said frankly. 'She was taken from me.'

'And believe me, my team and I are doing everything we can to find out who did this.'

'Well, I do hope so.' Janet turned to Hannon. 'You on work experience?'

Townsend smirked at Hannon, who scoffed.

'I'll take that as a compliment.'

'I would,' Janet said as she placed a hand against her own cheek. 'Botox is expensive, dear.'

Hannon chuckled, and despite the devastation of losing her daughter, Janet was putting on a brave face for the rest of the room. She explained to the three of them that she wanted this to be a celebration of Rachel's life, and she didn't want to wait for the police to return her body for everyone to have the chance to do so.

'I understand. And of course, you'll be able to give Rachel a proper burial once we find out who did this.'

'You mean once you charge that man you arrested?' Janet's eyes searched King in confusion. 'Jamie.'

'What do you know about Jamie's relationship with Rachel?' King asked, avoiding the question.

'Not much.' Janet shrugged. 'I mean, Rachel never told me that she was having an affair. I guess she thought I'd disapprove, but to be honest, I just wanted her away from Jason. I just wanted her to be happy.'

King nodded, but her focus was beyond Janet and on Connor Davis, who seemed in an intimate conversation with the same woman. Both she and Hannon and noticed his hand resting on the small of her back.

'Sorry, Janet…can I ask…who was the woman you were speaking to when we arrived?'

Janet flashed a glance back through the throngs of mourners.

'Oh, that's Penny. Lovely woman. Her and Rachel were best friends growing up. Like a second daughter to me back then.'

Hannon and King once again locked eyes, but then Townsend reached into the inside of his jacket and pulled out his phone. His eyebrows raised.

'Excuse me.'

Before King could say anything, he turned back to the door, nearly colliding with a small woman with dark brown hair who was moving swiftly to the door. Townsend held the door open for her as she rushed through, and he stepped outside into the rain and answered the call.

'Sir.'

'*Jacky boy,*' DCI Lowe greeted him disrespectfully. '*Jesus, where are you?*',

'At a memorial service.' Townsend frowned at the elements, and watched as the woman raced to a red car and then pulled out of the courtyard. 'How can I help you, sir?'

'*Beckford,*' Lowe said, snapping Townsend to attention. '*We've got a lead. Turns out, Jamal ran with the 1EZ gang out in Wembley. You heard of it?*'

'Of course not.'

'*Nasty fuckers,*' Lowe said disapprovingly. '*Back when we worked CID for the Met, I was in charge of a task force that was cracking down on the rise in gang violence in Wembley. 1EZ was the fucking top of the pile. Anyways, Beckford used to run with those boys apparently, and he has a previous arrest for trying to assault a police officer during a raid of one of their hangouts.*'

'Is he still affiliated?' Townsend asked, the rain slapping

against his face. 'Trust me, I know how ingrained in your bones those gangs can get.'

The reference to his past life undercover seemed to hold some weight with Lowe, who dropped the arrogant tone.

'*We don't know. The task force was cut due to budget bullshit, but a colleague of mine still works out of Brent Police Station. Heads up the CID there. DCI Alfie Staunton.*' Lowe sighed. '*I've called in a favour, but I can't share the files with him right now and I can't get out there this evening due to a meeting.*'

'Can't one of your team go?' Townsend asked, looking back towards the social club and wondering what King would do if she could hear the conversation.

Lowe's friendly tone lasted a minute.

'*Jesus Christ, Townsend. You wanted to be kept in the loop and I'm asking you to help.*'

'Okay, sir.' Townsend understood. 'Send me the details and I'll be there.'

'*Good,*' Lowe said with authority. '*I'll let know DCI Staunton to expect you. Oh, and don't worry Jacky Boy…I won't tell Mummy you're playing away behind her back.*'

Lowe hung up the call before Jack could respond, and Townsend stashed his phone back in his jacket and took a moment. As the rain lashed down, he contemplated how betrayed King would feel if she found out that he'd agreed to deliberately disobey her.

But he thought of Simone Beckford.

Her heartbroken wails of grief.

He'd made her a promise and even if it meant he had to work both cases day and night, he'd get to the truth.

Every victim deserved justice.

Just as he reached for the door with his soaking hand, an ear-piercing scream of terror echoed within the building, and as he burst through the doors and back into the social club, he saw the crowd gathered round, as Penny

Durant and the man she was with tending to Janet who had dropped to her knees, screaming in terror. Townsend pushed through the crowd, and Hannon and King were already at the table, their eyes wide as they stared at the open shoe box on the table beside the modest, home-made spread.

Townsend stepped forward, peering over the edge of the box.

He saw the blood.

He knew what was inside.

The entire room had become a crime scene.

CHAPTER TWENTY-THREE

The entire afternoon became an escalation of anger and frustration as King had shut down the memorial service and informed everyone they needed to remain both calm and within the building until their details could be taken down. With many of the attendees stopping by on a lunch break, or with other commitments such as childcare or doctor's appointments, the hostility in the room rose to match the genuine fear that had begun to pinball through the venue. Swiftly, three police cars had arrived, and Townsend led the officers into the room where the process of logging the attendees began.

Someone in that building had placed the tongues on the table, and Janet, who had been visibly shaken by the presentation of her daughter's severed tongue, confirmed that the box hadn't been there before they arrived.

Which meant someone had planted it.

Someone knew something.

Townsend had swiftly approached the owner of the social club who was pitched up behind the modest bar, and the man had chuckled behind the beer taps at the idea that the venue had security cameras.

'This ain't the fuckin' Ritz, mate,' he'd said dismissively.

As King sat with Janet and talked her through her shock, Townsend and Hannon went about helping the uniformed police take down the names and statements, and unsurprisingly, nobody knew or saw anything. As the photo of Rachel looked out over the commotion, Townsend could feel his frustration growing.

This was a message being sent.

Whoever was doing this had just proven that this was more than just murder.

This was planned.

The crowd began to thin as the uniformed officers went to work, and Townsend approached King and Janet and shook his head sorrowfully.

'I am so sorry,' he offered. Janet dabbed at her eyes with a tissue.

'It's okay. I just…I don't know who would want to do that to my beautiful Rachel.'

King looked across the room to Hannon, who was approaching both Connor and Penny, and she lifted herself from her seat.

'Jack, do you mind?'

'Not at all,' Townsend said as he took his seat, and he placed his hand over Janet's to comfort her. With purpose, King strode across the social club towards the duo, who seemed a little intimidated by her approach.

Good.

'Mr Davis.' She nodded as she stopped next to Hannon. He smiled weakly, and she turned to Penny. 'DI King. And I've been informed you're Penny Durant?'

'That's right,' Penny said with a slight unease.

'You knew Rachel from way back, right?' King asked, pulling out her notebook more for show than anything, as she knew Hannon would be making the required notes. 'When did you last see her?'

'Oh, gosh. Years ago.'

'Mrs Jennings said you were like a second daughter to her,' King said with a smile. 'So you must have been close?'

'We were. But…that was like twenty years ago. We just drifted apart over time.'

'Just drifted apart,' King repeated, almost accusingly. 'Did you see anything that happened here today?'

'No, not at all,' Penny said before she frowned. 'You're not accusing me, are you?'

King held up her hands in surrender.

'I didn't suggest anything like that. We're just asking what people sa—'

'She was here with me,' Connor interrupted. 'We were just talking about the Marlow Christmas Lights tomorrow evening. Are you attending?'

King shot Connor a glance that told him he was in trouble. The man visibly gulped as he stepped backwards slightly.

'Probably not.' She gestured to the room. 'As you can see, we're a little busy.'

'I didn't see anything.' Penny stammered once more, before she pointed towards the door. 'Although I did see a woman hurrying out of the door moments before.'

Hannon and King looked to each other.

'A woman? Can you describe her?' King said with urgency.

'Erm, I just saw the back of her head. Brown hair. Shoulder length.'

'Coat?'

'It was black. But seriously, it was like two seconds and then your detective over there, he opened the door for her, and she was gone.'

Penny pointed towards Townsend, and King had a

horrible feeling they'd been closer than they thought. Hannon noticed Connor gently reach up and tenderly squeeze Penny's elbow, and she flipped her notebook shut and smiled.

'Thank you, Mrs Durant. Let me walk you out.'

The situation was clear, and Penny shot a worried glance to Connor before she followed Hannon across the room, sliding on her coat as they approached the door. Connor watched on with concern before his eyes were drawn back to the stern scowl of King. He shuffled uncomfortably before once again making eye contact.

'I didn't see the woman myself but…'

'You lied to me,' King said sternly. He tried to look innocent, but King knew she had him.

'W-what about?'

'Four years ago. You invested money in a business venture that Jason Gallagher was starting up.'

'Oh. That.'

'Mr Davis, you do know lying to the police during a murder investigation is a crime, right?' King took a step toward him and lowered her voice. 'And it's a really fucking stupid thing to do.'

'Look, I just…I just don't want my wife knowing,' he said under his breath, as if his wife was actually there. 'She'd made it quite clear her disdain for the man and…'

'And what?' King shrugged.

'Jason was one of my oldest friends. Was he a prick? Yeah. But he told me he'd kicked the drugs, kicked the booze, and that he was starting up a window cleaning firm and he had a business plan and everything. It seemed legit.'

'But it wasn't?'

'What do you think?' Connor said with venom. King clocked it.

'How much we talking here?' King asked, already knowing the figure.

'About ten grand,' Connor responded glumly. 'Do you know how hard it is to hide a ten-thousand-pound hole in your accounts from your wife?'

'Not if you're an accountant,' King said with little sympathy. She'd dealt first hand with a lying husband and wasn't going to cut this one any slack. 'You should have told us this, Mr Davis. I've a good mind to drag you back to the station, but as you can see, we've got a bit of a situation.'

'Can I go?' he asked with hope.

'For now.' King took another step closer, a proven tactic to assert her authority. 'But I want you to bring all that paperwork he gave to you and everything that pertains to that company and what happened. Do you understand?'

'Yes, Ma'am,' Connor said submissively.

'Otherwise, I'll drag you out of your house and explain exactly why to your wife,' King threatened. 'And I'd rather not be the cause of any problems.'

With that, she let the man scamper off, watching him make a hurried effort to the exit. She stood, shaking her head, not just at the door where he'd exited but at the whole situation. Chief Inspector Hall had made it clear he didn't want the case to escalate, and now she stood in the middle of a complete clusterfuck.

Lying friends.

Secret business deals.

And now the mocking display of the severed tongues, of which the stories would spread like wildfire. One of the officers was already outside dealing with one of the local news reporters who'd got wind of the memorial service and the sudden surge of police cars to the venue. The SOCO unit had arrived, only adding to the spectacle.

The whole thing was threatening to spiral out of control, but the worst part of it all was she had a horrible feeling that the person they were after had passed right through them.

As the uniformed officers finished up with the last of the impatient guests, Townsend offered to drive Janet home, but she promised she had other arrangements. She thanked them for their work before taking her leave, and King looked to the bar and the cheap bottles of wine that were undoubtedly open in the fridge, and had to summon all her willpower not to ask for one.

But there was too much to do.

Too many things to sort out.

And what was nagging her most of all, is one of those things just happened to be the detective who was about to drive her back to the station.

CHAPTER TWENTY-FOUR

What Townsend would have given for DS Michelle Swaby to have been in the office to lighten the mood.

The drive back to the station had been as tense as the one heading out to the social club, and when they'd pulled up, King had flung open the door and marched inside without a word. Townsend followed, along with Hannon, and when they stepped into the SCU office, King was staring up at the board, lost in the case.

She addressed them as they walked in but didn't turn to them.

'What a mess.'

'Hear, hear.' Hannon said as she lowered herself into her chair, thankful for the strain taken from her spine.

'How did this happen?' King asked out loud, shaking her head as she turned to them both. 'Mrs Jennings was adamant that the box wasn't there before we arrived, so someone in that room had those tongues ready to go.'

'We'll find them, guv,' Townsend said assuredly as he leant back against his desk with his arms folded. 'We got everyone's name and contact information. We just need to follow the process, right?'

'Did we get everyone?' King said with a hint of accusation. 'Penny Durant said she saw a woman hurrying to the door just before Mrs Jennings screamed and *you* opened the door for her when you took that phone call.'

'Me?' Townsend said with a confused frown.

'Think, Jack,' King demanded. Townsend racked his brain. He'd been so distracted by the call that he hadn't paid any real attention to what was happening at the time.

Then his eyes widened.

'Shit.'

'There was a woman.' King confirmed for him. 'Did you get a look at her?'

Townsend felt sick to his stomach.

'No, I didn't even think. We got to the door at the same time, and she seemed in a hurry—'

'Come on, Jack,' King said with desperation.

'She had brown hair.'

'Like the woman at the reunion.' Hannon helpfully chipped in, trying to bail him out.

'And she got into a red car.'

'That's it.' King sighed and shook her head. She stormed towards the murder board and slapped the grainy, CCTV photo of the blurry woman. 'She was right there.'

'Guv, I'm sorry.'

'What was the call, Jack?' King said, clearly irritated. 'Because I said we can't have anymore distractions…'

There was no use lying to her. Townsend knew their entire effectiveness as a team worked on trust.

'It was DCI Lowe.'

Instantly, he saw the look in King's eyes. It wasn't of anger or of annoyance.

It was much worse.

It was a look of betrayal.

Townsend tried to explain.

'He was just calling me with an update on the Beckford

case. Says an old colleague, DCI Staunton knew something about him and…'

King held up a hand to cut him off, and took a moment to find the right words. Townsend looked to Hannon, who could only offer him a look of sympathy.

'I admire your commitment, Jack. I really do. But you *have* to leave that case to Lowe and his team. Like I said before, if you're not one hundred per cent here when I need you to be, then you're no good to me. Mistakes happen. Details get missed if you stretch yourself too thin.'

'Yes, guv,' Townsend said feebly.

'We needed to get on top of this before it became a shit show and now…'

'Oh, it most definitely is a shit show.'

Once again, Detective Superintendent Hall timed his entry to perfection, only this time, the usual warm charm and fatherly approach had dissipated. The man had a face like thunder, with a brow so furrowed it almost touched the tip of his nose.

'Sir.' King addressed him, as she and Townsend stood up straight. Hall motioned to Hannon not to bother as she attempted.

'I've just had the mayor and the Deputy Commissioner on the phone for the past hour, doing their level best to ram my police helmet up my arse over this. So please, please…someone in here tell me we know what we're doing. Because I specifically said this needed to be contained and handled quietly and now, the press is all over the fact that not only do we have a potential serial killer on the loose, but one that turns up at the memorial service attended by three of my fucking detectives.'

Hall wasn't usually one for swearing and hearing him curse sent a shudder of shame through Townsend's body. He had been distracted, and he took his eye off the ball. Before King could answer, Townsend stepped forward.

'It's my fault, sir,' Townsend said with his chin held high. King looked at him in shock. 'I allowed a suspect to leave the building before the incident, the woman we now believe to be involved.'

Hall turned and faced up to Townsend, and his angry posture relaxed slightly. There was always something admirable about someone who could face up to their mistakes, and Hall knew that they happened.

'Well, I appreciate the honesty, DS Townsend. But this unit, it cannot afford to make mistakes.' Hall addressed the entire team. 'This police service looks to you as specialists. It's in your goddamn name. So please, just for me and my peace of mind, let's not make any more.'

'Yes, sir,' all three of them said in unison.

'Oh, and I take it Langley is off the table now,' Hall said curtly. 'Let's not leave a wrongly arrested man chained to his hospital bed longer than needs be.'

King looked to Hannon, who pushed herself up out of her chair.

'On it,' she said as she shuffled to the door.

'Tell him not to go far,' King called after her, and then turned to Hall who looked at her sceptically. 'Just because he didn't deliver the tongues to the service doesn't mean he didn't remove them.'

'It does if you can't prove it,' Hall retorted. 'So find some proof. Find this sick bastard before this gets even further out of control.'

'Yes, sir,' King said with just a hint of defeat. Hall turned on his heel and then addressed Townsend once more.

'And no more fuck ups,' Hall said sternly, with the threat very clear in his voice.

'No, sir.'

Hall marched from the room and once he was gone, only then did Townsend realise he was clenching his fists.

The shame of letting the team down was heavier than he first thought, and he dropped into his chair and dropped his head. After a few moments, King took a few steps towards him and squatted down to eye level.

'Head in the game, Jack.' She reached out and patted his shoulder. 'You're no use to anyone wallowing in self-pity.'

She was right.

King was as demanding as anyone he'd ever met, sometimes bordering on unreasonably so, but she strived for success. It made her a better leader than she thought herself to be, and Townsend knew if he tried to tell her that, she'd just bat it away.

King wasn't one for opening up or sharing her feelings.

But she was a hell of a leader.

'I think Hall's got it wrong,' Townsend eventually said. King turned her attention to him.

'What do you mean?'

'He says we have a serial killer on our hands, but I don't think that's the case.' Townsend stood and headed to the murder board. 'I mean, our killer had killed more than once, but I don't think it's just a random killing of a married couple. They were targeted and there *is* a reason for it.'

'Jason wasn't the most likable of people.' King joined him by the board. 'From what we heard, he gambled, he drank, and he pissed people off.'

'Enough to be murdered for?' Townsend asked. 'Enough for them to then target his wife in such a brutal way?'

'Maybe.' King tapped the photo of Connor Davis. 'He did his old friend out of ten grand.'

'This guy? He doesn't seem like the killing type.'

'Did Baycroft?' King asked.

'Touche.'

'Remember, Jack. We can't dismiss *anything*. Not without proof. Right now, we have two things to go on. Mr Davis and the fact that he lied to us about the money Gallagher took from him.' She then tapped the grainy image of the mystery woman. 'And little miss unknown right here.'

The two of them stood for a beat, staring at the wall and trying to make sense of it. Trying to understand why the Gallaghers were murdered and what everything meant.

The severed tongues.

The suicidal displays.

They needed to start connecting dots because at that moment, they had no clue if it would happen again or who was a target. As Townsend's eyes scanned the board, King looked up at him.

'For the record. Stay away from DCI Staunton if you can,' King said with a level of hatred in her voice. 'He's a nasty piece of work.'

Townsend nodded, feeling another flicker of guilt in his stomach at what he'd agreed with Lowe. King had made it clear what she expected from him, and as he looked up at the photos of the murdered couple, he knew she was right.

He needed to get his head in the game.

He needed to put things right.

But he also had a promise he couldn't walk away from.

CHAPTER TWENTY-FIVE

'Last card.'

Eve smirked over the lone card in her hand, and Townsend scowled at the vast number he was holding. Despite doing a thorough shuffle of the Uno deck, somehow, his daughter always ended up with the power cards that would result in his hand growing in tandem with her cockiness. As he sifted through them, he threw down a 'pick up' card, only for Eve to slam down the same one to once again win the game.

'You know you don't have to let her win anymore, right?' Mandy said dryly from the stove, where she was overlooking the final preparations for the risotto she was concocting.

Townsend turned to her with a frown.

'I don't.'

'I'm just really good at it,' Eve said and then stuck her tongue out at her dad, who reciprocated. Mandy laid out three bowls across the kitchen counter.

'Have you done your homework, missy?' Mandy asked, without turning.

'Yup.' Eve nodded and then turned to her dad. 'I need to do my reading. Can we do that before bed?'

'Absolutely,' Townsend said as he cleared away the damned cards and then went about setting the table. Moments later, the three of them were tucking into another wonderful home cooked meal. Despite her modesty, Mandy was a hell of a cook, and Townsend was envious of people who found comfort or enjoyment from preparing a meal. Beyond his specialty omelette or a barbeque, he was useless in the kitchen. After the dinner, Townsend fetched Eve a bowl of ice cream, and not long after, she'd been bathed and then he sidled up next to her among her cuddly toys on her bed to do her reading. The school had her reading one of Roald Dahl's more famous books, and after reaching the target page, he carried on for a few more until she was sleeping soundly. He placed the book back in her bag, ticked her reading card, and then turned off the light.

Downstairs, Mandy was sitting on the sofa, legs wrapped in a blanket, with her laptop rested on her lap. A glass of red wine was on the side table, and she peered up over her glasses as he walked in. He raised his eyebrows in surprise.

'I've taken my contacts out,' she proclaimed, as if reading his mind. He chuckled and fell onto the sofa next to her.

'I like it. You look like a sexy secretary.' He joked, and then frowned. 'I hope your boss doesn't think like that.'

'I've told you before, Jack. Daniel would be more interested in you.' She smiled, casually reminding him of her boss's sexuality. 'Besides, the only real thing that man is interested in is his business.'

'How's it going?' Townsend asked sincerely. As she looked at him, he offered her a warm smile. His job meant his mind was so wrapped up in a case that he often forgot to check in with her. She'd passed her probation in her role as Daniel's VA, and even though the concept of a virtual assistant still baffled him, it was clear she was good at his job. Mandy was a smart woman and Townsend often joked that she'd make a fine detective, and he wasn't surprised that her tenacity and attention to detail made her a valuable asset to the company. Over the past five months, she'd explained numerous times about the software they produced, and how more and more of the larger companies were signing up to it. But it was a world that was alien to him.

He was a rough detective who was built on some of the roughest estates in the country.

The corporate world was as alien to him as the *cantina* in *Star Wars*.

Mandy pulled her blond hair back and readjusted her hair tie and tilted her head to him.

'It's fine, babe.' She smiled. 'I know your mind is elsewhere.'

'I want to know,' Townsend demanded, even though she was right.

'Well, I could walk you through the presentation notes I've prepared for Daniel for the tech roundtable he's attending tomorrow with a few banking firms,' she said jokingly, amused by his blank stare. 'Or, I could just tell you to go and meet that detective in Wembley, even though I don't think it's the best idea.'

'It's like we share a brain, isn't it?' Townsend chuckled. 'Which is pretty scary.'

'One mind, babe,' she said with a cheeky grin, but it quickly turned to concern. 'But I know you, Jack. You're the most strong-minded man I've ever met. I know you want to do whatever you can to help that family, but it's just going to clash with your loyalty. I mean, what happens if Izzy finds out that you went behind her back?'

'She'll hand me my arse, I'd imagine.' Townsend shrugged.

'And is it worth it?' Mandy turned and faced him, looking deep into his eyes. 'Is it worth the problems it could cause?'

She was right.

Ever since Townsend had made it out of his under-cover job after three long years, he had strived for some-where to belong. The Merseyside Police had tucked him away in an office under the pretence it was for his safety, when in reality, it was because they'd handed him the promotion as a make-good. In truth, even King wasn't sold on the idea of having him in her team, but with her guid-ance and trust, he'd seemingly found his calling.

He owed so much to her.

But he'd made a promise to Simone that he'd find out who killed her husband, and it was something he just couldn't shake.

As his mind began to connect with clarity, he could tell from the look on his wife's face that she'd already accepted his decision.

'I have to, babe,' he said with clarity. 'If there is a chance I can find out what happened…'

'Then go.' She nodded her approval. 'But if what that Lowe says is true, then you need to be careful.'

'I'm always careful.'

Mandy let out an uncontrollable laugh.

'Bullshit, Mr Townsend.' She shook her head. 'You'd run headfirst into a speeding train if it could offer you the truth. And I love you for it, I really do. But just remem-ber…that little girl upstairs, she needs you just as much as those people out there do. We both do.'

Her words hit him hard, and he took a few moments before he let out a deep sigh. He then leant forward, kissed her tenderly on the lips and then stood up.

'I know. And I'd walk through hell to get back to you both, you know that.'

'We know,' Mandy said with a nod. 'But we don't want you to. Just make sure you're around for her. That's all she needs.'

'Yeah. And I am,' Townsend said to himself more than his wife. To remind himself of the progress he'd made with Eve, and where their relationship was. 'I have to do this, Mandy. But believe me, I'll fight like hell to keep my word to that kid.'

'I know.' She looked up at him with pride. 'Now go get 'em, Tiger.'

With his wife's endorsement ringing in his ears, Townsend marched to the front door and lifted his coat from the hooks that ran along the hallway wall. As he pulled open the front door, the darkness of the night was illuminated by the sensor operated light from above. The rain lashed down, and the bitter cold of winter rushed towards him like a long-lost friend.

Townsend stepped out into the night and headed to the car, stopping to look back at the home he was leaving behind. As the downpour quickly drenched him, he gazed up at the window of his daughter's room and wished her a silent good night.

Then he dropped into his car and headed for the capital, knowing it was going to be a long night.

It just had to be worthwhile.

CHAPTER TWENTY-SIX

It's funny how, no matter the setting, you could recognise a police station when you saw one.

With the street lights basking the downpour in a rich glow, Townsend peered up through his windscreen as he approached Brent Police Station, and even in the darkness, the building felt familiar. It was drab and grey and in serious need of an upgrade, and the fixtures looked like they were clinging to the brickwork with their final grip. Even the sign, this one emblazoned with the Metropolitan Police badge, was faded, and one of the spotlights designed to proudly illuminate the sign had burnt out.

It was a concrete block that housed some of the most important work in the country, but like so many other areas of every police service, it had been neglected and abandoned by a government who thought the country could be policed on a shoestring budget.

Same as the Merseyside Police Service.

Same as Thames Valley.

Townsend pulled his car into one of the few spaces made available for the public and stepped out into the rain, and as he looked up at the building once more, he almost felt a modicum of sympathy for Staunton and his team.

They were all in the same boat.

But then he remembered King's warning, and he marched towards the entrance of the station with a renewed vigour. Whatever his pre-conceived notions of Lowe's comrade were, he needed to shift them to the side. He was there for Simone Beckford, and to find out what had happened to her husband.

Who had slit his throat?

Who had left him to die alone and in the dark?

There was a chance DCI Staunton could help, and if that was the case, then Townsend was willing to play nice. As he pushed open the door, the brightness of the waiting room greeted him like a hard slap to the face, and as he looked around the room, he noticed it was just as unwelcoming and as bland as the one he passed through on a nearly daily basis.

Uncomfortable plastic seats bolted to the tiled floor.

A raft of posters pinned to the wall, ranging from a neighbourhood watch promo to warnings about littering.

Behind a Perspex screen, a young officer sat busily typing away on a computer, and as Townsend approached, the officer barely gave him the time of day.

'DS Jack Townsend from Thames Valley Police,' Townsend said with authority. 'I believe a DCI Staunton is expecting me.'

'About fucking time, son.' A voice boomed from behind him, and Townsend swivelled to see a bulky man approaching. The man stood over six foot two, and was as broad as a heavyweight boxer, but the slide into his mid- to late-forties had seen him loosen round the edges. The cheap lights above reflected off his shiny, bald head and his cruel smirk was framed by a thick, gingery beard that was now speckled with flecks of grey. He walked towards

Townsend with the Cockney swagger that matched his voice. 'You ready, Scouse?'

'Excuse me?' Townsend said, slightly combative. Staunton smiled and headed towards the door.

'Come on. Let's go for a drive.'

Without an explanation, Staunton shoved open the door and disappeared out into the rain and Townsend took a quick glance at the young officer who gave him a mournful look.

Clearly, King wasn't the only one who knew about Staunton's reputation.

As he darted out into the car park, he saw the flicker of a lighter and then a plume of smoke, and the hulking figure of Staunton disappeared around the corner of the building.

'Hey…where are we going?' Townsend called, jogging to catch up. As he rounded the corner into the car park, Staunton chuckled as he unlocked his flash sports car.

'Just get in the fucking car, son,' Staunton ordered, before taking a long drag on the cigarette then flicking half of it into the darkness. 'I don't want to be babysitting all fucking night.'

Townsend went to remonstrate, but caught his tongue. Despite the clear disdain Staunton had for him, Townsend had to remember the man was doing him a favour. As Staunton dropped into the driver's seat, Townsend went to open the door, but it was locked.

With a sigh, he rolled his eyes and rapped his knuckles on the window.

Staunton unlocked the car.

Townsend pulled the handle.

Staunton locked it again.

Townsend huffed and then the locks clicked once more and he yanked the door open, easing into the seat to be welcomed by the smell of stale smoke and childish laughing of the brutish detective.

'Fucking cheer up, Scouse.' Staunton laughed as he pulled out of the spot. 'I thought you fuckers were meant to be good crack.'

'Yeah, that was hilarious,' Townsend said dryly as he clicked his seat belt. 'So, what's the plan?'

Staunton pulled out of the station and hit the main street before answering.

'The plan is I don't get paid overtime for this shit, so whatever it is you want from me, make it snappy,' Staunton said, his eyes locked on the road. 'Marcus and I, we go way back. We worked these streets for years, and trust me, they're a shite-sight worse than the fucking villages you run around in.'

'Trust me. I've seen worse,' Townsend said defiantly. They stopped at a light and Staunton spun in his seat.

'Yeah, the big bad Scouser, right?' Staunton chuckled. 'They've told me about you. Undercover. Got himself into some right shit along the way. That's impressive and all, but this isn't about how fucking hard you are. Trust me, if it was, I'd be commissioner of this goddamn police service. This is about knowing the streets. Knowing how these fuckers work and how they move. You spend a few years with a gang, you get some knowledge. You do this for twenty-two years, son…and you're one of them.'

Staunton pulled off the main road and down a few relatively nice residential streets that spat in the face of the bad reputation Wembley had. But just as Townsend was beginning to appreciate them, they turned again and just minutes later; they were cruising through a rundown high street, with graffiti laden shutters and more boarded-up windows than those with glass panes.

'So you knew Jamal Beckford?'

'I knew of him,' Staunton said with a shake of the

head. 'Mouthy little prick. Only a matter of time before someone shut him up.'

'So he had enemies?' Townsend asked with a raised eyebrow. There was something about Staunton that made him question his own ability. Especially when Staunton chuckled once more.

'Fucking hell, son. You really are playing the Izzy King playbook move by move ain't ya?'

'You worked with DI King?'

'Yeah. Back before she had that stick surgically implanted up her arsehole.' Staunton shrugged. 'But she was out here with us, running these fuckers down and stopping them from getting too far out of sight.'

'What do you mean?' Townsend asked with genuine interest. Staunton may have been an unapologetic brute, but he had been a detective for nearly quarter of a century.

The man was experienced, if nothing else.

'Look around, Scouse,' Staunton said with his eyes on the road. 'The people who live in these estates, they don't have the same faith in the systems or the laws we have. They are fighting every fucking day, and to them, the law isn't something to follow, but just to avoid. Drugs. Women. Weapons. Most of it floods through these streets like a fucking rat infestation, and my team, we work hard to make sure the supply lines get cut off, or that the shit doesn't swim too far downhill. We just face a lot of push-back from the gangs around here, and trust me, after years of fighting it, some people want to piss off for an easier life.'

'Is that why King and Lowe moved out?' Townsend asked, realising a hint of resentment in Staunton's voice. The gruff detective's lips drew into a thin line of frustration, and then he indicated and turned onto a run-down estate that reminded Townsend of home.

Not Flackwell Heath.

But the real home where he was built and shaped.

'She wanted out,' Staunton said. 'They started fucking, decided to get married, and then she wanted a family. Marcus, he was my go-to guy, but I guess he did what he thought was best. Trust me, son. I heard you put him on his arse in the boxing ring, and that's no easy feat. But believe me when I tell you, that guy might be a prick at the best of times, but you don't want anyone else kicking down a fucking door of one of these flats than him.'

They sat in silence for a few moments, as Townsend contemplated the idea that Lowe was *actually* a good detective. Despite the man's permanent aura of arrogance, he had a flock of loyal detectives, and was seen as the golden boy by nearly every senior figure within the Thames Valley Police. The man ran CID and, by the account of Staunton, had been an asset to his team during his days in the Met.

Maybe it was time for Townsend to not let the personal issues between King and Lowe affect his own relationships.

Maybe he didn't need to pick a side.

Just do his job.

The car came to a stop, and without one ounce of consideration for his passenger, Staunton lit up another cigarette.

'So this is where Beckford was from?' Townsend said, looking out the window.

'It's where he ran about, yeah.'

'The NX Gang?'

'Someone's been doing their homework.' Staunton took a long pull and then pushed open his door. 'You got questions, right?'

Townsend stepped out of the car, and the rain hit him instantly. His coat did little to protect him from the freezing, relentless wind, and he squinted through the elements at the run-down community centre before them. The iron gates were locked, pulled together by a thick padlock that looped between the bars. What little greenery it had was overgrown, and the entire front face of the build was a hodgepodge of different coloured spray paints.

Every window was boarded up.

The metal front door bolted shut.

The place was as broken and as neglected as the rest of the surrounding estates, and Townsend felt a sense of unease as Staunton stepped round the car and began to march around the side of the building, following the chain-link fence to a side alley. As he approached the alleyway, he stopped and gestured for Townsend to go first.

'Come on, pretty boy. This is your fucking investigation, not mine.' Staunton's face was twisted into a cruel grin. 'Lead on.'

With his wife's plea to be careful ringing in his ears, Townsend paused for the briefest of moments. The warnings from DI King also echoed through his mind, as the spectre of the Gallaghers murders, and her worries that Townsend was spreading himself too thin hung over him like the storm clouds ahead.

Maybe he should just turn back.

Toe the line.

But some things were worth crossing the line for, and despite his gut telling him nothing good awaited him down the alleyway, he marched forward with purpose, took the invitation and headed down the dark alleyway, hoping to find some answers.

CHAPTER TWENTY-SEVEN

The alleyway led to a break in the fence, and Townsend shoved his way through it, crawling through the gap and soaking his hands and knees in the grimy, litter covered mud. Staunton, rather unhelpfully, showed him that the nearby gate was open and shrugged at Townsend who stared daggers at him.

'I didn't say anything.' Staunton chuckled, then nodded towards the rear of the building, which, like the front, was covered in graffiti. As they approached the back door, Townsend's boots crunched on broken glass, and the wall was lined with discarded roaches and even a few syringes. Townsend yanked open the door, which hung precariously on its hinges and Staunton stepped through as he cupped his hands around the cigarette hanging from his mouth as he sparked it to life.

Somewhere inside the community centre, they heard a discussion come to a hushed conclusion, before an angry voice yelled out from somewhere in the darkness.

'Yo, who the fuck is there?'

The aggression was clear, and Townsend looked to Staunton who just raised his eyebrows.

'It's your fucking rodeo, son.'

The smirk on Staunton's face told Townsend he wasn't going to get any help, and with his fists clenched, he strode down the narrow corridor to the doorway where the voice emanated from. As he stepped through, he heard the shuffling of feet and the community hall was bathed in the dull light of a few lamps that were set up in different parts of a room that had long since fallen into disrepair. The paint on the walls had been damaged by the mould and damp, and a few slits of moonlight crept through the cracks in the wooden boards that were hammered over the windows. Lining the room were bags of rubbish, along with broken pieces of furniture from a time before.

But in the middle of the room was a beaten leather sofa, along with a few chairs, and standing in front of all of them were five young men who had their eyes locked on Townsend. All of them were in their early to mid-twenties, and each one of them stood in their own aggressive stance, as if offended that someone had dared to intrude on their patch. As Townsend took a few steps further forward, one of the young men took one step forward, pulled back his hood, and stuck his hand in his pocket.

'That's far enough, bruv.' The voice was recognisable as the one that had shouted out earlier, and as Townsend watched the others shift into formation behind, the young man was clearly the leader. 'I'd say you're a long fucking way from being lost right now.'

Townsend glanced over his shoulder, but there was no sign of Staunton.

He'd left him.

Alone in the lion's den.

Townsend held up his hands in a show of surrender.

'I'm not here for trouble, lads…'

'What?' The leader did a comical cupping of his ear.

'Bruv, I don't understand a fucking word you just said. You a tourist or summin?'

'I just need to ask you some questions.'

The group began to laugh, a few of them shoving the others in an over-the-top display of disrespect to their guest. Townsend stood strong, determined not to show one ounce of the fear that was beginning to bubble within him. Hand to hand, he was confident he could handle any of them. His years being hardened on the streets of Toxteth and in the boxing ring would see to that, and the traumatic time undercover allowed him to quickly assess who was truly a threat and who was just 'playing gangster'.

But up against five?

Alone and in a part of the country that had been forgotten about, he didn't fancy his chances.

As the gang calmed down, the leader straightened up and fixed him with an icy stare and shook his head.

'I'll tell you what, I'm feeling like a generous guy today.' He held out his hand, and Townsend shuddered as one of the larger members of the group placed a large machete into it. The leader then pointed it towards Townsend with intent. 'So how about you put your phone, your wallet, your watch…fuck, anything you white boys pay stupid money for, on the floor, and back the fuck up out of here before I cut you from hole to hole.'

The threat was real, and Townsend could see in the man's eyes that he wasn't playing around. Behind him, a few of the other members swayed anxiously, telling him that some of them were only in this to a certain level.

It meant that five on one advantage had decreased.

His next move was a potential life ender, and he saw a mixture of hatred and apprehension flood the room as he held up his police lanyard.

'I am a detective for the Thames Valley Police.' He

began, scanning the group as he took a step forward. 'And I just have a few questions for you.'

'Yo, Jordan…the man's a fucking fed,' a voice whispered from the group, and Jordan snapped his neck to them to quiet them. The mood had shifted, and Jordan kept the machete pointed at Townsend as he considered his next step.

'Thing is…we don't like the fucking police. They ain't welcome round these streets, you know?' Jordan took a step forward. 'But you…you cocky little bitch…you ain't even from round here. This motherfucker isn't even part of the Met, blud.'

'But I am.'

Staunton's gruff voice boomed from the corridor, exploding in a fearsome echo through the room, and the bulky detective marched into the room as he took a long, satisfying pull on his cigarette before flicking it irresponsibly into the corner of the room. Townsend didn't show it, but his body tensed with relief as Staunton emerged from the shadows. Judging by the look on the faces of the group, they knew Staunton. With venom in his eyes, Staunton glared at Jordan, who slowly lowered the blade.

'There's a good boy,' Staunton said cockily.

'The fuck you doing here, Alfie?' Jordan said with an arrogant shake of his head. 'You know we ain't on some shit.'

'My associate here has a few questions for you that I can't answer for him.' Staunton looked around the room and then sniffed. His face grimaced with disgust. 'Stinks like shit in here.'

'Yeah, that's because your little bitch here shat his pants,' Jordan said, turning to his crew for support to try to save face. But the mood had changed, and for all the bravado they'd shown before, the gang seemed a little more compliant.

Townsend wondered just how far Staunton's reputation preceded him.

As the silence hung in the room, along with the dank smell, Staunton looked at his watch and then slapped Townsend on the back, hard enough to make him take a step forward.

'Come on then, Scouse. It's getting late.'

'Jamal Beckford,' Townsend began, and he saw the recognition on their faces. 'When did he leave your gang?'

'Man, why you bringing that pussy up?' Jordan sneered. 'That name is dead around here.'

As Jordan nodded to his crew, who all agreed, Staunton chuckled.

'Bad choice of words, son.'

'What you talkin' bout?'

Townsend stepped in.

'Jamal Beckford is dead,' Townsend stated coldly, watching all their reactions. 'Somebody slit his throat four days ago and left him to die not too far from his home.'

The shock was genuine. All five of the young men looked at each other as if someone would have the answer to the question they all had. Then swiftly, Jordan realised it was the same one that Townsend did.

'That ain't anything to do with us.' His voice was stricken with panic.

'No? Because from what you were just saying to me a minute ago, and the fact you were waving that blade around like Jason Voorhees, makes me believe you might have been a little pissed off he walked away from…' Townsend looked around the room. '…whatever life this is.'

'Yo, fuck you.' Jordan snapped. 'Come walking in here with your fucking fancy coat and your shitty shoes, judging us. Judging the lives we lead. We gotta be out here grinding. We gotta be out here making moves, because mother-fuckers like you hold us down.'

Townsend was growing in confidence, and he could sense the almost proud smile on Staunton's face.

'Like you said…I'm not from even round here.' Townsend spoke sternly. 'But I am investigating who killed Jamal Beckford, and my eyes are on the mouthy little twat with a machete.'

The insult sparked a red mist in Jordan, and with the expectant eyes of his crew locked on him, he dropped the blade and lunged at Townsend. It was telling that none of his crew joined him, and that seemed to sprinkle an element of doubt in the man's eyes as he approached Townsend. But he was too far in to turn back, and he wildly threw a right hand at Townsend, who spun, allowing the fist to fall over his shoulder, and then Townsend clasped his hands on the man's arm. Using the man's momentum, Townsend arched his back into Jordan's body, flipping him over and driving his spine down onto the rotten titles beneath. Jordan grunted with pain as the air was driven from his lungs, and in one swift yank, Townsend turned him over onto his front and then wrenched his shoulder until the tendons screamed for mercy.

'Fucking get him!' Jordan screamed from the ground. Two of the crew looked willing, but backed down as Staunton took a step forward.

'Don't even fucking think about it.'

With his crew stationary, Jordan felt the fight leave him, and Townsend knelt on one knee, locking Jordan's arm against his own spine.

'Shall we try that again?' Townsend said softly.

The entire room was silent, and the balance of power had irreversibly shifted. As his crew watched on, and Staunton stood guard, Jordan sighed before speaking.

'Look, man. Jamal left. We didn't want him to, told him you don't walk away from the NX, but that man had been sprung.'

'Sprung?' Townsend asked for clarification.

'Some bitch who lived out in the fucking sticks. Met her online. We thought he'd just tap it a few times and come back, but the idiot fell in love. Said he wanted that normal life. Hell, he even took on her kid.'

'So you killed him for it?'

Jordan's eyes widened in panic.

'We didn't kill him. Jamal goes way back with another member of our crew. Higher up, you know? They gave him their blessing and Jamal split. That's it, man. That's the truth. I swear down.'

Townsend looked up at Staunton, who nodded.

'Fine.' Townsend released his grip and lifted himself off Jordan, who rolled over and scrambled back to his crew. Townsend stared them all down and then pointed at Jordan. 'Next time, take a second to think before you swing like that. You made it easy.'

Jordan muttered something under his breath before turning back to his crew who all ceremoniously turned their backs on the duo. Staunton patted Townsend on the arm and headed to the exit, and neither one of them spoke until they were back at the car. Staunton was smirking as he lit a cigarette.

Townsend, with the rain lashing down on them both, called to him across the roof.

'What's so funny?'

'I already checked them out a few days ago when Marcus was given the case.'

Townsend felt his fists clench and his muscles tighten.

'What?'

'We knew the NX Crew from way back, and Beckford. We've run into him a few times.' Staunton took a puff and then pointed at Townsend with the cigarette. 'But you embarrassed the fuck out of him when you laid him out a few months ago. Kudos to you, son. But Marcus, he's a petty bastard. Hell of a detective, but a petty bastard. He wanted to shit you up a little bit. So I said I'd take you into the belly of the beast and see what they do.'

'You set me up?' Townsend said with fury.

'Mate, I'd never let them do anything.' Staunton flicked the cigarette into the street and allowed the rain to wash it away. 'You're a cop. That means something to me. Besides, I have to say. You handled yourself pretty fucking well back there. No wonder Marcus is threatened by you.'

Before Townsend could respond, Staunton dropped back into the car and this time, he didn't mess about with the lock. Townsend took that as a mark of respect and the two travelled in silence back to the Wembley nick, with the empty roads meaning for a swift return. As soon as the car came to a stop, Townsend threw open the door and marched back towards the exit. Staunton called after him, and Townsend stopped, turned and was surprised to see an extended hand.

'You're all right, Scouse,' Staunton said.

Townsend took the hand and shook it.

'Next time, don't fuck me around,' he said, but was unable to hide the smile forming on his face.

Mutual respect was hard to find.

It was even harder to command.

Staunton stepped back, fished out another cigarette, and then smiled.

'Hopefully, there won't be a next time.'

With that, Townsend headed back to his own car in the visitor's car park, and he shot one final glance back, as the burly detective disappeared round the back of the building in a plume of smoke.

Townsend headed back to his own life, knowing that whoever killed Jamal Beckford wasn't a ghost from his past.

As with the Gallaghers, it meant death was in High Wycombe.

Right on his doorstep.

CHAPTER TWENTY-EIGHT

'Jesus Christ, Izzy. You look like hell.'

As ever, Detective Superintendent Hall cut straight to the point, peering up over his glasses at DI King, who stood sheepishly in front of his desk. He was right, King had to admit, as another sleepless night had almost stretched her to breaking point.

The pressure of the Gallagher murders was building, not just within the confines of the case or in the ever-growing interest of the media, but in her own head.

Every possible theory was fighting for clarity in her mind.

Every minute that passed meant they were closer to losing control of the situation and worse, drifting further away from the truth.

As she'd spent the night forcing herself to try to sleep, the only thing her body truly craved was a drink.

Just one.

Just to take the edge off.

Just to calm the nerves.

But she knew she couldn't give in. One small glass

would lead to another, which would inevitably lead to a bottle.

A hangover.

A day filled with regret and the only thing it would truly accomplish would be the betrayal to the Gallaghers who, although dead, were relying on her to bring meaning and justice to their murders.

As she'd lain in bed, the guilt of letting down the five women who'd been mercilessly slain by Gordon Baycroft had taken hold of her brain, whispering to her to just give in to her addiction and take a drink.

But she hadn't, and while she felt stronger for it, she knew she looked how she felt.

Like she'd been dragged through hell by her hair.

'Thank you, sir,' she finally responded dryly, and he motioned for her to sit. 'I'm fine, sir.'

'Look, Izzy.' Hall often used her first name in private, establishing a friendship that would spawn loyalty. 'I know what you're going through. I've never been there myself, but trust me, you're not the first officer to walk these halls who's had to battle back these demons.'

'I know, sir,' King said with a little self-hatred. 'But I won't let them beat me.'

'How long's it been?' He rocked back in his chair as he looked at her.

'A hundred and forty five days, sir,' King stated proudly. 'Not since Baycroft.'

He nodded his respect to her and then leant forward. 'You know I'm here for you whenever you need me, right? For support. For a friendly chat. But I need you at one hundred, Izzy? Not walking in here looking like death warmed up. So if you need to take a little time…'

King cut him off immediately.

'That won't be necessary, sir,' she said defiantly. 'This is *my* case, and I won't let this get ahead of me.'

Hall clasped his fingers together as he regarded her, and eventually, he smiled.

'Then go get 'em,' he said with a firm nod. 'But remember, Izzy, this can't spiral out of control. Not again.'

The warning was clear, even if it was delivered with a sense of friendship, and King turned and marched out of Hall's office and down through the empty corridors of the police station. The night shift was returning, ready to hand over to the early risers, and on her way through to the SCU office, she stopped off at the canteen for a coffee. She took it to go, mumbling pleasantries she didn't mean to a canteen worker she didn't know, before her autopilot took her through the corridors to the hub of the Specialist Crimes Unit.

As she stepped through the door, DS Townsend already sitting at his desk, catching him stretching back in his chair, mid-yawn.

'Late night?' she asked, stepping past him towards the murder board. He quickly spun in his chair, covering his mouth with a little hint of embarrassment.

'Kids,' Townsend said dismissively, swallowing the guilt of lying to King who didn't seem to notice. Her attention was turned to the murder board. 'Any thoughts, guv?'

'Hmmm. A few,' she said vaguely and then turned to him. 'Did Sykes have any information regarding Jason?'

The question caught Townsend off guard and King knew from the look of bewilderment on his face that it had slipped his mind.

He scrambled.

'I'll get on to him today and—'

'Jack. Remember what I said about stretching yourself too thin?' King said sternly. 'Three days. That's a long time in this investigation and we need to move fast. So please, get yourself down to Paradise—'

'Sounds fun,' Hannon said with a smirk as she

walked in. Her coat was dripping with rainwater, but in her hand, she carefully balanced a cup holder with three cups of piping hot coffee. As the two of them descended upon her like zombies in a horror film, she chuckled. 'Don't even ask me how I managed to balance these in the car.'

'You're a lifesaver,' King said as she gratefully scooped up the cup.

'I second that.' Townsend followed, grateful for the interruption.

As the two of them guzzled their drinks, Hannon slid her coat off.

'I like to think that as a team, we've all got each other's best interests at heart. And that we can be honest with each other.'

'Go on…' King nodded to her.

'You both look like shit,' she exclaimed, and the two of them smiled.

Then chuckled.

One of Hannon's talents, of which there were many, was being able to slice through tension with a well-placed comment. As she took her seat, King sent one final stern look towards Townsend, that told him everything he needed to know.

No more mistakes.

Head in the game.

Blowing out her cheeks, King turned back to the board and tried to absorb everything. Her brain was too tired to process every single detail, but there had to be something.

Anything to give them something to chase. As if reading her mind, Townsend piped up from behind her.

'Shall we bring Connor Davis back in? Push him on the financial aspect?'

'I already put the fear of God into him yesterday,' King replied, not taking her eye from the board. 'If he had any sense, and if he has nothing to do with this, he'll bring us all the information and walk us through it himself.'

'He's going to the Marlow lights tonight,' Hannon said. 'Might be worth going along?'

'I'm already going,' Townsend said, and both women looked at him. 'Shock horror. My little one wants to see the lights turn on.'

'Okay for us to tag along?' King suggested, not really asking for permission.

'Oooo, yeah. Finally, we get to meet Mandy.' Hannon smiled. 'We can discuss your habits.'

'What habits?' Townsend said with a scowl and Hannon raised a mysterious eyebrow.'

'Let's park that until later.' King brought the conversation back to the matter at hand. 'If Davis doesn't show tonight, let's get him at the switch-on. Until then…we need something…'

'Well, it's a good job you have me,' Hannon said with a grin, and beckoned them both to her desk. 'While you two were busy being old and tired last night, I decided to do some more digging, and I found this.'

She opened up a few windows on her laptop and then dragged them across to the bigger screen on her desk. They were the write-ups from the uniformed officers who had been at the memorial service, and who had clearly put in some overtime to get the reports onto the system so swiftly. She highlighted the same name on three separate statements, and King read it out loud.

'Gemma Miller,' King said blankly.

'I've not heard that name yet,' Townsend added, looking to his boss.

'No, because it hasn't come up before,' Hannon said excitedly, as she pulled up a list of names who'd given statements. 'These three people all said they knew Rachel Gallagher from school, right? And all of them mentioned

Gemma, with one of them lumping her in with people they knew from school.'

'So Gemma went to school with them?'

'It seems like it,' Hannon said but then smiled. 'But here's the kicker...she's not on the list of people interviewed. Meaning...'

'Meaning she wasn't in the building when we locked down the building.' King's eyes lit up. 'Nic, sometimes I could kiss your brain.'

'I mean, it's just a theory, but there's a good chance we now have a name for your mystery lady.'

As Hannon spoke, King was already marching to the murder board, and underneath the grainy photo of the lady, she wrote the name Gemma Miller. As she clicked the lid back onto her pen, she turned to the team with a new sense of purpose.

'Nic, start digging. Find out whatever you can about this Gemma Miller. If she's smart, and she is behind this, I can't imagine her digital footprint will even exist, but I want you to flip every stone and check every corner of every database.'

'I'm on it,' Hannon said merrily, spinning in her chair and dropping her eyes down to the keyboard. King turned to Townsend.

'Jack, get back to the school. Find out if Gemma was in attendance at the reunion and then pull out any records they have on her. I want confirmation of a connection to our victims, and anything else we can link between them and her.'

'Yes, guv,' Townsend said, as he finished his coffee and pulled his jacket off the chair. 'I'll call by Sykes on the way back.'

King gave him a thankful nod, and Townsend threw his coat on and marched out of the office, almost colliding with DCI Lowe as he did.

'Easy, Scouse,' Lowe said with a smug grin. 'You're not in Wembley now.'

'Good one,' Townsend said dryly, but held his tongue before he could shoot off a snarky reply. Staunton's words still echoed in his mind, and the idea that behind all the smugness and the bravado, a decent man and detective existed within Lowe. Townsend more than anyone knew what it was like to keep up a charade, and the toll it took to keep up appearances. As Lowe stood waiting for the reply, Townsend just offered him a smile and patted him on the arm. 'Have a good day, sir.'

The respect seemed to catch Lowe off guard, and as Townsend marched off down the hall, Lowe called after him.

'Good work last night.'

It was all he could muster, and although Townsend didn't look back, he felt a small part of a long bridge slowly being built.

What he didn't know was that a few feet away, just inside the doorway to the SCU, DI Inspector King heard every word of it.

CHAPTER TWENTY-NINE

As Townsend pulled into the car park of the school, it was significantly harder to find a parking space than at the weekend. With lessons in full flow as the curriculum headed towards the end of the year, the entire faculty was in house, meaning Townsend had to park in one of the reserved bays.

If anyone had a problem with it, his identification would probably calm them down swiftly.

As he marched from his car to the front door, he could see interested faces peering from the windows, as the teenagers that comprised the school's intake were intrigued at the mystery man who was arriving at their school. He paid them no attention, keeping his eyes on the automatic door to the reception and his mind on the task at hand.

Who was Gemma Miller?

As he entered the reception area, he noticed Carly Roberts, who he'd spoken to a few days before, and her head shot up like a meerkat from behind the desk. She quickly rose from her desk and scurried through the door and welcomed him.

'You're back?' she said, somewhat startled.

'Indeed, I am,' Townsend said with a smile. 'I need some more information I'm afraid.'

'I mean, it's the middle of a school week,' Roberts said, seemingly anxious. 'Let me call Mr Hollis.'

Townsend had done enough research to know she was referring to the head teacher, and after a quick phone call, a confident man came striding down the corridor towards him. Roughly the same age as Townsend, Mr Hollis had lost his battle with his hairline and given up the ghost, but made up for it with a thick, greying beard. Dressed in a well-pressed suit, the head of the school greeted Townsend with a tight handshake.

'How can I help you, officer?' Hollis asked.

'DS Townsend.' He corrected him. 'Can we maybe speak somewhere a little more private?'

'Of course.' The head teacher motioned for Townsend to follow, and he shot a glance back towards Carly and the other woman who worked in the front office. Hollis opened the door to his office and welcomed Townsend inside. Townsend let out a whistle at the nicely furnished room, which was immaculately tidy. The desk was small, but neat as a pin, and there were two comfy looking chairs opposite it. The wall was lined with a bookshelf that was stocked with the usual 'high performance' books, written by gurus who promised self-development by the chapter. The wall was adorned with numerous framed certificates, presenting the man's credentials, and as Mr Hollis took his seat behind his desk, Townsend stood to admire them.

'Ah, those old things.' Hollis faked his embarrassment. 'It seems to put the parent's minds to rest to see I'm at least qualified for my job.'

'You should be proud of them,' Townsend said, without turning. 'Nothing wrong with being well educated.'

'Indeed. You'd fit in well here.' The joke caused

Townsend to smile, and he turned and took the seat being offered by the head of the school, who placed the tips of his fingers together. 'How can I help?'

'As you've probably been made aware of by now, alumni of this school, Jason Gallagher, went missing from the reunion that was held here last Friday.' Townsend began flipping open his book.

'Yes, I heard.' Hollis sighed.

'Well, I need to gain access to some records pertaining to a student who we believe might be able to help.' Townsend regarded the headmaster carefully.

'Absolutely.' Hollis nodded. 'The last thing we want is for this mess to spread through the school. Lord knows these kids are distracted enough as it is. Let's go and speak to Amy.'

'Amy?' Townsend's eyebrows rose.

'Yes, she works with Carly in the front office. She's a godsend,' Hollis said with a smile. 'Carly is fantastic with the students, but put her in front of a computer and, well…'

He tailed off, and Townsend wasn't too surprised. Carly hadn't seemed like the most useful of people.

'Did you attend here when you were younger?' Townsend asked as Hollis stood and headed to the door.

'No, no. I went to the grammar school just outside of Marlow,' Hollis said proudly. 'Do you know it?'

'I mean, you know I'm not from round here,' Townsend said with a smile, and Hollis chuckled. As they marched back towards the front office, Hollis reprimanded two teenage boys for running, and Townsend smiled with approval. The school was a world away from the rough school he'd attended, where the teachers cared less than the students did. As they entered the office, Carly spun in her chair as if she'd been caught watching something illegal.

'Is everything okay?' she asked with a little panic.

'Yes, yes.' Hollis waved her off. 'DS Townsend needs access to some student records is all.'

'Oh. Amy is in the back.'

The two men walked through to the small, darker office at the back, where a small woman looked up from her desk with annoyance more than intrigue. Her glasses magnified her eyes almost comically, and her unwashed brown hair was pulled into a messy ponytail. The desk was immaculate, however, and Townsend offered her a smile as Hollis introduced her and gave her the remit.

'The files from back then have been digitised,' she stated as a matter of fact. 'Well, whatever ones we could.'

'Is there a chance you won't have any?' Townsend asked with a little concern.

'You're talking twenty-five years ago.' Amy spat back. 'We weren't in charge of the filing system back then.'

Seemingly offended by the accusation, Amy tapped away on the keyboard, as Hollis explained to Townsend how Amy was the one who introduced the digital database for students and had led the upload of all files onto the new system. Before she'd come along, it was just cabinet after cabinet of paper files.

'What was the name?' Amy interrupted.

'Err...Gemma Miller,' Townsend said hopefully.

Amy clicked the required keys, looked at the screen and then shook her head.

'Nothing.'

'Nothing?' Townsend echoed.

'No records.' Amy sat back in her chair. 'You're welcome to check yourself.'

Townsend took the offer, and after twice entering the name and twice returning no results, he typed in Jason Gallagher and a few files returned. As did Connor Davis.

But no Gemma Miller.

'Damn,' he muttered under his breath.

'I'm sorry, DS Townsend.' Hollis shrugged. 'They are very old records and…'

'Do you have a yearbook?' Townsend shot a glance up at Hollis, who seemed taken aback. 'In your library. Are there editions of the yearbook?'

'I think so,' Amy said from behind them, her eyes on the screen as she returned to work. 'They have a pile of them in the back of the library.'

'Thank you.' Townsend turned back to Amy, who completely ignored him. With a roll of the eyes, Townsend turned back to Hollis, who led him through the school towards the library. They passed a few groups of teenagers, all of whom stopped their conversation at the appearance of their head teacher, and all of whom giggled once they were a few steps ahead of them.

Townsend would likely be the talk of the school before long.

As they entered the library, a class of the older children all spun in their chairs, and Hollis instructed them back to their lesson. As he led Townsend through to the back room, the light automatically clicked into action. As it burst into life, it illuminated several rows of shelves, all of them packed with thick, dusty books.

'Mrs Lynan has a thing about throwing out books…' Hollis offered feebly, as Townsend looked at him with disappointment. Without a word, Townsend began slowly walking the aisles between the shelving units, his eyes scanning over the spines of the books, some of which he had to rub clear of the dust.

Encyclopaedias reaching as far back as the seventies.

Old curriculum books that were no longer fit for purpose.

Until finally, yearbooks.

With an excited lunge, he pulled down the one for

Gallagher's school year and brought it back out to the light. Hollis watched on with intrigue, as Townsend began to flick through the worn, faded pages, skipping through the alphabet until he reached the letter M.

Miller.

As he flicked to a page that was dotted with faded, uncomfortable smiles, with the final girl on the page a Kathryn McGillis.

He turned the page.

It was missing.

The remaining torn paper was still embedded in the spine of the book, and Townsend tipped the book upside down, but nothing fell out.

Someone had removed the page.

After triple checking the page wasn't stuck, Townsend slammed the book down angrily on the desk and turned to Hollis, who looked embarrassed.

'Do you have any extra copies?' Townsend asked, knowing the answer before Hollis shook his head. He sighed. 'Is there CCTV in here?'

'Not in the library. No.'

'Fuck,' Townsend said quietly. Hollis frowned. 'Sorry.'

'No worries,' Hollis said, as he casually looked at his watch. A not-so-subtle hint. Townsend straightened up and gestured for Hollis to lead the way, and a few minutes later, he was heading back to his car. As he dropped into the driver's seat, he took a moment before he thumped the steering wheel with frustration.

They were no closer to finding out who Gemma Miller was.

But they did know now…that somebody didn't want them to find out.

CHAPTER THIRTY

'Any luck?'

Hannon looked up at Townsend as he walked in through the door to the SCU, but the glum look on his rain-soaked face told her. In his hand, he held a coffee holder, and she couldn't help but smile at converting him to her favourite coffee shop.

'Oat milk, right?' he said as he handed her the cup.

'Yes, sir,' Hannon said with a grin. 'I bet you just loved ordering that.'

'None more so than ordering a skinny latte.' He joked back, drawing a small chuckle.

'So, dead end?' Hannon asked as Townsend collapsed into his seat. He reached across to her desk and pulled a biscuit from the packet.

'Not exactly.' He looked around. 'Where's the gaffer?'

'Here,' King called from her office, before appearing a few moments later. Her eyes flickered with pleasure at the sight of the coffee. 'So, how did it go?'

'Well, the head is a pretty strict guy. Seems to be on the ball.' Townsend shrugged. 'But they digitalised all their records a few months back. They've got some really unso-

ciable hermit working in a back room who did it all, but…
you know…twenty-five-year-old records…'

'Her record didn't make it into the system.' King drew
the conclusion.

'But, more interestingly, I dug out the yearbook from
Gallagher's year, and guess what page has been removed
from the book?'

'No way?' Hannon sat forward, before regretting it
instantly as a pain shot up her spine.

'Yeah. Someone doesn't want us to know what Gemma
Miller looks like.'

'Good work,' King said, running her tongue on the
inside of her lip in concentration. 'Anything else?'

'Yeah, I took a little trip to Paradise on the way back,'
Townsend said, waggling his eyebrows at the mention of
the strip club. 'Old Sykes was just thrilled to see me, as you
can imagine. Asked after you though, Guv.'

'I'm flattered.' King rolled her eyes.

'But he didn't have much to say. Said he's not really in
the business of sharing his customer's lives with the police.
I did remind him about what happened with Lauren, but
he said this was different. I guess his loyalty is more to the
girls than the drooling guys in the cheap seats.'

'Say what you want about that place. He does look
after his workers,' Hannon said begrudgingly, her disap-
proval of the establishment clear.

'Never any trouble?' King turned back to Townsend.
'No incidents?'

'A few times he got his knuckles wrapped for being a
little too forward with the girls. Kicked out once for drugs.'
Townsend shrugged. 'Nothing that doesn't already fit his
character.'

King rubbed the bridge of her nose.

They were hitting brick wall after brick wall.

'We spoke to Langley,' she said as she lifted her head.

'Told him we weren't going to charge him with the murder right now due to new evidence, but I've told him he needs to stay where we can find him.'

'You think he will?' Hannon asked, looking up from her screen.

'Yeah. That man is broken by what happened, and I think I managed to scare him a little,' King said. 'But right now, we need to find out who Gemma Miller is and where the hell we can find her. Nic, anything?'

King and Townsend turned their attention to Hannon, who was mid-sip of her coffee, and she almost dribbled as she put it down.

'Erm, nothing on Gemma. Anywhere,' she said coldly. 'However, I did do some digging and there is something in our archives from around their time at the school that might be something. There is a very minimal, and I use that word lightly, report on a teacher called Mr Calvin Miller who worked at the school. Apparently, there was a complaint made against him by one of the parents, but judging from the report, the officer at the time didn't take it seriously.'

'Who was the officer?'

'PC Brian Welling.' Hannon read from the screen. 'Long since retired.'

'Well, no harm giving the old boy a call.' King turned to Townsend. 'Leave that one with you?'

'No problem.' Townsend nodded and smiled.

'Oh, that's not all.' Hannon spoke up. 'I did as much digging as I could, and Calvin Miller did leave his employment at the school a few months before Gallagher's year finished. He never worked in teaching again, judging by the government records.'

'How come?'

'Because he died later that year,' Hannon said sadly.

The announcement of his death seemed to affect the

room entirely, and all three of them exchanged thoughtful glances, as if all three of them were trying their hardest to slot in the puzzle piece.

It meant something.

It had to.

As they all sat in silence, King rolled her wrist and glanced at her watch and then stood.

'Right, I've got a meeting, but Nic, dig in as far as you can on Calvin Miller. Where he died. How he died. I want to know everything.'

'Yes, guv.'

'Jack…' She turned to Townsend who was finishing his coffee. 'Reach out to PC Welling, see if he can remember anything.' She rubbed her chin. 'Might even be worth checking in with that girl at the school to dig up any employee records.'

'Can I just call her?' Townsend said with a smile. 'She's not exactly the welcoming type.'

'Whatever,' King said dismissively, but then motioned for him to stand up. 'Can I grab a quick word?'

Townsend looked to Hannon before he stood, and she shook her head with no clue. He followed King into her office, and as he stepped in, she was already gathering her pad for the meeting.

'Everything all right, guv?'

'Yeah, I just thought I'd give you a quick update,' King said, looking him dead in the eye. 'I spoke to DCI Lowe, who said they've ruled out any involvement from Beckford's old London gang with regard to his murder.'

Townsend put on his best poker face.

'Oh, really?' he said as surprised as he could muster. 'That's progress, right?'

'Yeah,' King said, again not breaking eye contact. 'He said his old mate, Alfie Staunton, remember I mentioned him? He went and spoke to his old running mates and they denied any involvement. He's since checked out their accounts and they're in the clear.'

She looked at him again, studying his face to see if there was any hint of guilt.

Of regret.

For lying to her.

Townsend played it straight, nodding his thanks.

'Well, thanks for the update, guv.'

King smiled, even as she felt her heart break slightly.

'No worries.' She kept up the façade. 'Anyway, I'll see you later tonight. Looking forward to meeting the girls.'

'Huh?'

'The lights, Jack?'

'Oh yeah.' Townsend shook his head with embarrassment. 'Yeah, it will be…interesting.'

King chuckled as she walked past him to the door.

'Remember, try to have fun tonight. Nic and I will keep an eye on Davis.'

Townsend smiled his thanks, and King disappeared, and only then did his body relax. Every muscle in his body had been rigid, and the guilt at lying to her was eating away at him like a cancer.

He knew he should have just told her. Come clean and admit that he disobeyed her direct order to keep his word to Simone Beckford.

But he hadn't.

He'd lied.

And as he stepped out of her office, he looked over to Hannon who was lost in her screen. His eyes found their way to the murder board, and after scanning the pictures of the deceased married couple, they finally rested on the grainy photo of the mystery woman.

Of perhaps, Gemma Miller.

And the guilt intensified, as despite her plea for him to

focus solely on the case at hand, he hadn't been able to bring anything to table.

As of right now, they were no closer to finding the killer than they were that morning.

They were failing.

Townsend shuddered and scolded himself.

He was failing.

CHAPTER THIRTY-ONE

Marlow high street had been turned into a Winter Wonderland, and Townsend found himself almost as transfixed as his daughter. They'd parked in one of the car parks just outside of the small town, as the street closures to accommodate the festivities meant the few open roads within Marlow were gridlocked. Townsend didn't mind, and once they'd stepped out of their car and zipped up their winter coats, he and Mandy walked hand in gloved hand as their daughter skipped merrily ahead. She'd spoken of the possibility of seeing her school friends that evening, with the idea of out of school socialising and staying up late seemingly energising the young girl.

Townsend couldn't help but smile as he watched her.

As they approached the main high street, they were immediately greeted by a number of brightly lit pop-up stalls, all of them offering cheap plastic trinkets, from bubble wands to light tubes at eye watering prices. Eve fell in love with a light-up wand, and Townsend felt his toes curl as he handed over the required ten pound note for the cheap tat.

'I should arrest him for that,' Townsend joked to

Mandy, who often teased her husband about his thriftiness. The high street soon split into two as it hit the roundabout, where the stone obelisk that shot up towards the sky had been wrapped in tinsel. They veered left, passing through the metal fences that had been put up to cut off the traffic, and joined the throngs of people who were shuffling further down the high street towards the large attractions nearer the end. As they walked, more salesman tried to entice them over with even more tacky goods, but Townsend did stop at one of the pop-up coffee trucks to treat his girls to a hot chocolate each.

As they neared the large open-top bus that had been parked smack bang in the middle of the road, a snow machine kicked in, pumping out thin circles of white confetti that sent the kids into an excited panic. Eve was spellbound by how magical it was, especially due to her crushing realisation over the years that the UK rarely had a Christmas as depicted in cartoons.

No frosting of snow.

No snowmen being built.

It was just bitterly cold and usually raining.

As they watched her spin gently in the fake snow, Mandy bobbed her head along to the Christmas music that was pumping out from the large speakers that sat either side of the bus, and soon, street performers decked out as Christmas characters or Disney princesses soon emerged, wafting through the crowds of people on stilts, waving to the kids and adding another layer of magic to the evening.

Mandy locked her arm in his and nuzzled her head onto his shoulder.

'This is nice,' she said softly.

Townsend smiled.

As his daughter and another young girl struck up a friendship in seconds, he looked across the group of families and couples who had braved the elements, until his eyes ventured further down the high street. There were more stalls, as well as a few burger vans, which had gathering crowds around each. Beyond that was the park that Eve loved to visit during the summer, with its expensive adventure playground and the usual suspects of an overpriced merry-go-round and bouncy castle. It also offered a lovely stroll down towards the Thames, where Eve loved to go and feed the ducks and marvel at the swans that dominated the water.

He turned to his wife and gently kissed her.

'I love you,' he said tenderly.

'Awwww.' Hannon's voice interrupted them, and Townsend sighed and turned to his approaching colleague. 'Turns out he's just a big softie.'

'Nic.' He rolled his eyes at Mandy. 'Mandy, you remember Nic, right?.'

'Oh, of course.' Mandy smiled and leant in for a kiss on the cheek.

'You really are stunning aren't you?' Nic said, looking at Townsend with her eyebrows raised. 'How the hell did you pull this off?'

'What can I say? I'm a charmer.' Townsend joked. DI King then stepped through the crowd towards them. Mandy noticed her approaching too. 'Guv?'

'Jack.' She smiled and turned to his wife. 'Lovely to see you again, Mandy.'

'You too, DI King.' Mandy extended her hand, but King just frowned.

'Please. Izzy.' She smiled and leant in for a kiss on the cheek. 'It must kill him to have both his bosses in one place.'

Mandy laughed out loud, and Townsend faked like he was offended. Instantly, he was reminded of when he had introduced Mandy to the team during a celebratory drink after the Baycroft case. Mandy had charmed them, as she did with everyone, and had been the talk of the office for the following weeks. However, before they could all catch up, Eve barged past King and Hannon to get to her parents.

'Dad. My new friend Stacy said she's going on the teacup ride…'

'How much is it?'

'Umm. Five pounds.'

Townsend baulked at the price, but then reluctantly stuffed his hand into his coat for his wallet as Mandy made the introduction for Eve. King and Hannon both remarked at how pretty her headband was and then caught him off guard by telling her how brave her daddy was.

'I know.' She beamed with pride. 'My daddy catches bad guys.'

King smiled.

Townsend felt his heart melt.

'Yes, he does,' King agreed and then stood up and winked at Jack. 'With a little help, of course.'

Townsend nodded his agreement and then handed Eve a five-pound note. Mandy quickly swooped in and plucked it from his fingers.

'I'll go with her.' She waved to both King and Hannon. 'Lovely to see you both again.'

'You, too,' King said after her and then turned back to Townsend. 'You have a gorgeous family, Jack.'

'Thanks.' He blushed.

'Seriously, how did you manage that?' Hannon joked, but Townsend looked at her in confusion. 'Oh, I'm riding solo tonight.'

'Oh?' King interjected. 'No Shilpa?'

'No. We had an argument.' She looked at Townsend who offered her a knowing smile and then she shook it off. 'It's fine. It'll blow over.'

'So what's the plan, guv?' Townsend asked, his arms

folded across his broad chest as his eyes scanned the crowd for his wife and daughter.

They were queuing for the ride, and Mandy, as ever, had struck up a conversation with whom he assumed were Stacy's parents.

His eyes widened.

King hadn't noticed.

'Well, we'll go for a walk, see if we can find Connor Davis and put a little pressure on him,' King replied.

'Guv…' Townsend began, but King continued.

'He didn't stop by with the paperwork we asked for, so I'm pretty sure us interrupting his family outing might just hammer home the message. He seemed pretty worried his wife might find out he'd given Jason Gallagher all that money and…'

'Guv.' Townsend tried again.

Hannon spoke over him, already on the same train of thought as her boss.

'If he thinks we might tell his wife, he might just start cooperating.'

'Exactly.' King wagged her finger. 'And you'd think, if he had nothing to hide, then he'd just do whatever he could to clear his name in an instant.'

'Guv…' Townsend tried one more time.

'Don't worry, Jack,' King said dismissively. 'You can stay here with your girls, and Nic and I will search the street for him. Nic, you start from back up there, and let's meet in the middle. Keep your phone on and…'

'Guv. Fucking hell,' Townsend said with a chuckle. 'He's right there.'

Townsend pointed beyond them both, and they turned to follow the direction of his finger. Standing by the teacup ride, and nattering with Mandy, was Connor Davis and his wife. He was holding hands with the girl Eve had struck up a friendship with, and it all clicked that it was his daughter.

As if he could feel the eyes of three people latched onto him, Connor turned his head and his smile swiftly evaporated when he saw them. Mandy seemed to notice his attention shift, and Townsend saw her point out that he was her husband.

Connor shifted uncomfortably and then relinquished his child so she could join Townsend's in the teacup.

His wife and Mandy continued their conversation, and he shot them one last look before he whispered something into his wife's ear and then marched off into the crowd.

'Let's follow him.' King ordered, and the three of them stepped forward, but she turned and placed a hand on Townsend's shoulder. 'Stay here, Jack. You're with your family.'

Reluctantly, Townsend stayed put and watched as his team filtered off, disappearing into the crowd from different sides of the street, as his wife continued her conversation and his child whooped with delight as her teacup spun wildly. As he watched her, he felt his chest thump harder.

Everything was for her.

Everything.

And as he stood, basking in the happiness of being a proud father, he failed to notice the familiar face sidle up next to him.

'Hello, stranger.'

Townsend turned and couldn't help but smile.

DS Michelle Swaby.

Instinctively, he threw his arms around her, and the two of them embraced for a few moments before he stepped back to introduce himself to her two boys.

'We know who you are,' one of them said with a smile.

'You're the one who stopped the killer,' the eldest said with a nod. 'Respect, man.'

'Thanks?' Townsend looked to Swaby, who rolled her

eyes, before she stuffed some cash in their hands and shooed them away.

'How are things?' she asked with a smile, although the bags under her eyes told Townsend she was tired.

'Yeah, not bad. Bit of a fucked-up case at the moment, but…'

Swaby held up her hand.

'No work talk, please. I don't have the headspace right now.'

'Shit, yeah. Sorry,' Townsend said clumsily. 'How's it going?'

As Swaby unloaded about supporting her husband during his loss and keeping the kids in school, Townsend realised how much she'd been missed in the office. Not just for her ability, and she was a high-level detective, but for her level headedness and more importantly, her positivity. The office had felt like a dark and dreary place, even though they were no longer in the basement.

Death and failure had filled the office from wall to wall, and someone like Swaby, who saw the good in everyone and every situation, would be just the tonic.

Minus the singing, mind.

'But yeah, I've booked the next few days off as annual leave just to make sure I'm present, but I'll be back next week.'

Before Townsend could respond, Eve ran and slammed into his legs, pleading dramatically for the chance to go on the ride one more time. Mandy joined her a few steps behind, but before Townsend could make the introduction, Swaby did it herself and within less than a minute, she and Mandy were chatting like old friends.

Townsend looked out to the crowd, but he couldn't see Connor Davis, or either DI King or DC Hannon.

All his attention belonged to Eve.

An announcement came over the speakers to begin the

countdown to the lights, and Townsend swept his daughter up in his arms, and shouted along with her as the numbers dwindled down to one. Then, to a resounding cheer that echoed throughout the street, every tree and shop front burst into colour, and the Christmas music thumped out once more.

Merriment and laughter ricocheted through the throng of people, and as Eve looked around at the lights in awe, Townsend couldn't take his eyes off her.

The entire street was illuminated in a festive glow, but to him, nothing shone brighter than his daughter.

CHAPTER THIRTY-TWO

Every second that passed as they walked the ten-minute stroll to the high street felt tightened the knot in Connor Davis' stomach, and by the time they rounded the corner, past the tackily decorated obelisk, he thought he was on the verge of a panic attack.

'You okay, babe?' Abby asked, her eyebrow arching up under her woolly hat. Stacy and Maddy were a few paces ahead, already bubbling with excitement.

'Yeah, I'm fine,' Connor lied, forcing a smile to hammer home the point. 'It's just been a long couple of days.'

His wife squeezed his hand lovingly, only adding to his guilt, and as soon as they passed the expensive stalls towards the waves of people surrounding the display, Connor could already sense his heart beating faster. It was supposed to be a nice family evening, mirroring the ones they'd attended over the past decade, but tonight, his mind was elsewhere.

He was trying his best to spot Penny.

His wife's voice broke his concentration.

'Where are you meeting later?'

'What?' He spun to her; his eyes wide. She looked confused.

'The guys,' Abby clarified slowly. 'You said you were meeting them for a few drinks.'

'Oh yeah.' Connor tried to play it cool. 'Not sure. Might be round here. Jay said he'll message when he finishes work.'

She bought it, and Connor breathed a gentle sigh of relief as she turned her attention to the girls. Maddy was looking up at one of the princesses looming over the crowd on stilts, as the fake snow danced on the bitter chill in the air.

Stacy was busy making friends with another girl of around the same age.

Then Connor saw her.

Penny.

And he felt a jealous rage shudder through his body like an extra pulse as he saw her husband, Stephen, drape his arm around her shoulder as he chatted heartily to another couple. Connor knew it was ridiculous, but at that moment, he hated the man for trying to claim Penny as his own, even though they were married.

If he only knew.

Connor was busy ticking off all the ways in which he felt superior to the man, when once again, Abby broke through his concentration.

'What are you smiling at?' she asked, and just as she began to turn her head in the direction of the Durant's, Connor spun her back and kissed her.

'It's Christmas.' He smiled, laying it on thick. 'Let's just have a nice time.'

Abby smiled, kissed him again, and was then dragged towards the teacup ride by their eager daughter. As she began to explain the ride to them, her new friend appeared with her mother, and they introduced themselves as Mandy and Eve. Mandy was one of the most naturally stunning women Connor had ever seen, and her accent was thick and alluring.

'I'm just here with my husband.' Mandy went on, nodding back towards him. 'He's just bumped into some work friends, so I need some sanctuary.'

'Well, welcome aboard,' Abby said, and the two women already seemed to be hitting it off. As the kids began to anxiously bounce on the spot as the ride began to slow down, Connor looked back across the crowd to see who was lucky enough to be married to such a woman.

Then he saw them.

The detectives.

Not only were they about to ruin his entire evening, he felt a twinge of jealousy for the rugged detective in the middle of being able to call Mandy his wife.

DI King, the woman who'd threatened to expose his secret dealings with Jason to his wife, locked eyes on him and he shuffled uncomfortably before turning back to his wife who was mid-conversation.

'Would anyone like a coffee?' he interrupted with a charming smile.

'Oh, I'd love one,' Abby said and then turned to Mandy with a silent offer.

'That's very kind of you, but I just had one.'

Connor pecked his wife on the cheek and then scampered off into the crowd, cursing himself for trying to impress Mandy with his devotion to his wife.

How pathetic.

He was planning on sleeping with another woman in a few hours.

As he headed into the growing crowd, he peered back over his shoulder, and could see DI King also slaloming through the rows of people, and he quickly darted off down a side road between two shops, that would lead to an alleyway that looped back onto the far side of the road. Once he was out of sight, he picked up the pace and turned behind one of the buildings and then fell back against the wall and tried to calm his breathing.

What were they doing here?

He pulled out his phone, opened the social media app, and checked to see if Mandy had messaged.

She hadn't.

Was tonight even going to happen?

He'd already booked a room at the Premier Inn just off Handy Cross roundabout, paying for it with cash that he'd taken out of the business under the loose term of 'petty cash'. The books would swallow it, and as long as he did the totalling up at the end of the month, Abby would be none the wiser. With his heart racing, he sent the location of the hotel and a time to her profile's messenger and then stuffed his phone into his jacket in shame.

He was going through with this.

Connor glanced down at his smart watch, checked his heart rate, and then briskly walked through the alleyway which acted like a wind tunnel. As he emerged from the other side, he joined the queue that had formed behind one of the coffee stands.

'This is my favourite coffee shop,' Hannon said, stepping beside him. 'What are the chances, eh?'

'What do you want?' Connor snapped, not even looking at her.

'I'll have an oat milk latte, thanks,' Hannon said with a grin.

'Haha. Very funny.' Connor shook his head. 'I'm with my family…'

'Not right now, you're not,' King said coldly, appearing over his shoulder and standing between him and the crowd of people he had glanced towards as an escape route. 'What's going on, Connor?'

'What, right now?' He looked at them both defiantly. 'I'd say tantamount to harassment.'

'Now who's being funny?' Hannon chimed in, before shuffling forward with a genuine intent for a coffee. 'You want one, Guv?'

'Usual,' King said, with her eyes locked on Connor. 'You promised you'd drop the information I requested off today and…'

Connor slapped his hand to his forehead in disbelief.

'I did, didn't I?' He was acting dumb and doing a bad job of it. 'Sorry, it's been a confusing few days…'

'Well, luckily your office is just round the corner, so maybe we could go now?'

'I would, but I don't have the keys with me.'

'Maybe your wife does?' King suggested and saw the anger flicker in his eyes. 'I'm sure she'd want to know about what is really happening in your business.'

King turned as if to make good on the threat, and Connor reached out and grabbed her arm. Instantly, he retracted it, and held his hands up in surrender as King stood him down with a thunderous expression.

'I'm sorry. Okay? I'm sorry.' He looked back and forth between the two detectives. 'I'm just…just not ready for the fallout of it and…'

'Mr Davis, I want to make it clear, I don't give a shit that you've been lying to your wife,' King said bluntly. 'I don't approve, but it's not my business. But two people are dead, and right now, we're doing everything we can to find out why and by who. I asked you to help with my investigation and I'd rather not waste any time turning your office inside out for it.'

'First thing. Okay?' He looked at her for mercy. 'First thing.'

Hannon beeped her card on the machine and gratefully accepted the two coffees and then handed one to

King, who kept her eyes locked on the pathetic man in front of her.

'First thing.'

It was an agreement.

It was a threat.

With the truth threatening to come out, Connor felt his mind race as he watched the two detectives walk away, and when he returned to his wife, he realised he hadn't even bought a coffee. He lied, again, telling her their payment system was down and he ducked into the nearest *Starbucks* and got her one and a muffin to make up for it. As he stood with his wife and two daughters, the lights came on and the crowd cheered but he wasn't there.

Not mentally, anyway.

He walked his family back to the car after the music stopped playing, kissed them good night, and then promised his wife he wouldn't be too late. As he watched them drive away, he felt the weight of the world in his gut, as guilt threatened to empty the contents of his stomach. But he stayed strong, booked his cab, and twenty minutes later, he found himself sitting in the small, dingy bar of the Premier Inn, nursing a pint.

Things were beginning to creak, and what was worse, he wasn't sure if he cared. Abby would be furious about his dealings with Jason Gallagher, and maybe, it would spark a situation where they would be able to get things off their chest.

Be honest with each other.

Admit where life had taken them.

As he'd given up hope of his evening mapping out the way he had planned, the automatic door to the hotel opened and Penny Durant marched in, her face stern as if she was in deep thought. He quickly hopped to his feet and approached her, but as he went to speak, she put her hand over his mouth.

'Don't. You'll just talk me out of it.'

She marched to the elevator, clicked the button and the doors pinged open.

She stepped in.

Like an obedient and desperate dog, Connor joined her, and they travelled up towards the room he had booked, ready to change their lives permanently.

CHAPTER THIRTY-THREE

From the moment she kissed him, Penny Durant knew it was a mistake.

It had been quite thrilling to reconnect with her high school sweetheart at the reunion, and she had to admit that, as a man in his early forties, Connor had certainly aged like a fine wine. The casual flirting had quickly escalated, and when he'd messaged her on social media, she'd felt a flutter of arousal.

Why?

She and Dan were happily married, and although the passionate spark that had once existed in their mid-twenties had died down, there was still a deep and honest affection between them, and she was hardly starved of sexual fulfilment. Her life had turned out wonderfully, with a lovely home, a doting husband and a career that she'd built for herself and was proud of.

So why did she entertain it?

Why had she agreed to share herself intimately online with a man from her past and then go one step further?

If it had been one of her coaching clients, Penny would have walked them through the idea of self-sabotage, a thread that human beings foolishly pull on when life gets too comfortable. When all the hard work and all the sacrifices have been proven to have been worth it.

But was that what she was doing?

As she leant over the sink in the bathroom of the crummy hotel room, she looked up at herself in the mirror through her blurry eyes, and saw the tears streaming down her face.

She'd talked herself out of going over ten times throughout the evening, and when Connor had messaged her with the hotel address, she hadn't responded. The guilt was so close to winning out, but she still found herself making an excuse to her husband about a coaching client on the edge of a nervous breakdown, and of course Stephen had been understanding.

He was a great guy.

When she'd arrived at the hotel, she didn't even say anything, as the very idea of small talk would have set her straight, but she'd taken Connor up to the room with enough conviction that the man was champing at the bit for them to close the door. As soon as they did, he cupped her face in his hands and planted his lips on hers, and instantly, the guilt began to pump through her body like a duplicate bloodstream. She'd tried to kiss back, to force the passion into her lips, but it didn't work, and as they undressed each other, she hoped that the feel of his skin pressed against hers would convince it was worth it.

It wasn't.

As the man thrusted and grunted on top of her, any desire for an affair faded, and she pulled him in close so he couldn't see the devastation on her face at the betrayal she'd committed. As soon as Connor had finished and collapsed on the bed beside her, she quickly scooped up her clothes and headed to the bathroom.

And she'd wept.

She hadn't kept track of the time, but they hadn't been in the room for too long, but her absence soon became suspicious.

'Everything okay in there?' Connor asked tentatively through the door.

'Yeah.' Penny dabbed at her eyes, scolding her reflection for what she'd done. 'I'll just be a minute.'

She heard Connor collapse on the bed once more, and it sent a shiver down her spine.

She just wanted to go home.

To be with her family.

To be herself again.

Quickly, she pulled her clothes on, pulled her hair into a loose ponytail, and then wiped her eyes once more. With a reassuring nod to herself, she pulled open the door and Connor sat upright on the bed in shock.

'You're dressed?' he exclaimed in panic.

'This was a mistake, Connor.' She swiftly marched across the small room to retrieve her bag as Connor comically tried to scramble from the mattress with his modesty intact.

'Penny, what the fuck?' His words were heavy with devastation.

'I'm sorry, I have to go.' She pulled open the door to the room and rushed out, not looking back as she hurried down the narrow corridor to the elevators. She clicked the button, but none of them were at her floor, so she flung open the door to the stairwell and took them two at a time. Her heart was racing, but as she flung open the door to the reception, she made a beeline to the exit. As she passed the exit, one of the lifts opened, and Connor lunged out, grabbing her shoulder.

'Penny, what the hell?' He looked heartbroken. She turned to him. His trousers were unbuttoned, and his T-shirt was half tucked in.

He hadn't even had time to put his shoes or socks on.

'Please, Connor.' She begged. 'Let's just leave it as it is.'

'No.' Connor raised his voice, drawing a look from the receptionist, and a few nosy late-night drinkers sat up in the bar. 'Do you know how much I've risked for this?'

'We both have, Connor.'

'So what?' He took an angry step towards her. 'I'm not worth it?'

'Please,' Penny said once more. 'Let's just go home.'

'This could fucking ruin my life.' Connor's eyes bulged with furious tears. 'I was willing to ruin everything for you.'

'Everything okay, miss?'

Both of them snapped their head to the bar, where a large man stood, his heavily tattooed arms folded across his broad chest. He was twice the size of Connor, and from the vicious glare, was more than happy to prove it. Connor took a tentative step back, but Penny shook her head and smiled.

'Everything's fine. Thank you.' She turned back to Connor. 'Just go home, Connor.'

He was crying now.

Like her, he had realised what he had done and all the guilt needed was the smallest of cracks in the psyche to seep in.

'But, Penny…' He feebly reached for her arm, but she pulled away and as she hurried across the car park to her car, she flashed one glance back, half expecting to see him running barefoot through the rain to her.

But he wasn't.

He was still standing in the reception, pathetically weeping and although she felt bad for seemingly breaking his heart or his reality, she was fresh out of guilt.

That was reserved for her husband, who deserved better than her.

Who deserved to know what she'd done.

On the drive home, she'd pulled over to a twenty-four-hour petrol garage and bought a packet of cigarettes, and she smoked a couple out of the window on a quiet street as she contemplated the next few hours.

Stephen would be devastated.

There was a chance he would leave.

Or ask her to leave, although he would never confuse her failings as a wife with her incredible bond with their kids.

He might ask for a divorce.

She might have kissed him for the final time.

As she ran through every permutation of how the conversation would go, the only thing she became certain of was that she'd never be able to move past what she'd done on her own. The truth would hurt her husband, but a lie like that would only rot their marriage from the inside if it was left unsaid.

Her mobile buzzed every five minutes.

Connor.

After the eighth missed call and voicemail, she blocked the number in frustration. She'd unblock it tomorrow, once they'd both had the chance to calm down and come clean, and she'd apologise and wish him the best.

She didn't hate the man.

Far from it.

But she needed him out of her life if she was ever to recover from what she'd done.

As she pulled onto her street, she could already see that the lights were off. The kids would have been shattered from the probable sugar crash from the evening, and she'd most likely find Stephen sitting up in bed, his eyes shut and his book open on his chest as he had fought valiantly to finish a chapter.

She began to cry.

The guilt became unbearable and with a shaky hand,

she reached across the seat for her bag, unaware of the figure that was lifting up from behind her seat in the car. As she clasped the pack of cigarettes and lighter in her hand, she sat upright in her seat, and with her last moments of consciousness, she saw a face she found vaguely familiar in the rear-view mirror.

Before she could scream, she felt a sharp prick in the back of her neck, and as she felt herself falling face first into the thick, leather steering wheel, everything went black before she felt the impact.

CHAPTER THIRTY-FOUR

The call had come in at just after five thirty in the morning.

An early riser had taken their dog for a stroll around Booker Common, a large open field just outside of Cressex Business Park, and as they'd strolled through the woodlands listening to a podcast, they hadn't noticed the car parked in the middle of the field.

It had only taken them one look to call the police.

Townsend had already woken by the time King had called him, working through his thoughts as he hammered the punch bag in his garage to keep his technique sharp.

'We've got another one.'

It was the words he dreaded whenever her name popped up on his phone, but fifteen minutes later, he was wrapping a crisp white shirt around his damp body, and Mandy stirred in the bed behind him.

'What time is it?' She said wearily, gently lifting herself off the pillow. Townsend fastened his final button and then walked around the bed, tucking his shirt into his trousers as he did.

'Time to go to work,' he said dryly, planting a kiss on his wife who dropped back onto the pillow.

'Be safe,' she called after him, as he quickly ducked his head into Eve's room, where she was still curled up in her bed, clutching her cuddly toy and lost in an innocent dream. The harsh winter would make the crime scene a nightmare he told himself, but Townsend was thankful for the clear roads that saw him zip through High Wycombe and up towards Booker. It was approaching seven when he finally arrived, pulling into the gravelly car park that was already full with the police cars and the SOCO van.

King was standing against her own car, the hood of her rain jacket over her head, and a cloud of vapour pouring out from underneath it. Townsend pull in beside her and stepped out.

'Guv.'

'That was quick,' she said, impressed. 'It's Penny.'

'Durant?' Townsend clarified, and she nodded. 'Shit.'

The duo approached the cordon that had already been placed across the entrance to the common, and the poor officer tasked with standing still in the rain lifted the tape for them. On the other side of the field, a few of the residents were already standing at the windows, watching with a morbid interest.

'Dog walker called it in. First on scene ran the plates on approach to confirm it.' King spoke with anger. 'We've already sent an FLO to her house.'

'Kids?' Townsend asked.

'Yup.' King nodded, on the same wavelength. 'Whoever did this just took this mother away from her kids.'

The fury was shared between the two detectives as they approached the SOCOs, who were battling the elements to preserve as much of the crime scene as possible. There were clear tyre marks running across the field to where the car had been left, and as they approached,

212

they could see the rubber hose that had been connected to the exhaust pipe with duct tape. They walked around to the driver's side of the car, following the hose as it snuck in through the small gap on the rear passenger window.

In the front seat, Penny Durant's body sat, slumped forward against the tightness of her seat belt.

'Well, at least she didn't feel anything.' One of the officers commented to both of them. King frowned at him.

'I doubt that.'

The front of her top was drenched in blood, which also covered the entirety of her chin.

If they opened her mouth, they both knew they'd find the savaged remnants of her tongue.

'Fuck,' King muttered under her breath as she stepped away from the car. Then she frowned. 'The engine is off?'

'Guv?' Townsend looked to her, but she scanned the area until she found the officer who was looking after the shaken dog walker. She marched across the mud towards him.

'Sorry, excuse me. DI King.' She held up her lanyard to hammer it home. 'I know this morning has been hard, but I need to know…was the engine of the car still on when you found it?'

'Errm…' The middle-aged man looked anxiously to the officer beside him.

'It's very important you remember,' King stated.

'No. No, it wasn't,' the man eventually replied.

'Are you certain?'

'Yes,' the man said with conviction. 'I thought it was just abandoned.'

'Thank you.' King smiled and nodded, before turning on her heel and stomping back towards Townsend.

'So it wasn't on?' Townsend echoed.

'No. Which means our killer waited until Penny was

dead and then killed the engine.' King's brow furrowed with anger. 'They watched her die.'

The clouds darkened as they loomed overhead, pumping down a heavier downpour. Townsend let out a large sigh.

'So another staged suicide.' He thought out loud. 'We've had a drug overdose, slit wrists, and now this.'

'Don't forget stuffing Langley with a stomach full of pills.'

'But he wasn't the target,' Townsend mused. 'They left him alive and with his tongue in his mouth. Which means this friend group is being targeted and these killings symbolise something.'

King nodded her agreement.

'Well, there's still one member of that friend group who hasn't been targeted yet,' King said through gritted teeth, making no effort to hide her dislike for the man. 'And I think we can speed up our meeting.'

'Want me to drive?' Townsend offered with a shrug. 'Not much else for us to do here.'

'No.' King shook her head. 'I want you to get to the office and get Hannon in as quickly as possible. Get her to try to track Penny's movements last night and go through the woman's social media or whatever she does. I want to know everything Penny Durant did in the last few days, who she spoke to, where she went. Everything. Then you need to get over to see her husband and let him know what's going on. It might be hard for him, but anything he can offer us could be crucial.'

'I'll check in with Mitchell, too. See if she has anything from Rachel that can help.'

'Good idea...' King began, but then shifted as her phone began to vibrate in her pocket. She pulled it up and sighed. 'It's Hall. Give me a sec.'

She answered the call and turned away from

Townsend, who turned his own attention back towards the car. His eyes were transfixed on the body of Penny Durant, helplessly slumped against the seat belt. The officer had been right, she wouldn't have felt her own death, but if what Mitchell had said before was true, and the same toxins were in her body as were in Jason Gallagher's, then Penny Durant would have felt her tongue being cut out.

Unable to move, bound to her seat.

She must have been terrified.

But all Townsend could think of was why?

Jason Gallagher, for all intents and purposes, had been a nasty piece of work, and the behavioural timeline they'd mapped out made his murder seem plausible.

Rachel, being his wife, could have just been an unfortunate victim by association. Same as Langley.

But Penny?

She hadn't been in contact with the Gallaghers for years according to Janet, and now here she was, stricken from the world in the same way they were.

But why?

Townsend could feel the frustration tightening his muscles, and when King hung up her call and returned to his side, he realised he had clenched his fists. The two of them stood for a moment, the rain lashing down upon them and the harrowing crime scene, and they both knew they were hunting a serial killer.

'Anything else?' She had offered him the opportunity. Townsend wanted to tell her about his trip to Wembley and just come clean that he hadn't obeyed her order. The trust the two had established ever since he'd saved her from Baycroft was now balanced on a betrayal that he knew would hurt her.

He had to tell her.

He would tell her.

But now wasn't the right time.

'No, guv. I'll be in touch,' Townsend said and turned and began marching back across the muddy field with purpose. As he was about eight paces away from her, King called after him.

'Hey, Jack,' she called out, and he turned. 'Find me Gemma Miller.'

Townsend nodded, then turned, pulled his hood up, and marched back to his car, tasked with finding a ghost that seemingly didn't want to be found.

CHAPTER THIRTY-FIVE

He couldn't imagine it.

Townsend pulled his car onto the drive of Penny Durant's home and brought it to a stop behind her widowed husband's. As the rain clattered on the windscreen, Townsend looked up at the semi-detached, four-bedroom house and wondered how many happy memories had been created in it. The front of the house was modern, with the adjacent garden as pristine as the season would allow. Tasteful Christmas decorations adorned the edges of the windows, and an elegant wreath was clutching to the front door for dear life as the wind blew.

With a mournful grunt, Townsend pushed open the door and stepped out. His feet crunched on the gravel beneath him, and as he approached the door, a Family Liaison Officer pulled it open and greeted him. She wasn't someone he was familiar with, but with the body count rising, Hall had clearly called in re-enforcements from neighbouring towns.

She showed him into the front room, where a broken Stephen was sitting on the sofa, his eyes bloodshot and his cheeks damp. His floppy, greying hair sat scruffily on his head and his well-groomed beard looked slightly ragged, which was understandable. Beside him, their youngest son was asleep on the sofa, wrapped in a blanket. The eldest didn't even acknowledge Townsend's arrival, with his eyes glued to the expensive TV as he hammered the controller in his hand, lost in whatever the latest shooting game was. Stephen went to stand, but Townsend waved him back down.

'Please, don't.' Townsend spoke softly before taking the seat beside him. 'Mr Durant, I'm so sorry for your loss.'

The widower blew out his cheeks, and Townsend knew his condolences meant little.

'I'll put the kettle on,' the FLO said, before making her exit as Townsend lifted himself from the sofa and took a few steps to the photos that sat on the shelves either side of the large screen.

The eldest son clattered the buttons some more.

'For Christ's sake, Nate, can you turn that game off?' Stephen demanded.

'Please, don't do it on my account,' Townsend said softly, before pointing to a picture of the family on an exotic holiday. 'This is a lovely picture.'

'I know.' Stephen sniffed. 'Rhodes. About two years ago.'

'I've never been,' Townsend said with a sad smile, before he took his seat once more. 'Mr Durant…'

'Stephen.'

'Stephen.' Townsend echoed. 'I know this is a horrible time for both you and your boys, and I can't imagine what you're going through right now. We'll offer you all the support you need, but I do need to ask you some questions. The quicker we can get on with things, the more chance we have of finding out what happened to your wife. Is that okay?'

'Yes.' Stephen took a deep breath, clearly trying to pull

his broken self together. Before Townsend could begin, the FLO entered with two cups of tea, and Townsend thanked her before turning to Stephen.

'Can you walk me through last night?'

'Err…we went to the Marlow lights and…'

'So did I,' Townsend said with a smile. 'Was pretty impressive.'

'Yeah, we do it every year,' Stephen said glumly. 'Well, we did.'

'Take your time.'

'Umm…we went there for a few hours. Met a colleague who was there with his family. Raj. Raj Chaudary. I can give you his details.'

'Thank you.' Townsend urged him to continue.

'We hung about for the lights, and then Penny said she had a work emergency to attend to.'

'Was that normal?' Townsend scribbled in his pad. 'In her line of work?'

'She is a…*was*…a life coach.' Stephen swallowed back his tears. 'Some of her clients weren't in the best state mentally, and a few of them really leant on her for support. I always said she should just send them to a licensed therapist, but that was Penny…could never turn away someone in need.'

'So this emergency?'

'She didn't say too much.' Stephen rubbed his eyes with his palms with frustration. 'If I'd known this would have happened, I'd have never…'

'Hey, hey.' Townsend got through to him. 'This is not in any way, name, shape, or form your fault, Stephen. Do you understand?'

'I just…I just don't know what I'm going to do.'

'We'll figure it out.' Townsend assured him. 'Like I said, we'll support however we can. But right now, I just need you to be strong for your boys, and to help us with any information you can.'

Stephen took a few deep breaths and nodded.

'Like I said, she didn't tell me much. Just told me she'd be a few hours maybe.' Stephen shook his head. 'I fell asleep reading in bed, and then the next thing I know, you guys are knocking on my door telling me my entire world's been shattered.'

'Look, Stephen. I know this is hard, but I need you to think. Has Penny mentioned anything or acted different at all recently? Any indication that something was wrong?'

'No. Nothing. Well…' Stephen seemed to be tossing something over in his mind.

'Well? Any information could be vital.'

'It's nothing really.' Stephen frowned as he searched his archives. 'She seemed a little off when she got back from her school reunion the other night. Then that fella, Jason, it spread across social media that he was killed. And then his wife, Rachel. Her and Penny were friends back in the day and I think it really caught her off guard.'

'Yeah, we spoke with her at the memorial service.' Townsend nodded. 'Her and a gentleman named Connor Davis.'

'Connor?' Stephen's eyebrows raised. 'She didn't mention he was there, too.'

'Would that have been a problem?'

'No, not at all.' Stephen shook his head. 'It's just…he was her first proper boyfriend, and I was teasing her about it before the reunion. She said she spoke to him, but she didn't mention he was there on Monday.'

'I believe they all went way back.' Townsend tried to ease the man from any troubling thoughts. 'We'll do some digging our end to try to track her final movements and see exactly where she went and as soon as we have some concrete information for you, I'll be in touch. Thank you for your time, Stephen.'

Townsend stood, and Stephen just stared vacantly ahead of him.

'Would she have felt it?' he asked, before turning his watery eyes up towards Townsend in hope. 'When she died?'

'Dad.' The eldest son finally spoke. 'Leave it.'

Townsend reached out a hand and squeezed Stephen's shoulder.

'It would have been peaceful.' Townsend assured him, ensuring he left out the gruesome details of the severed tongue and the other information he knew. 'I'll be in touch.'

As Townsend stepped back, he turned to the teenage boy sitting across the room, who despite trying to put on a tough act, was clearly just as broken as his father. Townsend offered him a nod and then looked at the screen.

'Your next game is about to start?'

It seemed to snap Nate's attention back to the screen.

'Oh, no.' He shook his head. 'I'm just in the lobby.'

'I don't know what that means,' Townsend said with a smile.

'It means I'm online, but I'm not playing. I can just join a game at any time.'

'We've come a long way since the Game Boy.' Townsend joked.

'What's a Game Boy?' Nate asked with a confused frown.

'Exactly.' He then arched his neck back towards Stephen on the sofa. 'Look after him, okay, Nate?'

The request seemed to spark a sense of responsibility in the young lad, who puffed out his chest as he sat up straight.

'Yes, sir.'

Just as Townsend went to leave, he turned back to Stephen, who looked up with interest.

'Stephen. Random question…did Penny have a yearbook from school?'

'A yearbook?' Stephen took a moment to think. 'I've never seen one. I can have a look for you.'

'If you could. Please let us know if you find one.'

Stephen collapsed back on the sofa, and the FLO stepped back into the room as Townsend made his exit. It was a relief to leave the house, as intruding on a family's grief was one of the worst parts of his job. The pain and loss they were experiencing were beyond anything they could imagine, and yet here was a stranger, asking them to put pieces of a puzzle together that they didn't even know existed.

But all of it was a puzzle.

And the SCU had barely even clipped two pieces together.

As he sat down in his car and slammed the door shut, Townsend flicked through his notepad. He stopped on the page he needed and then keyed the phone number into the phone.

Janet Jennings answered on the fourth ring.

'Hello?'

'Mrs Jennings,' Townsend said in his friendliest voice. 'It's DS Jack Townsend from the Thames Valley…'

'I know. I couldn't forget that accent if I tried.'

'Sorry to bother you, but can I ask a question?'

'Anything.' Her voice was full of hope. It was the only thing those lost in grief could cling to.

'Did Rachel have a yearbook from her time at high school?' Townsend asked. 'I'm trying to locate one.'

'I think so.'

'Really?' Townsend leant forward in his seat.

'I remember it being expensive.' Janet tutted. 'Jason didn't allow her to have much in the house, but she has bags and boxes of her things in my attic. My son's coming down this afternoon to help with the arrangements. I can get him to have a look for you.'

'Janet, you're a star,' Townsend said. 'I'll be in touch.'

'God bless you, Jack.'

The grieving mother hung up the phone, and Townsend tossed his onto the passenger seat. He took one more look up at the Durant house and then threw the car into reverse.

He was surrounded by grief.

A devastating ripple of murder.

And as he backed out onto the road and then shifted into first, he launched forward down the street, heading as fast as he legally could back to the station.

They still didn't have pieces to the puzzle.

So it was time for him to start making them himself.

CHAPTER THIRTY-SIX

By the time Connor had made it home the night before, he was already drunk. After Penny had shattered his reality by walking away from him, he'd posted up at the hotel bar hotel and ordered drink after drink after drink until it closed just after eleven. Not only did it help him deal with both the guilt and the heartbreak, but it would help hold up his end of the façade that he was out for a few drinks with his friends.

He needed to smell like alcohol when he got home.

The taxi ride back to the house felt like it took over an hour, as he half expected Abby to greet him at the door with his bags packed and a remorseful Penny by her side.

But the house was dark when he pulled up, and when he stumbled in, he could sense that his family were asleep. He'd like to have thought that it was his thoughtfulness that took him off to the spare room to fall into a drunken slumber, but it was the shame of his actions that kept him from his marital bed. He stripped down to his underwear, set an early alarm, and then clambered into the spare bed for a restless few hours of sleep. When his alarm did go off, his hangover clung to his skull like a shower cap, and after a brisk, cold shower, he headed downstairs and began his first steps to retribution.

Stacy was the first one to greet him, emerging from the stairs with tired eyes to be greeted by a massive hug from her father.

He promised her any breakfast she wanted, and when she requested pancakes, he jumped to action and began whipping up the mixture in a bowl. Just as he poured it into the pan, Abby stepped into the kitchen.

'You're awfully chipper,' she said, slightly astounded. He turned and planted a huge kiss on her. 'Good night?'

'Yeah, it was nice,' he said with a smile. 'But Harry was talking about his problems at home and it just really made me appreciate how good we have it.'

His lie made Abby smile, and he swallowed back to the vomit the guilt was trying to push up his throat.

Maddy soon joined them, and he overcompensated for his guilt by putting on a show of flipping the pancakes and promising them all a wonderful weekend ahead. Abby kept asking him if he was okay, and Connor knew he had to dial it down a bit.

He was usually pretty strict with the girls, and rarely was he as playful in the mornings. It was usually an agitated rush to get them ready for school, but he just told her he wanted to turn over a new leaf.

Appreciate what they had in their home.

Love his family.

Abby finally relented, drew him in for a kiss, and told him she liked that idea, and as she ushered the girls upstairs to get ready for school, the doorbell rang.

'I'll get it,' Connor called up from the kitchen, frowning as he looked at his watch. He pulled open the door and his face dropped.

Detective Inspector Isabella King.

'What the hell do you want?'

'Morning.' King smiled and then looked up at the rain. 'Can I come in?'

'No,' Connor said, and slammed the door. King put her foot in to block it.

'It's really in your best interests for us not to do this the hard way,' King said, before nodding her head to the side. Connor looked over her shoulder and his stomach dropped at the sight of the police car. 'If I recall, the idea of being dragged out of your house and put in a police car wasn't something you were especially keen on.'

'Fine.' Connor stepped to the side and opened the door. 'Make it quick.'

King stepped in, making a show of wiping her feet before looking around at the expensive furnishings in his house.

The man clearly did well for himself.

'Nice house.'

'What do you want?' Connor snapped. The pleasantries weren't working. King sighed and straightened up, taking control.

'You owe me that information.'

'Yes, and I said I'd bring it first thing.' Connor spat through gritted teeth.

'It is first thing.'

'Oh, fucking come on.' Connor raised his voice and then shot a worried look towards the kitchen and quickly lowered it. 'You know I've got kids to get ready for school.'

'Babe…everything okay?' A voice echoed from further in the house, and Connor looked devastated as Abby emerged in the hallway and startled at the sight of the strange woman in by the door. 'Who are you?'

'Detective Inspector King.' She extended her hand, which Abby took with a confused look at her husband. 'Your husband has been helping us with our investigations.'

'Oh, the Gallaghers.' Abby nodded. 'Horrible business.'

'It is.' King agreed.

'But Connor's already given his statements about what happened that night. What else could you need?'

She looked at King, who just raised her eyebrows and looked at Connor. Abby's brow furrowed, and she turned to her husband.

'Just go back upstairs, dear,' he offered and, as he placed his hand on the back of her arm, she pulled away from him.

'What is it, Connor?'

'Look, it's nothing…'

The dots were starting to connect.

'You said you had nothing to do with that man.'

'And I don't.' Connor barked and then jabbed an angry finger in King's direction. 'These fucking morons are just out of ideas.'

King cleared her throat and claimed control of the room.

'First off, watch your mouth.' The threat was clear. 'Your aggression won't be tolerated for long. And second, seeing as how this is getting boring for me, the situation is that your husband had a financial connection to Jason Gallagher five years ago and decided to lie about it to us when we questioned him.'

Abby threw an angry slap that caught Connor on the shoulder. King stepped in before she could deliver another.

'Mrs Davis, I understand you're upset. But please don't do anything you'll regret.'

'What else, Connor? Huh? What else have you not told me?'

'We just need to take him to collect the information and then have him walk us through it,' King said.

'I didn't kill anyone,' Connor said meekly, unable to

look his furious wife in the eye as she leered over King's shoulder at him.

'No. You haven't got the fucking balls,' Abby spat.

'Mrs Davis. Final warning,' King said with authority. 'I have a police car outside, and I'll have them drag you out in your pyjamas if you want?'

The threat worked and Abby took a deep breath and a step back. Their eldest daughter appeared in the doorway.

'Mum, what's going on?'

'Go upstairs, baby,' Abby said, instantly snapping back into her loving tone. 'I'll be up in a sec.'

'But I heard shouting.'

'Just go,' Abby demanded, and the shift in tone sent Maddy scattering back towards the stairs. She took another breath and then fixed her husband with a furious stare. 'You promised me.'

'Look, I can explain.'

'You said you barely spoke to Jason on Friday, yet here you are, making deals with the man.' Abby shook her head. 'Feeding me bullshit that you were chatting with Penny all evening.'

'I was,' Connor insisted. 'You can ask her yourself. We had a few drinks and a catch up. Seriously, message her if you don't believe me?'

What was he doing? Connor couldn't believe he was dangling his mistress towards his wife like bait.

'I'm afraid that won't be possible,' King said softly. She turned to Connor and looked him in the eye. 'Penny Durant was found dead this morning.'

The announcement drove all the air from Connor's lungs, and as he tried to steady himself, his grief connected with his guilt and flipped his stomach. He pushed past both women to the toilet under the stairs, and emptied his guts, vomiting into the bowl until nothing but translucent bile dribbled from his throat. As he cried, he looked up at Abby, who shook her head in disgust.

Had she pieced it together?

After a few tense moments, Abby wiped a tear from her eye and turned to King.

'Just take him.' She shook her head. 'Do what you want with him. Just don't fucking bring him back here.'

'Abby wait…'

Connor reached up to her, but she just marched away from the door, leaving her pathetic husband quivering on the floor of the bathroom, leaning against the toilet bowl. King watched Abby leave and then leant against the door frame, her arms folded. She felt no pity for the man.

He was a liar.

Judging from his reaction to the news, potentially an adulterer, too.

She'd dealt with that pain herself, and her sympathy was entirely with Abby, who had shelved her heartache to go and be a mother.

She was stronger than Conner.

She deserved better than him.

As Connor stood and washed his mouth out in the sink, he turned to King, defeated.

'I take it the cuffs won't be necessary,' King said dryly.

He just shuffled past her to the door.

'Let's just get this over with shall we?' His voice was defeated, and as she marched him to the police car, he looked back up at the house, as Abby glared at from the upstairs window and then angrily drew the curtains.

She was shutting him out.

Despite having the seemingly perfect life, Connor had been unable to stop himself from shattering it to pieces. Now, as the police car pulled away from the curb and the house disappeared behind him, Connor knew that when he got home, there might not be one to piece back together.

CHAPTER THIRTY-SEVEN

This was the job.

That was what DC Hannon had told her partner, Shilpa, when in the midst of yet another argument, her phone had lit up, with her boss's name appearing on the screen.

'Don't answer it,' Shilpa had demanded in anger.

'I have to, Shilp,' Hannon said with a sigh. 'You know I have to.'

'Of course. Because it's more important, right?'

'That's not fair,' Hannon had snapped, with a shake of her head, before taking the call.

It was brief.

It was direct.

Penny Durant had been found dead. Same as the others.

Staged suicide.

Tongue taken.

As she hung up the call, Hannon took a deep breath, pulled her fiery ginger hair into a ponytail, and then turned to her girlfriend.

'I have to go.'

'Sure. Off you go then.'

'Shilpa. Look. I love you, you know I do.' Hannon stepped towards her. 'But I can't just commit to something because your parents are putting pressure on you.'

The issue had been bubbling ever since they'd announced their relationship to Hannon's parents back in the summer. For too long, Hannon had hidden her homosexuality, worried about the impact it would have on her relationship with her strict, traditional parents. They surprised her with their love and support, and now, at the age of twenty-six, she finally felt like she could be her true self.

It felt like freedom.

They had welcomed Shilpa into their family, with her father particularly getting on well with her, and for the first few months, it was the happiest Hannon had ever been. But with their relationship now official, as well as their co-habitation, Shilpa's parents now viewed their relationship at a whole new level. They were more than willing to accept their relationship, but now, her parents were posing the idea of grandchildren. And despite Shilpa being one of the strongest women Hannon had ever met, it was one of the main reasons she loved her, there was a blind spot when it came to her parents.

And Shilpa was pushing the pressure she was feeling onto Hannon.

As Hannon gathered her bag, Shilpa stood, arms crossed, shaking her head as she held back tears of anger.

'Off you go then.'

'Shilp.' Hannon reached out to her, but she pulled away and marched through their flat until she slammed the bedroom door behind him. Hannon stood for a few moments, wanting nothing more than to follow her, make things right, and prove her love to Shilpa in the most tender way possible.

But she couldn't, and with an anger simmering inside her, Hannon headed for the door and another early start.

This was the job.

By the time she'd arrived at the office, Shilpa had sent one message that simply said *Talk later*.

She couldn't wait.

She took five minutes to enjoy the coffee she'd picked up on the way into the office, speculating it would be the only five minutes of pleasure she'd experience that day, and straight away, she began making the necessary calls to gain access to the CCTV footage from Marlow the night before. The local operators were usually very helpful, and the man she dealt with, Stuart, with was more than happy to oblige. As he collated the footage for her, Hannon pulled up Penny's driving record and quickly located the license plate for the car that was insured in her name. Thankfully, with most of the world going digital, paying for parking via an app meant it didn't take her too long to discover that her car had been parked in the car park just outside of Marlow high street, tucked behind Sainsbury's.

She called Stuart back, and requested all the footage for the car park, and a few minutes later, the video files began to filter through into their encrypted shared folder. She booted up the video from the car park and sped to the time where Penny paid for the parking and watched as she and her husband got their boys out of the car, and the four of them walked happily towards the exit. They were wrapped up for the evening, and Hannon even felt herself smile when she saw Penny and her husband link their hands and walk side by side.

She pulled up the other cameras and followed as Penny and her family joined the festivities on the high street, and once they linked up with another couple who they seemed to know, they seemingly stayed in one place for the duration of the event. Once it was over, they headed back to the car park. Only her husband and boys got into an Uber while Penny, after a long hug with all three of them, got into her car on her own and sat for a few moments.

Did she know?

Hannon followed the car through the streets on the way out of Marlow, as it headed towards the A404, where she was either heading to Maidenhead or back towards High Wycombe, and once she turned off the roundabout and made her choice, Hannon pulled up the cameras that surrounded the Handy Cross roundabout. She pulled the camera back to the same time that Penny joined the motorway and watched intently, and after five minutes, Penny cruised onto the screen, navigated the roundabout, and then turned off down towards High Wycombe. Hannon followed her, and watched with interest as she pulled off the main dual carriageway and down towards the Handy Cross business estate, which was predominantly filled with car showrooms. The large High Wycombe leisure centre dominated one length of the business park, along with a chain supermarket, and as Hannon tried to scramble through the available CCTV footage, she finally picked Penny up on the camera overlooking the car park for the Premier Inn tucked away in the corner.

'What are you up to, Penny?' she mumbled to herself.

'Beg your pardon?'

Townsend's voice startled Hannon, who hadn't even registered that he'd arrived. She sat back from her screen and blinked the fuzz of the screen away.

'Sorry. I didn't realise you were here.'

'Should I be offended?' Townsend joked as he approached her desk and then nodded at the screen. 'You got something?'

'Yeah…I think so.' Hannon began clicking open the

various windows of the CCTV footage, and then she began to drag them around her dual screens, lining them up in chronological order. The skill and speed that the young woman operated a computer often blew Townsend's mind. As she prepared the incoming slide show, Townsend offered to grab her a coffee from the canteen. A few minutes later, he returned, coffees in hand, followed swiftly by King, who had a face like thunder.

'Everything all right, guv?' He knew it was foolish to ask.

'No,' King said with a scowl. 'Another woman is dead, and I just watched a man lie to his wife's face. So not the best morning.'

'Here.' Townsend handed her a coffee, which seemed to lighten her mood. 'Nic's got something.'

King shuffled across the room and joined Townsend as they loomed over her shoulders.

'I *think* I've got something.' Hannon was busy running through some footage and lining up the window with the others. 'Give me a sec.'

As Hannon continued, Townsend turned to King and sighed.

'Penny's husband didn't have too much to say.' Townsend shook his head. 'The man is devastated.'

'I can imagine.' King sipped her coffee. 'Any luck on Miller?'

'I'm chasing down another yearbook. Rachel's mother said she might have one for me.'

'Good.' King nodded and Hannon turned in her chair. 'Ready?'

Hannon walked them through the footage she'd been collating, outlining all Penny Durant's movements from when she arrived at Marlow the night before, to her arriving at the Premier Inn.

'Her husband said she'd gone out for drinks with friends,' Townsend said, slightly confused.

'At the Premier Inn?' King rolled her eyes. 'Do we know when she left?'

'Yes.' Hannon held up a finger and then clicked the video. The grainy footage showed Penny rushing from the entrance of the hotel.

'Why is she in a hurry?'

'I don't know, but...' Hannon paused to build up the suspense. 'It could have something to do with him.'

She clicked on the final video, and roughly an hour or so after Penny had departed, they watched as a cab pulled up outside the front of the hotel, and unmistakably, Connor Davis exited the hotel and got into the backseat. As the cab pulled away, Hannon swivelled in her feet and held open her arms, waiting for the applause.

'So he was the last person to see her alive?' King said with venom on her tongue.

'Your hunch that they were having it away appears to be correct,' Hannon said.

'You think he did it?' Townsend asked, his arms folded and his brow furrowed. 'You think he killed her?'

'I don't know.' King rubbed her temples. 'But I'm going to find out. Nic, great work.'

'A-thank-you,' Hannon said slightly comically.

'Fancy making this creep squirm in his seat with me?' King offered, without a hint of jest in her voice.

'I'm happy to sit in,' Townsend offered, but King shook her head.

'No, I want you to go to that Premier Inn, and I want their CCTV footage. I want proof of them together, and I want it now,' King said coldly. 'I want to drag him over the coals with it.'

'Yes, guv,' Townsend said, trying his best to hide his

disappointment. Once again, it felt like King was keeping him a little at arm's length.

Could she sense that he hadn't been honest with her?

As King turned back to the screens with Hannon, Townsend swiped his coat from his chair and marched back out of the office, heading to the Premier Inn to watch some of the final moments of an innocent woman's life.

Potentially spent with the man who had ended it.

CHAPTER THIRTY-EIGHT

As Townsend pulled into the Handy Cross business estate, he began to feel a little seedy. The evidence was pointing to the fact that both Connor Davis, and the recently deceased Penny Durant were having an affair and, as the Premier Inn loomed large in the far corner of the estate, Townsend felt an unease of how tucked away it was. The idea of ever betraying Mandy had never once crossed his mind, even during the years he had spent undercover.

The opportunity had presented itself on numerous occasions.

In some instances, his cover was almost blown by his refusal to act upon a woman's advances, but there was a line he wouldn't cross.

He had taken drugs to maintain his cover.

Even exacted acts of pretty grim violence.

But breaking his vow to Mandy was never one of them, and as he pulled into the hotel car park, his heart went out to the grieving Stephen, who had no idea that in her final moments, Penny wasn't with her beloved family.

She was in the arms of another man.

Townsend was often quick to point out that in their

role as detectives, they should never be in a position to judge someone for their circumstances.

But at that moment, as he killed his engine and looked up at the hidden hotel, he hoped that King and Hannon were dragging Connor Davis over the fucking coals.

As he dashed in through the automatic door and in from the rain, Townsend was greeted with a warm smile by the woman behind the desk. Although he was nothing but polite, that smile faded when he announced himself and showed his lanyard, which was a common reaction. The woman exaggerated her foreign accent to avoid a proper conversation and scurried away to find the manager as Townsend looked around the reception area. Like every chain hotel, it was bland and unwelcoming, and he looked beyond the vending machine to the eating area. The bar was locked, hidden behind a wooden shutter, but a few of the tables were occupied by guests who were persevering through the unappetising looking breakfast buffet.

'Hungry?'

The voice snapped Townsend out of his thoughts, and he turned to face the smiling manager, who thrust his hand into Townsends.

'I'm fine, thank you.'

'That's a fine accent,' the portly gentleman said, still shaking the hand. 'Liverpool?'

'Bingo,' Townsend said with a smile as he retracted his hand. He loomed over the man, who'd given up the ghost with his thinning hair and shaved it to the scalp, but his round face was framed with a neat beard.

'Thomas Manning. How can I help?' The manager said boldly.

'Can we speak in private?'

'Right this way.' The manager beckoned Townsend as he marched beyond the reception desk and into a small room that could barely pass as a broom cupboard, let alone an office. As Thomas squeezed into the gap between his chair and the desk, he turned to Townsend, who tried to find a comfortable place to stand. 'What seems to be the problem?'

'I can't divulge too much information, but we're currently in the middle of an investigation and need to double check that a person of interest stayed here last night.'

'Sure, what's the name?'

'Well, that's the thing. We already know that he checked in under a false name.'

'Ah, right.' Thomas sighed. 'We get that a lot.'

'And you approve?' Townsend said and then scolded himself. 'Sorry. That was unfair.'

'No, no.' The man waved his hand. 'It is what it is. We're a cheap hotel near a motorway and a lot of people use it as a place to…err…'

'Play away?'

'Sadly.' Without thinking, Thomas ran his thumb over his wedding ring.

'Do you not require a photo ID to check in?'

'Not anymore.' He shrugged. 'Just an online booking and if we did we'd be turning away half of our business which would see us shut down faster than a burger van with a rat problem.'

'Well, can I check the CCTV footage?' Townsend demanded more than asked. 'We believe he was only here for a few hours.'

'Absolutely.' The helpful manager turned back to his desk and began clicking through the programs on his PC. Townsend gave him the timeframes, and sure enough, Connor Davis emerged into the reception area, checked in, and then posted up at the bar. They fast forwarded through a few drinks and then Penny Durant arrived, and Townsend felt a little morbid watching the final moments of the woman's life. She took Davis by the hand and straight to the elevator, but there was no greeting or any signs of affection.

'Can we see where they went?'

'I don't have cameras in the rooms, if that's what you're after?' Thomas said with a wry smile.

They followed them out of the lift, and again, the body language conveyed that only one of them seemed excited by what was to come next. They disappeared into a room, and Townsend hit the fast-forward button. It didn't take too long for a distressed-looking Penny to burst from the room and rush hurriedly towards the stairwell. Minutes later, Connor stumbled out through the door, dressing himself as he ran to the lifts.

'Back to the reception,' Townsend ordered, and the manager handily linked the cameras up to the right time to show Penny throw open the stairwell door just as the lift opened and Connor stumbled out. He reached out and grabbed her, spinning her round, and seemingly irate at the woman who was clearly crying.

'You don't have audio?'

'I'm afraid not.'

Townsend leant in, watching closely as Connor's face twisted in an angry snarl as he yelled at her. Penny was crying, racked with guilt at what she'd done, but their attention was then drawn away by a large man who appeared at the bottom of the screen. Penny said something to him and then darted out, leaving a broken Connor stood in the reception, half dressed and wallowing in self-pity.

After a few moments of silence, Thomas blew out his cheeks.

'That didn't go well for him, did it?'

'No.' Townsend shook his head. It had gone worse for

Penny, but the manager didn't need to know that. 'Can I have a copy of this?'

'Yes, of course.' Thomas scrambled around his desk, pulling open the drawer that slammed into his gut. 'Let me grab a stick for you.'

As the manager went about fulfilling his request, Townsend stared at the screen, where the image had stopped on a devastated Connor Davis. They already knew the man was under extreme pressure, with his private dealings with Jason Gallagher threatening to come to light and impact a marriage the man clearly didn't care about.

He kept lying.

A sign of a man at the end of his rope.

His entire life was wrapped up in his family, as he and his wife ran their business. If things started to come out in the wash, who knew what might happen? Similarly, if he had been willing to risk it all for Penny Durant, what would he have been willing to do had she walked away from him?

Heartbreak was a powerful motive, but the need to keep her quiet was even stronger.

But was Connor Davis capable of killing?

Townsend wasn't sure, but as the man finished up his transfer of the files to him, he knew that whatever the answer was, Connor Davis was the last person to see Penny Durant alive.

Townsend pulled up his phone, dialled his boss, and she answered on the second ring.

'Jack.'

'Have you started?'

'Not yet,' King said cruelly. 'Wanted to make him sweat a bit.'

'Think you can hold on another ten minutes?'

'Yeah, why?'

The manager handed Townsend the USB stick, and Townsend nodded his thanks as he headed back to his car.

'Because I have something you need to see.'

CHAPTER THIRTY-NINE

It was the same interview room he'd been sitting in a few days before, but this time, the walls felt closer.

The ceiling felt lower.

In all aspects of his mind, Connor Davis felt like the world was closing in on him.

There was no hiding from it now.

Abby would have headed straight to the office as soon as she'd dropped the girls off at school, and once she knew where to look, she'd pull out all the information pertaining to the money he'd lent to Jason Gallagher and the lengths he'd gone to to hide it. The very real danger he'd put their livelihood in, just to hide things from his wife.

Their future, and that of the girls, were wrapped up in the business, and now it would be clear for all to see, that he had jeopardised it.

But the reason the world really felt like it was caving in had nothing to do with any of that.

Penny was dead.

It had never really occurred to him that he'd been unhappy with his life until she'd walked back into it, and that sudden spark of excitement had consumed his every waking moment since they'd reconnected. When she'd arrived at the hotel the night before, he was certain that it was the first step on a complicated road that would destroy two families but would ultimately lead to happiness.

Now, it was over.

She'd made it clear to him that she hadn't felt the same as he had, but there would be no chance to win her over.

He'd sacrificed everything for a woman he could no longer have.

The door to the room finally opened, and he was met by the disapproving glare of DI King, along with DC Hannon who had a habit of getting under his skin. He turned to Rupa Patel, the duty solicitor who had been sitting silently beside him for over an hour.

'Sorry to keep you waiting,' King said insincerely as she sat down and plonked her paperwork onto the table. 'DC Hannon, do you mind?'

Hannon leant across and turned on the recording device, announcing who was in the room after the long high-pitched noise. Connor looked to Patel, who just nodded for him to cooperate.

'Right, Mr Davis…' King said with a sigh as she shuffled the papers in front of her. 'Tell me about Penny.'

'What about her?'

'Look, I don't want to stretch this out…'

'Funny. You kept me waiting here for over an hour. It hardly seems like speed is high on your list of priorities.'

'When did you last see Penny Durant?'

Rupa Patel leant forward.

'I thought this was about the financial dealings between Mr Davis and Mr Gallagher?'

'It is,' King said respectfully. 'However, there are a few other things we'd like to discuss with Mr Davis, and I assumed he'd rather not have done that in front of his wife.'

King shot a disapproving glance to the man, who squirmed in his seat. King nodded to Hannon, who began.

'When did you last see Mrs Durant?'

'Yesterday.' Connor sighed with frustration.

'Could you be a little more specific?'

'Yesterday evening,' Connor snapped. 'She was at the Marlow lights. You guys should know that. You were there.'

'And you spoke with her and her husband?' Hannon continued.

'No. I didn't speak to her. You asked if I saw her. And I did.'

'And that was the last time you saw her?'

Connor's eyes flicked nervously to King, who bore a hole through him with her unblinking stare.

'Yes.'

'Connor, I'm going to be very real with you here.' King leant forward a little, her hands clasped on the table. 'You've already lied to us once regarding your interactions with the people who've been killed this past week.'

'Like I said.' Connor folded his arms in protest. 'That was the last time.'

King sat back and sighed and motioned to Hannon. All eyes turned to the laptop that Hannon swivelled round, and she hit play on the CCTV video she had ready to go. The colour drained from Connor's face as he relived the moment in the hotel reception, as Penny pulled away from him. A silence hung in the air for a few moments, and Rupa Patel whispered something into Connor's ear.

'Mr Davis, just for the recording, can you confirm that the video we just played for you showed you and Penny Durant at the Premier Inn in Handy Cross business estate late last night?'

Connor looked to Rupa who gave a slight shake of the head.

But he broke.

'Fine. Yes, it was me. We've been talking since the reunion and last night, we went up to that hotel room and we fucked. Okay?' The gentleman had all but left him. 'What do you want from me?'

'The truth.' King slammed her hand down on the table, sending him shooting back in his chair. 'This woman is dead, Mr Davis. She was left in a field, her tongue cut from her mouth, and her lungs long since obliterated by carbon monoxide. While you're sitting here giving us bullshit, her *husband*, who loved her dearly, and her two boys, are sitting at home, knowing they'll never get over this.'

The gravity of her words hit Connor like a sledgehammer, and his eyes began to water. He dipped his head and began to weep.

'She regretted it.' He eventually sniffed. 'I knew, I knew…when she got there, she didn't want to go through with it. She was convincing herself the entire way up to the room, but I was just so…locked in that this is what we wanted, that I never asked her if she still did.'

'Did she say no?' Hannon demanded. The insinuation was clear.

'No, god no. I didn't rape her.' Connor looked offended. 'But the second we finished, she went to the bathroom and then she said goodbye and stormed out.'

'What did you do?' King asked bluntly.

'I panicked. Ran out after her half naked and begged her to not leave.' Connor wiped a few tears. 'I was just so sure this was what we both wanted, and we had so much to lose…'

'Where did you go after you left the hotel?'

'Home,' Connor said sternly. 'I didn't kill her, if that's what you're thinking.'

'She did walk away from you after everything—'

'I loved her.' Connor spat through his tears. 'I have a video doorbell. You can check the fucking logs.'

He slumped back in his chair, clearly no better for clearing his conscience. King looked to Hannon, who pursed her lips a little and raised an eyebrow.

Did they believe him?

As Connor wept some more, Hannon slid a packet of tissues across the table to him. He took one, grunted a thanks, and then dabbed at his eyes. King flicked a glance to the two-way glass that ran along one of the walls, knowing that Townsend was standing behind it, likely with his arms folded over his chest and a face like thunder.

It was hard to pity a man who would betray his family in such a way.

'Mr Davis,' King began once more. 'Do you know a Gemma Miller?'

Connor frowned, and then let out a deep sigh as he sat back in his chair.

'That's a name I haven't heard in a long time,' he said weakly. 'I don't know her, but she did go to my school a long time ago.'

'What about a Mr Miller?' Hannon asked, looking at her notes. 'We haven't been able to find much about his tenure at the school when you were there, but we do know that he taught at the same time and…'

Hannon stopped and King sat straight as Connor Davis went white as a sheet, as if he'd connected some dots that they weren't privy to. Then, to the shock of everyone in the room, and undoubtedly Townsend who was observing, Connor broke down into uncontrollable tears. Hannon looked at her boss for guidance, but King just stayed calm, knowing whatever emotional response he was experiencing, they had to let it play out.

But it was what Connor said that changed the mood in the room.

It changed their entire investigation.

'We didn't kill him,' Connor eventually said, as if begging for mercy. He took a few moments to compose himself, taking large deep breaths as if he realised he was out of rope.

The truth needed to come out.

'What do you mean?' King said with authority.

'I said we didn't kill him,' Connor said and then straightened up, ready to face the music. 'But it was our fault he killed himself.'

CHAPTER FORTY

A haunting silence had fallen over the room, and all eyes were on Connor, who had requested a cup of water before he went any further. Hannon had obliged him, and as he sipped from the plastic cup, he tried to calm himself.

He'd never spoken about Mr Miller before.

Not since Jason Gallagher had threatened him into an eternal silence.

He'd threatened all of them.

Rachel.

Penny.

Even Shelly, who had nothing to do with what had happened.

It was a secret they'd sworn to take to their graves, and for three of them, that had been the case.

But now, with two detectives and an exasperated solicitor by his side, Connor was ready to finally shed some light on a secret that had been eating away at him for the past twenty years like a slow-acting tumour.

'We were just kids,' Connor began, his voice cracking with guilt. 'You know. We fucked about at the back of the classroom. We were late. Nothing too bad. Anyways, Jason and I were on both the football and rugby teams. Star players. I mean, you've seen the size of Jason, right? He was that big when we were fifteen.'

Connor took another sip and then glanced at the recording device, understanding that everything he said would be archived. He continued.

'Well, we were a little group—'

'We being?' King wanted clarity.

'Me. Jason. Rachel. Penny. We were a little foursome. It sounds so ridiculous now as adults, but we were the cool kids. Star athletes. Penny and Rachel were the prettiest girls in the year. The other kids looked up to us, you know?'

'And Shelly?' Hannon asked. 'She's been mentioned.'

'Shelly Lawson?' Connor's eyebrows raised. 'Yeah, she sort of joined us. She was more Penny's friend than ours, but she hung around with us a bit. She did *not* like Jason.'

'They fell out?' King asked, her eyebrow raised.

'They just never got on. I think she saw through his bullshit way before any of us did. Once we left school, I never heard from her again.' Connor took another sip. 'Anyways, there was a girl in our year, Gemma. Gemma Miller.'

'What was she like?'

'Quiet.' Connor shrugged. 'Not unattractive, but unlike Penny and Rachel, she didn't really make a big effort. Her dad was the Head of English, but he had a big interest in rugby, so he also coached the team. A real hard arse. I mean, times have changed, but even back then, he'd lay into us. Said it was toughening us up. Anyway…one training session, Jason turned up late and he stank of weed, and Mr Miller went ballistic. Chewed him out in front of the entire rugby team, and to try to save face, Jason took a swing at him.'

'He hit a teacher?' Hannon asked in surprise.

'Tried to,' Connor corrected. 'Like I said, Mr Miller

was a mean old bastard, and he moved and shoved Jason to the ground. Everyone laughed at him, and I think that was the first time I saw what was underneath Jason's macho bullshit. He was scared, and to be fair, he was just a teenage boy with a bad attitude, and nowadays, Mr Miller would be reported, and it would be handled appropriately.'

'But not back then?' King poked.

'Jason wasn't going to tell on him. His dad was a drunk who would have knocked ten shades out of him if he heard he'd been pushed around by a teacher. No, Jason had a different way of getting back at Mr Miller.'

'Gemma.' Hannon connected the dots and Connor nodded.

'Yup. Jason started paying her attention whenever he could, and that was the thing. Despite all the horrible stuff you've heard, he could turn on the charm. He was a good-looking guy, popular, and for someone like Gemma, who was on the outskirts of the school because nobody wanted to be too close to one of the head's daughter, that attention meant something.' Connor shook his head in disgust. 'I should have fucking stopped him.'

'What happened, Connor?' King asked bluntly.

'He led her on. Compliments. Kind gestures. The usual stuff and then he invited her to a house party and took her upstairs.' Connor's eyes watered and he shook his head in shame. 'Basically, they got undressed and started fooling around and then he ran out in just his boxers, but he took her clothes with him.'

'Poor girl,' Hannon said, glaring at Connor. 'I take it you all found it funny?'

'Yep. We were that young and naïve that this poor girl had to call her dad from the house phone, wrapped in a towel, while Jason made it pretty clear people weren't allowed to help her. When Mr Miller arrived to collect her, he didn't say anything, but he knew what had happened. And what was worse, he knew why.'

'So what happened?' King asked. 'How did he react?'

'In a way that really got to Jason. Gemma never came back to school. He took her out of that environment and as a father now, I'm sickened by what we did to that girl. But Mr Miller started making Jason's life hell. Detentions. Extra laps in training. Not picking him to start matches. Everything to shatter his armour of being the coolest kid in school. It was petty, but I guess he wanted to teach Jason a lesson.'

Connor asked for another drink, and this time, the door opened, and Townsend stepped in, having clearly been listening on the other side of the glass. King nodded her approval for him to stay, and Connor took the cup with a shaky hand.

'Thank you.' He took a sip as Townsend stepped to the back wall and leant against it. 'So, Jason started a rumour. I think this was the moment Shelly and eventually Penny stepped away from us.'

'What was the rumour?' Hannon demanded.

Connor shook his head, and fresh tears began to slide down his cheeks.

'Connor,' King said calmly. 'What was the rumour?'

'That Mr Miller touched him. That, after practice, Mr Miller cornered Jason in the shower and grabbed his penis and tried to molest him. Jason pushed him off and got out of there and…' Connor broke again. '…and I confirmed I saw it happen. And even worse, I had to agree that Mr Miller had tried to do the same to me.'

'Jesus.' Townsend's voice echoed from the back of the room. Connor was weeping.

'I knew it was too far. I told Jason we needed to stop it. But he just kept pushing and pushing, and the rumour spread through the school quicker than a fire. Eventually, our parents were called in and we swore it was the truth.' Connor took a breath. 'Mr Miller even begged us to admit we were lying, but Jason just doubled down, turning on the waterworks and said how he had nightmares about it.'

The room was silent, and all eyes were on Connor as he tried to collect himself.

'Mr Miller left soon after that. He became known as Diddler, and within a week, Jason was back to his old self. He even boasted that he fought off a paedo and the other kids respected him for it.'

'And you?' King asked, visibly shaken by the story.

'I knew there was more to come. There was no social media back then, and the only way news spread was through gossip. Soon, one parent had heard that Miller's wife had taken Gemma and left him. Another one said he was now under investigation from the police.' Connor sighed, running out of energy. 'The final rumour was that he'd killed himself. The second we heard that, Jason threatened us all and swore us to secrecy, and Penny never spoke to me again.'

Connor fell back into his chair, letting out a deep breath of relief. It had clearly been a weight he'd carried for quarter of a century, and although his face was pale and his eyes were red, he seemed somehow healthier for unburdening. King scribbled a few notes and then handed them to Hannon, who lifted herself from the chair and left the room. King turned to Connor, who lifted his cup with a trembling hand.

'Do you know where Gemma Miller is nowadays?'

'No.' Connor shook his head. 'We never heard from her again, but I could have sworn I saw her at the reunion.'

'The thing is, Connor, we can't find her. Nothing.' Townsend stepped forward. 'No records in the school database. Not even a picture in the yearbook.'

'She'd left before the year finished.' Connor shrugged.

'But they used our pictures from the beginning of the year, so maybe she was in it?'

'Do you have a copy?'

He shook his head.

'It won't shock you to know I kind of wanted to block out what had happened in those years. It's why, over time, I pushed Jason away.'

'Until he came asking for money?'

'Well, he did have a pretty big hand to play. Told me he'd go to the police about what we did if I didn't help him out.' Connor scoffed in disgust. 'What a prick.'

'Mr Davis. If what you're saying is true, then we have a very serious belief that your life is in danger. Your alibis for the times of death for Jason and Penny check out, so we're not arresting you for that. But we have strong reason to believe that you'll be targeted.'

'Fuck.' Connor uttered under his breath.

'But we can help. We can put you in a safe place with police protection, but we need you to help us,' King said firmly. 'No more lies. No more bullshit. I know you've got some issues going on right now, and I know you want to put them right, but for your own safety and possibly even the safety of your family, I need you to work with us. Do you understand?'

After a few moments of reflection, Connor shot a glance to Rupa Patel, who nodded her agreement.

'Yes,' he finally answered.

'I need you to stay here for a little while,' King continued as she stood. 'I'll be back as soon as I can. I just need to make the arrangements.'

King nodded her goodbye to Patel, and then beckoned for Townsend to follow. He took one more look at Connor and saw the definition of defeated staring back at him. As they stepped out into the hallway, King took a huge pull on her vape stick, and then waved away the frown of a passing constable.

'Fucking hell.' She sighed, letting the plume of vapour out into the corridor.

'What's the move, guv?'

'Hannon's double checking the doorbell at his house, but I have no reason to think he's lying.' King took another danger puff and then pocketed it. 'But I need to speak to Hall. He'll be thrilled that we need accommodation.'

'What do you need from me?'

'Stay here. Watch him.' King jabbed her thumb at the door. 'Once we're good to go, we'll take him to a safe house and then move on to the next bit.'

Townsend nodded his understanding, looked at the door to the interview room, and then back to his boss.

'Which is?'

'Finding Gemma fucking Miller.'

CHAPTER FORTY-ONE

Things were starting to slot into place.

For the past five days, Townsend's mind had been racing, weaving in and out of blind alleys, and chasing shadows he knew he'd never catch. It was the part of the job that was the most thrilling and most devastating in equal measure.

He was responsible for tracking down a killer and bringing him or her to justice.

But the longer he took, the more irreparable damage he allowed to happen.

He'd been the one to latch onto the name Gemma Miller, and it was through his relentless searching that they'd been able to bring her into the frame. The CCTV footage from the party. The missing records and mysterious missing year book picture. It should have seen him vindicated in the eyes of DI King, but the way she'd told him to watch Connor was a sly way of telling him to sit on the sidelines.

Did she know?

Ever since he'd saved her life and stopped Gordon Baycroft in the summer, their bond had grown and the trust they'd developed had been nigh on unbreakable. Usually, she'd pull him into the conversations, coaching him without him realising as he came to the right conclusions.

But not this time.

Now, she wanted him out of the way, sticking him on babysitting duty while Hannon got to piece together a jigsaw puzzle that Connor Davis had just tipped out in front of them.

Had Lowe said something to her?

In his mind, he knew she was right. His entire focus needed to be on tracking down Gemma Miller and bringing a woman who'd potentially killed three people to justice. But in his heart, he couldn't just walk away from Simone Beckford, the grieving woman who he'd given his word to, and the broken family Jamal Beckford's death had left behind.

Don't make promises you can't keep.

King's advice was wise, and certainly came from experience, but Townsend just couldn't take it on board.

He intended to keep his word.

If it meant working every hour he could, he'd find justice for all the families that had been touched by the hand of death.

Janet Jennings.

Stephen Durant.

Simone Beckford.

All of them were in the depths of grief, and all of them were looking to him for answers.

As he stood, his thick arms folded across his broad chest, Townsend looked at the fragile Connor and realised he too was going through grief. He'd gambled his entire world on a new beginning with Penny Durant, and now the life that he'd thrown away and the life he'd chased were now lying in pieces.

It was hard to feel sorry for the man, but gone was the confident, successful businessman they'd met a few days earlier. Now, grief had reduced him to a husk, and as he solemnly sipped on the cup of tea Rupa Patel had retrieved for him, Connor stared into the void.

Lost.

After a small, quiet discussion, Rupa Patel gathered her things and said a courteous goodbye to Townsend, leaving the two of them in the room together. Connor avoided eye contact, and Townsend stared at the man as he tried to connect Connor's harrowing story to the case in hand. He'd been certain that the staged suicides had been symbolic, and if what Connor had said was true, then it could have been Gemma Miller putting her victims through what her father had been through.

Make them relive the pain and suffering that had father had.

There was also the severing of the tongues, which could be linked to the idea of speaking out of turn.

By spreading rumours.

As his mind raced, Townsend tried to collate his theories into a palatable order, with the hope that maybe he could bring DI King back onside. Deep in thought, Townsend startled as the door beside him rocked with a hard knock. Connor jumped in his chair, and Townsend held up a calming hand, turned, and pulled it open.

DI Lowe.

'Sir?'

'Can we talk?' Lowe said. It wasn't a request.

'I can't right now…' Townsend turned to Connor, and Lowe dipped his head into the room and frowned.

'He's fine,' Lowe said with a sneer. 'Two minutes.'

'King told me to watch him and…'

'She also told you to keep your nose out of my case, so don't play the boy scout with me.' Townsend looked to

Connor, who peered up at him, and with an angered sigh, he stepped out of the room and pulled the door closed. Lowe smirked. 'There's a good boy. In here.'

Lowe pushed open the door to the interview room opposite without knocking, gave a pointless look inside before he stepped in.

'What's up?' Townsend asked, his arms folded.

'We made an arrest this morning,' Lowe said, rubbing his eyes with the balls of his hands. 'Turns out, a member of a rival gang's phone was pinned to High Wycombe less than an hour before the call came in for Beckford's murder.'

'No shit,' Townsend said excitedly.

'Yes, shit.' Lowe huffed. 'Turns out, this fucker has previous. Nasty piece of work. Staunton led a raid on his residence this morning, dragged him out of bed in his undies.'

'Did he let him get dressed?'

'You've met Staunton, right?' Lowe said with a grin. 'Anyways, search of the premises found a knife. It's been sent off to be analysed, but we're pretty confident it will come back with Beckford's blood on it. These boys think they clean their blades, but they always miss a spot.'

'And if it does come back clean?'

'Then we're up shit creek with a very flimsy paddle.' Lowe admitted. 'But, like I said, this guy has previous. He's had beef with the NX in the past, and for all intents and purposes, he has no business in High Wycombe.'

'Doesn't mean he did it?' Townsend said thoughtfully.

'Fucking hell, Jack. You're hard work sometimes.' Lowe shook his head.

'I'm hard work?' Townsend took a powerful step forward. 'I'm not the one who sent you into a fucking firing zone for a laugh.'

Lowe rose to the bait, and he also took a step forward, his eyes locked on Townsend.

'Think of it as a hazing.' Lowe gently lifted a fist and brushed it against Townsend's jaw. 'You won't always be able to land a lucky punch.'

'If you fancy a rematch?' Townsend offered, and after a few tense seconds, Lowe finally chuckled and stepped back.

'Like I said, you're hard work, Scouse.' He nodded approvingly. 'So am I.'

Townsend also relaxed a little, and yet again, he had this unnerving feeling that he and Lowe were beginning to forge a mutual respect. As he turned to reach for the door handle, Townsend looked back to the Detective Chief Inspector.

'Thank you for the update, sir.'

'No worries.' Lowe shrugged. 'Just don't go running to Mummy about it.'

Townsend resisted the urge to tell his superior officer to *fuck off*, but he did yank open the door to the interview room. Respectfully, he stepped to the side and let Lowe step out of the open door.

It wasn't the only one in the corridor.

CHAPTER FORTY-TWO

Things were moving at a mile a minute.

As DI King rushed through the halls of the High Wycombe Police Station, she thumbed through her phone to pull up Detective Superintendent Hall's number. As she took the stairs two at a time, she cursed silently as he failed to answer his phone, and she sped past the open-plan office of CID where she used to work and made a beeline to his office at the end of the corridor. She rattled the door with a closed fist.

'Come in.'

Hall's voice boomed from beyond, and King pushed open the door with a scowl.

'Sir.' King greeted him as she stepped into his office. 'I tried calling.'

'Apologies, I was on another call.' Hall sighed as he stood from behind his desk and began to gather his things. 'Make it quick, Izzy. I've got a meeting to attend.'

'It's Connor Davis, sir. We believe he's the next target for our killer.'

Hall's white eyebrows shot upwards above the thin frame of his glasses.

'I see. Do we have evidence?'

'Nothing concrete, sir,' King began. 'However, he just relayed to us a serious motive for who we believe to be the killer. The other three victims, they were all part of a rumour that saw a teacher kill himself twenty-five years ago, and it all stemmed from their bullying of his daughter.'

'And Davis has proof of this?' Hall asked as he slid on his suit jacket. 'Because I ran my eyes over the updates on the case, and it would appear that Davis was the last person seen with Mrs Durant before her death, and also one of the last people to be seen with Mr Gallagher.'

'I know, but that's circumstantial.'

'Is it, Izzy?' Hall snapped in irritation. 'You're the one who always says to follow the evidence. Leave all those wild theories to DS Townsend.'

'Sir, I think we need to take the threat to his life seriously…'

'What threat? Have we seen any actual evidence of a threat towards his life?'

'No, but we have footage of a woman we believe to be the daughter of the deceased teacher…'

'Believed to be?' Hall sighed. 'Look, Izzy. I know you and your team are working round the clock to get on top of this situation, but I've got my superiors, the PR team, and the mayor so far up my arse on this one, I'm practically flossing with their shoelaces.'

'I understand, sir, but—'

'Then follow the evidence. This man has lied about his connections to Gallagher and has a significant link to Durant. I want you to pick apart his life and find out exactly who he is.' Hall demanded as he stepped past her and to the door. 'In the meantime, do what you can to verify his story and for God's sake, find this Gemma Miller and then, if it all adds up, I will back you to the hilt. You know that.'

'Yes, sir.'

'But right now, I have to go and brief our PR team as to why a body was dumped on Booker Common this morning, and why a story about severed tongues is starting to gain traction.' Hall pulled open his door and looked back at a crestfallen King. He sighed. 'Look, Izzy. You and your team…this is what you do. You figure out what others can't. So go and do what you do best.'

Hall held the door open, signalling the end of their meeting, and King swallowed her disappointment and gave him a reassuring nod.

'Yes, sir.'

As she marched back down towards the SCU office, DI King knew that deep down, Detective Superintendent Hall was right. He'd been one of her key allies ever since she'd relocated to the Thames Valley Police, and although her issues with Lowe had threatened to derail her career, Hall had ensured she'd stayed on the right track. He was the only person in the entire organisation who knew about her struggles with alcoholism and had offered numerous times to attend meetings with her as a show of support. She'd rejected the offer, but it helped to know that she wasn't alone.

But now, with Hall unlikely to sanction a safe house for Davis on the basis of his "story" alone, she suddenly felt a little abandoned.

She wanted a drink.

As she approached the door to the SCU, King stopped a few feet from the handle and gave a quick, cursory glance back down the hallway to check the coast was clear. She took a quick puff on her vape and shook out her hands.

'Head in the game, Izzy,' she uttered to herself and

then pushed the door open to find Hannon ferociously tapping away on her keyboard. 'Nic. Update.'

'I'm trying to build a timeline for Gemma Miller, but there isn't much to go on. I've been able to track down the documentation for her parent's divorce, along with her father's death certificate. Which is pretty sad.' Hannon frowned and then sat back in her chair, adjusting the backrest. 'But as for Gemma, she went to university in Bristol for three years, studying to become a veterinarian, and then studied another three years with the BVA to become fully qualified.'

'BVA?'

'British Veterinarian Association,' Hannon continued. 'She passed with flying colours, but that's where the trail ends. No practice. No social media. It's almost like she just disappeared.'

'Or she didn't want to be found.' King theorised. She looked to the board, and at the grainy photo of who they believed was their killer. 'Perhaps she changed her name?'

'If she did, she didn't do it legally.' Hannon grunted. 'Nothing from deed poll. I even checked for a death certificate for her just to be sure, but nothing. We're chasing a ghost.'

'What we're doing is chasing a smart woman with a very serious grudge,' King said coldly. 'If she studied as a vet, she'd understand anaesthetics, which means she'd know how to administer them correctly. Contact a local vet, get a list of all the drugs they use and then cross check with Dr Mitchell with what she found in Jason, Rachel and Langley. She won't have gotten to Penny yet, but we can safely assume the same will be in her blood as well.'

'You know what they say about assuming, right?' Hannon said with a wry smile.

'Yeah. Don't fucking do it.' King blew out her cheeks. 'But right now, we need to find a woman who seemingly doesn't exist anymore, and I need to go and take care of Connor Davis.'

'Am on it, guv,' Hannon said as she stretched out her back and then cracked her knuckles. As she returned to her screen, King set off down the hall, wondering if perhaps her cold shoulder to Townsend was a little hasty. When they were hunting down Baycroft in the summer, they'd all been blinded by factual evidence pointing in one direction, when it was Jack who'd questioned it all, working tirelessly to disprove what the evidence was telling them.

She needed him with her.

Needed him back onside.

So when she walked around the corner towards the interview room, her heart sank as she saw the door adjacent to Connor's room open and Lowe and Townsend emerge. As she approached, she could see the panic spread across Townsend's face, and he shot her a devastated look as she rushed to the open door to Davis's room.

He was gone.

CHAPTER FORTY-THREE

With every step he took, Connor Davis didn't know what he was doing.

For what felt like an eternity, the imposing Townsend had loomed large from the back of the room, his eyes locked on Connor the entire time, enough to make him squirm in his seat. Although the detective's face was a blank slate, Connor knew that his entire private life had become public knowledge.

The dodgy deals with Jason Gallagher.

His affair with Penny.

The awful rumour they'd spread that had seen an innocent man take his own life.

As much as he willed it to happen, the ground just wouldn't open him up and swallow him. He'd have to face his shame head on, and he knew that Abby would never forgive him. She'd been the most wonderful partner over the past few decades and wasn't just an amazing wife, but a brilliant mum. Their business had thrived off their partnership, and he'd thrown it all away.

He had to see her.

Had to make things right.

His stomach flipped as the guilt tried to manifest itself in an avalanche of vomit, but he pushed it down. It had been just over twelve hours since he'd been lying in bed with another woman, dreaming of a new life. Penny's body was probably still warm, yet he was already trying to move on and rebuild.

He hated himself for it.

A knock on the door caused him to lift from his seat with fear, and a belittling glare from Townsend caused him to look away in shame. The door opened, and an older detective peered in. Like Townsend, he was tall and broad, but with black skin and a neat, greying beard. The man summoned Townsend with a sarcastic authority, and Townsend obliged him.

Connor was on his own.

For some reason, he was compelled to get up from his seat and after a few moments of gentle pacing, he decided to try the door.

It opened.

He peered his head out into the corridor, to find it was completely empty and without thinking, he stepped out, retracing the steps he'd taken when he'd been led to the room that morning. If anyone stopped him, he'd make an excuse about needing the bathroom.

But nobody did.

He followed a distracted police officer through the card activated door to the front desk, and as that officer spoke to the desk sergeant, Connor seized the opportunity and headed to the exit. His pace quickened, and before he knew it, he was stepping out into the freezing winter, with the bitterly cold drizzle announcing his new-found freedom with a cold slap to the face.

He kept moving.

As he hadn't been under arrest, he still had his phone,

and as he marched up the hill, beyond the post office, he turned down a side street and called Abby.

She didn't answer.

He continued up the hill for a few minutes, turning right at the top and into the entrance of the High Wycombe Rail Station car park, and went straight to the taxi rank. The gentleman parked at the head of the queue welcomed him with the usual spiel about the weather, and Connor grunted and gave him the address to his office, and then made it quite clear he wasn't interested in small talk.

As the car made its way back down the hill towards the magic roundabout, Connor felt a thrill as they passed the police station, where he was sure his absence would soon be realised.

Why was he doing this?

The only emotion he could draw on was his guilt, and the panic at losing the life he'd built for himself and pushed him to make things right, even though he'd been more than happy to throw it all away for Penny.

That wasn't possible anymore, and he knew he was too pathetic to rebuild a new life on his own. As the taxi pulled onto the A404 from the Handy Cross roundabout, Connor stared out of the window as the trees rushed by. It was a brief drive, with the driver turning off at the next junction, before he navigated the series of small, inconvenient roundabouts on the approach to Marlow. As they pulled onto the road of Connor's office, he felt his heartbeat quicken at the sight of Abby's car parked in the usual spot.

'Just here, mate.'

The taxi pulled in behind the car, and Connor paid and then stepped out. Without the keys to the office, he pressed the intercom button and thankfully, with the rain picking up, Abby buzzed in to let him into reception. Connor stepped in, shaking the rain from his coat, as Abby appeared at the next door with a face like thunder.

'What the hell do you want?' she demanded as she opened the door.

'Please, Abby. Let me explain.'

She glared at him once more, drinking in how pathetic he appeared, before she stepped back in and left the door open as an invitation. Connor took a deep breath and then followed, ready to lay on the charm that had won her over so many times before.

Make promises he would be determined to keep.

Grovel if he had to.

But as he stepped into the main office of their accountancy business, he saw his suitcase leaning against his desk, and Abby leant against hers with her arms folded.

'You've got two minutes,' she stated coldly. Connor looked at his suitcase.

'What is this?' he asked, ramping up the pain in his voice.

'One minute fifty.'

'Okay, okay.' Connor held up his hands. 'I fucked up, Abby. Jason came to me a few years ago, and he threatened to go to the police about Miller. I told him it wouldn't do anything, but he said he'd go to the press and drag our name and our business through the mud.'

'You should have told me,' Abby insisted.

'I know.' Connor shook his head and took a step towards her. 'Together, we can face anything.'

He reached out a hand with a smile, but as he brushed Abby's arm, she jerked away from him. Angrily, she lifted his laptop from the desk, flipped it open and then spun it round and shoved it into his arms.

'Explain that then.'

With his hands shaking, he tapped in his password, and the screen opened up on the private messages of his social media account. Abby knew his passwords and had opened up the chat with Penny.

270

It was all there in front of him.

The sickening flirting.

The confirmation he'd sent that he thought she looked great naked.

The plans to meet up.

The lies he'd tell Abby about meeting the guys for a drink.

The desperate messages he'd sent after she'd left the hotel and hadn't picked up her phone.

All the evidence that Connor Davis was a lying, cheating rat and as he turned to his wife, his heart broke at the sight of the angry tears running down her face. Symbolically, she pulled the eternity and wedding rings she'd proudly worn on her left hand, and dropped them onto the laptop keyboard. She then dropped the car keys on top as well.

'You can keep the car.'

'Babe, please…' Connor began, but Abby just lifted her hand to cut him off. She took a deep breath, wiped her tears, and then fixed him with a look of pure hatred.

'You can keep the car,' she repeated. 'But I'm going to take everything else from you. Now get the fuck out, Connor.'

With tears sliding down his cheeks, Connor realised he had no fight left in him. This was a mess of his own making, and as he feebly turned, he slid Abby's wedding ring into his pocket and then tucked his laptop under his arm. As he dragged his suitcase to the door, he heard his wife weeping behind him and he stepped out into the rain and dumped his suitcase in the back of the car.

He drove.

There was no real direction, and no real attention paid to the road, and after three or four hours of mindless miles, he realised he'd basically looped Buckinghamshire a few times and was now heading down towards Beaconsfield.

He pulled into the car park of a quaint little hotel and checked his phone.

Out of battery.

Probably for the best, and although he wanted to call Abby and try to work things out, doing it while he was drunk probably wasn't a good idea.

And he planned on getting very drunk indeed.

As he stepped out of his car and headed to the entrance of the hotel to enquire about a room, he stopped to allow a red car to pull into the car park space beside him, and he wandered in.

They had room.

He paid whatever.

He didn't care.

As the sky darkened and the rain picked up, Connor sat in the corner of the hotel bar, looking limply out into the darkness, and intermittently lifting and sipping his pint. Instead of getting wasted, he'd decided to freshen up, get a decent meal, and then try to collect his thoughts over a few drinks.

He charged his phone, but he still hadn't had the nerve to turn it back on.

He's assume it would have been peppered by the insufferable Detective Inspector King, who was likely hunting him.

What was he going to do?

He drew up a plan in his mind to smooth things over with the police, and then do whatever it took to win Abby back. With a worried sigh, he booted up his phone, and instantly messages and voicemails began to ping. As he processed the avalanche of messages, the young waitress in the bar placed a drink down on his table. Confused, he looked up at her.

'Sorry, love. I didn't order this.'

'It's from the woman at the bar.' The young woman

arched her neck towards a brunette sitting with her back to them. She then gave Connor a wink. 'I guess she doesn't want to drink alone.'

Connor chuckled to himself. Throughout all the turmoil of the past twenty-four hours, he was still drawn to the idea of being desirable to women.

Abby had told him to get stuffed, after all.

He knew it wasn't worth the hassle, but the least he could do was go and thank the mysterious brunette and indulge her in a conversation over the drink she'd sent his way.

'Well, I better go and thank her then.'

The waitress smiled and went about her job, and Connor lifted the drink up as the woman turned.

Did he recognise her?

Either way, she lifted her drink from across the room and he did likewise and took a big gulp.

It didn't take long for the drugs that she'd slipped into it to take effect.

CHAPTER FORTY-FOUR

The temptation to have a drink was getting stronger by the hour, and King knew if she didn't leave the station, she'd have been in the pub by now.

Or worse, sprawled out on her sofa with an empty bottle of wine in her hand, another on the table, and a hangover from hell to look forward to. Hall had roared into her office with a face like thunder when the news of Davis's disappearance had filtered through to him and after he read her the riot act, King had taken it out on the rest of the team.

Townsend had taken the brunt of it.

She knew there was an escalating situation brewing between her and her detective, but right now, there were bigger things to worry about than her perceived betrayal. Townsend might have been bullish at the best of times, downright stubborn at others, but his heart was in the right place.

But right now, his mind wasn't.

And DCI Lowe wasn't helping matters either.

As soon as Townsend had tried to apologise, she'd barked at him to get his arse out on the streets and find

Davis. Her tone was so sharp, that even Townsend knew not to push back. With him out of the way, poor Nic had taken the brunt of her mood, as her inability to track down Gemma Miller just riled King up even more.

King tried to call Connor.

The call wouldn't connect.

She tried again and again.

She left message after message, and eventually, she got through to Abby Davis, who informed them that Connor had turned up at the office, but she'd sent him packing. King didn't blame her.

She knew firsthand what it was like to discover that your husband was a snake.

The only useful bit of information they had was that Connor was in Abby's car, and she put out an ANPR on the vehicle and prayed that they'd get a hit.

Soon, the already darkened sky turned black, and the town mocked her as it burst into festive brightness, with the automatic Christmas lights that lined every fence and lamppost exploded to life.

All King wanted was a drink.

It had been five long months since she'd last let a drop of it touch her lips, but the willpower she'd clung to for so long was spilling from her like a leak.

Just one drink would be fine.

As Hannon intimated that she needed to leave, King grunted at her, making a sly remark about dedication and Hannon left dejected.

It was cruel.

King regretted it immediately.

But the addiction was seeping through her every decision, clouding every thought. No one ever truly recovers from alcoholism, or any addiction. Every day was a continuous fight to not fall back into that familiar, reliant pattern and every morning, when you'd made it through another day, you promised yourself you'd take another step further away from the person you used to be.

But the person King used to be was able to push the pressure away with a bottle of wine and as she stared up at the board, with the faces of the deceased staring back at her, she felt her body shaking. The names of the women murdered by Baycroft once again filtered through her mind, and the brutal assessment from the murderous priest that her drinking had let them all down.

But the Gallaghers and Penny Durant were dead, and she hadn't touched a drop.

So why bother with sobriety if it didn't make a difference?

Townsend returned, soaked through and in need of a supportive word, but all King could muster was a 'talk tomorrow' and then left him to wallow in his own worry.

And she regretted it now.

Now, as she sat at the back of the community hall, she looked around at the other people doing their best to overcome the struggle of alcoholism, and she wondered if any of them had been so cruel to the people they needed most. It wasn't the usual meeting she attended, which she'd selected to ensure she was far enough away from her life so as not to be recognised.

This one was slap bang in the middle of town, as when Hall finally told her to leave the office, she knew there was only one other place she would go.

And it wasn't home.

With the myriad pubs along High Wycombe High Street all offering a warm chair and a chilled glass of house wine, it took every bit of her willpower to walk past them and to the meeting. It hadn't been laid out in the usual circle, and the chairs were in neat rows as if people were attending a seminar. But she'd quietly shuffled to the back row, slumped into a chair and bowed her head. She absorbed the words of the other people, all of them sharing their pain and the reasons why they wanted to be better.

She remembered hers.

Lauren Grainger. Natasha Stokes. Michaela Woods. Irena Roslova.

She had three names to add to the list.

She didn't want to add anymore.

Her phone buzzed, and she quickly made her exit, ignoring the few heads that turned to watch as she slid her chair across the tiled floor.

They had a hit on Connor's car.

Within minutes, she burst through the doors of the High Wycombe Police Station, her lungs burning from the sprint she'd just undertaken. She threw her wet coat onto one of the chairs of the SCU and booted up her computer, opening up the CCTV footage she'd demanded from the officers who'd located the car and checked out the venue.

It had been spotted in the car park of the Western Barn Inn, a small, expensive hotel in the more rural parts of Beaconsfield. It had lovely grounds, and although the prices were extortionate, it was seemingly very popular with the inner-city crowd who wanted a taste of the coun-tryside. The two officers had spoken to the manager, who confirmed that Connor Davis had checked in, but the last he'd seen of him was in the bar. A discussion with the bartender led them to the CCTV, where they confirmed her claims that he seemingly hit it off with a woman at the bar and the last she saw, he was drunkenly following her out to her car.

King opened the CCTV footage of the car park and felt every muscle in her body tighten to breaking point.

The clear footage showed Connor stumbling through the door, before a petite woman with brown hair looped his arm over her shoulder and led him to a car. Even from the black and white footage, she could make a logical guess it was a red one.

She also knew that Connor Davis wasn't drunk.

From experience, and from her knowledge as a police officer, it was clear that he was under the effects of drugs.

With no one around to question her, the woman pushed him into the backseat of the car, and just before she got into the driver's seat, she looked up towards the camera and King saw her face clearly for the first time.

She was looking at Gemma Miller.

As the car reversed back into the car park and then drove out of shot, King lifted her phone and called Townsend, not giving a damn about the time.

He answered on the third ring, and he didn't seem pleased to hear from her.

When she spoke, she got his attention.

'She's got Connor.'

CHAPTER FORTY-FIVE

A dull ache in the back of his head slowly drew Connor Davis awake, and as he tried to open his eyes, he felt the sharp brightness of the spotlight pointed right at him. He tried to sit up, but was pulled back against the metal unit and the collision sent another shockwave through his skull.

His brain felt like it was in a blender.

Carefully, he tried to move, but thick, plastic zip ties around his wrists dug into his skin, causing him to grunt with pain before relenting.

He was tied up.

His head was pounding, and just as he began to question how many drinks he'd knocked back, fragments of the evening began to appear.

The woman at the bar.

The free drink.

Had he been drugged?

Unable to move, a panic began to set in and as he screamed for help, a voice cut him off from somewhere in the darkness.

'No one can hear you.'

It was a woman's voice.

The one from the bar?

'Please, what is this?' Connor asked, trying to focus his blurred vision beyond the bright spotlight. He was in some kind of hardware store, pinned to one of the thick metal units that were stacked with large pallets. He was halfway down a long aisle, and beyond the relentless glow of the spotlight, the entire building was bathed in shadow. From the aisle behind him, he could hear the clanking of feet on metal, and moments later, a thick cable dropped down onto his lap.

The end was tied in a noose.

The realisation set in, and Connor felt his heart begin to pound in his chest.

'Please. Whatever this is, we can figure it out.' Connor yelled into the darkness, as behind him, he heard someone shuffling down a ladder. The footsteps thumped up the aisle, fading in volume, before they grew again, and a masked figure emerged into the light. The frame was small, clearly a woman, but the black balaclava over her face sent a shiver down Connor's sweaty spine. 'Please, I have a family.'

The masked woman took a step towards him and then squatted down, mindful to keep her distance.

'You were happy to throw that family away yesterday,' the woman sneered through the mask. 'So don't try to use them as a bargaining chip.'

'What do you want?' Connor looked up at her. 'If it's money, I can give you money.'

'I don't want money.' The voice was cold.

'Then what? Come on, we can figure something out.' Connor begged, and the woman disappeared once more, and moments later, Connor heard the snap of a ladder shutting, and then the footsteps headed back in his direction. 'The police are looking for me. They'll be here any minute.'

'No, they won't,' the woman said with little emotion, stepping back into the light and carefully setting the ladder up a few feet from the man. 'Nobody knows you're here.'

The reality was terrifying, and Connor once again pulled against the cable ties with all his might, the sharp plastic breaking the skin and drawing blood. He hoped it would act as a lubricant, but when he shifted the open wound against the plastic, the pain thundered up to his already thumping skull and caused him to yell in pain.

The woman's head snapped towards him, and she marched over and once again squatted near her.

'The more you struggle, the worse this will be for you.' She peered at him with hatred in her eyes. 'Now…this might sting ever so slightly.'

Connor's eyes flickered to the small leather pouch she laid out on the floor, and he gasped in horror as she opened it, revealing a syringe and a vial of liquid.

'Please. I'll do anything.'

'Then hold fucking still,' she barked, and despite his best efforts to dodge it, she managed to plunge the needle into his neck and pumped the drugs into his body. 'This is a nifty little drug. Well, a combination of them, really. It relaxes your muscles, which makes you a little more obedient. But the best part is, it heightens any sensation to a nerve ending.' She leant in and whispered into his ear. 'Which means what happens next will hurt like hell.'

Connor's eyes widened with fear, but as he tried to fight against his restraints, he could feel the drug sweeping through his bloodstream, and as she'd warned him, he felt his muscles weakening.

The fight was leaving him swiftly.

Knowing what awaited him, he was unable to do anything as the woman draped the slack noose over his head, fixing it nicely across his clavicle, and then she pulled it tight, the cable pulling tightly against his neck.

He murmured something, probably begging her to stop, but he couldn't manage it.

All he could do was sit and let her position him for the afterlife.

The woman smirked through her mask, and reached out with a gloved hand and roughly pulled his jaw up to face her.

'You really should have kept your mouth shut.'

He could see the pliers in her hand, and although he tried to resist, she yanked his mouth open and clamped them down on his tongue. The sensitive muscle sent pain screaming up into his brain, but he couldn't move.

Couldn't fight it.

The woman lifted a box cutter and slid the razor-sharp blade out, and Connor roared with agony as she began roughly severing his tongue from his mouth. Blood gushed down his chin, across his teeth, and he gurgled it as he screamed in agony.

It was over in six seconds.

It had felt like six hours.

The woman stepped back, her gloves and sleeves coated in his blood, and she looked at his tongue and then simply dropped it on the floor. Connor was heaving, the pain unbearable, and the tears poured from his eyes as he slumped forward, the bloodied stump of his tongue like a flame in his mouth.

He felt the cable ties snap from his wrists and he fell forward, catching himself on his trembling hands before he hit the ground. The pain was inconceivable, and it took everything within his weak body not to pass out. He reached out with quivering fingers for his tongue, but the woman pressed her boot down on his hand, pinning it to the floor. As she squatted down, he could feel the pressure breaking the bones in his hand.

'Climb the ladder,' she commanded.

He shook his head.

Tried to tell her to fuck off, but it came out as just a bloodied dribble.

The woman sighed and pulled off her mask and then yanked his head back by the hair. His eyes widened with horror.

Although the years had been kind to her, and she was now a striking woman, Gemma Miller's furious scowl burrowed into him. He thought back to Friday night, when he thought he'd seen her at the reunion, and now, as their eyes locked, he understood exactly what was happening.

She was there to kill him.

No matter what.

'Look at this.' Gemma held up her phone, which had a picture of Abby dropping the girls off at school. 'I took that this morning.' She grinned. 'While you were at the police station. I know when and where your family are at what time, so if you don't want me to add their three tongues to my collection, then I suggest you get up the fucking ladder.'

Connor felt the sudden surge of fear manifest itself within him, and in his panic, he emptied the contents of his stomach on the floor before him. The vomit was thick with the blood he'd swallowed, and as Gemma took a step back from it, Connor managed to push himself to his knees and began to weep. Gemma just stared at him, patiently waiting, and sure enough, Connor pulled himself up via the first few rungs of the ladder and slowly began to climb. There was enough slack in the cable that had been looped through the metal fixtures, and when he finally got to the top of the ladder, Gemma marched out of the spot-light and into the darkness.

He was too weak to move.

The drugs pumping through his body had stripped him

of any real movement, and it was only his love for his kids and for Abby that had pushed him to the top of the ladder.

The agony was unrelenting.

The blood loss was beginning to add to his nausea.

He felt the cable tighten around his neck as Gemma yanked it back through and Connor almost collapsed from the ladder. It was now digging into his skin, and any sudden movement from the ladder would be fatal. The cable was fastened somewhere in the darkness, and Gemma once again appeared in the light, looking up at her victim with hatred in her eyes and vengeance in her soul.

His life began to race through his mind, peppered with moments of happiness from his childhood, to the milestone moments of his wedding and the birth of his beautiful girls.

Gemma took a step towards the ladder.

Connor tried to say sorry, but all he could do was feebly dribble onto his blood-soaked shirt.

'Don't say a word,' Gemma whispered sinisterly, and then, as the final image of Abby and his daughters flashed in Connor's mind, she booted the ladder out from underneath him. Gravity summoned him to the ground, but the cable snapped tight, and Connor gasped for air as his body twitched, doing whatever it could to survive. As he felt the vessels in his eyes begin to burst, he took one final glance at Gemma, who watched him unflinchingly.

He feebly clawed once or twice.

His body gave a final few twitches.

Then Gemma turned, pulled her mask back on and disappeared into the darkness, leaving Connor Davis's corpse hanging in the air, with a small dribble of blood trickling onto the concrete below.

CHAPTER FORTY-SIX

Connor Davis's body was discovered shortly after seven a.m. by the shop's security guard and the young assistant manager who had passed out at the brutal sight of the man's execution.

The police and ambulance were called to the hardware store, and as the morning traffic began to build along the main road, public interest in the swarm of emergency vehicles grew and spread across social media like a virus. A group of interested onlookers had gathered by the wall, which the uniformed police were using as a cordon, while another young officer braved the elements and the morning rush-hour impatience to direct the traffic on the main road to allow for more emergency vehicles to gain access to the store car park.

The same young officer guided Townsend through the steadily building chaos, and he pulled up beside the SOCO van, with the team already inside the building to preserve the crime scene. As he stepped out into the cold drizzle, he felt the water splash against his face, clinging to the thickening stubble that clung to his face as evidence of a long and tiring week. The bags under his eyes also weren't helping, as a disgruntled King greeted him.

'You look shattered,' she said, her tone indicating he still wasn't in her good books.

'I hardly slept,' Townsend responded.

Neither of them had. When King had called Townsend the night before to confirm Miller had Connor, he'd insisted on coming back to the office. Mandy hadn't been thrilled, and he knew he run the risk of her wrath as he threw on his coat and headed for the door.

This was the job.

They both knew it.

But the intensity of the case, and the relentless chasing of ghosts, had begun to push him away from the family.

He was missing dinners.

He'd made no more progress with his reading of *Matilda* with Eve.

And the lack of sleep and the pressure of King's cold shoulder had ebbed away at his patience. That only worsened when he'd arrived at the station to get to work, and King stuck him on CCTV duty. He wanted to be out on the streets, chasing down leads and doing his level best to save Connor, but he had to follow orders.

He had to accept that he was being sidelined.

The two of them entered the building, checking their names with the officer at the door, before they followed the commotion down aisle fifteen. As they approached, Townsend scanned his eyes over the display of new lawnmowers that the shop offered, and accepted his descent into middle age as he made a mental note to come back and buy one.

Connor's body was hanging motionless from the cable.

Both King and Townsend stopped for a second as they rounded the corner, appalled by the horrific scene before them, and Townsend's heart went out to the two staff members who had discovered him. As they approached, they could see the long streak of blood that slathered his chin and the front of his shirt. He'd long since bled out, but the shiny, red puddle beneath him showed it would have taken a little while.

The tight cable around his neck told them his death would have been quick, albeit painful.

'Jesus.' King uttered as they approached. Beneath the body, one of the SOCO members was snapping photos, collecting the visual evidence, while the others tagged a few items that had been left behind.

A battery powered spotlight.

A ladder that lay strewn across the floor a few feet away.

A bloodstained box cutter.

A severed tongue.

The urge for a drink lapped at the edges of King's mind like a rising tide and she rubbed her temples with frustration.

'You okay, Guv?' Townsend asked.

'I'm fine,' King snapped. 'This is just getting out of hand.'

'You can say that again.' The booming voice of Detective Superintendent Hall echoed behind them, and the two detectives spun and stood to attention. Usually, the cordial senior officer would have waved off their respect to his rank, but not today. Instead, he beckoned King with his finger. 'Izzy. A word.'

King shot a glance to Townsend.

'Eyes open,' she stated, before purposefully marching back down the aisle. Hall had taken himself down another aisle for privacy, and when King approached, she realised it wasn't for another private pep talk.

'Sir, we are well aware how this looks—'

'Are you?' Hall cut in angrily. 'Because let me tell you, Izzy, it looks pretty grim from where I'm standing.'

'We have a theory that her murders are based on suicides because—'

'Not the fucking crime scene,' Hall barked quietly through gritted teeth. 'I mean for you. And your entire SCU. Do you know what happens when a specialist team doesn't deliver on its supposed speciality? It gets canned, Izzy.'

'Sir, come on.'

'Look. I've given you all more than enough rope,' Hall insisted, struggling to keep his voice down. 'I have backed you all to the hilt. I always have, Izzy. You know that.'

'Yes, sir,' she agreed sadly. It was true.

'I even stepped in when your personal issues became a problem. I protected you, and you promised me you had them under control.'

'Sir, I haven't touched a drop—'

'Then fucking act like it,' Hall said firmly. 'You've got a detective working alongside CID on another case, and now we've got the local media swarming around and sensationalising the idea of another serial killer in town. You told me on Monday you had this under control, Izzy. It's now Thursday and we've got two more dead bodies and what? A ghost? A name we can't track down?'

'Sir, we are doing everything we can.'

'Well do more,' Hall said and then sighed, shaking his head. 'Izzy. There are some things I can't protect you from. Now, I'm going to head out there and face the media and I'll put up as much of a wall as I can. But get your head straight, get your fucking team in order and, for god's sake, find me this killer.'

It was rare for Hall to speak with such aggression, but King knew that the pressure he was applying was just a fraction of that being placed on him. She looked back through the large, metal shelving fixtures that separated the aisles, and could see the SOCOs hard at work.

She wondered how much of their conversation had travelled via echo to the rest of the team.

Finally, she turned back to Hall.

'Yes, Sir.'

Hall huffed once more and straightened his jacket and then stepped past her. As he did, he gave her a reassuring pat on the shoulder, and then stomped away, his boots echoing loudly against the concrete. King took a moment, fighting the urge to head straight to a pub, and then she marched back to the crime scene, where Townsend was squatting down, inspecting the box cutter.

'Come on, Jack. Let's go.'

'Might be worth checking with Mitchell if this blade matches the one used on—'

'I said let's go.' King snapped, drawing a few looks from the masked SOCOs, and Townsend slowly got to his feet. Not waiting for him, King marched back through the store, her head swirling with the constant reminders of pressure, the need for her results, Townsend's reluctance to listen and the wave of her alcoholic craving crashing on top of all of them.

She needed some air.

As she burst out through the door and into the car park, she could see across the empty lot that a group of reporters had gathered near the far wall and Hall was already laying on a charm offensive.

He'd tell them to remain calm.

Not to spread panic.

To respect the privacy and grief of those who had lost loved ones.

But they would do none of it.

As she scanned the growing crowd of onlookers, Townsend finally caught up with her.

'Guv, you want to tell me what that was about?' he said with a frown.

'I gave you an order, and you weren't listening.'

'This isn't the army,' Townsend retorted. 'I know this is going to hell in a handbasket, but don't take it out on me.'

'That's the thing, Jack. Twice now, *twice*, it's on you.' King unloaded. 'You've been so caught up in trying to prove yourself to Lowe that you've been sloppy. I told you that you were spreading yourself too thin, but you just didn't listen.'

'That's unfair,' Townsend said, genuinely hurt.

'Is it? Because if you weren't on the phone to him on Monday, you wouldn't have just let Gemma Miller walk away. Or better yet, open the fucking door for her.'

'You were there, too. Remember?' Townsend felt the need to defend himself. 'You were the one trying to put the shits up Connor Davis, and I suggested he hadn't done it.'

'But we didn't know that, did we?'

'Nor did we know that Gemma was at the service.' Townsend shook his head. 'What is with you lately? Whatever it is, you need to sort it out.'

'Do I?' King could feel her temper rising. 'Maybe I should have a cosy chat with my ex-husband and let the one person we knew was a target leave the fucking police station. Do you want to tell his wife and kids what happened?'

It was a low blow.

Essentially, laying the blame at Townsend's feet wasn't her intention, but her mind was rattled. Everything was beginning to crack, and the only idea she could cling to was the bottle of wine she needed to pick up on the way home.

Her words had clearly hurt Townsend, who looked completely deflated.

The silence sat between them for a few moments, with

both of them hoping the downpour would wash away the broken pieces of their trust that had just shattered before them.

Townsend eventually shook his head.

'I've got work to do,' he said through gritted teeth.

'Take the day off,' King said coldly. 'In fact, take the next couple.'

'Don't take me off this case,' Townsend pleaded.

'Just go home, Jack,' King said with a shake of the head. 'Or better yet, ask Lowe if he has a spare desk in his office. He could always use another lap dog.'

Townsend went to respond, but King just pulled her collar up and marched past him towards her car. As she walked, she could feel her conscience trying to wrestle control of her body and spin her around to apologise.

But she kept walking.

Maybe, on some level, it would be good for Townsend. Would refocus him.

Sharpen him up.

He was a good detective, and better still, a good person. But even the best people needed reasons and opportunities to grow.

That's what she'd tell herself, she thought.

At least until she could drink enough to wash away the five names that had kept her sober for the past five months.

And the four new ones that had led her back to the brink of the bottle.

CHAPTER FORTY-SEVEN

There were three empty cups of coffee dotted around Hannon's desk, and with a long, drawn-out yawn, she reached for the fourth. King had called her when they'd confirmed that Connor Davis had been abducted, and she'd slunk out of bed carefully so as not to wake Shilpa to take the call.

Fifteen minutes later, she was on her way to the station, and had been met by a highly strung King, who looked like she was on the verge of snapping. As much as she admired her boss, Hannon couldn't help but think that things would be easier for DI King if she just opened up a little more, or extended a hand for some help, but the admirable determination would never allow it. King had curtly cut off Townsend when he'd suggested a few avenues of investigation, and she'd dumped him in a corner with the monotonous task of tracking CCTV footage to try to pinpoint her car.

Hannon felt for him.

While she hadn't been privy to the conversations that had seemingly escalated between the two, she'd pieced together enough to understand that two very powerful personalities had collided.

King was about following the facts and dedicating every millisecond of thought to the case in hand.

Townsend was slightly more mercurial, following his instincts, which, in his brief time in the SCU, had proven to be just as effective.

It was an irresistible force colliding with an immovable object, and although King was right when she'd stated that the Beckford case was now the responsibility of CID, there was no way that Townsend could walk away from it until it had been solved.

King had taken Townsend's frequent chats with DCI Lowe personally, although Hannon felt that Townsend having to spend time with that insufferable man was punishment enough.

Nevertheless, the tension in the team was beginning to weigh them down and no matter how strong a bond was, if you apply too much pressure to it, it would snap.

When the call came in that a body had been found, Townsend and King had disappeared, and Hannon had continued her own lines of investigation. She'd been researching the components of anaesthetics used within the veterinary world and had sent a message to Dr Mitchell at the local hospital to get in contact as soon as she could. Minutes after Hannon had been left to her own devices, her phone buzzed.

'DC Hannon,' she said as professionally as possible.

'Nic.' It was Mitchell. 'That's a very formal greeting.'

'Well, I like to be polite,' Hannon said with a grin. Even on a wet, dreary winter morning overshadowed by another murder, Dr Mitchell had a way of bringing some sunshine. 'Sorry to have messaged you so early.'

'Oh, don't be silly. How can I help?'

Hannon proceeded to fill Mitchell in on what they'd discovered, and the possibility that their killer had extensive training as a veterinarian, which would explain her proficiency when it came to the drugs she'd been using. She rattled off a list of components used to numb or put animals to sleep, and Mitchell asked for a few moments to cross check them against her own findings in the bodies of the deceased Gallaghers. She had sent off for the bloodwork to be done on poor Penny Durant, but it hadn't come back yet.

But sure enough, there were traces of pentobarbital, which in high doses could render an animal unconscious.

Pump enough into a human, and the same thing would occur.

Hannon thanked her and hung up, and started the arduous process of shifting through veterinary clinics to try and find any record of Miller. She knew it was a fool's errand to start with, and quickly moved on to try and locate any digital footprint for the woman.

It was a dead end.

Her head pounded.

She needed another coffee.

Hannon headed out into the rain and up the hill to her favourite coffee spot, and she must have looked as tired as she felt as the burly owner told her this one was on the house. Reggie held a lot of respect for the boys in blue, and often gave Hannon a discount, but today he told her it looked like she needed a pick-me-up.

He wasn't wrong.

By the time Hannon had wondered back down the hill to the station, she'd decided to try a different line of enquiry. There were over thirty statements taken from the memorial service on Monday, when Gemma Miller hand delivered the tongues for the world to see.

A few of them mentioned her by name.

Was there anything else?

She spent the next hour and a half trawling through the recorded statements, finding herself judging the varying levels of competency from the uniformed officers. Some of them were barely a few sentences long. Some of them were extensive, offering more detail than necessary.

But then her eyes widened with excitement.

One of them might have been a golden ticket.

As she read through the statement again, her attention spun to the door as a soaking wet DI King marched in, her face seemingly in a perma-scowl.

'You okay, guv?' she asked, and then waited a few moments. 'Where's Jack?'

'He's gone home,' King said curtly, her tone suggesting that it wasn't for his health, nor would it be wise to offer a follow-up question. She sighed as she looked at Swaby's empty desk. 'We could sure use Michelle right now.'

'I know. Just her singing alone would be a nice distraction,' Hannon said with a smile. 'I spoke with her last night. She's coming back down today. Rich and the boys should be back next week. You could call her? She might be able to get in—'

'No, no.' King waved off the idea. 'She's got enough on her plate at the moment.'

'So…how was it?'

'Grim,' King said as she moved Connor's photo to the top of the murder board alongside Miller's other victims. 'The man had been hung from the rafters.'

'Jesus,' Hannon said to herself. 'And his tongue?'

'She left that on the floor for us this time.'

'How considerate.'

'Yup. I know you didn't like the man, Nic, but he does leave behind a pretty devastated wife and two kids.'

'I know,' Hannon said firmly. 'We do this for them.'

'We do this for them.' King echoed with pride.

'Well, I might have something,' Hannon said, turning

back to her screen and King strode across the room to her. 'I went back through the statements from Monday and you know how a few people said that they saw Gemma Miller?'

'Yes.'

'Well, this one here says that he saw her at the school last week.'

King shook her head and sighed.

'Connor Davis already said that he was sure he had seen her at the party on Friday. We have the CCTV footage.'

'No…this person said he was pretty sure he saw her there last week when he picked his daughter up from school.'

King stepped back in confusion and then leant in and read the statement. As she got through to the end, her eyes lit up and she patted Hannon on the shoulder.

'Great work, Nic. Call this…Stephen Lewis and confirm it. If he does, then we need to get to the school immediately.'

Hannon wasted little time, and after reassuring a nervous Mr Lewis that they just wanted to confirm what he said in his statement, he seemed relatively sure that he'd seen Gemma Miller at the school last week.

'You know when you recognise someone but can't place them exactly? But yeah, I'm pretty sure that it was her.'

Hannon thanked him, and minutes later, she and King were heading towards the car park. Just before they made it to the door, DCI Lowe called after King, and she sighed and excused herself for a few moments. Hannon made an excuse and headed to the bathroom, and when she returned a few minutes later, King was waiting, seemingly deep in thought.

What had Lowe said to her?

As they approached King's car, Hannon glanced across to the empty space where Townsend had been parked when she'd arrived late last night, and she felt saddened that his and King's relationship had deteriorated to the point that he'd been sidelined.

Perhaps she could talk King round on the way to the school?

It was an opportunity, but Hannon knew that King wouldn't want to talk about it.

It wasn't who she was.

It was clear she was going through something difficult, but was too proud or too stubborn to share.

Besides, the only topic of conversation was one they started as soon as they slammed the car doors shut and the engine roared to life.

Had Gemma Miller been within reach this entire time?

CHAPTER FORTY-EIGHT

As he blew out his cheeks and rocked back in his chair, Lowe looked across the various stacks of paperwork that had managed to find their way to his desk.

Reports.

Statements.

Meeting minutes.

A budget plan that he needed to *get on board with* that had been designed and signed off by people who had never run a case or walked the beat in their life.

Holiday requests he'd have to turn down.

Basically, an endless sea of written words that would pin him to his desk for the next few hours, keeping him from finding out who had left Jamal Beckford to bleed out alone and shivering in the winter rain.

This was the job.

It was one that he took great pride in, and one he had been doing for nearly two decades. From as young as he could remember, he'd wanted to be a police officer and he knew it was his dad's influence that had pushed him down that path. Growing up in East London in the early eighties as a black kid had been tough at times, but it paled in comparison to what his father had faced when he'd moved to the UK with Lowe's grandparents in the late sixties. Although his grandparents found a Nigerian community to connect with, racism was still rife in the country's capital, and Lowe's father worked his fingers to the bone to provide a better life for his son than the one he had gone through.

He worked two jobs, while Lowe's mother worked part time as a cleaner and raised him and his two older sisters.

Lowe watched as his father did everything he could to provide and to keep Lowe away from the gang culture that infested the inner-city estates where they grew up.

During his teenage years, as Lowe flirted on the fringes of the local gang, his father simply had one chat with him that would change his life.

'Marcus. You are old enough now to determine what kind of man you want to be. A man who tries his best to leave a better world behind him, or a man who only adds to its decay. There's goodness inside you, son. But it's up to you whether you let it out, or you hide it from the world.'

His father passed away two weeks later from a heart attack.

From that moment on, Lowe dedicated his time to his studies, achieving straight A's at his GCSEs before achieving the same at college. With his attention turned to law, Lowe studied criminology at the University College of London, refusing to move away for the 'student life' so he could help his ageing mother in the early stages of her dementia.

She at least survived long enough to see him attain his distinction and pass out as a Metropolitan Police Officer one year later.

After his mother moved on to join his father, Lowe found that success and attention came easily. He was a strapping man at six foot two, with an impressive physique and the gift of the gab. His silver tongue made him a tremendously effective police officer, especially when, on the rare occasion his words didn't work, his brawn would often suffice.

Senior figures took note, and when the time came for him to take his detective's exam, Lowe was already high on the list of rising talent within the service. The fact that he was from a minority background was an added bonus.

He excelled in CID, forging a tremendous partnership with Staunton, as well as his blossoming romance with Isabella King, and as he now sat in his office, he sometimes regretted how things turned out with her.

She wasn't a bad person.

He had just treated her badly.

As they'd approached their thirties and their thrill of the job slowly morphed into the thrill of parenthood, they moved out to the sticks, only to discover that their ability to conceive was compromised.

Lowe knew his behaviour was befitting his name, but he found a new comfort in the arms of Maria, and his marriage to King drew to its conclusion.

The only way to face the potential backlash, and his deep hidden self-loathing, was to act boorishly ignorant of his behaviour and it soon became as natural as breathing. He had the record to back up his arrogance, and the swagger and good looks to own the rooms he walked into.

That would have been enough to take control of CID as he moved up to Detective Chief Inspector, but the fact still remained, he was a damn good detective.

Which was why he was hellbent on giving DS Jack Townsend such a hard time.

The man reminded Lowe of himself. Only the cocky swagger was replaced by a calm understanding of himself. Everything about the man seemed considered, and even in the face of Lowe's aggressive provocation, Townsend had kept his cool.

Hell, he'd even shut Lowe's lights out in the boxing ring.

Sending him to Wembley had been a way of putting the Scouse detective in his place, but it was also to see what he was made of.

It was one thing being calm when being run down by a DCI.

It was another thing entirely to be calm in the face of a dangerous gang.

But Townsend had done what he'd expected, and that was walking into the lion's den and pulling the lion by its tail.

The man had no fear.

Had proven, through his time undercover and by the way he charged in to stop Baycroft from murdering DI King, that he was willing to go above and beyond for the right thing.

DS Jack Townsend was going to be a hell of a detective, and Lowe knew in his gut that if he could convince him to come to CID, then the sky was the limit for the lad.

A notification flashed up on his screen.

It was time for a briefing with the higher brass about the Beckford case. Although his ex-wife played the victim of being under immense pressure from Hall to tie up the increasing deaths, there was still sustained pressure on him to find out who had murdered Beckford and left him for the world to find.

What annoyed Lowe most, however, was the lack of attention people were paying to it.

Four white, middle-class people had been killed and the whole town was going into a panic. But a young black man found with a stab wound just didn't seem to register with them as a concern.

But it did to Townsend.

That was why Lowe had kept him in the loop.

Winding up King about it was just a bit of fun, but as he headed to his meeting, Lowe saw his ex-wife and DC Hannon headed for the car park.

'Izzy…' he called out and the two women turned. 'Can I grab a word?'

He watched as she sighed, and then Hannon shuffled off to the bathroom as Lowe approached.

'What?' she said with a shrug.

He deserved even less courtesy.

'Are you okay?' he asked sincerely. 'I know things are a bit rough right now but I—'

'I'm fine.' She snapped. He knew when she was lying, but he smiled and nodded.

'Okay. Just make sure if you're struggling to reach out.'

'To you?' She scoffed. 'What do you want, Marcus?'

'I heard you sent Townsend home.'

'Yeah. Because he's too busy working with you and it's impacting our investigation.'

Lowe lifted his hands apologetically.

As his father had said – he could either let his goodness out or hide it from the world.

'That's on me,' Lowe said. 'Townsend was following orders from me, and I made it clear I was his superior. So, give me grief if you have to, but you and I both know that you have a better chance of finding your killer with Jack onside.'

'And why is that?'

Lowe sighed.

'You're going to make me say it?' He raised his eyebrows. King waited. 'Fine…because he's a damn good detective. And plus, he has you with him.'

The kindness caught King off guard, and Lowe's phone buzzed.

He was late.

He turned and walked away from Izzy, knowing she'd struggle to believe his act of kindness. But he'd meant it.

Not for any other reason other than they had two separate ongoing murder cases, and neither one was helped by Townsend's absence, or their seemingly endless rivalry.

Sometimes, Lowe knew, he needed to curtail his own ego for the good of the case.

It was on him to put the necessary pieces together, to get them working properly.

He was the head of CID.

He was the best detective in the Thames Valley Police.

But he was also, deep down, the same young black kid who had a choice, one which Beckford had made for himself and now had his new life taken away.

And Lowe was working day and night to find justice for the man, his family, and perhaps, maybe for himself.

This was the job, he told himself.

This was the job.

CHAPTER FORTY-NINE

There was a palpable excitement flooding through the school as DI King and DC Hannon arrived, with the students once again speculating as to why the police were becoming a continued presence at the school. With her patience on the wane, King had little time for Carly's bumbling uselessness when she asked about Gemma Miller, and King asked if she could call the head teacher. Townsend had spoken of the man in glowing terms, and King was hopeful he'd be able to assist them.

'He's just in with a parent at the moment,' Carly said anxiously, weary of King's annoyance. 'But if you'd like to take a seat, I'll send you right through when he's done.'

'Fine,' King said with a little agitation and took her seat as Hannon looked beyond Carly into the office.

'Is the other lady here today?' she asked. 'We're after some records and our colleague said she'd be the person to speak to.'

'Who, Amy?' Carly suggested. 'I'm afraid she's been off for the past couple of days. I think there's something going around.'

Hannon thanked her and took her seat beside King, who was angrily picking at the clear polish on her nails.

'You all right, guv?'

'Yes. Stop asking.'

'Sorry. It's just—'

'It's just what?' King looked at Hannon, who turned away. King sighed. 'Sorry, Nic.'

'It's a shit time. I get it.' Hannon shrugged. 'But more hands and all that. Whatever's going on with Jack, he'd be more use to us out there doing his thing than sat at home with his thumb up his arse.'

Hannon had the inexplicable ability to put a smile on King's face, and as she looked at the young detective, she felt a sense of pride in how far the young woman had come in such a short space of time. Having Townsend watching her back had certainly helped, but Hannon had drawn upon her own strength and sense of belonging to really come into her own. She had proudly come out as homosexual, and now held herself with the same respect that King did.

It was pleasing to see.

'It's not that easy.'

'I know. You and Lowe are still at war.'

'We're not at war,' King said through her teeth.

'Then what is it?'

'Jack knew where his focus needed to be. I made it clear he was to leave the case to Lowe, and not once, but twice, big fuck ups have happened because he was looking the other way. He has to own that.'

Hannon looked at King and knew there was something else gnawing at her. Something she'd never willingly share.

But sensing the woman was in need of some sort of comfort or support, Hannon reached out and squeezed her hand.

'Fair enough.'

Just then, a door down the corridor opened, and a well-groomed middle-aged man strode out, mid-conversation with a woman who was hanging off his every word. As they approached, his conversation fell within in earshot.

'And trust me, Mrs Lo, we will make sure that Kaira receives all the support from our staff.'

'Thank you, Mr Hollis,' the proud parent said with a smile. 'We'll be in touch.'

Mr Hollis saw her out of the door, and then looked to Carly for an explanation for the two women sat in the waiting area.

King beat her to the punch as she stood.

'Mr Hollis. DI King, Thames Valley Police. This is my colleague DC Hannon.' They both extended their hands, and he shook each in turn.

'You've already been here this week?' Hollis arched his eyebrow.

'My colleague, DS Townsend. Yes, of course. He said you were very helpful.'

'Well, we of course will help in anyway we can.' Hollis said with a warm smile. 'But could we discuss this in my office? I'd rather not talk police business in earshot of the students.'

King gestured for him to lead the way, and the two detectives followed him back down the corridor, past the large noticeboard and a glass cabinet that proudly displayed the numerous sporting trophies that the school had won over the years. The duo stepped into the neat office, and he gestured for them to take a seat on the small sofa as he headed to the cabinet on the far side of the room and retrieved a bottle of water and some glasses.

'Oh, we're fine thank you,' King said politely, but the hospitable headmaster still placed it all on the table between them. He then took his seat, looped one leg over the other, and clasped his hands together.

'I'm not too sure how much more help we can offer,' he said warmly. 'Your colleague searched our database—'

'Which didn't have the records we were after,' King cut in.

'Yes. I know. I mean, we've only digitalised our historic records once Amy brought in the new system.' Hollis leant forward, trying to hide his confusion. 'We did go through all this with DS Townsend.'

'We're not here to look through the records again,' Hannon said with her usual upbeat smile. 'But because someone we interviewed said that a Gemma Miller was seen here at the school in the last week.'

'Miller? Miller?' Hollis said to himself, trying to place her. He found it. 'Ah yes, that was the name your colleague searched for. She was a student here twenty-five years ago or so?'

'Yes, she did. Her father taught here, as well.'

'That is quite before my time.'

'We know. Like we said, we're not here for historic records.' King was feeling her patience thinning. 'But one of the parents of a student at this school, who attended this school themselves back then, was certain he'd seen Gemma in this school just last week.'

'I can categorically tell you that Gemma Miller doesn't have a child who attends this school, nor does she work here.' Hollis shook his head. 'They must have been mistaken.'

'Perhaps she visited?' Hannon offered. 'We had to sign in when we arrived…'

'Of course.' Hollis stood. 'Let's go and have a look.'

King looked at Hannon and nodded her approval, and the three of them rose and headed back down the corridor, just as a few gossiping teenagers were walking idly down the hall. Hollis gave them some stern encouragement to get to class, confirming what Townsend had said about his strictness. As they approached the office, Carly watched on anxiously as they entered through the side door.

'Carly, can you pass us the logbook?'

'Of course.' Carly obliged them and turned on her chair with interest. 'Everything okay?'

'There have been reports of a woman being seen in the school last week,' Hollis said in a calm tone as he flicked back through the pages. 'I don't see the name Miller.'

'May I have a look?' Hannon asked, and Hollis stepped aside and allowed her access. As she flicked through the pages, Hollis stood, arms crossed, seemingly worried that an unidentified woman had been on the premises. It was clear he ran a tight ship at the school and wore that with justifiable pride. King looked around the small, pokey office, and she looked towards the back where Townsend had told her about the hermit who handled the records.

Amy.

Townsend said that despite her lack of people skills, the woman was pretty smart, and it would have potentially have been useful to pick her brains about it. Maybe they could call by her home on the way home if she was up to it?

As Hannon flicked through the pages and battling with a desperate sense of defeat, King's eyes scanned the notice-board on the wall beside Carly and she stopped suddenly. Without breaking her stare, she walked towards it, sending a worried Carly shuffling to the side and as she walked, she called out to the room.

'Who the hell is that?'

'Who?' Hollis said, looking around in confusion.

'That.' King slammed her finger on the woman in the picture. It was of Hollis and a number of the faculty, all sat around picnic benches in the school field, all of them smiling and looking towards the camera over bowls of what looked like pumpkin soup.

'Oh that. That's Amy,' Hollis confirmed. 'That was our staff Harvest Festival Day. Carly here made the most delicious pumpkin soup.'

But King had stopped listening.

Despite the woman doing her best to shield herself, her face was as clear as all the others in the photo.

King had seen it before.

From the CCTV footage from the Western Barn Inn less than twenty-four hours ago.

It wasn't the face of Amy.

DI King was looking at a photo of Gemma Miller.

CHAPTER FIFTY

The feeling of failure was overwhelming for Townsend as he had headed home, with King's admonishment ringing loudly in his ears for the entire drive.

'You've been so caught up in trying to prove yourself to Lowe that you've been sloppy. I told you you were spreading yourself too thin, but you just didn't listen.'

Had that been the case?

For Townsend, gaining the approval of DCI Lowe had never been a factor. He'd made a promise to Simone Beckford and her son, Tyler, that he'd find out who'd murdered Jamal, but on some level, was he trying to get on even ground with Lowe? The man had a lot of sway within the Thames Valley Police and having him as an ally rather than an enemy would certainly make his life easier.

But one thing that King had been dead right about was he had been sloppy.

She had warned him countless times to step away from the Beckford case, and that his entire focus needed to be on the Gallagher murders, and as more bodies piled up, the more his breaking point was being reached.

The fact of the matter was, he *did* open the door for

Gemma Miller to leave the memorial service. And what was worse, he had turned his back and allowed Connor Davis to escape their protection and now the man had been brutally killed and left two daughters without a father, and a widow who despite their issues, would be grieving her loss.

He'd let them all down.

The Gallaghers.

The Durants.

The Davis.

The Beckfords.

King. Hannon. Even Lowe.

His own family.

When he returned home, he was aching for the warm embrace of his wife, but Mandy was nowhere to be found. He sent her a message to see where she was, and she responded saying she was actually in the office that day, and she'd told him the day before.

Once again, he'd been absent.

His whole life, both inside and outside of the force, was dominated by the need to find these killers.

Mandy followed it up with another message to inform him that she had a work dinner after hours, and that Eve was with her best friend, Amelia, who she also did ballet with.

Ballet. Townsend made the note.

That was tomorrow.

With nothing to do and nobody in the house, Townsend tried to pass the time by finally picking up the odd jobs around the house, and he went about fixing a wobbly door handle on the bathroom door, as well putting together a new side unit for the front room that Mandy had bought online.

It kept him busy.

But his mind was still elsewhere.

He ventured to the garage and hit the bag for twenty minutes, hoping a trip down his boxing past would alleviate some of the tension, but it was no use. With sweat dripping down his neck in spite of the cold, Townsend went to the kitchen and whipped up some poached eggs, and once he'd polished them off, he reached for his phone.

Nothing from King.

From anyone.

Feeling isolated, he found Hannon's number and lifted the phone to his ear.

'Jack,' she said quietly. 'I can't really talk.'

'I'm going mad here, Nic.'

'Look, we might have something,' she whispered. It sounded like she was in the bathroom. 'Guv and I are headed back to the school right now. I'll keep you posted.'

'Tell the guv to send something my way. I'm no use on my arse and you guys need the hands.'

'I think she said she's going to reach out to Michelle and get her back early,' Hannon whispered. 'She's back down this way and…'

'Yeah, I saw her at the Marlow lights. She said she was coming back at the end of the week.'

'Right, I gotta go,' Hannon said sadly. 'I'll speak to her and see if she can see sense.'

'Thanks, Nic. Don't get into shit on my behalf.'

She hung up.

Whatever they'd found, it must have been important for them both to head to the school. Was it another thing he had missed?

Had his sloppiness overlooked another vital clue?

Townsend caught a glimpse of himself in the window, and his reflection didn't lie. His stubble had thickened, and was beginning to looking scraggy, and his hair was a mess. The bags under his eyes were proof of his lack of sleep, and he felt as terrible as he looked.

He marched upstairs and took a shower, and then neatly trimmed his stubble back. Once dried, he put on jeans and a thick hooded jumper, and then returned to the mirror.

He looked himself again.

'Head in the fucking game, Jack,' he barked at his own reflection, before he headed back down the stairs, determined to find some use for himself that day. The afternoon had got away from him, and the sun had departed a long time ago, bathing the streets outside in darkness, and the customary shower of rain.

His phone buzzed.

Janet Jennings.

'Hello, Mrs Jennings,' he said as cheerfully as he could muster. 'Is everything okay?'

'*As well as it can be I suppose,*' the grieving mother replied. '*It's just, I found that yearbook you were after. Would you like me to bring it to the station?*'

Townsend perked up and was already heading to the door.

'No, no. I'm not at the station right now.' It was the truth. 'But I can swing by and collect it now. Send me your address and I'll be right there.'

He was already halfway down Millionaire's Row between Flackwell Heath and High Wycombe when the address came through, and he pulled into the petrol station on the roundabout and tapped the address into the satnav. As it predicted, eleven minutes later he was pulling his car onto the driveway of Rachel's mother's house. She'd clearly been waiting for him, as not only did she open the door before he had exited the car, but there was a hot cup of tea waiting for him when he stepped in.

'Thank you, Mrs Jennings.'

'Please. Like I said before. Janet.' She smiled and

gestured to the yearbook on the table. 'I can't look at it myself. Seeing those poor people as innocent kids.'

'I understand,' Townsend said comfortingly. 'Do you mind if I do?'

'Knock yourself out.'

Townsend took a seat at the table and flicked through the alphabetised book until he came to the page with Kathryn McGillis. He turned the page, landing on the one that was missing from the book in the school archives.

Gemma Miller wasn't in it.

Frowning, he flicked back and forth between the pages. But there was no record of Gemma Miller.

There was a Benjamin Mills, a scrawny-looking teenager, which meant the book was intact. Connor had said Gemma left before the yearbook was made, and in light of what had happened, it was likely they'd left her out of it.

'Damn it,' Townsend uttered.

With frustration coursing through his body, he flipped back to page one and began to turn the pages one at a time. He found Connor Davis first.

The same arrogant smile.

Penny Durant was up next, and she had a shy smile creeping at the sides of her mouth.

Jason Gallagher looked more menacing than happy, and Rachel Jennings was as photogenic as anyone Townsend had ever seen. He sighed.

'No luck, dear?' Janet asked and Townsend just shook his head as he flicked through the pages until he got to Shelly Lawson.

His body tightened with shock.

Then it shook with fear.

He stood, made his apologies to Janet and thanked her for her help, and then, with the book in hand, he darted for his car, ignoring the torrential downpour as he raced towards the driver's side door.

He tried calling King.

He tried calling Hannon.

Nothing.

He roared the engine to life and sped off into the rain, hoping he was wrong.

Michelle Swaby wasn't answering her phone either.

But he'd just seen her smiling face, above the name Shelly Lawson in the yearbook.

The same Shelly Lawson who'd been part of the gang who had all been brutally murdered.

CHAPTER FIFTY-ONE

Losing a parent was one of the few things in life DS Michelle Swaby was genuinely afraid of.

She was thankful that both her mother and father were still in rude health, and beyond her mother's slightly high blood pressure, the two of them were more active in their seventies than most people were in their thirties. It was why, when her husband Rich got the call to say that his father had suddenly passed after a stroke, she knew she had to be a rock for as long as needed.

Rich had always looked to his father as a hero, the same way their boys looked to him, and the sudden departure of his idol had hit him harder than he could have ever imagined. They'd shot up to the family home to be with his mother and sister, who had also brought her family along, and for almost an entire week, Swaby had run a household of four adults and five teenagers, all in varying stages of grief.

It had been tough.

But she knew, when the inevitable day came that she had to say goodbye to one of her parents, Rich would do the same for her without batting an eyelid.

She'd missed work.

As much as she loved being a mother, Swaby was so proud of being a detective for the Thames Valley Police, and being away from the job was always difficult. It was probably due to her inquisitive nature, but the thrill and rush she got from helping piece together evidence was as fulfilling as parenthood.

She loved her team.

Moving to the SCU hadn't even needed a discussion, as her longstanding friendship with DI King and blossoming one with DC Hannon had made the decision for her. DS Townsend was a big softie in her eyes, and although he was certainly rougher around the edges than almost anyone else in the station, she'd seen enough banter from him to know that he was just a gentle soul.

Plus, her singing drove him up the wall.

In fact, it had been wonderful to spend an hour or so with him and his family at the Marlow lights show a few evenings before, and she couldn't wait to spend time out of work with him and his wife. She and Mandy hit it off right away, with their passion for interior design and seemingly winding up her husband, generating an instant connection.

It would be nice to get back to the office.

Back to normality.

The original plan had been for Swaby to drive back to High Wycome with the boys, but neither of them wanted to leave their dad when he was still upset. Rich knew Swaby's compassionate leave was already over, and he encouraged her to return home on her own and that he'd feel better with the boys, anyway. As she packed up the car, he gave her the tenderest kiss of their marriage and then thanked her.

'Go and have a few days looking after yourself.'

Even with his heart broken, Rich could see how much she'd done for him and his family.

The drive back was long and rain-soaked, with the motorways regularly rolling to a standstill as people panicked at the idea of driving in the rain. Swaby didn't mind the stoppages, and as she indulged herself in podcast after podcast, she didn't even realise the time when she pulled onto their driveway and made a dash through the rain to their home.

It smelt stale.

With her Alexa blaring out the latest hits, Swaby went about putting the house in order. First, she ordered a take-away, and a opened a bottle of wine, and then went about stripping the beds and refreshing the sheets. As she boogied around the house as she did her chores, she completely forgot about her phone, which was buzzing almost constantly. Unlike most people, Swaby wasn't addicted to the screen of her phone, and found the idea of social media apps to be the bane of society.

Ninety per cent of it was negativity, and the other ten was some social or political narrative being pushed upon people as news.

It wasn't for her, which meant she hadn't had a whiff of anything that had been going on in the local area for the past week or so.

Sometimes, ignorance really was bliss.

The takeaway arrived, and she gorged on a few slices of pizza before heading off to the utility room to put a wash on, when the doorbell went again. Frowning, she dumped the washing in the machine and headed to the door.

A woman was standing in the rain.

A woman she sort of recognised.

'Shelly.' The woman smiled. Swaby winced.

Nobody had called her that in over twenty years.

'Hello?' Swaby was trying to place her.

'It's me. Gemma. Gemma Miller. From High Wycombe High School…I don't know if you remember?'

The surprise almost hit Swaby for six, and she stepped to the side and opened the door.

'Jesus. Gemma. Wow.' She beckoned her in. 'Come in, it's pouring.'

'Thank you.'

The petite woman stepped in gratefully and wiped her feet on the mat. Swaby took her coat for her and put it over the bannister and then looked at the woman with confusion.

'Would you like a drink? I've got a wine on the go?'

'That would be nice.'

Swaby gestured for the woman to follow and they moved through to the open-plan kitchen of the house, trying her hardest to figure out why she was there.

She was a detective.

Just ask her.

Swaby poured herself and her unannounced guest a glass of wine, handed it to her and then took a sip.

'I mean, it's been years,' Swaby said. 'What brings you this way? Not that I mind…'

'No, it's fine.' Gemma smiled, tucking her soaked brown hair behind her ear. Swaby remembered the poor Miller girl as a bit of a recluse, whose overbearing father meant she wasn't allowed to make-up or fancy clothing during their teen years. Now, she'd blossomed into quite a stunning woman. 'I'm just…you heard about what happened to my father, right?'

Swaby felt a sloshing of guilt in her gut.

She'd been 'part' of the group who'd started such a vile rumour, but it had been the straw that broke the camel's back, and she'd walked away from the social group then and there.

'Yes. I do,' Swaby said glumly. 'I'm sorry for your loss.'

'Thank you. That means a lot.' Gemma smiled. 'Well, I just feel like I lost a lot from that time in my life and I've been trying to reconnect to who I was before it all happened.'

Swaby nodded, hummed her agreement, and took a sip. Something didn't feel quite right.

'Well, that sounds healthy. My husband just recently lost his father.' Swaby tried to make conversation as she tried to remember where she'd left her phone. 'It can take a long time to get over a loss like that.'

The utility room. She remembered.

Swaby smiled at Gemma, who had fixed her with an awkward gaze, and she held up an apologetic finger as she walked across the kitchen to the door that led to the utility room.

Her phone was on the counter, and she snatched it up and the screen illuminated.

Eight missed calls.

All from Townsend.

'You must deal with a lot of loss in your job as a detective.'

Gemma's voice echoed from the kitchen.

'Yep,' Swaby said distracted as she went to open the messages that her colleague had also sent.

Then she clocked what had been said and her head snapped upwards.

How did Gemma know she was a detective?

Just then, she felt a warm sensation in the back of neck, and her hand sloppily flapped up to pat away the needle that Gemma was pulling from her skin. Instantly, she felt her legs turn to jelly and just as she felt like she was falling towards the ground, Gemma's arms looped under her own, and the strange guest lowered her to the ground.

Immediately, the edges of her vision began to blur and

darken, and as the panic began to set in, the last thing Swaby saw was Gemma's striking face peering over her.

The last thing she heard sent fear pulsing through her immobile body.

'You were always the nicest one of the group to me.' Gemma sounded regretful. 'So, I'll try to make this as painless as possible.'

Then everything faded to black.

CHAPTER FIFTY-TWO

'Come on. Answer the fucking phone!' Townsend yelled angrily as the ringtone echoed through his car speakers. As had happened multiple times before, he was greeted with the same jovial message.

You've reached Michelle Swaby's phone. I can't come to the phone right now but leave me a message and I shall grace your ears shortly. Ta ta for now.

The phone beeped and Townsend angrily slapped the screen of his dashboard to end the call. As he veered around a roundabout and navigated the back streets of High Wycombe, he peered through the lashing rain for signs that would take him towards Princess Risborough. It was a quaint town, roughly twenty minutes out from High Wycombe itself. As he hurried round the roundabout, he saw the petrol station where Irena Roslova was murdered five months ago, and it hammered home the potential danger his friend was in.

He didn't know that Gemma Miller was heading for Swaby.

But he had a feeling.

As he pushed his foot down on the pedal to pick up speed, he commanded his car to call DI King.

It rang.

She didn't connect.

'Fuck.' Townsend grunted, as he whizzed past a few rows of stranded houses surrounded by fields. 'Call Nic Hannon.'

He hated talking to his car like a child, but the voice activation system whirled on the screen and then Nic's name flashed up.

It rang.

Hannon answered the phone.

'Jack. What's up?'

'It's Gemma,' Townsend yelled. 'She's after Michelle.'

'What?' Hannon sounded confused. 'We need to speak, Jack. You remember that woman at the school…'

'Nic. Did you hear me? Michelle is in danger.' Townsend slammed on the brakes as a tractor inconveniently pulled out from one of the gated fields and joined the road, slowing everyone down. Angrily, Townsend veered to overtake it, but the narrow country round and the oncoming headlights put an end to that idea. 'I'm heading out there now.'

'Jack, slow down.' Hannon sounded flustered. 'What's up with Michelle?'

'She's home tonight, right? Getting back from the in-laws'.'

'Yes, she's coming back but you're not making any sense.'

'Michelle is Shelly. Shelly Lawson.' Townsend angrily waved a hand at the tractor to speed up. 'We just didn't connect the dots.'

'Jesus,' Hannon exclaimed. 'How do you know she's in danger?'

'I don't. But she's not answering her phone, and if we're getting close, then if I was Miller, then I'd want to finish what I started while I still had the chance.'

'Well, we are close,' Hannon said proudly. 'Like I was saying, that woman…the creepy one you said worked in the school.'

'Yeah?'

'She *is* Gemma Miller.'

'What the fuck?'

'We had a tip that someone had seen at her at the school, and guv saw her photo and it matches the woman who took Connor from the hotel,' Hannon continued. 'So either this Amy is some rando or…'

'She changed her name and got access to the records.' Townsend shook his head. 'Fuck.'

The tractor indicated and headed off down a muddy side road, and Townsend once again slammed his foot down, whizzing through the village of Saunderton and continued down the dark, wet country road toward Princes Risborough.

'I'll try Michelle and tell her to…'

'No, don't bother. She's not answering her phone,' Townsend yelled into the screen. 'Send uniform as soon as you can. I'm five minutes out.'

'I'll tell the guv…and Jack…don't do anything stupid.'

'No promises.'

Townsend hung up the call and sped towards the signs of Princes Risborough, and as he approached the high street, he slowed, turned off the main roundabout and headed towards the quaint residential strip until he found Swaby's road. He pulled the car in roughly onto the curb and threw open the door, not even reaching for his coat as he ran as fast as he could through the rain to the front door.

He hammered it with fists, screaming Michelle's name in a hope to draw her attention.

If she was home but asleep, he'd certainly wake her, and he was begging for her to yank the door open and give him both barrels for the scene he was making.

But there was nothing.

No answer.

He tried the doorbell a few more times, and then stepped back, looking up at the house.

The lights in the front bedroom were on.

He leant down and called through the letter box, noting that there was no pile of mail on the other side.

Someone was home.

Townsend scoured the front of the house, catching from the corner of his eye the curtain twitching from the neighbouring house. He stood, soaked through, with his T-shirt stuck to his muscular frame and his wavy, dark hair pasted to his skull. He looked to the side for another way in and then he double took.

A red car.

The same one that was from the CCTV footage of Connor Davis's abduction. The license plates were different, which was expected, but that was enough for Townsend.

'I'm coming in, Michelle,' he yelled, before he lifted a large rock from the pebbled driveway and smashed it through the glass panel on the front door. If it meant saving her life, he'd gladly foot the bill. As the majority of the pane shattered and fell into the house, Townsend used the rock to brush away the remaining jagged fragments still in the door before he looped his arm in and opened it from the inside.

The thumping of a bland dance tune emanated from a speaker somewhere, and Townsend followed the tempting smell of pizza towards the large, expensive kitchen that was the centrepiece of the house.

No one.

'Michelle?' he called.

No answer.

He ventured further, heading through the open French doors into the front room, where his eyes widened in horror.

Swaby was lying motionless on the floor.

Without thinking, Townsend darted towards her, dropping to one knee and yelling her name to illicit a response. When he didn't get one, he pressed his fingers to her wrist to check for a pulse and sighed as he found one. As he checked her for injuries, he noticed that there was no blood around her mouth.

Meaning that Gemma Miller hadn't been able to finish the job.

As it dawned on him that he'd interrupted her, he heard the final footstep behind him, before a gloved hand swung down and he felt the instant, burning sensation as the razor-sharp scalpel embedded in the top of his pectoral muscle, and Gemma's small frame collided into his back. The two of them went sprawling forward, and Townsend roared with pain and Gemma grasped onto the blade, and tried pushing it further into Townsend's chest. With his adrenaline pumping, and with a sizable weight advantage, he managed to push himself upwards, and he reached back with both hands, grabbed her by her hair and collar, and launched her over his shoulder. Gemma slammed into the thick oak dining table against the far wall, the wind driven from her lungs on impact. As she hit the ground, she groaned in pain, and Townsend looked down at his chest, where the handle of the scalpel protruded from the growing bloodstain on his shirt. Thankfully, it was just in the muscle.

Unfortunately, it hurt like hell.

Not wanting to exacerbate the bleeding by removing the blade, Townsend launched forward just as Gemma was trying to push herself from the ground, and drove his elbow into the centre of her spine, drilling her to the ground once more. As he gritted his teeth to push through the pain, he pulled both of her arms behind her back and pinned her to the ground with a knee to the base of her spine.

She wriggled a little, but when he applied more pressure, she finally relented.

They both knew it was over.

As she gave up the fight, Townsend adjusted his grip of her wrists to just one hand and pressed his other to his chest to try to stimy the bleeding. Beyond the large bay window that ran around the far wall of the house, the world was being illuminated with intermittent flashes of blue as the uniformed back-up arrived on the scene.

Swaby was alive.

Gemma Miller had been stopped.

And although he was doing his best to get through the pain of being stabbed, Townsend was still in one piece. He may have been sidelined by King, but he was still a detective, and he still had a job to do.

'Gemma Miller, I am arresting you for the murders of Jason Gallagher, Rachel Gallagher, Penny Durant, and Connor Davis, and the attempt murder of Detective Sergeant Michelle Swaby. You do not have to say anything, but it may harm your defence if you do not mention, when questioned, something which you later rely on in court. Anything you do say may be given in evidence.' Townsend pressed his knee down a little firmer. 'Understood?'

Gemma didn't reply.

As the police came through the door and Townsend

directed them to Swaby, Gemma Miller didn't move a muscle.

She didn't try to struggle.

She didn't try to fight back.

It was over.

And Gemma Miller didn't say a word.

CHAPTER FIFTY-THREE

The entire street was awash with activity, and by the time King and Hannon arrived, DS Swaby had already been taken off to High Wycombe Hospital for treatment. The paramedics had assured Townsend she'd be fine, but due to the drugs that had been pumped into her bloodstream, they needed to monitor her to ensure that she recovered without issues.

Police cars had blocked off both entrances to the road, and while the nosy neighbours either braved the rain and gathered at the cordons, or just watched the crime scene unfold from their windows. Uniformed officers, wrapped up in their high-vis coats, patrolled the front of the house, and King and Hannon approached PC Boyd, who'd drawn the unfortunate straw of standing guard on the driveway with an increasingly sodden list.

'Your boy's over there.' Boyd pointed, and King and Hannon turned their attention to the ambulance parked across the road.

'Oh god,' King said with worry, and she and Hannon raced across the road to the back of the ambulance, their shadows bursting across the street in the light of the police headlights. As they approached the doors, they both breathed a sigh of relief when they were greeted by the casual smile of Townsend.

'Evening, ladies,' he said with a slight grimace. He was shirtless, but his left pec and shoulder had been heavily taped up. 'You haven't got a spare shirt by any chance have you?'

He nodded towards the ruined T-shirt on the bench beside him, which was soaked with blood and had been cut from his body by the paramedic.

'Jesus, Jack' Hannon barked. 'You had us worried sick.'

'Is he okay?' King looked to the paramedic who was finishing off the bandaging.

'Yeah, he's fine.' The paramedic said without looking up. 'Just a few stitches, but he'll live.'

'It hurts like hell, though,' Townsend said with a smirk.

'You're a big boy.' The paramedic joked. She then strapped his arm up in a sling and pulled it tight. 'That will keep your arm in the best position for the stitches to hold.'

'Jack, you should go to the hospital,' King stated as the paramedic stepped back through the ambulance and jumped out, heading out of their conversation.

'I'll be all right,' Townsend said grimly, turning stiffly so as not to disturb his sling. 'Where's Miller?'

'She's on her way to the station,' King said. 'She'll spend the night in the nick there and then tomorrow morning, we'll go through the process and bring this to an end.'

'Cool.' Townsend eased off the step, drawing a few eyes from the onlookers of the shirtless man in the downpour. He handed Hannon his keys. 'Can you grab my coat for me?'

Hannon swiped the keys and jogged a few cars down to Townsend's car to retrieve his coat, and Townsend looked to King who was staring up at the house.

'Michelle will be fine,' he assured her.

'I know. And that's because of you, Jack.'

'It's because of all us,' he responded. 'I just happened to be the one who connected the final dot.'

King turned to him and smiled.

'Well, I should read you the riot act for running into that house with no backup or safety gear, but if you hadn't, who knows what would have happened?'

'I wouldn't have been stabbed,' he joked, and King chuckled as Hannon returned and draped the jacket over his shoulders. Despite their protests, Townsend removed his sling and gingerly eased his arms through the sleeves.

There was no reasoning with him with regards to his injuries.

All King knew was DS Jack Townsend was a tough bastard.

Tougher than most.

'Go home, Jack,' King said with an approving nod. 'We'll handle Gemma in the morning.'

'With all due respect, guv. I want to be in that room,' Townsend replied, and King made a show of weighing up the decision. They were still on shaky ground, but Townsend needed to see it through to the end.

'Okay, fine.' She finally agreed. 'Eight o'clock.'

Townsend nodded and then turned to Hannon.

'Now I get to go home and have Mandy kick my arse for this.' He joked and Hannon chuckled. 'Can someone give me a lift?' Hannon offered, and as Townsend followed her to her car, he could feel the eyes of every detective, officer, and local resident on him. They all knew what he'd done.

He'd raced into a potential murder scene with little care for himself.

He'd saved DS Michelle Swaby's life.

But as he lowered himself with some difficulty into Hannon's car, he refused to be thought of as a hero.

This was the job.

And it was one he did with pride.

Mandy, however, didn't see it like that when he arrived home, and she was in floods of angry tears as he peeled off his jacket and explained what had happened. Eve was asleep upstairs after a long day at school and her friend's house, and Mandy had to make a concerted effort to keep her voice down.

'For crying out loud, Jack. You could have been killed.'

'Could being the operative word.'

'Very funny,' Mandy said with a scowl. 'What if that blade had gone into your throat? Or a few inches in and your heart?'

'If I hadn't gone in, Michelle would be dead,' Townsend said defensively, stood against the countertop of their kitchen as he looked at the hurt on his wife's face. 'I didn't have a choice.'

Deep down, she knew that, too.

Despite how much it filled her with worry, her husband's relentless commitment to doing the right thing was his most admirable quality. A small part of her had resented him for the years he'd spent under cover, as it had denied them the time other married couples had. It had denied him the chance to bond with their daughter during her early years.

But he'd done what needed to be done.

And one thing Mandy could guarantee, even more so than Jack Townsend's commitment to the cause, was that he would always find his way back to them.

Even if he had to walk through hell barefooted, he'd force himself through every step.

She took a deep, calming breath and then wiped away her tears.

They headed to the front room, and Townsend lowered himself onto the sofa, and Mandy promised him a cup of tea. She headed back to the kitchen, quickly whipped one up, but when she returned, Townsend was fast asleep, slumped back on the sofa, with his bandaged arm propped up on a cushion. Mandy smiled, put the tea down on the table, and then planted a loving kiss on his forehead. She draped her blanket over him and pulled the door closed and took herself off to bed.

When she woke the next morning, he'd already gone.

She knew he needed to see it through to the end, but she felt a little saddened by his absence.

She pulled out her phone and tapped out a message.

Remember. 5.30. Don't miss it. x

He responded back immediately.

Had to be in early. Wouldn't miss it for the world. X

Mandy turned her head towards the stairwell as she could hear the first few shuffles of Eve in her bed, and the process of getting her up school was about to begin. Their daughter had blown her away with her commitment to ballet, and the burning passion for it was something Mandy knew would last a lifetime.

It would break Eve's heart if her father missed her first ever recital.

Mandy needed to make sure Jack knew that, and then sent one more message that would resonate more than she could ever know.

Don't make promises you can't keep.

CHAPTER FIFTY-FOUR

For the first two hours, Gemma Miller refused to speak. Rupa Patel had once again been drafted in as the duty solicitor, and even she encouraged the killer to cooperate. Frustrated, King decided to call for a break and when they returned just before midday, King took her seat and waited as Townsend slowly lowered himself into the chair beside her. He grunted as he shifted his taped-up shoulder, and rested his arm on the table and glared at Gemma, who met his stare and held it.

King reintroduced everyone for the purposes of the recording, and as soon as she finished, Townsend spoke.

'This hurts like hell, by the way.'

Gemma tilted her head, but she didn't blink.

'It could have been worse,' she finally spoke for the first time. Her voice, just as Townsend remembered, was soft and gentle. King looked to Townsend and encouragingly nodded.

He'd got through to her.

'So, should I call you Gemma or Amy?' he said with a smile. Hannon entered the room with a cup of water for

Gemma, and then she swiftly left, returning to her position on the other side of the glass.

'Gemma.' She nodded. 'Amy was just a way back here.'

'Back home?' Townsend suggested warmly.

'This place is not home. It hasn't been for a long time.'

'Is that because of what happened?' King chimed in. Gemma fixed her with a hideous glare and refused to answer. King sighed and turned back to Townsend.

'What DI King means is what happened to your father.'

'What happened to my father has been with me every day of my life,' Gemma spat.

'And what did happen?' Townsend asked, gingerly adjusting in his seat. 'All we've heard is Connor Davis's account of things.'

'Then all you've heard are the words of a liar.' Gemma had returned to her calm voice. Sitting in the chair, she looked smaller than everyone else. 'My father was a brilliant man. He was respected, and he was one of the best teachers in this town.'

'He taught at your school, didn't he?' Townsend probed.

'Yes. I was actually pretty proud of it. You get the odd comment from other kids who he had told off, but you shrug them away. It was quite nice to be in a place where your dad was.'

'I bet,' Townsend said with a smile. 'My father was a policeman back home in Liverpool. One of the best. Loved by everyone.'

'Is that why you joined?' Gemma asked, and then sipped her water. 'To work alongside him.'

'Unfortunately, he passed before I could join.'

'I'm sorry to hear that.'

The woman's kindness caught both King and

Townsend a little off guard, and eerie feeling had begun to fill the room like a fog.

'Thank you.'

'Was he taken from you like mine was?'

'He died from cancer.'

'Then no,' Gemma stated. 'My father, who did everything he could to make my mum and me happy, had his name dragged through the mud. Those horrible rumours…none of it was true.'

'Connor said as much…'

'But he still said them.' Gemma's pretty face was beginning to morph into a mask of fury. 'All of them did. All of them spread the lies that my father did unspeakable things to them, and instead of trying to help clear his name, the police, the school, the community…They all turned their backs on him. Even my mother did.'

'And you?' Townsend asked calmly, trying to lower the tension.

'Never.' Gemma shook her head defiantly. A tear was forming in the corner of her eyes. 'I wasn't allowed to see him at first. My mother thought it was for the best. We moved away, I changed schools. Then we found out about his first suicide attempt. An overdose.'

King looked to Townsend.

Just like Jason Gallagher.

Gemma continued.

'When they brought him back from that, he slit his own wrists, only he didn't do it vertically, so they saw it as a cry for help. Sectioned him, put this incredibly smart man through the mental health system to see why he was self-harming. All that talking, but nobody ever listened to him when he said he didn't do anything…'

'Then he committed suicide?'

'Eventually,' Gemma said, swallowing a lump in her throat. 'He tried gassing himself, but a neighbour stopped him. Tried hanging himself in a hotel but the light fixture broke. Eventually, he was put in a hospital for his own safety, but my father wasn't ill. He was broken. There is a big difference.'

'How so?' Townsend said, shuffling in his seat. King and Patel listened on intently.

'Illness, you treat. Medicines and what not. Broken… you fix. You find out what was broken and why and help them piece it back together. No one ever did that for my father, and one day, he managed to get into the pharmacy and took an overdose of painkillers.' Gemma wiped away her tear. 'He went to sleep and never woke up.'

'And you blamed them?' Townsend asked with authority. 'The victims?'

'Victims.' Gemma cackled wildly. 'They were not victims. They spread the evil that eventually took my father away from me, broke him down until the only way out for him was to kill himself. I can save you some trouble, both of you. I killed Jason Gallagher. I killed his bitch wife, Rachel Gallagher. I drugged and killed Penny Durant, and I did the same thing to Connor Davis.'

'You're confessing to these crimes?' King asked, and Gemma snapped her head towards her. Her eyes seemed darker now, consumed with hatred.

'They were not crimes. They were comeuppance,' Gemma said cruelly. 'But these weren't good people. They cheated on their spouses. Betrayed their families. Took drugs. Stole money. Yet they…*they*…were the ones who drove a good man to his death. So yes, I confess to killing them, but I do not confess that these were crimes.'

'So, just for the record…' King said. 'You plotted and murdered the Jason Gallagher, Rachel Gallagher, Penny Durant, and Connor Davis.'

'Yes,' Gemma said coldly. 'It wasn't hard. Building a fake identity is pretty easy these days and arrogant people like those four are too self-centred to ever realise someone following them. I volunteered at the school so they didn't need a National Insurance number, and it wasn't hard to confuse that idiot in the office with digitalising their databases.'

'And that gave you access?'

'To everything I needed. Their parents' names, addresses, numbers.' Gemma shrugged. 'Whatever GDPR nonsense that gets sprouted, most places just shove old records in a storeroom and forget about them. After that, it was pretty easy to locate each of them and then learn their routines. When they were alone. Where they went. Who they fucked. Once I had all of that…'

Gemma shrugged as if she'd just cooked an easy meal. The gravity of her crimes didn't seem to register with her.

King looked to Townsend, who shifted a little uncomfortably.

'Tell me, Gemma. Was staging their deaths to look like suicides a message to us? Or was it just to confuse the investigation?'

'Both.' She smiled proudly. 'I figured you'd start making connections to further down the line I got. So if I could blur the truth of what was happening long enough, I'd be able to get the justice my father deserved.'

'Why deliver the tongues to the memorial service?' King interrupted. 'Wasn't that a risk?'

'Maybe. But it shook everyone up. Made them feel terrified. Made them feel targeted.' Gemma's voice hardened again. 'Just like my father.'

'But why go for DS Swaby?' Townsend asked. 'She didn't spread the rumours. From what we've heard, she walked away from them when they started.'

'Just because she didn't spread them doesn't mean she didn't condone it. She never spoke up to say they were lying. She was more concerned with her own social standing.' Gemma shook her head. 'She would have been regrettable but, you stopped that.'

'Yes, I did,' Townsend said firmly. 'You do understand the severity of your charges, don't you? Before we finish, is there anything you don't understand?'

'Like what?'

King cleared her throat.

'That you will be charged with the murders of Jason and Rachel Gallagher, Penny Durant, and Connor Davis? And you will spend the rest of your life in prison.'

Gemma turned her face to the King, and once again, returned to her gentle demeanour.

'I understand. And I accept whatever comes my way.'

King turned to Townsend, seemingly ready to wrap things up, but Townsend still had his eyes locked on Gemma, who turned her attention back to him.

'Just so you know, Gemma. Penny Durant had two sons she leaves behind. Connor Davis had two daughters. You might think you've earnt justice for your father, but in reality, you've taken a parent from four other children.' He shook his head. '*You* have put them through what you went through. I want you to know that.'

Gemma scoffed and shook her head.

'I've opened their eyes to who their parents truly were. I knew who my father was, and he wasn't the man he was made out to be. I wasn't allowed to fight for him back then, but I have done now. And tell me, Detective Townsend, what wouldn't you do to protect the ones you love?'

Her words hit Townsend hard.

Not for the reasons he would have thought.

King clearly noticed something trigger in Townsend's mind, and she brought the interview to an end and then informed Gemma and Patel that uniformed officers would be in shortly to take her to be processed. She then swiftly followed Townsend into the hallway, where Hannon had already arrived.

'That's it right?' Hannon asked eagerly. 'This is over.'

'Nic, you're a video game nerd, right?' Townsend asked, drawing an immediate scowl from King. Hannon raised her eyebrows in confusion.

'Task at hand, Jack,' King cut in.

But Townsend shrugged her off.

'Can you check a console at an address at a specific time?'

'Well, yeah. You might need to get round a firewall and maybe…'

'Good.' Townsend pulled out his notepad, winced in pain, but then scribbled down a time, a date, and an address. 'Can you check to see if any console was active at that time?'

'I mean, yeah but…'

'Jack, what the hell?' King asked.

'Sorry, guv.' He turned and began walking away. 'I need to speak to Lowe.'

The mention of DCI Lowe's name seemed to deflate the balloon of euphoria for catching the killer. Townsend quickened his pace and disappeared around the corner just as the two uniformed officers arrived to collect Gemma from the interview room. King and Hannon stepped to the side, and the young DC looked to King, who was failing at hiding her sadness. Hannon went to offer a comforting comment, but King brushed it off.

'I need a drink,' she barked and then headed towards the exit.

Hannon stood, watching her leave, wondering how, when they'd just caught a serial killer, their team felt so far apart.

CHAPTER FIFTY-FIVE

It felt odd to be sitting in a car with DCI Lowe and it not be rife with tension, but Townsend was pleased that two of them had been able to build some bridges. Although Lowe was arrogant at the best of times, underneath there was a good detective who did care about his job.

When Townsend had intruded on his briefing that afternoon asking for a word, Lowe had obliged him, and once DC Hannon had confirmed his suspicions, he laid it all out for Lowe to digest.

He did so sceptically.

'And you're sure?' Lowe had asked. 'Because if you're wrong, this is going to backfire on you big time.'

Townsend had staked his reputation on it, and now he and Lowe sat waiting for DS Ramsey to give them the all-clear. Ramsey had been by Simone Beckford's side the entire week, and as one of the most experienced Family Liaison Officers, she'd warned them of the situation inside the house.

Tensions were high.

Simone Beckford had fallen into the seven stages of grief, going through each one to its most wicked extreme.

Her son, Tyler, had become a shell of a teenager, void of most emotions, and had lost his appetite.

It had led to a few arguments, and something this big could cause an irreparable crack in the family.

Lowe looked up at the house and frowned.

The outskirts of High Wycombe town centre either offered pristine, countryside living or, as with the road that the Beckford home had been crammed onto, a way to keep your head just above the poverty line. Townsend could tell that Lowe was anxious, having taken the case on with the respect and dedication it deserved. As a successful black man in a prominent position within the community, Lowe was a driving force for equality in the town.

It wasn't something he advertised, despite his mammoth ego, and Townsend knew it was because it was something he held dear.

It was something real to him.

DS Ramsey appeared at the door of the house and beckoned them, and Lowe gave a groan.

'You better be right about this, Scouse.'

The two of them opened the doors of the car and stepped out, walking briskly through the rain to the house, and they entered the cramped hallway.

Tyler's coat hung over the bannister, just like a week ago.

'DS Ramsey,' Lowe greeted her with a respectful nod. Before she could say anything, Simone Beckford appeared, looking confused.

'Detectives.' She looked back and forth between them, and then to Ramsey. 'What are you doing here?'

'Mrs Beckford. Can we take a seat for a minute?' Townsend asked, gesturing to the doorway to the front room. But the woman was locked in the 'anger' stage of grief and was already put on the back foot by their unannounced arrival.

'No.' She turned to Ramsey. 'What are they doing here?'

Lowe answered for her.

'Mrs Beckford. Is Tyler here?' he said with an air of resignation. The penny was about to drop.

'Oh, fuck off,' she yelled, her eyes beginning to water. 'You are kidding me?'

Drawn by the noise in the hallway, Tyler appeared at the top of the stairs.

'Is everything okay, Mum?' he called down. He caught a glimpse of the two large men in the hallway and froze slightly.

'Go upstairs, honey,' she barked, as angry tears began to roll.

Lowe stepped forward.

'Come down here, son.'

Despite his mother's protests, Tyler did as he asked, and Townsend greeted the boy with a pained smile.

'Tyler. Last Friday, I came here. Do you remember?'

'Yeah.' The boy shrugged. 'Because someone killed Jamal, right?'

'Yes.' Townsend nodded. 'When I arrived, your jacket was hanging on this bannister just like this. Only it was soaking wet. Now, I thought it was because I hung mine over the top of it, but the wetness seemed excessive.'

'Wow,' Simone snapped sarcastically. 'A teenage boy's coat gets wet in the rain.'

Townsend ignored her.

'Because you were upstairs, weren't you? Playing your video game?'

Tyler nodded anxiously.

'I saw another young lad this past week, playing the same game, and he told me that you could hang around in some kind of lobby beforehand. Basically, be online but not be involved. Is that true?'

Tyler looked to his mum. Then to Lowe.

The boy was panicking.

Townsend didn't need him to answer, and he continued.

'The thing is, Tyler, we can check that level of activity. And for a ninety-minute period last Friday afternoon, when you were up here on your computer, you weren't actually playing the game.' Townsend could see the fury building in Simone. 'Because you weren't here, were you?'

'Get out!' Simone screamed, launching across Ramsey and striking Townsend with a balled fist. The blow hit him hard in the chest, sending a shockwave of pain pulsing from his fresh stitches, and he fell backwards slightly, as Ramsey restrained her.

'Mrs Beckford,' Lowe bellowed. 'Do you understand the severity of assaulting an officer?'

'It's okay.' Townsend held up his hand, trying his best to mask the pain.

'Get the fuck out of my house,' Simone screamed. She was just a woman, protecting her young.

'It's okay, Mum,' Tyler eventually said. 'It's okay.'

'Tyler. Go upstairs, right now,' she demanded. The boy began to cry.

'I did it,' he said, shaking as he took a seat on the step. 'I killed him.'

The announcement hit the room like a freight train, and Simone collapsed into a heap, wailing into the arms of DS Ramsey who looked up at Townsend with an accusing look.

The family had been through enough over the past week, and she'd been right by their side to experience it all.

But Townsend couldn't walk away from the truth.

He'd promised Simone Beckford he'd find out who had killed her husband.

He wished with every fibre of his being that he'd come to a different conclusion.

The confession seemed to hit Lowe hard as well, and he swallowed back his sadness and took a step towards the stairs, extended a comforting hand onto Tyler's shoulder.

'It's going to be okay, son.'

'Why, Tyler?' Simone screamed from the floor, weeping uncontrollably as her world fell apart at the seams. 'Why would you do this?'

'Because he was hurting you, Mum.' Tyler was weeping, too. 'He hit you and you couldn't fight back. When I tried to, he threatened me, and I couldn't allow that anymore. I told him that I was being bullied and that the kids who were doing it hung around that car park after school and…'

'And then you snuck out?' Townsend said wearily, struggling as he watched this young boy confess to a crime that would ruin his life.

'Yeah,' Tyler said sadly. Lowe patted him on the shoulder and Tyler sniffed back the tears, took a deep breath, and stood. 'I killed Jamal to protect my mum. I'm not ashamed of it.'

The boy was facing his future bravely, and as his mother cried herself hoarse, Lowe begrudgingly read him his rights, and then forewent the handcuffs as he led the boy down the final few stairs. He then let Tyler drop down to his mother, allowing him to hug her and apologise before he led him to the door, as Simone Beckford cried out his name with anguished wails.

Lowe marched Tyler towards his car and opened the back door for him to get in. The young boy was clearly terrified, and Lowe would do everything he could for him.

But the future didn't hold anything for Tyler.

Not anymore.

As Townsend went to leave, Simone looked up at him with rage filled eyes that were red from soreness.

'You did this.' She spat angrily. 'You have ripped this family apart.'

Lowe appeared back in the doorway to pull a clearly affected Townsend out into the rain, and said his goodbyes to Ramsey, who assured him that she'd look after her. There would be a backlash against the arrest from certain members of the senior hierarchy, as well as the black community who felt they were targeted by the badge.

Lowe knew he was in for a constant stream of shit.

But they'd done their jobs.

As the rain lashed down on the roof of the car, Townsend peered through the raindrops at the young kid, who sat frozen with fear in the backseat.

'Good work, Scouse,' Lowe said through the downpour.

'It doesn't feel good, sir.'

'No. It doesn't.' Lowe shook his head. 'Just another young black kid lost to the system. But...I'll do what I can for him.'

'Thank you.' Townsend nodded.

Lowe extended his hand.

'If you ever fancy a change, there's a desk in CID.'

Townsend took the man's hand and experienced one of the most unlikely handshakes of his life.

'Thanks, sir.' Townsend smiled. 'But I already have a desk.'

Lowe smirked.

'Need a lift?' he asked as he rounded the car to the driver's side.

'I'll walk.' Townsend said looking up at the rain. 'I think I need to clear my head.'

'See you around, Scouse,' Lowe said respectfully, and Townsend watched through the rain as Lowe pulled away, taking the young man on the first steps of a long and hard journey ahead. With the guilt threatening to overwhelm him, Townsend looked at his watch.

Four o'clock.

He had a half-hour walk back to the station, and he hoped the rain would wash away his grief for the Beckford family before he got there.

All he wanted was to see his family.

To look upon his little girl.

To hold her tightly.

Ignoring the pain in his chest, and the feeling that his heart had broken, Townsend pulled the hood of his coat over his head and began his march back to town, hating the fact that he was good at his job.

CHAPTER FIFTY-SIX

The glass of red wine had sat on the bar for over half an hour, and DI Isabella King stared at it indecisively. The barman had cracked a joke about her nursing it, but when he realised there was more to it, he'd shuffled away and left her alone.

Five long months.

That was how long King had been sober, and she knew throwing it all away was as easy as just lifting the glass and tipping it back. All the meetings she'd been to, all the hard nights when she'd wrestled with her demons.

All washed away.

All washed down in that beautiful, tangy drink.

Detective Superintendent Hall had been by her side through it all, and she knew that by turning her back on her sobriety, she'd be turning her back on him. He'd supported her through some rough nights, even sat with her in meetings and never said a word if she shared her struggles, or if she hid away within herself.

He believed in her.

Even when she failed to believe in herself.

The past week had been one of the hardest of her career.

Not just because of the pressure of running a manhunt for a serial killer, or the rising tide of public distrust in the police to keep them safe. Nor was it completely due to the fact that four people, regardless of how they lived their lives, had been snatched from the world, leaving behind nothing but broken lives and shattered families.

It was because she felt like she was losing control.

Usually, when the notion to reach for a drink got too strong, she could rely on her team to pull her out of it. She'd never shared with them her problem, even though she knew she probably should, but they did it by just being themselves.

By being there for her.

But the past week had seen that connection begin to fray at the seams, and King could feel Townsend in particular drawing away from her.

Or was she pushing him?

Was her hatred for her ex-husband the driving force for her attitude towards her fellow detective? In fairness, Townsend had failed to listen to her, and his sloppiness had hindered their case on a few occasions. Despite his age, he was still new to the role, and he looked to her for guidance.

Not punishment.

He had solved the case in the end, once again following his own intuition to stop a murderer before any more blood could be shed. He'd thrown himself into the path of a killer, and would have a scar on his chest to remind him of it every day. But instead of taking the time to celebrate with the team, Townsend had gone running to Lowe.

It felt like her ex-husband had managed to needle his claws into her friend, and the inevitable was about to happen.

He'd leave her team.

And she'd watch him prosper under Lowe's magnetic tutelage.

With a sigh, she reached out for the glass, running her fingers up and down the stem of it, feeling the moisture sliding down the glass.

'You going to drink that?'

King spun on the bar stool, and a soaking wet Townsend stepped towards her, flapping the rain from the sleeves of his sodden coat. She wanted to smile, but instead, she just turned back to the glass.

'Thinking about it,' King said glumly. Townsend took the seat beside her but waved away the barman as he approached. 'How did you know I was here?'

'She told me.' Townsend nodded beyond King, and Hannon took the other stool beside her. 'Said she was worried about you and when you walked away, she had a feeling you were going to break your sobriety so she followed you, then gave me a call.'

'My sobriety?' King tried to act offended.

'It's okay.' Hannon reached out a caring hand and rested it on the back of King's.

'You are both way off the mark.'

'Come on, guv,' Townsend said softly. 'I spent three years in some of the worst places you could imagine. I know when someone is struggling with an alcohol problem.'

King wanted to protest, but she knew it was useless. Annoyingly, her team were some of the best detectives she'd come across.

Rough around the edges.

A few flaws.

But they were damn good at their jobs.

Finally, she sighed and bowed her head.

'Why didn't you say anything?' she finally asked.

'Wasn't our place.' Townsend shrugged, and he looked

to Hannon who nodded her agreement. 'End of the day, you're a grown woman. These decisions are yours to make, but if you do make them, guv…make sure they're made for the right reason.'

'You're also a fighter.' Hannon chimed in with a warm smile. 'By far the strongest woman I know.'

King could feel her heart racing, and she took a few deep breaths to hide the emotions that were ricocheting through her body.

'It's just been a hell of a week.'

'I know. It has been. For all of us.' Townsend agreed.

'Yup,' Hannon continued. 'Shilpa's been pressuring me about starting families and all this crap. Trust me, hunting down a serial killer has felt like a week in a spa compared to that.'

King chuckled.

As always, Hannon had her way.

Townsend leant against the bar with his elbow and made eye contact with her.

'And I've not helped. I know.' He grimaced. 'I'll have to live with the fact that I messed up and people died because of it. But you were right. I pushed myself too far. Spread myself too thin.'

'It's because it's who you are.' King finally spoke with the authority she usually did. 'You're a good man, Jack Townsend. Don't let anyone, even me, keep you from being that.'

'Especially Lowe.' Hannon sneered and then followed it up with a downward thumb and a raspberry sound. It drew another chuckle.

'How did it go?' King finally asked, resigning herself to losing him. 'With Lowe?'

'We caught the killer,' Townsend said glumly.

'Wow. Two in a day,' Hannon said, impressed. 'Is that a record?'

King ignored her and continued.

'How do you feel?'

'Like shit, guv,' Townsend admitted. 'He's just a kid trying to protect his mum. Just like Gemma trying to protect her dad.'

'And Lowe?'

Hannon also looked to Townsend. Although she'd never shown it, she too was afraid she'd lose a good friend who had brought her out of her shell.

'He offered me a job pretty much.'

King scoffed.

'Figured he would.' She shook her head. 'Unfortunately for me, you're a good detective.'

King and Hannon both shuffled uncomfortably at the thought of Townsend heading up one flight to CID.

He smiled.

'Well, unfortunately for you both, you're stuck with me. I told him I already had a job, and one that I'm damn proud of.' The smiles spread across his colleagues' faces. 'We're the Specialist Crimes Unit for a reason, right?'

'Hell yeah.' Hannon slapped her hand on the bar enthusiastically and turned to the barman. 'Can I get a gin and tonic and a Diet Coke, please? Jack...pint?'

King was looking at her watch and her eyes widened.

'Five fifteen, Jack.'

'Is it?' He checked his watch, too. 'Fuck.'

'Go,' King said. 'Send our love to the girls.'

'Will do.' Townsend stepped up from his stool and headed to the door. Before he opened it, he turned back to King.

'We good?'

King made a show of pushing the glass of wine away from her and offered him a nod.

'We're good.' She smiled. 'Good work, Jack. Now get going.'

With that, Townsend pushed open the door, racing against the clock to make it across town in time for what was important to him. King had a mountain of paperwork and an endless list of emails that needed her attention. But she was willing to put time in with what was important to her.

Her team.

As the barman passed over their drinks, she turned to Hannon, and asked her to talk her through her problems to see if she could help. If not, it would allow the young woman to unburden herself a little.

Maybe, it would make them both feel better.

They'd just caught a serial killer, but that didn't mean the world stopped turning. There was still work to do, and in King's world, there was still a team to look after.

This was the job, she told herself.

And as she sipped her Diet Coke and listened to her team member begin to unload, she knew she wouldn't trade it for anything else in the world.

CHAPTER FIFTY-SEVEN

'Don't worry, baby,' Mandy said softly as she hugged Eve, who was struggling to hold back the tears. 'You know your daddy's job is really important.'

'More important than me?' the young girl asked, her innocence breaking Mandy's heart.

'Of course not,' Mandy stated. 'Trust me. When you're older, like, an adult like Mummy and Daddy, we'll tell you all about the things he's done for us.'

'But he said he'd be here.' The tears began to roll down Eve's cheek, and Mandy caught them with her thumb before they splashed down onto her ballet dress.

'I know, baby.' Mandy crouched down to meet her eye level. 'And if he isn't here, it means something really bad has happened, and he needs to fix it.'

'Places!'

A voice echoed behind them, and Mandy turned to see Miss Alex, the ballet teacher, calling the other girls into a line. With an understanding smile, Miss Alex beckoned Eve to the line, and Mandy gave her little girl a cuddle and a kiss on the cheek.

'I'll be in crowd.' Mandy smiled. 'Look for me, okay, baby?'

Eve nodded glumly and rubbed her eyes. Mandy felt her heart break a little more as Miss Alex took Eve by the hand and guided her into the line of girls, all of them looking adorable in their pink dresses and their fairy wings. A round of applause echoed from the community hall where the show was being held, as the year below Eve's class brought their performance to a close.

'Damn you, Jack,' Mandy muttered to herself as she wiped away a tear and then took a deep breath and made her way back to the main hall to find her seat. All in all, there were over a hundred seats laid out in symmetrical rows, all of them filled with proud parents, adoring grandparents, and bored siblings. Mandy politely weaved through one of the rows, apologising for the intrusion as she made her way to her seat. As the younger kids curtseyed once last time as the applause came to an end, Miss Alex walked out, enthusiastically applauding and ready to announce Eve's class.

Before she could, the door to the community hall flew open, and the swirling wind and rain accompanied the man who stepped through.

Mandy turned like everyone else.

Although unlike the scowls and the shakes of the head for the intrusion, she felt her heart piece back together and then burst with happiness.

Jack.

Townsend held up an apologetic hand, pulled the door closed, and then strode down the aisle looking for Mandy. He was soaked through, with the rain sliding from his parka jacket, leaving a slippery trail behind him, and his boots squished with every step. Rows upon rows of parents looked on disapprovingly, but Miss Alex just smiled warmly, turned and gave a nod to Eve behind the curtain.

Townsend found his seat, lowered himself into it, and turned to the stage.

'Made it,' he whispered.

Mandy slid her hand into his soaking wet palm and then kissed his cheek. The music began, and sure enough, the girls all walked out and fell into formation, standing with feet in first position. Eve's face was a picture of happiness as she strode out, and as her eyes locked with Townsend's, her smile pushed her face muscles to their limits.

Mandy looked up at her husband and could see the pride in his eyes.

She could feel the tears in hers.

After the show, Townsend kept another one of his promises, as he drove them to the large McDonalds near Cressex Business Park, and after tapping their order out on the screen, they took a seat, as the two parents fussed over how great Eve's routine was and how she'd done so well. As Eve then lost herself in her Happy Meal, Townsend turned to his wife who gently reached out and stroked his face.

'How did it go?'

'I got 'em,' he said proudly. 'Both of them.'

Townsend never spoke in any detail about his job within earshot of Eve, and Mandy smiled.

'Proud of you.'

'Thanks, Mummy,' Eve said, not looking up from the cheap toy that accompanied her meal. Townsend and Mandy giggled, and he reached across and tickled her under her arm.

'She was talking to me, Pickle.'

Eve giggled, wriggling away from him and shuffling down the booth. With both cases out of his mind, Townsend found his thoughts veering towards Christmas and found his heart warmed at the thought of a quiet time in their new home, starting new traditions as their life in Buckinghamshire was beginning to take shape.

Eve was flourishing in her new school, making friends, and in ballet, she'd found her first real passion in life.

Mandy was enjoying her job in a role he still didn't understand, but the extra responsibility her manager had sent her was a testament to her, and she seemed to be thriving now she was back in the working world, and although he couldn't relate to the work, he loved listening to her talk about her day.

It always seemed much more pleasant than his.

But he wouldn't change it.

He was starting to truly find his feet as a detective, even though the lessons he'd learnt over the past week had been tough and would likely haunt his quieter moments for the rest of his life. The bond with his team now felt stronger for what they'd been through, and bridges had been built with Lowe, which was something he'd never have expected. The week had been mentally and physically painful. He'd have the scar to prove it, and it left behind a number of broken families, some of whom may never pick up the pieces.

Janet Jennings would have to bury her own daughter in the coming weeks, a thought that chilled Townsend to the bone, and King had already put it in all their diaries to attend.

Stephen Durant would need to raise his boys on his own, never knowing that his beloved wife had actually betrayed him in her final moments on Earth.

And Abby Davis would need to steer a family and a business on her own, all because her selfish husband had been part of a rumour that had devastated a young girl and had pushed her father to his death.

It had been a heavy week.

But with the bond between him and his team as strong

as it had ever been, and with his incredible family waiting for him when he came home, Townsend knew that he was built for the job.

His thoughts were broken by the echoing rumble of a mobile phone, and he looked down at his on the table as it shook.

It was DI King.

Townsend lifted the phone, took a few seconds and put it back down.

'It can wait,' he said, and Mandy smiled.

It began buzzing again.

Townsend looked to Mandy, who sighed.

Eve reached out and picked it up and offered it to her father.

'It might be important,' she said firmly, and Townsend shot a shocked glance to his wife, who beamed with pride.

'Are you sure?' Townsend said, accepting the phone. 'I don't want to leave you two.'

Eve leant in and threw her arms around Townsend's body and pressed her head against his stomach. She then sat back up and smiled as she spoke.

'This is the job.'

GET EXCLUSIVE ROBERT ENRIGHT MATERIAL

Hey there,

I really hope you enjoyed the book and I'd love for you to join my reader group. I send out regular updates, competitions and special offers as well as some cool free stuff. Sound good?

Well, if you do sign up to the reader group I'll send you **FREE** copies of **THE RIGHT REASON** and **RAIN-FALL**, two thrilling Sam Pope prequel novellas from my best-selling Sam Pope series. (**RRP**: £1.99/$2.99 each)

You can get your **FREE** books by signing up at www.robertenright.co.uk

BOOKS BY ROBERT ENRIGHT

For more information about the DS Jack Townsend series and other books by Robert Enright, please visit:

www.robertenright.co.uk

ABOUT THE AUTHOR

Robert lives in Buckinghamshire with his family, writing books and dreaming of getting a dog.

For more information:
www.robertenright.co.uk
robert@robertenright.co.uk

You can also connect with Robert on Social Media:

facebook.com/robenrightauthor

instagram.com/robert_enright_author

Milton Keynes UK
Ingram Content Group UK Ltd.
UKHW031436311024
2498UKWH00011B/38